SURRENDER

Lily didn't have Gitan's patience. She'd fought the urge to come here as long as she could, and finally she gave in. She didn't just want him; she needed him. She needed to feel his hands on her skin; she needed to watch as he rose above her. She needed to feel the play of hard against soft, and warm against cool. More than anything, she needed to feel alive again, vitally important to someone, even if it lasted only for a moment or two. Morning would come soon enough with glaring clarity, and she would be forced to face her mistakes and poor judgment, but tonight in the soft shadows of his screen porch, with the fireflies drifting outside, incandescent green specks against the black velvet night, she refused to think about it . . .

IN
AT THE
KILL

S.K. McCLAFFERTY

ZEBRA BOOKS
Kensington Publishing Corp.

ZEBRA BOOKS are published by

Kensington Publishing Corp.
850 Third Avenue
New York, NY 10022

ISBN 0-7394-5955-4

Printed in the United States of America

For Faelan, my "wonderful little dog" who waits for me at Rainbow Bridge . . . And for Frazer, who came after, filling my empty mornings with boundless Sheltie enthusiasm and unconditional love . . . And for dogs everywhere, who give so much and ask for so little in return.

CHAPTER ONE

The day dawned hot and hazy in southern Louisiana, and closed in a sweltering heat that even the coming of nightfall failed to alleviate. Outside the open windows of a room crowded with canvas waiting to be stretched, tubes of oil and acrylic paints, paper, and ink, the night air was alive with noise. The ever-present symphony of frog and cicada filtered through the window screens, softened by the ceiling fan turning slowly overhead. Gitan could have closed the windows and cranked up the air conditioner, but that would have lessened the sensory experience, and he needed the night sounds to enhance his recall.

The studio was hot, and he'd stripped off his tank top. As he leaned in to add the final brush stroke to the portrait, a thin runnel of perspiration zigzagged its way with maddening slowness between his shoulder blades. Gitan barely noticed. He was fully focused on the portrait of the young woman.

Something was missing.

Was it the angle of the light? The crook of her

seductive smile? The highlights in her hair, or the way she glanced back at him over one bare shoulder? Had he gotten the perfect symmetry of brow, cheekbone, and jaw just right? The slant of her brows?

For seven years and nine months he'd been thinking about the portrait, considering every facet of her angel's face, deciding on the angle of the light striking the right side of her face, casting the left in subtle shadow.

Unconsciously, the paint-smeared fingertips of his right hand smoothed the heavy satin of the scar cleaving his chest from the clavicle to just a few inches above his navel. It had proven impossible to separate thoughts of Lily Martin from the horror of that last night in her father's study . . . the searing fight for each breath, the beep of the cardiac monitors, the uniformed officer standing guard just outside the ICU. So much time had passed and so much had happened. Seven years and nine months behind prison walls, and there had been no photographs to remind him how she looked, or the reason he was no longer a free man. Only his memories, and a smile he couldn't seem to forget. . . .

Through the open windows came the scream of a rabbit caught in the jaws of a predator. Gitan left off studying Lily long enough to cock his dark head and listen. There was something about the sound that cooled the sweat on his bronze back and sent an instant shiver up his spine. Maybe it was the loneliness of the caught creature's cry that got to him . . . or maybe it was because he knew how it felt to be the rabbit, caught by something bigger and more powerful than himself, scared beyond anything he could have imagined, with no way out and nowhere to turn to make things better.

Sometimes death was better, Gitan knew.

At least in death, there was freedom.

The scream died and the night was silent for the space of a breath. The rabbit had found release, but there was no satisfaction in that knowledge for the ex-con. Just an unease he couldn't brush off, or easily explain away. As he cleaned his brushes and turned them on end to dry, then turned out the lights, he decided to drive by *Tante* Rose's place on Tupelo Avenue to make sure everything was okay. His brother Mason seemed troubled these days, and though everything was probably as it should be, he wouldn't sleep until he could be certain.

He hit the light switch, glancing one last time at the portrait of Lily Martin resting on the easel. As he closed the door on her bewitching smile, he realized what was missing. That haunted look in her pretty blue eyes.

Mason Boudreaux and Jerry Gonzales skipped school on a Wednesday morning in late September and headed out onto the green-brown waters of Bayou des Cannes. The school year was new, but Mase was already bored with the routine and ripe for a little rebellion. He had a couple of joints of marijuana recently purchased from a friend of a friend, and Gonzales had a six-pack of cold beer confiscated from his old man's fridge, along with a "borrowed" skiff that belonged to his uncle. They'd been planning the getaway for a week.

Mase knew that his brother, Gitan, would ream him out if he got wind of what he was up to, but he figured his chances were better than sixty-forty he wouldn't be found out. The timing, for one thing, was perfect, since no one was home that day. *Tante* Rose volunteered every Wednesday at the recreation hall behind the Catholic church, where a group of ladies from the parish got together and cooked dinner for the folks in the parish who were either too old and decrepit or too damned lazy to cook for themselves. She would be gone until late afternoon, when she would breeze through the door with two plates full of leftover fried chicken, biscuits, and gravy for supper.

As for Gitan, he was too preoccupied with other things to notice what Mason was up to, at least during daylight hours. He was working hard to get back on his feet. *Tante* Rose claimed he was rebuilding his reputation, but as far as Mase was concerned, seven years, nine months served of a twenty-year sentence for murder in the second degree was all the reputation a man would ever need to keep anyone with a lick of sense from trying to fuck with him. There were days when Mason envied him that, but not today. Today he just wanted to escape, and maybe kick back for a while with a beer or two and a few tokes of some second-rate weed.

Catfish Point was deserted, a lonely, spooky spot on a dead-end dirt road where the century-old Catholic church called St. Bartholomew's still stood. The whitewash had faded from the clapboard facade, and all but a few of the windows were broken. Only a few shards of glass clung in most of the weathered frames, partially held in place by the vines that had overtaken the ghostly shell of a building.

Mase didn't like it a damn bit, and he said so. "This place don' even look like a church. What we doin' here, anyhow?"

"Just lookin'," Gonzales said. "Jesus, man! What the fuck's eatin' you?"

"Nothin'." Mase turned his head and spat. "This place gives me the creeps, that's all." They'd put the skiff into the cove, drifting until the bow scraped on the mud of the shallows. "What are we groundin' it for? I thought we were gonna catch us some cats?"

"We got all day, don't we? Besides, I need to take a leak and I ain't about to pollute the bayou." Gonzales jumped onto the muddy bank and lost his footing, landing on his knees in the mud. The joint he'd just finished smoking made him giddy, and he laughed as he pushed to his feet. "Come on, man. Let's have us a look around. The serious dopers come out here sometimes to meet. Maybe we'll get lucky and find us a stash. Dealers, they make all kinds of cash. If we find something, we can sell what we don't smoke, and have us a real party. Hey, maybe your brother can hook us up. I bet he knows a lot of guys into that sort of shit."

Mase just glared at him and reluctantly followed. "Gitan knows some bad-ass guys, him, but ain't no way he'd hook us up. He says that was another life, and not one he's anxious to do over."

Gonzales snorted. "Shit! He works at the Chop Shop. Ever'body knows—"

"Nobody knows a goddamn thing!" Mase shot back. He wasn't sure why Gonzales's comments bothered him, but they did. Maybe it was because he knew how it felt to have someone look at him and decide who and what he was at a glance. It didn't matter that a moment ago he'd been thinking along the same lines. Yet Gitan was *his* brother, not Gonzales's. "Gitan's legit, and he don' do drugs. Never did. Now, drop it, will you? I don' want to spoil my day off by talkin' about Gitan."

"All right, all right. No need to take my head off. Jesus, you on the rag, or what?" Gonzales was silent for a few seconds, but as they neared the old church, he nudged Mase with his elbow. "Check it out, man. You think it's haunted? I heard some talk—"

"It's a church, stupid. Churches don't have ghosts."

"Yeah? What about the Holy Ghost?"

Mase gave Gonzales a shove. "Asshole."

"C'mon, chickenshit, let's have a look." Gonzales headed across the churchyard, choked with waist-high weeds.

"Nah. I'm goin' back to the skiff. Somebody steals it and we're in trouble."

"*I* stole it, and we're already in trouble." He stuck out his chin. "You really are a waste. I don' know why I hang wid you. Got to find me a better class of friends."

"I ain't afraid of nothin'," Mase insisted. "There just ain't nothin' in there I need to see, that's all. Didn't skip school so I could go to confession. But since you're so hot to go inside, let's get it over with. Otherwise you'll been whinin' about it all afternoon." It might have been the combination of the beer and the weed, or just plain reluctance, but Mase's legs felt like they were made of lead. His heart had lodged in his stomach, its beat abnormally sluggish and slow. He'd never liked dark, smelly places, and the old building was both. The only light was a shaded sickly green that filtered through the vine-shrouded window frames, the smell one of must, dirt, neglect, and something else. A metallic taint that set the fine hair on Mase's forearms straight on end. Several small rust-colored puddles marred the cypress plank floor of the vestibule. "What the hell is that?"

Gonzales seemed reluctant to say what they both were thinking. "I feel a change of plans comin' on. What'dya say we get out of here?"

"Now, who's a chickenshit? We've come this far;

ain't no goin' back now." Mase stepped through
the shadowed doorway and into the chapel sanctuary. "Anybody there?" His voice echoed slightly
in the stillness. "Man, do you smell that? There's
something dead in here. Somethin' big, too."

Mase took a step forward, and the sunlight broke
through the tangle of vine, playing over the horror
hanging over the altar. A man, naked and suspended
on the large wooden cross in an upside-down position.
On the floor below, the broken plaster replica of
Christ stared sorrowfully up at the one who'd taken
his place on the cross. The corpse's eyes appeared to
be open, but they had gone cloudy in death. His
arms were outstretched, as if he would embrace
them, his mouth slack, his face a ghastly black from
the slash under his chin.

Gonzales gagged. "Holy shit. Is that—is it—real?"
As a fly landed on the blood-covered face and started
to crawl inside the corpse's mouth, he lost the beer
he'd consumed all over the last pew.

Mason heard him stumble outside, but he couldn't
seem to follow. His sense of self-preservation screamed
for him to go. *Move now! Run!* But he couldn't seem
to will his paralyzed muscles into action . . . kind of
like the nightmares he sometimes had, in which he
knew he had to escape, but he couldn't, and he felt
like he was standing in quicksand. Every movement
frustratingly slow, overly hard to execute.

Heart flailing against his ribs, throat closing against
the putrid odor filling the chapel, Mase stood there,
staring, details washing over him.

A man.

Murdered.

Crucified. Feet toward the ceiling.

He couldn't seem to shake the sick feeling that he

recognized the man under the tar-like mask. It looked like . . . Father Dugas?

The skin of the back of Mase's neck prickled, and he felt sick. A priest, for Christ's sake. *Not just any priest,* he mentally corrected. *His* priest. One unsteady step back, legs quivering, then two, and somehow he broke free of the shock-induced paralysis and stumbled from the old church.

Jerry Gonzales waited anxiously by the skiff, his round face still pale from being sick. "What the hell was that?" Gonzales cried.

"Father D-Dugas," Mase stammered. "It was—Father D—"

"How the hell did it get there?"

Mase shook his head, gulping fresh air. "Somebody killed him, Jerry. Oh, Jesus! They killed him! Let's get to a phone. We got to call the cops."

An hour later, Sheriff Hugh Lothair and his deputy, Alan Crebs, had cordoned off the area with yellow crime scene ribbon. The kids who had found the body stood off to one side, looking as if they wished they could disappear. Neither one was supposed to be here. Hugh had never had any truck with the Gonzales kid, though he'd cited his old man a few weeks back for DUI. The other one, he recognized. "Hey, kid. Aren't you Gitan Boudreaux's brother?" He noticed the hunching of the boy's shoulders at the mention of his older brother's name. So there was animosity between Gitan and the kid. Now, that was unsurprising.

"The name's Mason. Mason Boudreaux."

Hugh made a notation on his note pad. "Mason Edward, that right? Ain't seen you since you were in grade school."

"Been around," Mase said. "Might be that you ain't been payin' attention."

"I'd watch that lip, if I were you," Hugh warned him. "It'll get you into a world of shit. You boys aren't old enough to have graduated high school, and as far as I know, today isn't a holiday, so why aren't you in school? You cut classes to come out here? What else you been up to?"

The Boudreaux kid went a little deeper into himself. Determined not to give an inch, a tendency, a hardness Hugh recognized. "We were goin' fishin', Sheriff," Gonzales offered.

"Fishin', huh? I hear that. Bayou's nice this time of day. Guess that beer I smell was an essential part of your afternoon. You mind tellin' me how you came by alcohol? It's pretty damned obvious you're both underage."

The Hispanic kid swallowed hard. "I took it from my old man's fridge, okay? Are we under arrest? 'Cause if we are, then I want to lawyer-up."

Hugh snorted. Jerry Gonzales seemed to know the ropes. "I haven't decided that yet. How about goin' over and havin' a seat in the back of that patrol car? I've got some business to see to before I decide what to do with the two of you." Hugh watched them get in and settle down in the seat.

Crebs had been back of the church, taking stock of the surroundings, evaluating the crime scene, and determining where the photographer should be. He rounded the church, giving the building a wide berth, careful where he stepped. The forensic team's ETA was fifteen minutes, and once they got there, they'd go over every inch of ground in their search for blood spatter and trace evidence.

The deputy took off his hat, blotting his shaved

head with a folded white handkerchief. The humidity was high, and the slightest exertion made the sweat pop from the pores. There was hot, and then there was *Lous'iana* hot. Crebs was a transplant, accustomed to a much cooler clime. "You takin' those two punks down to the station for questioning?"

"Hell, I don't know. They've given a statement, and I guess they've had enough of a scare for one day. If we need anything else from 'em, I know where to find them."

Hugh's plan of action obviously didn't sit well with Crebs. "You smell the grass on 'em?"

"I caught that," Hugh told him. "And I'm going to let it pass, this time. Quite frankly, I've got more important things to do right now than to bust two kids for smokin' a marijuana cigarette. Unless, of course, you happen to find any on 'em?"

"No, sir. Clean as a whistle. I figure they ditched their stash before they called us."

"Which would indicate there's no evidence, am I right?"

"Yes, sir, Sheriff."

"End of discussion. You think you can handle this on your own for twenty minutes or so? I'll send Fred over to help out—meanwhile, I've got some calls to make."

Crebs couldn't imagine what could possibly be important enough to drag Sheriff Lothair away from the scene of a gruesome murder, and he didn't ask. There was a tightness to the set of the man's mouth that didn't encourage questions, so for now, he let it go and got back to work.

Hugh walked back to the squad car, but he stopped short of getting in. Instead, he went a few yards farther, almost to the banks of the bayou, and with the green water lapping softly a few feet below where he stood, he took out his cell phone and dialed her number.

Her machine kicked on after four rings. "Lily? It's Hugh."

Robert "Gitan" Boudreaux was putting the finishing touches on the custom paint job John Akins had commissioned for his Harley. It was an intricate geometric design done in shades of red that was striking and extreme. Gitan made the final sweep of the airbrush when Ruben Early tapped on the paint bay. "Hey, Gitan. You in a good place to walk away from that tank?"

"Give me a second." Gitan stripped off his goggles and respirator and laid them on the workbench, readjusting the rolled and faded red handkerchief on his forehead as a sweatband as he followed Ruben Early outside.

The mystery as to why his boss had called him away from an important job was short-lived. Hugh Lothair's squad car was parked at the curb. The lights were off, but Gitan caught sight of a figure slouched in the backseat and felt a familiar tension coil in his gut. He kept his movements deliberate, unwilling to let his uneasiness show.

"Thanks, Ruben," the sheriff called after Early. "I'll catch up with you later."

"Sure thing, Sheriff. Gitan," Ruben said, ducking his head as if embarrassed. "You take all the time you need."

Gitan's gaze slid from his boss's retreating figure to that of the sheriff. Hard to believe they'd been friends once. When he thought back on those days, they were always drenched in sunshine and golden haze that had had no place in his childhood, borrowed memories from someone else's life that had little to do with the man he was now, or the boy he'd been then. "Hugh," Gitan said, not bothering to use the title Lothair had won in the last election. "You dragged me away from my job—you mind tellin' me what the hell you want?"

The expression in Hugh's blue eyes was hard as he glanced at the patrol car. "That's right, I forgot. A steady job's a serious matter since it's a condition of your parole. I sure wouldn't get a wink of sleep if I was to jeopardize your brand-new start."

Always a twist of the knife, Gitan thought. A little goading, a touch of sarcasm, that air of superiority Lothair kept up to cover the fact that he'd always felt a little nervous around him. It rolled off Gitan's hard exterior like water off oilcloth, leaving him wary but largely unaffected.

He crossed his arms over his chest and waited, unaware of how he looked or how it affected Hugh.

It was clear he didn't give a damn. Hugh felt something ignite deep inside and burn to soft white ash. From the faded sweatband that held back hair the color of walnut stain, to the tattoo of a spider's web on his right shoulder, Gitan was the image of the outlaw.

It wasn't so much what he did—Hugh had monitored his activities closely since his parole six months ago, and the man was disappointingly clean—it was in his stance, in his glance, in the way he carried himself. He was tough, and he was seasoned, and he was impossible to know, and Hugh hated him for it.

His dark good looks, his quiet, slightly mysterious nature, combined with a gift for sleight-of-hand petty larceny had earned him the name Gitan, French for "gypsy." It fit him perfectly, and he'd worn it so long and it had become such an essential part of his persona that these days he answered to Robert only when cashing his weekly paycheck and during visits to his parole officer.

Gitan wadded his chewing gum into a wrapper and tossed it into a trash can a few feet away. No cigarettes, Hugh noted. Now why did that surprise him? Gitan hadn't smoked since the night he had murdered Justin Martin, Lily's father, the night Gitan himself had nearly lost his life.

"I got no time for this, Hugh. So do me a favor and state your business, then get outta my face. I ain't done nothin' wrong, recently—and nothin' in the past I ain't already paid for."

"Nothin' you'll admit to, anyhow," Hugh said. "That right?" That cold ash that filled his chest had a bitter tang to it. It edged up the back of his throat so that he could taste it on his tongue. "Truth is, I'm here to do you a courtesy. I got somethin' that belongs to you—sort of." Hugh motioned toward the patrol car. "You Boudreauxs sure have a knack for findin' trouble, I'll give you that. Your brother, Mason, skipped school with Jerry Gonzales, and they headed over to Catfish Point in a borrowed skiff. Little while later, I get a panicked call from the Gonzales kid that they found a body out there."

Gitan said nothing, gave nothing. He waited. Calm. Unaffected. Hugh's bitterness surged up, and he couldn't quite resist playing with him just a little.

"Not the least bit curious as to what we found?"

"At St. Bart's? Could be damn near anything. From what I hear, it's a real popular place. You gonna cut the kid loose, or charge him with somethin'?"

"St. Bart's. Funny you should call it that. Were you talking about the church or the inlet?" Hugh smiled a little, but his gaze was far from friendly and he knew it. "Not too many folks call it that way these days. They're more specific . . . St. Bart's for the church . . . Catfish Point for the spit of land by the inlet."

"Is there a point to this," Gitan asked, "or are you just runnin' at the mouth and takin' up my time for no good reason?"

Hugh shrugged. "Just wonderin'. It's a bit of a coincidence, that remark, since the victim was found inside the building. Not a careless slip, though, since you're a seasoned criminal."

A flicker of something shot through Gitan's dark eyes and then evaporated. Surprise? Regret? Or something else entirely? He said nothing.

"It'll be all over the news soon enough, so there's no point in not tellin' you. It was Michel Dugas we found out there, strung up on the altar cross—crucified. From the looks of things, our perpetrator didn't just want him dead—he wanted him to suffer." Hugh shook his head, glancing back at the patrol car. "Not a pretty sight, so don't be surprised if it gives the kid nightmares. Who would've thought something like this could happen to someone like Michel Dugas? The saintly parish priest. Everybody loved him, right? The whole damn community—and let's not forget Lily. Hell, they were almost inseparable back in the day. I always wondered why someone like Lily, beautiful, sexy, would waste her time with a pudgy little nobody like Michel. But then, there's a lot about Lily's taste in men I never could understand."

"*Mais*, yeah, brother, me too. Hell, she married you, didn't she?" Gitan's comment was dry as sunbleached bone.

She'd married him, Hugh thought angrily, but he hadn't been able to hold on to her, and the fact that the cause of most of his marital troubles stood a few feet from him, looking like he was carved from dark granite, bit to the marrow. "Yeah, she did, didn't she? That's more than you'll ever get from her. Listen . . . I ever tell you about our wedding night?" Hugh said with that same small, unfriendly smile. "Man, she must've spent an hour in the bathroom of our suite just getting ready, longest hard-on I ever had. Thought she'd never come out of there—and then the door opened, and there she was . . . surrounded by this filmy white thing that floated out around her. Virginal . . . angelic. You think a lot about Lily while you were at the Farm, Gitan? About how she looked? That soft, sweet-smellin' perfume she used to wear? Um, um, um. You remember her perfume? Christ, I sure do."

"You know, Hugh," Gitan said softly, meeting Hugh's gaze without flinching, "you never did know enough to shut your mouth." It was said without any trace of rancor, just an observation by someone who had known him for a lifetime. Then, without a word, he went to the patrol car and reached for the rear door handle.

As he opened the door, Hugh was at his elbow. "What the hell do you think you're doin'?"

Gitan spoke with his back to Hugh. "You want me to give Clairée Broussard a call? I hear she's takin' on clients. Maybe she can tell us if it's a crime to find a body. If you're gonna charge him with somethin', you do it now, and I'll make that phone call. But you're not gonna detain him another damn second so that you can fuck with me." Gitan opened the car door, bending just enough to peer in. "Mason, you come on outta there."

Mase Boudreaux looked from his older brother to the man in uniform, but the sheriff just stood back to let him climb from the car. "Inside," Gitan snapped. "Now! I'll deal with you in a minute." The kid's shoulders slumped under the weight of his brother's cold fury, and suddenly Hugh felt a shred of sympathy for the younger Boudreaux. He knew firsthand what it was like to live in Gitan's deep shadow. Not an easy thing for anyone. "We through?" Gitan asked, but it sounded more like a statement than an inquiry.

"Yeah, we're through—for now. Keep that kid in line, will you? I don't want to see his face in my rearview mirror again."

Gitan didn't say anything; he just turned his back and walked away, dismissing Hugh as effortlessly as he had when they were children.

Gitan entered the garage, hanging the goggles and respirator on a Peg-Board over the workbench as he did at the end of each and every day. Mason was crouched by one of several motorcycles in various stages of construction. Ruben Early and his employees built custom motorcycles to fit his clients' needs, dreams, or desires. Choppers, to be exact, long, low to the ground, sleek, and powerful. Ruben put his personal stamp on every machine that came out of this business, and the Chop Shop was just starting to gain more than regional recognition. The one Mase looked over was little more than a frame with elongated front forks, yet the kid's eyes had lit from within as if it were Christmas morning and he was once again five years old.

"Don't look like much right now," Gitan told him, "but it will."

"You work on this one?"

"No, not me. Ruben has me in the paint booth till

orders get caught up; then I'll come back out on the floor." He glanced at the clock on the wall. "Eight forty-three. *Tante* Rose know where you are?"

"Asshole out there didn't give me no phone call."

"Hey, you watch that mouth. You might have the man pegged, but you still owe that uniform a little respect."

Mason looked up at Gitan from under his brows. "Don' feed me that line of shit. You don' like him, either." He was quiet for a few seconds. "I heard ever'thing. Why you let him mess with you like that? You could snap him like a twig. What's more, the man knows it."

"You don't know nothin'," Gitan said, the words sharper than he'd intended. He paused long enough to pull together the ends of a frayed temper. Losin' it didn't do any good. Hard lesson learned the hard way. He might be stubborn, but he sure as hell wasn't stupid. "Puttin' Hugh Lothair in his place ain't on the agenda, Mase. It ain't worth it, and it don' solve a god-damned thing. Trust me." Gitan sighed without making a sound. "Hugh's full of hot air. He always was, and it ain't about to change. Get used to it. I have."

"He's a fuckin' douche bag, *and* he's in a position of power."

"Better him than me," Gitan told him. It pained him to look in Mason's eyes and see himself at that age re-flected back at him. He didn't want Mase walking the same path he had, and he sure didn't want to walk into a prison on visiting day and talk to Mase about normal things, knowing they'd come drag him back to a cell when the visit was over.

Gitan didn't want that for himself, ever again, he didn't want it for the lanky kid staring up at him, and it sent an icy chill straight through him to admit to

24

S.K. McClafferty

himself he might not be able to stop either from becoming reality.

Shit happened, and the best of intentions sometimes flew in the face of the law and civilized society. "Here's some change. There's the pay phone. Go call Rose. She's probably walked a hole in the carpet by now. Then, we'll see about gettin' you home. First thing tomorrow, you and I are gonna have us a little talk about you missin' school and bein' brought home by Hugh Lothair." Gitan slapped Mason on the shoulder as he got to his feet, forcing him to skip a step. "You get a good look at the backseat of that cruiser?" Mason just looked disgusted. "Ain't no handles on the inside of those doors, you catch that? No way out, Mase. You remember that."

"I hear you."

"You damn well better hear good. You screw up, Mason Edward, I'm gonna kick yo' scrawny coon-ass so hard, it'll be riding up 'tween your shoulder blades. Ain't you gonna look funny then?"

Soaked to the skin from a five-mile sprint in the teeth of a heavy downpour reminiscent of Louisiana, Lily Martin rounded the corner for the last leg of her evening run and saw the red and blue strobe of the cop car reflecting off the wet pavement in front of her building. Lt. James Delmar blocked the entrance, but Mrs. Mira from the third floor spotted Lily anyway. Wringing her handkerchief, she reached out a hand whose joints were knotted with arthritis. "Lily, she done it. She done it. Oh, Lord! Lord have mercy on her soul!"

The lieutenant turned slightly, glancing at Lily, his expression contemptuous. "Ambulance out front of the building and a lawyer shows up. Coincidence?" A dark chuckle. "I don't think so."

Lily and the plainclothes officer weren't exactly on friendly terms. He'd been the officer at the scene when Mary Nevers had been attacked in this very stairwell three months ago. The Nevers case hadn't received the priority it deserved, however, because the victim happened to have a troubled past. As a former member of the Los Angeles County District Attorney's Office, Lily knew how the system worked, and it had pissed her off. She'd tangled with Delmar more than once, and more than once, the Nevers case got shoved back.

As if it were nothing . . . as if she'd asked for it. . . . And Lily's anger burned.

Lily pushed past Delmar, careful not to get too close. There was something about the way he looked at her she didn't like. She'd seen that sort of look before, and it made her skin crawl. "I'd like to tell you what you could do with your attitude, Lieutenant, but I'm afraid you'd enjoy it a little too much." She turned her back on the officer, concentrating on her elderly neighbor. "Mrs. Mira? What happened?"

"It's Mary, from across the hall. She didn't pick up her mail for two days, so I called the super. She cut her wrists—"

"Oh, God, no," Lily said.

"Bled out in a warm bath," Delmar said, unaware, or uncaring that Mrs. Mira's eyes welled with tears. "Another recovering addict bites the dust. Cryin' shame, ain't it?"

"You self-serving ass," Lily shot back. "You got what you wanted. You can put this one to bed, and you won't have to think about it again."

Delmar scowled down at her. She was half his size

and dripping a puddle on the hallway floor. With no makeup, and her short blond hair streaming water down her neck, she hardly resembled the successful attorney she'd been a year ago. Up and coming, on the rise and the side of Right—but that was then, before it all started to disintegrate. "What's up your ass, anyway?" he asked, then leaned in close. "Or maybe that's it, huh? You been too long without it. I could fix that for you. Maybe it'd loosen you up some, without ruinin' your reputation as a man-hatin' dyke."

"With you?" Lily said, getting in his face. "I'd rather bleed out in a warm bath."

Lily sat with Mrs. Mira and nine concerned neighbors for several hours. Mrs. Mira, a widow of nearly two decades with no children of her own, had unofficially adopted Mary, and Lily didn't leave until she was certain the elderly lady was going to be okay. When she finally dragged home, it was getting on toward midnight, and her hair and sweats were almost dry. She inserted the key in the lock, unable to think of anything but Mary. She should have known. She should have paid closer attention. She should have been able to do something to prevent it from happening.

For a long time, Lily stood in the shower, the hot water sluicing over her skin, wishing she could find the tears she kept locked away inside. She should have been able to cry for Mary. If she had ever cried for anyone, she should cry for Mary, a hopeless girl with few connections, and even fewer options.

She should have been able to cry, damn it . . . but the truth was that Lily hadn't cried in years.

Wrapped in a white terry robe, Lily padded barefoot to the kitchen, turned on the TV, and picked up the portable phone, needing to hear Michel's voice. Maybe Michel could make sense of Mary's desperate life and lonely end. Michel would try to assure her that something better awaited lost souls like Mary Nevers on the other side, and it really wouldn't matter that Lily couldn't believe him.

Michel believed enough for them both.

She dialed the number of the modest room at the St. Bartholomew's rectory, worrying a short thumbnail as she listened to it ring. It was late, but he wasn't one to keep early hours, and he should have been there. "Pick up, Michel, please. Will you please pick up?"

She finally clicked the phone off and put it back on the base, noticing the blinking indicator light on the answering machine. Pushing PLAY, she listened to Hugh search for words, then finally give up, "Lily, it's Hugh. I need you to call me back as soon as you get this message. It's important."

She knew Hugh Lothair as well as anyone could, and she could tell from his tone of voice that something was wrong. As she reset the machine and played the message again, something unpleasant sprang to life and slowly unfurled deep inside Lily. A sense of dread she hadn't experienced fully in years. Her mind screamed not to listen, but it was important—too important to be ignored, so she gave it her full attention this time.

There was a note in his voice that she hadn't heard since he had received the divorce papers, a disgust he couldn't quite cover up, underscored by something else. She'd heard that voice he used often enough during their two-year marriage to recognize it. It was his career law enforcement voice—the all-business Hugh who had won the office by a small landslide the previous November after Vance Pershing had retired.

Lily picked up the portable phone again and dialed the sheriff's headquarters, pacing the tiny kitchen as the dispatcher picked up. "Angelique Sheriff's Department, how may I help you?"

"Sheriff Lothair, please," Lily said.

"Who is calling?"

"His ex-wife, Lily Martin," she answered automatically, thinking how much Hugh had hated her insistence on keeping her maiden name. She'd had her reasons, but Hugh had chosen to view it as a rejection of sorts, and it had been one of a thousand small things that had rubbed their marriage raw.

"I'm sorry, Ms. Martin. The sheriff's out on a call. Would you like to leave a message?"

"No," Lily said too quickly. "That won't be necessary." She was about to hang up the phone when a bright blue ribbon scrolled across the bottom of the television screen.

> *The body of a local priest was discovered outside the small Acadia Parish town of Angelique, Louisiana. Details are not being released at this time, pending an investigation by local authorities, but the death is being ruled a homicide. . . .*

Lily heard Hugh's voice again and this time it sounded as if it were inside her head, *Lily, it's Hugh. . . .* They hadn't talked in six months and his tone screamed that he would not have called tonight if it hadn't been vitally important. A priest dead, murdered, Hugh's voice, and suddenly, Lily knew.

CHAPTER TWO

By the time Lily boarded a red-eye flight at LAX, Michel's death had made the national news and was in all of the local papers. The manner of his death was so sensational, so cruel, that it proved an irresistible lure. A real ratings grabber. Some of the smaller TV stations, seemingly not bound by any code of journalistic ethics, were already speculating as to whether or not there could be a tie between Michel's murder and the scandal raging in the Church over pedophile priests. Lily, numb, disbelieving, couldn't listen without wanting to commit a few crimes of her own.

Someone had murdered Michel, and the truth was getting lost in the media scramble to find new angles to the story. WAS THERE ANY HINT OF SCANDAL IN THE PRIEST'S BACKGROUND? WAS HE TRULY A DEVOTED SERVANT OF CHRIST . . . OR DID HE HAVE SOMETHING TO HIDE?

Lily was outraged. Nothing could have been further from the truth. Michel had been one of those rare individuals who viewed the world through optimistic eyes. He had seen a basic goodness in humanity that Lily couldn't see, because he'd gone out of his way to look for it . . .

"The world's a cesspool," she'd told him during one of their more recent telephone conversations. "A man was murdered a week ago a block from here for pocket change. *Pocket change!* The son of a bitch who knifed him got a dollar and seventy-six cents. The victim left a wife and six kids behind, and the prick that killed him is going to walk because of a technicality. What the hell is wrong with this picture?"

"God's plan may not always make sense to us, Lily," he'd said, that same smile in his voice he always had when he talked to her. "That doesn't mean there's no method to the madness. It's just that we can't see it yet. If you can get me the contact information, I can raise donations. That poor woman shouldn't be left to fend for her children alone."

"Throwing money at it doesn't make it go away. It can't bring back her husband, or erase the fact that her kids no longer have their father. If this is God's plan, then He's seriously screwed up, and if you can't see that, then the Church has you brainwashed. When did you become so disgustingly naive?"

"Probably around the same time you became jaded and cynical," he'd said with a laugh. He'd always been patient with her temper, understanding and kind. "There's a light that will illuminate your way, Lily. But you need to turn it on. There's a purpose to everything. It isn't important that we don't see it, but we have to trust that it's there. Can you do that?"

"No."

"Well, try," he'd said. "Do it for me."

But Lily hadn't made any promises. . . .

There was a soft thud as the plane's landing gear

came down and locked into place, jarring Lily back to the present. "You're so wrong, Michel," she murmured as the seat belt sign continued to flash. There was no purpose in his dying, no reason to believe that any good would come from the torture and slaughter of a good and innocent man. And in his absence, no wisdom would be gained. There was nothing but the bottomless void he'd left behind, the loneliness, the ton of unanswered questions. . . .

Her anger burned, a constant fire in her belly. She'd lost whatever faith she'd had in the system the day Mary Nevers took her own life, so her expectations that Michel's killer or killers would be found and punished appropriately were almost nonexistent.

There was no justice for the Mary Nevers of the world. It was that simple.

Lily had seen how the system worked from the inside—the finagling, the fabricating of evidence, the coercion and manipulation of the truth. Evidence withheld, testimony suppressed, or twisted so badly by cross-examination that truth was ignored, or worse, buried under a heap of smoke and mirrors, cleverness and lies.

During her time with the prosecutor's office, she'd witnessed too much corruption on both sides to put her faith in the justice system . . . and L.A. was far more sophisticated, more up with the times than Angelique, Louisiana.

Hugh Lothair was a good cop, but hardly an objective one, and he was up to his ass cheeks in Louisiana's good-old-boy network. If that wasn't bad enough, Hugh's world was strictly black and white. He seemed incapable of separating fact from his own personal prejudices . . . and he had never liked Michel.

Lily knew better than to think that her opinionated and inflexible ex would care enough to look beyond the obvious to uncover the truth about Michel's murder.

Unfortunately for her, the truth was what she needed most. If she were to survive this—the worst blow she'd suffered in nearly eight years—with her sanity intact, then she had to know what had happened.

After the short, tense flight, Lily rented a car and drove to the small backwater town where she'd grown up, and which her Aunt Virginia still called home. She hadn't set foot in Acadia Parish since she had left for university at the age of eighteen, and she'd sworn then that she would never come back here.

It was bad enough that she dreamt about it, unsettling, fragmented dreams she didn't fully comprehend— dreams about childhood, and the night her father died. She'd thought that once the divorce was final and she'd accepted the offer in L.A., the dreams would cease.

A new town, a new opportunity, a chance to turn her back on her past and make a fresh start. Not to mention putting distance between her and her bitter ex-husband. It had all looked so promising, and for a while, it seemed like it might work out. Then, she was assigned to the State of California versus Ellen Bailey case, and everything she'd worked for, fought for, believed in, started to unravel.

Aunt Virginia didn't know about her downward spiral. Lily hadn't mentioned it because she hadn't wanted her to worry. She didn't need her mother's criticism, or Hugh's I-told-you-so. Except for Michel, she'd told no one.

Typically, Michel had begged her to rethink her plans and come home. "I know a young attorney who just hung out her shingle. I'd be willing to bet that Clairée Broussard would jump at the chance to take on a partner, especially one with your credentials. It might be tough at first, but you've got family here, you've got friends. It's home, Lily. Think about it."

"Lily don' want no partner, sugar," she'd quipped with a hollow-sounding laugh. "Lily wants a Lexus." The irony had been that even while working for the DA, she couldn't have afforded a used car in that particular price range. What she didn't say was that while Angelique might be home to Michel, it wasn't home to her.

The steamy little bayou town was the place of her birth, of her imprisonment, the place where hope had lived for a few brief months before Gitan Boudreaux was sent away, and where it had died.

Virginia Martin's door was always open, at least figuratively. Early in childhood, Lily discovered that her father's sister's house on Mill Creek Road was a refuge. When life became too overwhelming, it was to Aunt Virginia's protective embrace that Lily ran. Years had passed since she'd seen Virginia or the house on Mill Creek Road, and she found it surprising that so little had changed.

Lily arrived at half past five the next morning, pulling into the drive at the side of the old two-story house, turning out the headlights. As she took her bags from the rear seat of the rental car, the tip of a Pall Mall glowed orange in the dim shadows of the front porch. Aunt Virginia, wrapped in a pale pink robe, stealing a clandestine smoke, stepped from the shadows by the porch rail and walked to meet her at the edge of the porch.

Virginia embraced Lily with one arm, the hand holding the cigarette resting on the porch rail. "My

God, Lily. Where have you been? I've been calling and calling, and I've been almost beside myself with worry."

"I'm sorry, Aunt Virginia. I didn't mean to worry you. There was a problem in my building, and then I found out about Michel. I caught the first flight out, but it was delayed."

"Well, you're safe and that's what matters." Crushing her cigarette out in an ashtray that sat on the railing, Virginia embraced her niece again, this time an all-out-my-God-I-missed-you hug. "I'm so sorry about Michel, sugar. He was a sweetheart of a young man, and I know how close you two always were. Makes you wonder what the world's coming to. This used to be such a quiet little town—but not any more. It's a rude awakening to find out that bad things happen here, too."

The house was quiet as they entered, only the rhythmic tick of the grandfather clock at the end of the hall and the soft scuff of Virginia's slippers as she walked Lily to the stairs broke the silence. "Have you eaten, darlin'? I can bring you a tray, if you like. I've got some molasses cookies in the cookie jar, and there's cold milk in the fridge."

"Thanks anyway," Lily said. "I'm not hungry." The truth was she hadn't eaten since yesterday, early, but food was the last thing on her mind.

"You haven't mentioned your job. Is it going well?"

Lily bit her lip. "I've taken a leave of absence," she said. She could still hear Gerald Mayer's voice in her head. The Orange County prosecutor had been livid that she'd blown the Ellen Bailey case, and not inclined to let it go.

"Major meltdown," was the term he'd used, "in front of Judge Weinstein, in front of the jury, in front of the press, Lily!" He'd ranted for almost an hour, but he couldn't berate her any more than she did herself.

"I'm sorry," she'd said. "I don't know what came over me, but it won't happen again."

Mayer's face darkened, and the veins in his temples seemed to throb. "You're goddamned right it won't happen again. Take some time off, see a shrink, climb a mountain in Tibet and *find* yourself, but don't come back here until you know what the hell just happened out there, and you can swear on your mother's grave it won't happen again. If you're lucky, you might still have a job."

Lily's mother was alive and well, but at the time, she'd been unwilling to argue. She'd taken time off, as he'd strongly suggested, moving from the loft to a smaller apartment in a less expensive part of town. She'd resumed her running, had taken a part-time job at a suicide hotline . . . but she hadn't seen a shrink, and she hadn't gone back to the prosecutor's office.

"Something came up," she told Virginia, "and I need some time to decide what to do."

Virginia stepped back, smiling at Lily. "Well, that's wonderful news. Not that you've put your career on hold, but that you'll be staying for a while. My God, I've missed you!"

"I missed you, too, Aunt Virginia." Lily felt the tightness in her chest, the swirl of bittersweet emotion, but her eyes were dry. Then, she pulled away, tense, uneasy—not with Virginia, but with this place, the situation.

Virginia pretended not to notice. She wiped her eyes with a tissue she pulled from the pocket of her robe. "I think I'll have some of those cookies and a glass of cold milk. I won't be able to sleep anyway, and I have to go in to the shop later on. Are you sure you're not hungry, darlin'?"

"Positive." Lily's smile was sad. Without another

word, Lily went up the stairs and through the first door on the right. Alone now, she kicked off her pumps and sank down on the end of the bed. The streetlight shone through the windowpanes, the tree limbs outside throwing an odd network of light and shadow on the rose-patterned rug.

She remembered the first time she'd slept in this room. She'd been eleven years old and her parents had been away for the weekend. Lily had been secretly relieved. The nightly arguments between her mother and father had taken their toll on her, and there were times when she'd fantasized that she wasn't their daughter at all, but lived in Aunt Virginia's big house, with the lace curtains and grapevine wrought iron trim bordering the broad front porch.

She remembered feeling very small in the big bed. Small, but safe. It had been the first time she'd slept soundly in longer than she could recall.

Something inside Lily urged her to squash the memory, but it seemed beyond her control. There were some things she couldn't help remembering. So many details flashed through her mind as she sat there, gripping the bedspread so hard the chenille grew hot and a little damp from her palms: Michel's round face and liquid brown eyes, the sound of his voice, his laughter. The scrape of the tree branch against the balcony railing at the Martin house on Kyme Road, his tap on her bedroom window.

His childish attempts to make her laugh when inside she was dying and nobody knew who could stop it from happening.

She sighed, a shiver of sadness that rippled out of her, leaving her empty.

Michel had always been there for her. He'd been her friend long before he convinced Gitan and Hugh

Lothair to let them tag along, long before they'd become a strange little foursome.

Remembering hurt. Lily put her face in her hands and wondered how to ease the ache she lived with day and night. Pain blossomed deep in her chest, not quite physical, but every bit as real. Dry eyes gave the impression of strength, but she knew that if the emotional dam ever burst, she would weep and weep, and never stop.

Pushing off the bed, she walked to the window, but she saw far beyond the panes of glass, beyond the streetlight's reach, back to a time and place she hadn't thought of willingly in years . . .

She'd been spending the weekend at Aunt Virginia's that September while her parents flew to Atlanta. Virginia Martin was a great believer in personal freedom, and she turned Lily loose with the light warning that she was to be home at suppertime—no excuses. Lily met her friends under the Angelique Oak at the edge of James Bryce's pasture a half mile away. Hugh was in a mood, and quarrelsome, as usual, but he didn't provoke Gitan.

Gitan Boudreaux knew twice what Hugh knew about everything, practical knowledge, like how to sneak past the bull to reach the live oak tree in the center of the pasture, and the proper way to set a catfish line in a roadside canal while keeping one eye out for cottonmouth snakes and alligators. Gitan knew how to fight, too, and his impenetrable black glance and fearless air kept the bully in Hugh effectively in line most of the time. He hadn't prevented Hugh from taking his mood out on someone smaller, weaker, less aggressive than he this time, however. Michel Dugas made a fine target, and Hugh Lothair was always out to impress.

"Hey, Gitan, watch this!" Hugh called up into the limbs of the oak where Gitan was balancing twenty-five feet off the ground, one hand resting on the rough trunk, one knee cocked.

Down on the ground at the base of the tree, Lily stared up through a curtain of Spanish moss and held her breath. If he fell, he'd be no more than a splat on the ground, and could break every bone in his body. Lily had never been to Gitan's home, though she'd ridden past it, and heard her mother's harsh comments about "swamp trash." She knew that Gitan's mother was sickly, and that his father worked at the refinery, and she wondered who, if anyone, would care for the reckless boy if he fell and nearly killed himself.

Michel, who had the unmanly habit of fainting at the sight of blood, cringed. "God, Lily! How's he gonna get down? Hugh, can't you make him come down? He'll kill himself, and then what'll we do? Folks say Mr. Boudreaux, he's a man don' take crap from anybody. He ain't gonna like it if we take a dead Gitan home."

"Shit!" Hugh said, turning his head and spitting into the grass to show his derision. "If he falls, we'll dump his worthless ass in the bayou—no way am I cartin' him home to his daddy, dead or alive! 'Sides, the gators got to eat, too." Having failed to get his friend's attention before, Hugh called again, "Hey, you, coon-ass! Watch this!" Picking up one of the apples Gitan had stolen from the fruit stand an hour before and which he'd piled at the base of the oak, he threw it at the cattle grouped by the fence.

Michel grabbed Hugh's arm. "Hugh! Don't! You're gonna make that old bull mad." His frightened gaze sought the bull which stood, switching flies with his tail. The animal turned his broad head and glanced in their direction, then went back to working his cud and swatting.

Hugh gave Michel a hard shove, knocking him on his rump in the grass. "What the hell, Dugas? Pillsbury Doughboy, you scared?"

"I'm not afraid. But what about Lily?" Michel persisted, picking himself out of the grass. "She's too small to reach!"

Hugh got in Michel's face, and Michel blinked. "Then she's got no business bein' here, does she?" Bigger, stronger, tougher, Hugh planted a hand forcefully in the center of Michel's chest and knocked him down again before letting fly with another apple and hooting with devilish glee.

"Lothair!" The warning drifted down on the still summer air. "Pick on somebody your own size!"

"Doughboy, here, he's twice my size! Around his middle, that is." He flung another apple and it bounced off a cow's cream-colored back. The cow bellowed and jumped and the bull broke from the herd to approach, head lowered. Laughing, Hugh jumped for the lowest limb and swung easily up into the tree, leaving Lily and Michel to face the threat alone.

Lily was too scared to scream as the animal approached, but her heart was thudding high in her throat, and she was certain that death was breathing down her neck. She heard the rapid descent as Hugh came tumbling out of the oak and landed with a grunt on his back in front of them, a stunned expression on his sunburned face, and then all of a sudden Gitan was there.

As Lily watched, mesmerized, he edged between them and eighteen hundred pounds of enraged beef. "Michel, take Lily and get her through the fence! Go now!"

Michel grabbed Lily's hand and ran, dragging her to the fence. Lily pushed through hastily, cutting her knee on the barbed wire, a one-inch gash that bled profusely. Blood streamed down her leg and into her tennis shoe before Gitan joined them. He took off his headband and tied it tightly around the cut. Michel looked everywhere but at the red stain. Strangely, Lily hadn't felt a thing. She was too taken by the young Cajun's nearness to feel anything but a slow heat filling her face as he lifted heavily lashed black eyes and regarded her with a grudging respect Hugh craved, but never seemed to get from him.

"Hey, *cher*," he said with surprising gentleness, "looks like you get to keep that leg." He grinned and Lily thought her heart would stop beating. But it only stuttered a little, then speeded up. "All that blood. You're pretty brave, ain't that right? Most girls, they would've cried."

"Lily never cries," Michel said, then looked as if he'd swallow his tongue for drawing the older boy's attention. "Not ever."

"That right?" Gitan said, looking back up at Lily, his grin fading, his gaze finding hers again. "Guess you and me got one thing in common, then. *Tout doucement,* Lily," he cautioned as he helped her up. "Easy does it. Come on, *cher,* let's get you home. . . ."

The memory faded, and Lily was amazed that Gitan's black gaze had the power to keep her breathless an eternity later, even in retrospect. She sighed and blinked to clear her vision. The sky was lightening by degrees and she was restless, so tightly wound that she would never be able to sleep. Later, she would begin to confront the fact that Michel was gone and deal with the labyrinth of unanswered questions. Right now, she desperately needed to run.

* * *

Gitan had been on the outside for four months and twenty-one days, and not a single morning had gone by that he didn't rise well before daylight and walk out onto the levee. He knew that *Tante* Rose thought he was crazy, tormented by nightmares she couldn't begin to imagine, but it wasn't true. He'd slept like the dead while on the inside. A man didn't just get used to the routine behind those concrete walls, he got *into* the routine, learning to take whatever pleasure could be found in little everyday things, and even anticipate them, like an hour's exercise in the yard, or the muscle strain that came with a long day's work in the fields. He hadn't minded the menial labor because it brought fatigue, and fatigue brought sleep, and sleep was a form of escape. The only escape available to him.

Fear for his safety hadn't kept him awake as it had some of the men he'd known. Angola was at times a violent place full of violent men, but though he wasn't a man who made friends easily, he didn't make enemies, either. He'd kept to himself, learned all he could learn, read everything he could get his hands on, and promised himself that if he ever got released, he wouldn't waste one damn minute of the freedom most men took for granted.

The freedom to sleep when he was tired and to open the door to his rental and walk out in the backyard when he felt like it. And he felt like it every morning. From his cell, he'd had a clear view of the barred window in the outside corridor, but the window had faced south, so in seven years and nine months, he'd never once seen the sun rise. The other convicts he'd had truck with talked endlessly about the things they missed, things only to be had on the outside . . . like taking a real bath in a genuine bath-tub. Gitan had just thought about the way the sky changed gradually, from black to indigo, gray to brighter, more magnificent reds, pinks, orange, and sometimes maroon. He'd been looking at the world with an artist's eye all his life, and he'd quietly hoarded the memories. Stupidly, he'd thought that they would last a lifetime, but in time the grayness of the concrete block hell that had become his reality began to chip away at the colors until they were faded and indistinct. Losing the sense of what morning in Angelique was like had been worse than anything he had endured, worse than almost anything he could imagine.

Making his way through the wet grass, he climbed the levee and stood on the dewy slope, watching the black bayou water. He remembered that first morning, on the bus trip home, how his heart had thumped vi-olently as he'd stared out the window, afraid to blink for fear he'd miss a moment of the dawn breaking. If he'd had a tear left inside, he would have wept for the beauty of it, and he'd thanked God for allowing him to experience the glory of it one more time.

Since that day, he'd risen each and every morning without fail. Rain, shine, or gale-force winds, it didn't matter; Gitan could work well past midnight, fall into bed tired and aching, and long before the black night sky turned gray around the edges, he woke again, made coffee, and walked out to face another day of freedom.

This morning had been different. He'd lain awake for a long while before sleeping, unable to get Michel Dugas out of his mind. For some strange reason, he had to keep reminding himself that the young priest was really dead.

Not just dead . . . crucified.

How the hell did something like that happen? Especially to someone like Father Dugas. When he'd closed his eyes, he could see him, serious in his black threads and white inverted collar as he'd sat across from him in the visitor's room at Angola. Michel had made the long drive to Louisiana State Penitentiary once a month without fail, despite the fact that they'd never been particularly close. At first, he'd suspected that Michel's visits had to do with Lily, and he'd resented the intrusion. Eventually, he'd relaxed his guard and accepted that hour every fourth Sunday as something Michel did because he wanted to, though at times it seemed a sacrilege to have someone so untainted, so pure of heart, coming to a place like that. Once his parole was granted, Father Michel continued to drop by *Tante* Rose's place, and now and again he showed up at the Chop Shop.

He had gone to sleep thinking about the last time he'd seen him, but he'd dreamt about Lily. In the dream, she'd been wearing the filmy white nightgown Hugh had described that afternoon, and as she emerged from the bathroom of an elegant suite on slim bare feet she came to *him*, not to her husband. He'd awakened abruptly, covered with a light sheen of sweat, thoroughly shaken, heart railing against his ribs.

By the time he'd showered and made coffee, he'd put the dream into perspective and regained his composure. Yet, even now, with the bracing effect of the black coffee and the damp morning air, the image Hugh had planted in his mind refused to leave him.

Lily was the ghost of his past, and she haunted him. Her mother still owned the red brick house on Kyme Road, but to his knowledge, Lily hadn't been home since the night her father died. Somehow, she had hooked up with Hugh after college and law school, and they'd tried to make a go of marriage while living in Baton Rouge. After the divorce, she'd moved to California.

Maybe to her, living in Los Angeles meant freedom— from the past, from Hugh, from everything hurtful and ugly that had occurred in her life. Maybe even from him. If that were the case, then he hoped Michel's death didn't bring her home, because freedom was unbelievably precious . . . hell, *freedom was everything.*

From somewhere down the levee came the sound of a runner, a woman, Gitan knew. A man would have hit the ground with more force and the cycle of breath would have been slower and heavier. Gitan listened for a few seconds, the ghostly image of his former love still something of a teaser, stirring his senses; then he turned and walked back toward the house.

The last thing a woman running alone needed was to come out of the darkness and encounter a strange man, especially when that man had a long history of trouble with the law, and could not afford to risk any misunderstandings about his intentions.

Lily rounded the bend and saw someone moving away from the levee. He was visible for only a second, a tall, dark-haired man with a wide shoulder span and the sleeves torn out of his denim shirt. His hair brushed his collar in back, giving him a reckless air . . . and then he moved into the shadows of the trees and was gone. A jolt shot straight through her; she faltered for a half step; then she got a grip on herself and regained her stride. For a heartbeat, she'd thought—but no, it wasn't him. It couldn't have been. Someone would have told her if Gitan Boudreaux had been released.

* * *

Alan Crebs tapped on the door to the sheriff's office, and at the answering murmur, he opened the door and held up the envelope. Hugh motioned him into the room without missing a beat in his phone conversation. "You can come on down here and file a complaint against him, but Alice, my hands are tied." He opened the envelope and dumped the contents on the center of the desk blotter. Crime scene photographs, graphic color shots, stark black and white; the subject: Michel Dugas. "Well, I know you don't like it, but Alice, the man has a right to wear whatever he wants in his own house. Yes, even his boxer shorts. Well, for starters, maybe you should try to avoid looking through his windows."

Crebs sniggered at the audible click as Alice Dunning hung up the phone. "That eardrum still intact, or do you want me to have Amy fill out an accident report for you?"

Hugh cupped his hand behind his ear. "Say again?"

Crebs laughed.

Hugh just shook his head. "I wouldn't even be taking the call except for her bein' my mama's best friend. Like I don't have more important things to do than to cite a man for violating Mrs. Dunning's dress code. Jesus." He flipped the photos down like he was dealing a hand of solitaire, not stopping until they filled the desk. "You take a look at these?" he asked, glancing up at the deputy, who was leaning against the doorjamb.

"They made an extra set, remember? They're on my desk."

"Well, that wasn't what I asked, now, was it?" Hugh knew Crebs well enough to know that he sometimes slacked off when he was on the clock. The younger man liked to hang around the Dew Drop Café. The reason for his interest in the greasy little dive had little to do with the coffee, and a lot to do with Marie Alamantz, a pretty little brunette who worked the register most weekday mornings. Hugh didn't mind his deputy taking an extended midmorning break as long as he kept his radio on and was on the ball when he was at the station.

Crebs reddened. "No, sir, I haven't."

"Well, how about you stop warming my woodwork, go out there and do that, and get back to me with any observations you might have. You were the first officer on the scene. It's part of the job description."

"Yes, sir, I'll do that."

"Amy?" Hugh said, holding down the button on the intercom. "Bring me some coffee?"

With Crebs gone, Hugh sat back to study the photos. He already had the notes he'd taken yesterday on scene, and a copy of the notes Crebs had taken, along with some detailed sketches, complete with measurements. Since the crime scene was inside the building, there was little chance of any evidence being destroyed by the elements, unless of course there was a direct hit by a hurricane. That had been a real stroke of luck from where he sat, since the technicians had the luxury of taking their time in collecting trace evidence. Hugh had supervised the operation, returning to the scene after leaving the Chop Shop, and staying there until the coroner came to pick up the body.

It had taken thirty gallons of hot water and a lot of soap to get the stink out of his hair and off his skin, and he never did get it out of his nostrils. It was a damn good thing he had a cast-iron stomach, or the coffee Amy brought him would have come right back up again. She refilled his cup, a half smile on her painted pink lips. "This came in last night," she said. "Lerlene left it on my desk."

Hugh took the slip of paper and read.

Call from Lily Martin, 11:45 P.M. No message.

"Thanks, sugar," Hugh said without looking up. "I'll take care of it."

He dialed Lily's home number, but it rang unanswered until the machine picked up. He didn't leave a message. He'd try to get back to her later. By now, she'd heard the news about Dugas. Probably just as well that she hadn't heard it from him. It would have been hell to have mouthed platitudes about a man he had never liked, mostly due to his friendship with his wife—a friendship he had never understood.

In his mind, he heard her correct him: *ex-wife.*

That grated a little. It wasn't that he didn't get that the marriage was over, it was that he still thought of Lily as his. It didn't matter that she let him know at every opportunity that the possessiveness went one way, and wasn't welcome. In his mind, she was still his wife, and he wasn't sure he wanted to get around that. For the moment, however, he was content to let it go.

The town—a town where the majority of the residents were practicing Catholics—had just lost a popular young priest, and the manner of his death was already sending shockwaves through the community. Amy was fielding most of the calls, letting only the high-profile callers through—and Mrs. Dunning—while Hugh began to dig into the investigation.

Like it or not, he was going to become intimately acquainted with every detail of Michel Dugas's life.

His friends, his lovers, his enemies, not to mention what he'd eaten before he'd gotten himself killed. He found it ironic that a man he'd disdained as a boy, and then later avoided, he could no longer ignore. Lily had always pressured him to get to know Michel, and she was finally going to have her way. "Too bad she won't be here to see it."

CHAPTER THREE

Mason pushed the shop broom as if he'd been assigned to work in the death house at Angola. He'd gone to school that morning, and had been in class all day. Gitan knew, because he'd checked. At 3:40 P.M., he'd come dragging his ass in the door of the Chop Shop as instructed, hangdog look on his face, and Gitan had put him to work.

Three hours later, the boy's enthusiasm was wearing down. Building a chopper with enough chrome to blind a man in full sun was one thing; sweeping up, cleaning ashtrays, and emptying the trash was something else again. Gitan was out of the paint bay this afternoon and in the main shop, spot welding the frame on a brand-new order, while doing his best to ignore the black looks Mase sent his way every few seconds.

Finally, Mase had had enough. "Damn it, Gitan. How long I got to push this broom?"

Gitan finished the weld and picked up the hand grinder. The toes of the boy's old sneakers were visible in his peripheral vision, but he wouldn't give him the satisfaction of giving him his full attention. "You sweep till that floor's clean."

"It's already clean enough for *Tante* Rose to serve Sunday dinner on it, and you know how she is."

"Then, I guess you'll keep on pushin' it till I tell you not to."

"Jesus Christ."

A razor-sharp glance. "What'd you say?"

The kid didn't back down; he had to give him that. He just planted his feet a little wider and tried his best to match him toughness for toughness. "Fuck, Gitan! Ain't I been punished enough? Look, I'll finish on the floor, if you let me help you with the bike. I know how to use a grinder, and I can take the burrs off the weld while you work on somethin' else."

Gitan put the grinder down and took a slow, deep breath. He hadn't asked for any of this and he wasn't quite sure how to deal with it. Above all, he wasn't cut out to play surrogate father to a fifteen-year-old with a bad attitude. "You'll damn well do what I tell you to do, and you'll do it till I say you can stop. What's more, I'm not takin' your lip, you hear me?" He withdrew the finger he'd thrust in the boy's face, and went back to work.

"It's shit work," Mase said, his dark eyes angry and resentful, and all of his animosity aimed at Gitan.

"Goddamn right, it's shit work," Gitan told him. "You think I'm gonna reward you for the stunt you pulled yesterday? I had a little talk with Jerry's dad, so I know about the booze and the weed, Mase. You ought to be glad you're not coolin' your scrawny ass in Hugh's holdin' cell."

"It's just marijuana. You're actin' like I had a nose full of coke."

"Well, maybe I missed somethin' while I was away. They legalize pot? 'Cause last time I heard, possession could get a man five years in the federal pen. You got an argument for that? Go on, lay it down, and I'll know for sure that you're a damn sight stupider than I thought."

Mase kicked at a wrench and sent it flying, and Gitan lost his temper. He got to his feet and in Mason's face. His hands rested easily on his hips, but if the kid was sufficiently full of himself to make a move, he'd put him facedown on that floor he'd been sweeping. "Pick it up."

"You pick it up. I'm goin' home."

"*Pick it up.*"

Mase turned his back, and Gitan grabbed a fistful of T-shirt, shoving him onto a low stool that Ruben used when he worked on the '25' Indian motorcycle he'd bought in Pensacola. With a shove, he sat him down hard. "Look around you, goddamn it! This is a place of business. You want to take your temper out on somethin', I'll give you that chance, but you don' kick tools around in here, or anything else that don' belong to you, you got that?" Then, when he didn't answer, "I said, '*you got that?*'"

"What? Next, you're gonna tell me you're grateful to Ruben Early for givin' you this job?"

"You're goddamned right, I'm grateful," Gitan shot back. "The man trusted me. If Ruben hadn't given me a chance, I'd be washin' dishes at the Dew Drop, and I'll be goddamned if you're gonna come in here and fuck it up for me." His voice had been sharp and angry, and he had to work hard to get the fury down a notch. "I don' give a rat's hairless ass if you like me, Mase. But you're gonna respect me, because you've got to respect somethin' in this life. You don', you'll end up in Angola, or maybe worse, and believe me, boy, you don' want to go where I been. Not ever. Ain't nothin' worth a man losin' his freedom."

"You must've thought she was worth it," Mase shot back, but his anger had withered, and his voice had a hollow sound. "You killed her old man. You must have thought she was worth it."

Gitan drew a deep breath, and wondered how the hell to reply. He'd never talked about that night—not to Mason, or to his aunt, or anyone, aside from his court-appointed lawyer, and even then he'd been closemouthed, aware how much they all had to lose.

Tell the lie and then stick to it.

Most cops just wanted to solve the case, and they would leap on anything, no matter how improbable, to put a murder investigation to bed. Vance Pershing hadn't been any less eager. The murder of the patriarch of an influential parish family, and Gitan's confession. Three people at the scene, one who didn't remember what took place, one ready to take the blame, and the victim, who couldn't exactly dispute anything that was said. "I ain't exactly proud of what I did, and I can't get those years back. All I can do is keep goin' and hope to Christ you have better sense than I had back then."

Mase's eyes were watery, but the tears didn't spill. "I ain't goin' to prison, 'cause I ain't done nothin'. I ain't you, Gitan," he said, "and you sure as hell ain't Daddy. You don' get to tell me what to do."

Gitan straightened to his full height and stepped back. "Go on. Get your sorry ass out of here, but you make sure you go home. You're still in hot water, and I'll know if you step out of line."

Mase got on his bicycle and tore off down the street, anxious to be anywhere but the Chop Shop.

Gitan turned back to the bike, but he had about as much enthusiasm for it now as Mase had had for the shop broom. He glanced at the clock, and then started to put away his tools. He couldn't blame Mason for being pissed, and he couldn't let on that he hated assuming the role of disciplinarian as much as Mason hated him for coming down so hard on him.

The kid was right about one thing: he wasn't anything at all like their father. He didn't have his way with words, his ease around the people he loved, or his innate wisdom, all of which Gitan desperately needed. He was struggling not only to restore his place in society, but to hold this family together. With Hugh two steps off his ass most days, and the conditions of his parole uppermost in his mind always, life was hellishly complicated. Add to that a rebellious teenage boy and an overly protective aunt, and he was in over his head and sinking fast.

Lately, he'd felt his daddy's absence more acutely than he ever had. John Boudreaux had been a solid family man, a hard worker who'd never had a hint of scandal attached to his name until his oldest son stabbed a man to death in that man's own home. Gitan had hurt both his parents, but his father had had the most trouble bearing the weight of the burden. Annie Boudreaux had turned to religion for comfort and understanding. John, never deeply religious despite his Catholic upbringing, had struggled with it, and Mason had been there to witness it all.

Two years into Gitan's twenty-year sentence, John died in a car accident on his way to his job at the oil refinery. He'd been forty-nine years old. Gitan had been unable to attend the funeral. Then, a few years later, a bout of pneumonia took Annie. With Gitan doing hard time and their parents dead, Rose

Boudreaux, John's youngest sister, had assumed guardianship of eleven-year-old Mason.

Tante Rose was a good woman, but she loved Mase to distraction, and she couldn't seem to understand that sometimes love wasn't enough. Gitan just wanted some sort of guarantee that Mason would be okay. Trouble was, life didn't come with guarantees.

Gitan hung the wrench on its brackets and when everything was in its place, he punched his time card and clocked out for the evening. His bike was parked in the back lot, the same Harley he'd bought secondhand two years before he went away. Sleek, black, and low to the pavement, the engine purred like a six-hundred-pound cat when he stepped on the kick-starter. As he settled into the motion of the street, he felt the wild urge to hit the highway without looking back.

He was worn out, and the unending grind of living on the outside was more than he could manage. He'd heard that Lily was still living in California. If he made it that far without getting caught, would she be happy to see him? Or would she turn him away? Would she even remember him after all these years?

He killed the crazy impulse before it took root. Rose couldn't handle Mason alone, and he wasn't free to leave the state without permission. Besides, he had a meeting with his parole officer in the morning that he couldn't afford to miss. It was all part of the process of starting over, and he'd worked too hard to get this far to fuck it up because of a woman he'd loved a lifetime ago.

Lily sat in the rental, watching the kids playing down the block from the Dugases' shotgun-style house. They were huddled in a loose knot, three boys and a girl, and when they broke apart, she saw that the tallest boy had a ball tucked under one arm. The little girl complained loudly about being the monkey again, but the complaints dissolved when she leapt and caught the ball they had been passing over her head. "Jenna Lynn, you got springs in those sneakers?" one boy crooned.

The girl threw back her blond head, and her expression was smug. "What if I do?"

"Then you're gonna tell me where you bought 'em. Dis chile be NBA-bound!" He laughed and gave her the ball, and Lily felt something pull tight in her chest.

Children and innocence were supposed to go hand in hand, but it didn't always happen that way. Somewhere in the dark recesses of her mind she heard her father's drunken voice calling: *Lily? Lily! Where the hell has that girl gotten to? Lily!*

It was a mere whisper, an echo so faint that she barely recognized the heat before she ruthlessly shut it down, opening the car door, stepping out into the sweltering heat. Virginia had said there hadn't been any relief from the heat this year. Temperatures had remained unrelentingly high through the early part of September, and the low-pressure system stalled in the Gulf held the promise of worsening conditions. Even with the air cranked up full blast, Lily's biscuit-colored linen trousers and yellow silk shell clung damply to her, and the hair she wore styled in a modified short shag curled at her ears and nape. As she hurried up the walkway toward the one-story building, a vehicle pulled in at the curb and the playing children scattered.

Lily didn't turn around, but there was no escaping Hugh. "Lily? That you?"

She drew a fortifying breath, and turned to face him. He was tall and good-looking in dark trousers, white shirt, and tie. From the brown hair that was always an appropriate length, to his polished black wingtip shoes, Hugh's image was carefully cultivated to project the air of experience and competence. The consummate professional, the career cop, he knew how to work the system to get what he wanted. "I didn't expect to see you here."

"I'm in the middle of an investigation, and they're the victim's next of kin. It's all part of the process. You here because you got my call? Or is there somethin' goin' on I don't know about?"

"I'm here for Michel," she said, unable to keep the tension she felt from infecting her voice. It was always this way between them. Tense. Strained. They were like two boxers in the professional ring, circling around one another, each expecting the other to try and land a blow, always looking for a chink in the other's defenses, always wary. "He was my friend." It was that simple, but she knew he would never understand it. Hugh had never allowed himself to open up to anyone—not even Gitan, and he'd been as close to the Cajun as anyone.

He nodded once and his hard mouth tightened, a sensual slash in a rugged, tanned face. "I wonder, if the shoe was on the other foot—if it was your husband they were preparin' for the crypt, would you still be here?"

"I don't *have* a husband," Lily reminded him. "The ink on the divorce papers has been dry a long time. Do me one favor, will you? Tell Elaine I'll come back another time. I have more important things to do than to stand in this oven and bicker with you."

She walked back to the curb and the rental, aware that behind the dark glasses he wore, Hugh watched her. When she pulled away, into the street, he turned and went slowly up the sidewalk. Her upset hadn't completely left her when she turned the Subaru onto Mill Creek Road and nearly ran over a bicycle lying on its side in the middle of the road. A car was stopped on the sandy berm a few feet away. A teenage boy passed a beer to a companion while they leaned against the bumper of a reconditioned classic '69 GTO and watched three others fight.

Fight, Lily thought, slamming the gear shift into PARK and getting out. *It wasn't a fight. It was a massacre.* One teen pinned the arms of a second behind his back while a third punched the hell out of him. The kid taking the beating appeared to be a good deal younger, but it didn't stop him from fighting back. He struggled and cursed and tried to break free from the boy who held him, but he was covered in blood and losing strength fast. Lily could almost feel the energy drain out of him and onto the slick grass.

They were going to kill him, and there was no way she would stand by and watch it happen.

She pushed herself between them, forcing the bullies to take a step back. "Back off!"

The kid holding the bloodied boy slackened his grip just enough for his would-be victim to break free, but instead of running, he swung a fist, landing a blow that knocked the other boy sprawling. Staggering slightly, he found his feet and planted them wider in a boxer's stance, growling through the streaming blood from a broken nose, "Come on, Willie, you cocksucker! Come on!"

The one who stood beaten and bloody didn't lay a hand on her. The kid who'd been punching him shoved Lily, trying to push her out of his way. Lily reacted instinctively, kneeing him in the groin. "I said that's enough!"

The young man whom the boy had punched wiped a trickle of blood from his mouth onto the back of his hand, refocusing his attention on Lily. "Hey, bitch! What business is this of yours? You don' look old enough to be Boudreaux's mama, and I can't imagine a puss like that satisfyin' a fox like you—no how, no way." He stuck out his muscular chest as the kid by the car hooted and laughed. Walking to where Lily stood, he slowly circled around her, his hot, belligerent gaze touching her in places she didn't want to be touched. She felt her heat rising, a blistering anger that a snot-nosed punk like him would dare to challenge her. "Touch me, and you'll wish the hell you hadn't."

The teen standing by the car whistled. "Willie, she gonna whup your ass! I'd leave her be if I was you!" Then, he laughed, lending a heavy sarcasm to his warning.

"Shit! I ain't scared o' no woman. She ain't much bigger than a willow twig—makes you wonder if those titties are real, or if they're plastic. Maybe I'll find out." He edged in, a slow step that brought him close. He smelled of beer and brake fluid, and the fermented spearmint tobacco that bulged in his lower lip.

"Leave her be, Willie." The voice came from behind her. Lily didn't turn away from the young predator in front of her, but she knew the warning's source. He'd managed to fight his way out of a bad situation, against unfair odds, and her stomach clenched at the thought of his taking on the punk leering at her breasts.

"Shut up, Boudreaux, or you're gonna get that clock cleaned, for sure. This chick and me, we got business." He reached for her, and as he did, Lily struck, folding her knuckles under at the first joint, throwing all of her anger into a single blow to his larynx. He made a strangled sound and folded like a rag doll, his eyes huge, his face gone chalk-white as he choked on his chew. By the time his friends got him on his feet and hustled him back to the car, he was drawing air and gagging, but it would be a long time before he forgot her. The car engine turned over and the driver flung mud all over the asphalt as he spun out. He didn't even attempt to miss the bicycle, but ran right over it, leaving a mangled mess in the aftermath.

Lily looked at the bike, then at the bloodied boy, wincing. "Your bike's ruined, and it's my fault. I'm sorry."

He tore off his shirt, mopping at the blood on his face. "No need to be sorry. It never did amount to much. Just somethin' I found in the junk pile and put back together." He was trembling with a post adren-aline rush, but he managed to laugh. "Shit! It was worth it just to see the look on Willie's face when you laid him flat." He laughed again, then groaned, be-ginning to feel the effects of the beating now that the adrenaline was wearing off. He tried for a deep breath, but failed, and in that moment Lily could see his resemblance to Gitan. It was evident in the set of his shoulders, the prominent cheekbones, but most of all it was there in his sloe-dark eyes. "Hey, I know you. You're Lily, aren't you?"

Not Lily Lothair, or Lily Martin . . . just Lily.

"Mason," she guessed.

He grinned. "I thought it was you. I was just a kid, but I remember."

His knees buckled and he almost fell. Lily grabbed his arm to steady him. "You need to see a doctor. I'll take you to the ER, and you can call your family from there."

"I'm okay," he said quickly. "Honest. Besides, if I went to the hospital, my aunt would freak. A lift home's all I need."

Lily threw him a skeptical look, but got him in the car, and the skeletal remains of the bicycle in the trunk. Then, she drove to Rose Boudreaux's on Tupelo Avenue.

Rose Boudreaux was framed by the homemade screen door, the picture of a worried woman. It was getting dark, and Gitan had called over an hour ago to tell her Mason was on his way home. He'd indicated the boy should stay indoors, no video games for the rest of the week, and he said he'd be by in a little while to discuss the situation with her.

Gitan was reliable. He didn't waste words and he meant what he said, but she knew that her brother's eldest son was disappointed in her. Gitan felt that she couldn't handle a fifteen-year-old boy, and maybe he was right, but Rose didn't have it in her to turn her back on either of her brother John's boys. She couldn't have loved them any more if they'd been her own children, and maybe that was the problem. Maybe, if she'd had kids of her own, she'd have had a better idea what Mason needed, besides someone to believe in him. In Rose's opinion, it was really all either of them had needed: someone to give them unconditional love and unshakeable loyalty.

Blood was everything.

Her brother John had been one of the finest men she'd ever known, so it followed she would love his boys to distraction. Gitan was John and Annie's eldest, and Mason the baby. How could she be hard with him when every time she looked in his handsome face, she saw John, the brother she'd idolized?

The video games quickly became a nonissue as the clock ticked off another hour and Mason didn't show. "Watched pots don' ever boil," Rose muttered, but she didn't move from her position at the screen door. She watched the road, and she listened, and beneath her breath she prayed, her mind going back years to the night she'd worried and watched with Annie and John for Gitan to come home.

He'd been out late, later than usual, and Annie had it in her head that something was wrong. Rose remembered trying to calm her, but she'd been edgy too, though John kept telling them both that Gitan was a man now and he'd come home when he was ready. Morning had come, and still no Gitan . . . Then they'd heard the police sirens screaming all the way out to Kyme Road, to the Martin house . . . and their Gitan, he never did come home for more than eight long years, if one counted his time before trial.

The direction of her worries nearly sent Rose into a panic. "Mason ain't Gitan. Remember that, you. He'll be by in a little while, laughing and sayin', 'Shoot, no need to worry 'bout me. I take care of myself just fine.'" But there was no sign of a bicycle flying down around that wicked corner on Tupelo Avenue. And no Mason. Just a black car that didn't belong in this neighborhood that approached slowly, then, amazingly, turned into the drive.

A prayer frozen on her lips, Rose pushed the door open and walked out into the twilight. A woman got out, a beautiful young woman, short blond hair, blue eyes, tanned skin that was so finely textured it looked as if she'd stepped off one of those television ads for department store makeup counters. "Something I can do for you, miss?" Rose said, then as the young lady opened the passenger door and reached in to help Mason out, Rose's knees buckled under her and she nearly fell. "Mason?" Her cry was horrified, grief-stricken. "Mother of God, Mason, what's happened to you?"

She rushed forward, but he shrugged away from her, from both of them. "It's not as bad as it looks, *Tante* Rose. I got into a fight, that's all. A little hot water—I'll be just fine. Lily, thanks for the ride."

"Oh, God." Rose covered her mouth with her hand as she watched him limp slowly toward the house. Then, she turned to face Lily. "I should thank you for bringing him home, but I won't. You got some nerve, comin' here."

Lily caught the brunt of the older woman's anger and managed to weather it without flinching. Maybe she deserved it. If it hadn't been for her involvement with Gitan, he would have been home that night instead of in her father's study. "Miss Boudreaux, don't you want to know what happened?"

Rose Boudreaux lifted herself to her full five feet three inches, glaring at Lily. "What happened?" she shot back. "Been waitin' all these years to know what happened, 'cause the story I got wasn't truth. My nephew never killed no one, him! I know dat boy! He ain't got murder in him!"

Lily took a deep breath and tried to resist the urge to apologize for something she'd been powerless to prevent. But had she been? Powerless? She squeezed her eyes closed against a sharp wave of regret, seeking a calm she was a long way from feeling. "I was talking about Mason."

Rose's temper exploded. "Get out of here, you! Get

back in dat little black car, and leave us alone! You got no right to be here! No right a'tall!"

A part of Lily wanted to run, and it took everything she possessed to push past the impulse and stand her ground. "You can hate me if you want. You've earned that right, but I'm not leaving until I know that Mason is all right."

Somewhere back of the house, the soft, throaty purr of a motorcycle sounded; then the sound died, and the back door slammed. A second later, the screen door pushed open and Lily's past stepped into the twilight. He was tall, tanned, and lethal-looking, from the spider's web tattooed on his bare shoulder to his impenetrable dark eyes, and all Lily could do was stare, unable to believe he was real. "Rose, Mason's locked up in the bathroom and I can hear the water running, but he won't answer. He still pissed?"

"You tell him," Rose said hotly, "then get out, and don' you come back here, ever!"

At that moment, Mason appeared at the door, a towel draped over his bare shoulders. Gitan glanced from Lily, to Rose, to Mason, and cursed under his breath. "What the hell's goin' on around this place?"

Mason hunched his shoulders and the tension between them was thick and furious. "Nothin'."

"Nothin', hell! You look like you got hit by a truck. You may not have noticed, little brother, but I ain't stupid. That truck's got a name. Who was it?"

"Nobody that matters."

"Shit!" Gitan ground out angrily.

"I took care of it, all right? Jesus, *va brasser dans tes chaudières!*"

Rose gasped. "Mason Edward!"

"Mind my own business?" Gitan asked softly. "You dumb little shit. You are my goddamned business!"

Mase turned to glare at Rose, both eyes swelling
shut, his nose scraped and swollen, possibly broken,
his lip cut. "Lily got me out of there. That's all you
need to know, 'cause it's all that matters. You hear that,
Tante Rose? I owe her. I owe Lily, and so do you! You
may not want her here, but I do!" His voice cracked
under the weight of his emotional display. Clearly embarrassed, he shot Lily a swift glance and stormed past
his aunt into the house.

"I'll go," Rose told Gitan, but as she swept past
him, he grabbed her arm.

"He's not a little kid anymore," Gitan told her.
"Give him some breathin' room."

Rose glanced back at Lily, obviously wishing she
could say something compelling enough to convince
him to walk away, but the look on his face must have
killed the inclination, if not the desire. She held her
tongue and went inside.

Lily's heart thudded heavily against her ribs. "No
one told me," she said. "I had no idea—"

He ignored the awkwardness of the situation,
smoothing it over and taking it all onto himself, just
as he always had. "I'm not surprised they didn't mention it. It's only been a few months, and a con gettin'
sprung ain't exactly front-page news."

"A few months." How many times had she spoken to
Virginia on the phone? How many long conversations
had she and Michel shared? And neither had mentioned that Gitan Boudreaux was a free man. "I wish
Aunt Virginia had said something. I wish I'd known."

"Why? So you could've met me at the prison gate?"
He shrugged it off, shrugged her off. "It's over, *cher.*
Forget about it."

His offhand manner stung Lily's pride. She didn't
know what she'd been expecting, but it wasn't this.

She swallowed hard, but she couldn't quite choke down her confusion, her irrational hurt. *What is wrong with you, Lily? What did you expect?* Her roiling emotions put an edge in her own voice. "Are you working? Early release must come with a lot of strings."

"Why you askin'? Virginia Martin need a yard man? Someone to take out the trash? Don' fret, *cher.* Ruben Early put me on right after my release. Ever'thing's right as rain. Ain't no need for your concern. Ol' Gitan ain't gonna fuck this one up."

"I never thought that, and I didn't mean to intrude—" Lily broke off, shaking her head. *Cut your losses and go, Lily, before you make an even bigger ass of yourself.*

Gitan sensed her frustration and anger, but he couldn't afford to explain. He'd dreamt of this moment a million times over the years, but he'd never imagined it would be so hard, or hurt so intensely. He kept his hands in his pockets to keep from doing something stupid and destructive, like reaching for her. Her voice was tight, her tone strangled with barely suppressed emotion, but her eyes were dry. Typically Lily. "I can't believe I wrote you. That I tried to visit."

"Only mail I got was from Mama. I figured you were busy, gettin' that law degree. Gettin' on with your life."

And Lily snapped, her anger barely contained now. "Yes, I got on with my life! What choice did I have?"

Reaching out, Gitan let his fingertips glide along the curve of her jaw. His touch was light, appreciative, but not possessive. "You didn't have a choice, *cher,* and neither did I. We can't change what's past, so let's get on with it." He took a breath and released it slowly. "So, you gonna tell me what happened to Mase? Or should I guess?"

"I found him on Mill Creek Road, just past the boat launch. There were four of them—all older, I think."

"Four against one. Lousy odds, that's for sure."

"Yes, but he's got backbone. He didn't back down, and he didn't run."

"I s'pose we can write that on his crypt when we find him lyin' in a ditch. He might be dead, but he sure didn't back down."

She started to turn away and he called her back, his voice somehow different, less hard, less callous, and less uncaring.

"Lily? I'm sorry about Michel. I know you two were tight, and he was a good man. No one can dispute that."

"Thanks," she said, but she didn't turn back, and she wouldn't look at him again. As she walked to her car, Gitan allowed the image of her in that white gown to form in the back of his mind; he let the anticipation build for a few seconds along with the acceleration of his pulse before he squelched it completely, reminding himself in the starkest terms who she was, who he was, and where he'd been. A young lawyer and a hardened ex-con struggling to gain a little self-respect, working his ass off to prove himself, to keep his family from disintegrating—and from the looks of Mase's battered face, not doing a great job of it. *It's a dead-end road, man. Let it go.*

He turned then and walked slowly back to the house, and the only satisfaction he gained from any of it came from knowing that Lily would never know what it had cost him to be so harsh with her.

Father John Bernaud worked in the rectory garden most mornings. One of his greatest joys was tilling the earth and watching his vegetables grow. There was

something about the newness of morning that reju-
venated the spirit. The rising sun, the singing birds,
the dew-soaked grass, the limitless patience of a
garden snake lying beneath a tomato plant as it
waited for a mouse, inspired and provoked thought.

Today was different. It was late afternoon before
Father Bernaud found the time to care for his flowers and plants. There was trouble in the diocese, big
trouble. One of their own had been murdered, and
speculation was rife as to why it had happened, and
who among them, if any, might be next. On his knees,
vigorously plying a short garden fork and pulling up-
rooted weeds, Father Bernaud failed to notice that he
was no longer alone until the hem of the bishop's scarlet robes entered his peripheral vision. He glanced up,
a little startled, hastily wiping his hands on his handkerchief and kissing the ring the other man offered.
After the show of respect, he struggled to his feet. "Your
Excellency. I thought I was alone."

"It's too warm to be working in the garden, isn't it,
Father Bernaud?"

"I have a tolerance for the heat, and I enjoy tilling
the soil. It calms my thoughts, brings me peace."

The bishop's expression was sour. "We could all
use a little peace of mind. These are troubling times.
Very troubling. Walk with me. It's shady under the
arbor, and the breeze off the water's quite refreshing.
You may enjoy the heat, but I'm afraid I don't. I miss
New York. The nights are cool there this time of year."

Father Bernaud waited, saying nothing, aware the
bishop had not searched him out to discuss the differences in climate between Louisiana and his beloved
New York. Before long, his patience was rewarded. The
bishop got to the point. "It's come to my attention

through Father Murdoch that you have requested retirement."

"Yes, your Excellency. I've had nearly forty years of service to God and this community. I feel it's time."

His Excellency looked pained. "Normally, I would give you my blessing and make the arrangements. Instead, I find myself asking you to consider delaying a little while longer. The diocese already suffers from a shortage of priests, and now that we have lost Father Dugas, you're needed more than ever."

Father Bernaud looked down at his hands, the fingers knotted with advancing age, and slightly stained from dirt and weeds. There was strength yet in those hands, from his physical toil; some of his colleagues turned soft, their hands tender and flesh pale. He hadn't allowed himself that luxury, but what about his spirit? Did he have the courage to continue?

He thought about that. Thought about Father Dugas, and the terrible death he had suffered, and it took everything he had to nod his head in agreement. "Yes, your Excellency. I can see that."

"Then you'll reconsider retiring from St. Bartholomew's until we can find a suitable replacement? You'll agree to lead the funeral mass?"

"If I am needed to serve my parish, then how can I refuse?" His voice was steady and quiet, but his hands were shaking, and he was secretly relieved when the bishop suddenly remembered an appointment and left him.

For a while, he sat in the shade of the arbor, feeling the breeze off the water caress his hot skin and trying to forget the visitor who had come to him last night. Words usually reserved for the shadows of the confessional had been whispered in the near darkness of the chapel, and he could have sworn he could smell the metallic taint of blood, heavy and acrid in the air. *Bless me, Father, for I have sinned.*

A familiar voice, heavy with the sorrow of a dreadful and inhuman act. A lost soul, seeking redemption for the unthinkable.

The trembling in Father Bernaud's hands crept into his arms, and his shoulders, and soon his thin frame shook with a violence that was more than a little frightening. He was responsible. The sin stained his soul, just as surely as it stained the murderer's. Father Dugas's death was a shared burden, a shared secret that gave birth to a moral dilemma. How was he to stand before Father Dugas's grieving parishioners and offer solace at his funeral mass without choking on his own hypocrisy?

CHAPTER
FOUR

Dusk had fallen by the time Lily arrived at Virginia's. Evening fell softly in southern Louisiana, but the humidity didn't lessen. The rise and fall of quiet conversation coming from the deep shadows of the neighbors' porch was a distraction as Lily came up the walk and mounted the steps to the porch. It had already been a bitch of a day, and when the tip of a cigarette flared in the nearly impenetrable shadows near the lightless windows, and she recognized her ex-husband's profile, her bone-weariness settled more heavily upon her.

"Glad you're home. I was beginnin' to worry."

"Hugh. What are you doing here?" It was amazing that she could be upright and functioning on the outside when on the inside she was falling apart. The last thing she needed right now was another confrontation with him.

"California didn't improve your temper any," he drawled easily, dragging on the cigarette again. "Or your manners, for that matter. The polite thing would be to ask me in."

Like a starving dog with a meaty bone, he pushed a point to its limit and beyond, and he never took no for an answer the first time, or the second, or third. It was the one thing that made him a damn good cop, and a nightmare of an ex, but Lily had had enough for one day. "Do me a favor, will you? Leave."

"I take it your visit to Tupelo Avenue didn't go as well as planned."

Lily had started to push past him, but now she stopped to glare down at him. "You followed me?"

"Not exactly. I just happened to be in the neighborhood, and saw your car parked in the drive. It's my job to keep an eye on things in this town, but maybe you've forgotten." One last drag and he crushed the butt into the standing ashtray beside his chair. "So, the kid got the shit kicked out of him?"

A tremor came out of nowhere to vibrate through Lily. She'd been treading water emotionally since she'd heard about Michel, and she could feel herself slipping. She couldn't deal with Hugh. Not now, so soon after. She needed quiet. She needed to think, but she wouldn't get either. He would push and push until she lashed out or exploded. "I shouldn't have to remind you that Louisiana has laws against stalking. You may be the sheriff, but you're not immune, so watch your step. I won't roll over and play dead if I find out you're watching me."

He tapped another cigarette from a pack, shoved it between his lips, and bent his head to light it. "I care about you, Lily. You're family. Since when is that a crime?"

"You aren't family, Hugh. In fact, you stopped being anything to me but a pain in my ass the day I filed."

"Let's keep it civil, shall we? I came here to talk."

"You came here to harass me, and I don't have time for this bullshit right now." Lily pushed the door open. She'd had enough of his attempts at manipulation and control to last a lifetime, and there was no way in hell she would ever allow herself to be drawn back in.

"Fine, then. You don't want to talk here, you can come down to the station. It's about the Dugas homicide. I'd think you'd want to do all you could to help out, given the fact that you and Dugas were such good friends, and all. But maybe I'm wrong about that, too? Seems like I'm wrong about everything— according to you."

Lily steeled herself against the wave of fury crashing all around her. Hugh knew exactly what buttons to push, and he knew that she would do anything for Michel. "Manipulative bastard."

"Now, that was immature."

"All right. All right! You can come in; just don't get too comfortable." It was the only way to get rid of him. A moment later, Lily watched as he sank into a chair at the kitchen table and took out a notepad and pen. "I'd like to say I hate to bother you with this, but that isn't exactly true. You were always close to Michel, and I have no reason to believe you cut ties with him when you left Louisiana." When she didn't argue the point, he continued. "When did you last have contact with the victim?"

All cop, part unfeeling son of a bitch. Lily hugged her arms tightly against her body. Experts in reading body language would have indicated she was feeling the need to protect herself from him, and they would have been right. "I spoke with him by telephone last Thursday evening."

"What'd you talk about?"

"I don't know," she said with a shrug. "Normal stuff, nothing important. The weather, the rectory garden, life."

"Dugas liked to garden?" Hugh said. "Somehow it's a little hard to imagine him gettin' his hands dirty."

"Not Michel. A fellow priest—Father Bernard—no, it was Bernaud. Michel enjoyed walking the meditation path. It had become a sort of ritual after morning mass. It's close to the gardens. He said it cleared his mind—helped him to think."

"Did he seem troubled about anything?"

"Not that he mentioned."

"Did he mention receiving any threats? Was there anything unusual that concerned him?"

"Michel was a priest. Why would anyone threaten him?" He bent a look on her and she shook her head. "If he was worried about anything, he didn't tell me."

"You happen to know who he was involved with? He have a steady lover? Or was he more the one-night-stand type?"

"Damn it, Hugh!"

"Lily, sex is a part of the human condition and whether you want to admit it, or not, Dugas was no saint."

"Michel was totally committed to fulfilling his vows—"

"Yeah? Well, so were we, and look how that turned out." He must have sensed that he had touched a raw nerve, because his tone softened the smallest bit. "*Was* Michel involved with someone? Sexually speaking?"

"Even if he had been, that isn't the sort of thing he would have confided in me."

He closed the notebook and returned it with the pen to his jacket pocket. As Virginia's car pulled in out front, he stood. "Guess that's it for now. If you remember anything else, give me a call. You know the number." He started to leave, then hesitated, turning back, and the look on his face was grave. "Lily, do yourself a favor and stay away from Gitan Boudreaux. That scar down the center of his chest isn't the only thing that's changed about him. He's been away for a long time. Accept it. The man you used to know doesn't exist anymore."

He pushed past Virginia on his way out, and left with a brusque good night to both of them. Worn out, Lily went down the hall and up the stairs. In a moment, Virginia knocked softly.

"It's open."

"What did Prince Charming want?" Virginia asked. She looked just as she'd always looked, impeccably dressed in a beige skirt and a soft white blouse, her blond hair neatly styled and not a hair out of place, despite the humidity. Lily didn't know how she managed it. Especially when *she* felt about as neat as an unmade bed after the day she'd just endured. It wasn't until the older woman turned slightly and the light from the hallway hit her aunt full in the face that Lily saw the lines that age and fatigue had etched on her face. "He's not pressuring you to take him back, is he?"

"He was here about Michel."

Reaching out, Virginia smoothed a gentle hand along Lily's cheek. "Oh, darlin'. I'm so sorry. That must have been difficult. Are you all right?"

Lily didn't reply directly. "I found Mason Boudreaux getting the tar pounded out of him this evening, and I took him home. Why didn't you tell me that Gitan had been paroled?" She was standing by the windows that overlooked the lawn. Beyond the glass, night was rapidly closing in. The cane field in the near distance was a ragged black sea, undulating in the moist night breeze. "Did you think I couldn't handle it? That I'd fall apart?"

"Of course not!" She sighed. "Honey, life was finally giving you what you've always deserved. You had a good job, and everything was working out. I didn't see any reason to upset that, especially when things are so uncertain for Bobby." Virginia stepped close enough that Lily couldn't ignore her look of concern. "You know I want the best for you. I always have, and that much won't ever change."

"I'm not a little girl anymore, Aunt Virginia, and I'm not made of spun glass. You didn't have to keep it from me. Gitan and I have been over for a long time." A fact he'd reinforced that very evening.

Her smile was tinged with sadness. "Maybe, but I don't like to gamble. Shoot, darlin', I don't even play the lottery!" She laughed, reaching out, tucking Lily's short hair behind one ear. "I wanted to give you every opportunity to be happy, that's all. And maybe I did it for Bobby too, on some level. It's not an easy thing for a man to start over, and he deserves a chance to get it right this time. The link between you two was always strong. I couldn't be sure what you'd do if I told you about his parole, so for once I decided it was best not to meddle." When Lily said nothing, just turned away toward the windows, Virginia let it go. "Well, I have a shipment arriving at the shop early, so I'll say good night. Get some rest, sweetheart."

Lily didn't know how long she stayed by the windows, staring out at the dark sea of cane and the moss-draped oaks beyond. Virginia's concern and Hugh's warning had been well meaning but futile. There was nothing between her and Gitan but a turbulent past, a past to which there was no going back. For just an instant, she could have sworn she heard the reverberation of a gunshot, a man's hoarse laughter, an angry curse . . . and then the door slammed and she pegged it for what it was: the echoes of some half-forgotten nightmare.

The bayou was a different world in the daylight. Brown-green water dappled by sunlight, hanging moss, and fan-shaped palmetto. A snow white heron stood silent and still in the shallows as a pontoon boat overflowing with paying tourists motored past. In the daylight, the swamp was a place of beauty and wonder, a sportsman's paradise, but at night the bayou evolved into something more sinister. The absence of light on a moonless night turned the brownish green water an oily black, disturbed only by the shallow wake of a cruising alligator, or the propellor of a motored craft. Gitan preferred the bayou after dark, when a man could get as physically lost as he sometimes felt himself to be.

Seeing Lily again had taken him back eight years, to a night he'd done his best to forget. Remembering served no purpose, and though he'd told himself at least a million times over the years that there could be no going back, he couldn't seem to take his own sage advice. He didn't even need to try to remember how he'd felt when he arrived at Catfish Point that night and she wasn't there. He'd waited twenty minutes while fighting down the gnawing certainty that something was wrong, and finally he'd hopped on his bike and set out for Kyme Road, and the Martin house.

The memory of Lily's terrified scream echoed through his mind, and Gitan's pulse kick-started. As tension rippled through him, hardening the muscles in his forearms, he ruthlessly shut the memories down.

That was then, and this was now, and there was little anyone could do to change the events of that long ago night. Better that he concentrate on the immediate future, on the meeting with his parole officer scheduled for the following morning, and on Mason, than to relive that nightmare one more time.

Absently, he rubbed the scar cleaving his breastbone nearly to his throat, and ending a few inches above his navel. Lily's return had everything to do with Michel Dugas's death, and nothing to do with dredging up a past that was better off dead and buried. The funeral mass for Michel would be held day after tomorrow; then Lily would catch a plane back to L.A. and he would get on with the day-to-day grind of restoring a life fate had nearly destroyed.

It was that simple.

Forgetting her, how she'd looked, the sound of her voice, the soft woodsy smell of her perfume . . . That was bound to be the hard part.

Hugh pulled into the parking lot at Homer Folley's Funeral Home in Point Breeze at two minutes of eight the next morning under a hazy, overcast sky. It was already eighty-two degrees and the humidity hung in there at a relentless ninety percent. Blue haze was building on the southern horizon, and now and then a rumble of thunder sounded low and ominous somewhere out over the Gulf. They'd have rain sometime later in the day, but it would bring little relief from the oppressive temperatures.

Hugh grabbed his jacket, opened the car door, and the heat hit him solidly in the face, making him think about the position he'd passed up in St. Louis last year, before he'd made the decision to run for sheriff. St. Louis could be hot in the summertime too, but nothing beat the sauna-like conditions of southern Louisiana.

He'd passed on the job opportunity because Angelique was home. He'd felt that by staying, he could make a difference, and sometimes it was just better being a big fish in a small pond. There was no chance of anonymity in a place this small, especially when his parents still lived on Oakley Avenue, and his sixth grade teacher three doors down from the firehouse. But who the hell wanted anonymity, anyhow?

He enjoyed the respectful nods he received when he walked down the street, the murmurs of "Mornin', Sheriff," from the folks at the café counter when he dropped by for a cup of coffee on his way to the office.

Life in Angelique was normally laid back and pleasantly uneventful. Most families sat on their porches of an evening, and until a young ex-reporter-turned-private investigator had uncovered a string of brutal killings the year before, committed by a local resident, murder had been an uncommon event. Fegan Broussard had been the one to break the case and expose the culprit, no thanks to the former sheriff, Vance Pershing. Pershing, who'd been quietly counting down the months to his retirement when the crisis began, had left office following Hugh's election the previous November, and for months, Hugh's small bayou town had run like a well-oiled, if antiquated machine. Quiet, orderly, with just enough domestic situations, drug-related crime, petty theft, and DUIs to keep things interesting. Until Mason Boudreaux and a friend walked into an abandoned church out on Catfish Point and turned Angelique on its proverbial ear.

Hugh slipped into his jacket on his way to the double-wide trailer which had recently been set up at one end of the parking lot. It was the kind of building sometimes purchased by construction companies for on-site offices, but its innocuous appearance was deceptive. Hugh rapped lightly, then opened the door, stepping into Homer Folley's world.

Homer, a tall, dark-haired man in his mid-fifties with a distant politeness and a proclivity for same-sex relationships, doubled as parish coroner. Hugh didn't consider himself a homophobe, but he couldn't deny that the funeral director-slash-coroner's smile made him slightly uncomfortable. "Sheriff Lothair, I was beginnin' to feel stood up. Come in, won't you? We're about to get under way. Would you like to suit up? There are lab coats, bonnets, and booties in that cabinet over there." He gestured to a row of cabinets on the north wall. "First cabinet on your left."

"Thanks, I think I'll pass," Hugh said, glad he'd resisted buying a sweet roll with his morning coffee. "I don't plan on getting all that close." Close or not, there was no escaping the unique combination of the astringent cleaner, formaldehyde, and decomposing flesh. Hugh held up a small jar of Vicks VapoRub retrieved from his coat pocket. "You mind?"

"Oh, sure. Go right on ahead." Homer uncovered the naked form of Michel Dugas and got down to business, speaking into a pocket-sized cassette recorder held by his assistant. "Subject is a white male, twenty-seven years of age. Two hundred ten pounds, five foot ten inches tall. Extensive insect infestation—" As Hugh watched, he extracted several maggots with tweezer-like instruments, placing them in a small glass jar filled with clear liquid. When Homer reached

for the head saw, Hugh excused himself and went outside for a breath of fresh air.

Two hours later, after a hot shower and a fresh
change of clothes, he arrived at the new St. Bartholomew's. The white stucco walls and red tile roof of the
church were shaded by towering oaks, a pleasant,
almost exotic change from Hugh's red-brick Presbyterian roots. Shady walkways curved to the left and the
right of the main entrance, past lush gardens rife with
yellow begonias and red and white calla lilies. He
checked his watch. He was a few minutes early, and
might as well have a look around.

The last thing Hugh expected was to find Father
Bernaud on his knees in a patch of earth, weeding vigorously. As Hugh approached, he noted the shirt
the old man wore was damp between the shoulder
blades and stuck to his skin in places. A visor shaded
his face and kept him from seeing anything but the
heavy foliage of the calla lilies, a little like a horse with
blinders on. "Father Bernaud? That you?"

Startled, the priest glanced up. His face was flushed,
his skin damp. "Do I know you?"

Hugh offered a hand to help the priest to his feet,
and was surprised at the strength in the older man's
grasp. "Sheriff Lothair, Angelique Sheriff's Department. I'm a little surprised to find you here. I would
have thought that you would have retired by now."

"Hugh Lothair," the man said. "Yes, yes, I remember you now. You soaped the rectory windows each
and every Halloween, along with the Boudreaux boy.
I recall that he was punished—made to clean those
windows—"

He let it hang, almost an accusation.

Hugh smiled. "Boys will be boys, I suppose. Gitan

and I did create some mischief, back in the day. I'm surprised that you would remember."

The priest wiped his palms on his handkerchief, scrubbing at a stubborn stain. "Not much escaped me back then. I had a keen eye, as they say." A small glimmer of humor entered his blue eyes. "Not here to clear your conscience, are you?"

"My conscience is just fine, thank you," Hugh replied. "Actually, I have an appointment to speak with Father Murdoch about Michel Dugas." Hugh was watching the man as he explained, and noted the change in him at the mention of Michel's name. He averted his gaze, stuffed his handkerchief into a pocket, then pulled it out again to rub at his stained palms. As he turned his hand over, the abrasion was clearly noticeable. An inch in width, between thumb and forefinger, dark in color. "Is that a rope burn?"

"What? Oh, this! Yes. I have an elderly aunt who lives alone in Dupré. I do her yard work, mowing, weeding. Her lawn mower has a rope pull that proves quite obstinate. Ancient thing, should have been replaced years ago . . . not unlike myself, actually."

Hugh digested the explanation without comment. "Did you speak with Father Dugas in the days preceding his murder?"

"Several nights ago. He came to my private quarters. He'd heard that I was considering retirement, and he wished me well."

"Was there anything else?" Hugh asked. He had the strange feeling that the old man wasn't telling him everything, but whether he was intentionally holding something back, or just naturally nervous at being questioned wasn't readily apparent.

"As I said, Father Dugas and I didn't often have

occasion to talk. I suppose you could say that we disliked one another."

"Really? And why was that?"

Father Bernaud shrugged. "I'm from the old school, Sheriff, and my beliefs are conservative. Father Dugas had different ideals. He sided with that radical element which is constantly pushing for reform."

"Reform? You mean like condoning the use of birth control?"

"Among other things." Father Bernaud's expression turned sour. "He believed that priests should be permitted to marry. He was careful not to speak openly, to his congregation, but he let it be known within the religious order how he felt. I'm afraid that I disagreed with him on most issues, but it was nothing personal."

Hugh nodded. It was time for his appointment, but he couldn't leave without one last question. "Do you have any ideas about who might have wanted Michel Dugas dead?"

"I can only say that it was a depraved act by a sick individual. May God have mercy on his soul. Now, if you'll excuse me, Sheriff, I must get back to my lilies."

Morning had come, but Lily was reluctant to leave the comfort of a soft mattress and cool, crisp sheets. Somewhere beyond her bedroom door, Virginia bumped around in the kitchen, but the noise was not intrusive enough to drag her from her dreams. . . .

Lily had left the window open despite her mother's warning that the air conditioning was running. It was the only way to listen for her friends' arrival. Gitan and Hugh had made plans to pole a skiff out onto the bayou and laze away the afternoon searching for the biggest alligator they could find. Lily had begged to go along, and even though Hugh had argued hotly against it, he'd been outvoted. She'd risen early, dressed in jeans and a T-shirt, and applied a generous cloud of insect repellent. Now, she waited anxiously by the open window for sounds of their arrival.

"Lily home?" A lone voice drifted up from the shadows of the porch, not what she expected.

The housekeeper answered. "Our Lily? What do you want with her?" A second's pause. "Wait a minute. Aren't you that Boudreaux boy from over on Mayfly Street?"

"*Mais,* yeah, that's me. Gitan." Slurred and easy-sounding, there was something about the way he said it that made Lily's heart start in her chest and kick into third gear. It didn't help that he was on the front porch facing down Pauline's inquisition. Pauline was the housekeeper and she ruled when Lily's parents weren't home. Lily ran down the hallway, jumped on the banister, and slid to the third step from the bottom, hopping off in a breathless hurry.

"Lord, girl!" Pauline said. "How many times you got to be told to come down those stairs like a young lady instead of some godforsaken heathen-child?"

Lily murmured an excuse about being in a hurry, slipping around Pauline, who stood glaring at Gitan, her hands on the waist of her gray linen uniform. "And just where you think you're goin'?" she demanded, her voice rising at the end of the question.

"Just hanging out, that's all."

"Since when did your mama give you permission to hang out with swamp trash?"

Lily stopped dead in her tracks at the slur, feeling the hurt Gitan would not allow himself to feel. Turning slightly, she met Pauline's hard stare. "He is not, and you'd better say you're sorry."

The housekeeper snorted. "Me, apologize to swamp trash get? Dream on, child!"

Lily did the unthinkable and balled one small fist. "You apologize, or I'll tell Mama that the money she thought she lost really wasn't lost at all."

Pauline's eyes widened. "What on earth are you sayin'?"

"I saw you," Lily said. "I saw you with your hand in Mama's purse."

Pauline hesitated, uncertain, and her dark eyes filled with hatred. She apologized, reluctantly, but as she disappeared into the house, Lily could hear her muttering about "eleven-year-old girls who hung on the boys coming to no damn good."

"C'mon," Gitan said. "Got my uncle's pirogue waitin' by the water. If we hurry, we can explore Blackwater Cove and be back in plenty of time for supper."

"What about Hugh and Michel?"

"Michel didn't call?" He furrowed his brow at that. "His mama's draggin' him to mass, and Hugh stepped on a nail and needs a rabies shot. Guess it's just you an' me."

Lily laughed. "You can't get rabies from a rusty nail!"

"Maybe the doctor don' know that," he said with unaccustomed levity. "Hell, sometimes I think he needs a rabies shot."

Lily thought about that for a minute or two and they both got very quiet. Quiet was uncomfortable with a lot of folks, Lily knew, but with her and Gitan quiet was okay. "Why's Hugh always got to be so mean?"

He shrugged. "Wants to be bigger than he is, I guess. Some folks are just like that. You got to learn to ignore him. That's what I do. Gets to him worse than a good thrashin' would. Not that he couldn't use one."

Lily didn't like to hear him talk like that. Nobody deserved to be beaten. Not even Hugh.

"Listen, you aren't worried about gettin' in trouble, are you? 'Cause if you are, I can go out there alone."

Lily shook her head. "Pauline won't dare tell, and Mama wouldn't remember, even if she did," she said, her voice seeming to shrink, even though she fought to hide it. Her mother's drinking hadn't slowed; in fact, it was getting worse. Cocktail hour started at breakfast and stretched into the evening, or until she passed out. It was one more thing in a very long list of things that Lily didn't like to think about, but couldn't seem to forget.

Gitan seemed to read her thoughts. "Lot o' folks like to drink, Lily. My uncle, he likes to tie one on every now and then. Drives *Tante* Rose up the wall, you know? She was so mad at him last year, she took back her maiden name. But for them, it's normal."

Lily said nothing, and in a minute, he took her hand and held it. "Listen, *cher* . . . if you need outta there, you just got to say so, that's all. I'll break the locks if I got to. *L'union, fait la force.* You got that?"

Lily nodded. "In union, there is strength. That means two of us are stronger than one."

"*Mais,* yeah, dat's right, sister! Together, we can conquer the world!" He flexed his muscle in a mock show of strength, and Lily laughed. "C'mon, *cher*! Let's get on outta here. Pir'oue, she's waitin' . . ."

Lily rolled onto her side, squinting at the bright morning light slanting through the lace curtains. The urge to pull up the covers and sleep the day away was strong, but she couldn't return to that long-ago day, no matter how badly she wanted to. She wasn't the same Lily she'd been back then, and it had been blatantly obvious from their brief meeting at Rose Boudreaux's that Gitan had changed too.

What on earth did you expect? Everybody said he'd changed, and maybe they were right.

She flashed on the image of him standing over her father, fists raised and bloody. Somewhere a woman whimpered, pleading with him to "get away." The scene was hazy, viewed through a clouded lense. Lily struggled with it, as she always did, struggled with the idea that there was something else lurking there.

Gitan had beaten Justin Martin bloody. That was fact, documented in Gitan's statement taken much later, underscored by Lily's memories. She knew that she must have been the one pleading for Gitan to get away, but that was where her recall ended. Gitan hadn't left the scene to save himself when she'd begged him to. At twenty, he'd considered himself invincible, and he'd never shown an ounce of fear of her father, or the damage he could do. He'd stayed, and somehow stabbed her father to death.

Lily should have remembered the events of that night with startling clarity. The images should have been burned into her consciousness—but she must have blacked out. Her recall, beyond the moment when Gitan stood over Justin, was a blank slate. Gitan's confession, combined with Virginia's explanation, had helped fill in the blank spaces in her memory. Gitan's fingerprints had been lifted from the murder weapon, a five-inch buck knife he carried when he went into the swamp. When Vance Pershing questioned Gitan in the hospital, he'd admitted that he had killed Justin.

They'd been planning to run away, and Justin had discovered their plans. When Gitan came to the house, the situation, already bad, had spun completely out of control.

The five days that followed were lost to Lily. The shock of her father's violent death and Gitan's injuries had taken their toll. Lily did not return to the house on Kyme Road. With the threat of a total breakdown a real possibility for her, Sharon had relented and allowed her to stay at Virginia's. The Boudreauxs had kept her from visiting Gitan in the hospital, fearing her presence would be too much for their son to handle during those first crucial weeks.

When Lily thought about that night, it was with the realization that it had been a turning point in her life. After two weeks in ICU and two months in the hospital, Gitan had gone to a cell in the Angelique Sheriff's Department to await his sentencing. Lily had done everything humanly possible to preserve his freedom, hiring a lawyer with the trust money her grandmother had left her, but all of her efforts had failed. He'd pleaded no contest to the charge of murder in the second degree, and received a twenty-to-life sentence in Angola Prison by a "lenient" judge.

Four years at Loyola University of New Orleans, three years in Loyola's School of Law, and during that time her brief, ill-fated marriage to Hugh, her only contact with Gitan had been through Michel. Gitan had wanted it that way. Michel had somehow been granted what she'd been denied, and Gitan had tolerated, if not welcomed, the intrusion into his life.

Lily shoved her memories into that place where they could not intrude, and got on with it. When she descended the stairs, headed for her morning run, Virginia was in the kitchen battling the garbage disposal. She rammed the handle of the plunger down the drain while Edna Mae Cummins crossed her arms and sent her disapproving looks. "Damned, infernal contraption!"

A bit of knocking about, and she pulled out the handle and turned on the switch. The mechanism emitted a deep-throated gurgle, then gave up the ghost completely. Virginia pushed a lock of hair out of her face and ground out a few choice words Lily had never heard her utter. "You didn't hear that!" Virginia said, pointing a finger at Lily. "And neither did you!"

"Oh, yes, I did." Edna Mae was smug.

"Aunt Virginia? What on earth is going on?"

"Edna Mae and I are having a disagreement, sugar. Her memory's been slippin' a bit lately."

"Excuse me?" Edna Mae said, indignant now. "I ain't the one who made the appointment to have that disposal serviced, then turned right around and canceled. My mind's as clear as a bell, and you know it! Slippin', my backside! You wanna know who's slippin' 'round here, you take a good look in the mirror!"

"It was a misunderstanding," Virginia insisted.

"Uh huh," Edna said, but her tone clearly said she wasn't convinced. She'd worked for Virginia for too many years not to be comfortable speaking her mind.

"Ignore her, sugar. *I do.*" As the women traded glares, Lily took a pitcher of orange juice from the refrigerator and poured a small glass. "I'm surprised Prince Charming hasn't been by," Virginia said. "I'm sure that by now he must know that you're home."

Lily paused, the pitcher poised above her glass. "Hugh was here last night."

"He was?" she said, her voice tinged with sarcasm. "Well, I'm sorry I missed him."

Lily felt a chill that had little to do with the air conditioning. "Aunt Virginia, you didn't miss him. He was here when you got home last night; don't you remember?"

Virginia looked startled for just a second. "Well, of course, I remember," she said with a laugh, but Lily could tell she was rattled. "I never did like that man. Small wonder I was able to put him out of my mind." She took a sip of her coffee, then glanced at her watch. "Well, for heaven's sake, will you look at the time? I've got to get goin'."

She picked up her jacket and handbag, bussing Lily's cheek. "It really is good to have you home."

Virginia went out and Edna Mae busied herself with a grocery list. The housekeeper might not be above giving her employer a hard time, but when it came to "outsiders," she was loyal. "How long has she been like this?"

"Stubborn as a mule? Her entire life."

"Forgetting things she should remember," Lily said. "Missing appointments? Memory lapses?"

"Now, Miss Lily, you know Miss Virginia ain't no spring chicken. A certain amount of forgetfulness is normal."

Maybe, but Lily didn't think so. Virginia had always been sharp, and at sixty-two, was far from ready for the boneyard. "Has she seen a doctor?"

Edna glanced over the top of her black framed glasses, a sidelong look that made her "What do you think?" seem like a redundancy.

"All right," Lily said. "It's my place. I'll speak with her."

CHAPTER
FIVE

Ruben Early was a self-made man. For thirty years, he'd worked at the refinery with Gitan's daddy, repairing and customizing motorcycles in his garage in his spare time. What Ruben didn't know about motorcycles hadn't been dreamt up yet. He modified a few bikes of his own, worked on outside projects as word of his talents got out, and finally began building custom bikes from the ground up. At age fifty-five, he'd decided to take the plunge and start a small shop of his own. He'd cashed in his retirement fund, got a business loan from the First Federal Bank, and he'd bought a building on the corner of Fourth and Main. Five short years later, he had a backlog of orders, six full-time employees, and a membership at the country club.

The leap from refinery grunt to entrepreneur hadn't happened overnight, and it hadn't come without a price. He'd worked long and hard to establish his business, putting in more hours than any of his em-

ployees the first three years, and as a result his twenty-
five-year marriage had come undone. His alimony pay-
ments didn't quite bankrupt him, and the future
looked promising. Still, Ruben didn't take anything
for granted. He gave more back to the community
than he took, he volunteered to coach softball for a
local youth team, and he'd given one ex-con fresh out
of Angola a fair break.

In turn, Gitan gave Ruben his best work. Throughout his youth he'd worked with a pad and charcoal
pencil, sketching the wildlife he encountered in the
bayou, or *Tante* Rose and his mother sitting on the
back porch steps, stealing a smoke and telling jokes
and laughing. He'd spent countless hours trying out
techniques to correctly duplicate the contour of a
human face so that it appeared three-dimensional, or
the realistic turn of a thumb.

From an early age, he'd recognized that he saw the
world through different eyes than most people. He'd
roamed the fields, woods, and swamps with Hugh
Lothair because they'd been of an age, but Gitan had
known that's where the similarity between them ended.
Hugh had always viewed the world in stark and un-
yielding contrast, while Gitan's universe was multi-
colored and multi-faceted, a place where even a
spider's web, suspended between two strands of barbed
wire and glistening with early morning dew, was a
thing of beauty and wonder.

High school art class had presented Gitan with a variety of mediums. He'd learned how to shade and
shadow, and how to create the illusion of light. When
his father had found an airbrush in a scrap heap near
the refinery, his means of expression had been chan-
neled into something more lucrative than canvas and
brush, and by the age of eighteen, he was earning

enough money to supply his artistic habits. Everyone 'round Angelique knew that Gitan Boudreaux could design and paint a set of flames to curl along the body of an old coupe which became the talk of the town, but the only one aware that the Boudreaux boy had bigger dreams than painting cars was Lily Martin.

Lily had been to his bedroom by way of the old porch roof the summer she turned sixteen, and she'd seen his sketch pads. Lily, alone, knew that Gitan dreamt of owning a place of his own someday, a real studio.

Dreams had a way of going up in smoke, and his had been set aside so long that it all felt like some crazy adolescent fantasy, too faded, too tired and worn to be salvaged.

Unlike his dreams, his talent with an airbrush was paying off. Ruben was a fair employer, and Gitan's uncomplicated lifestyle didn't require much in the way of amenities. The job at the chop shop kept the wolf away from the door, his parole officer off his back, and even allowed him to save a little money. For now, it was enough.

Arley Malloy was grinding the burrs off the weld on the metal gas tank he'd just finished fabricating when Gitan walked in, but he paused long enough to give a two-fingered salute. Malloy was in his late thirties, short and wiry with a reddish ponytail that hung down his back. "Hey, Gitan, what are you workin' on this mornin'?"

"Got the fenders and tank in the paint bay for Billy Williams's Fat Boy. Why?"

"I sure could use some help with the new project. I'm way behind on the weld, and I never did get the hang of this old dinosaur. When do you suppose Ruben's gonna break down and get us a real welder?"

In the background Ruben's voice rose a notch or two, his chair squeaked, and the office door slammed, but the room wasn't soundproof, and it didn't contain his anger completely. Gitan adjusted his sweatband over his dark hair, taking a closer look at Arley's work. "I'm guessin' it ain't gonna be today," he said. "Guess I can give this a few minutes. You got somethin' else to do, I'll see to it."

Arley looked relieved. "I need to check in with the chromer and make sure the parts we dropped off are gonna be finished on time. Ruben was gonna take care of it; then Junior stopped by for his weekly shake-down, and he's been on a tear ever since. Can't say as I blame him, though. That kid's a waste of oxygen."

"Willie was here this morning?" Gitan took a welder's helmet down from its place on the shelf. "He takin' the day off school?"

Gitan didn't care for Willie Early, and he wasn't alone in his dislike of him. Willie had that air of entitlement that kids who have unlimited access to their parents' money too often have. Gitan had known kids like Willie growing up in Angelique, and he'd known a few in prison as well. Money bought a lot of things, and solved a lot of problems, but it couldn't stop a young man bent on self-destructing from throwing away his future, or from taking the people who loved him along for the painful ride.

Arley snorted. "Hell, no. The little shit quit school. Ruben's threatenin' military school, but Charlotte won't hear of it."

Gitan said nothing, and after lingering for a few minutes, Arley left to call the chromer. He had enough problems keeping Mason on the right track to comment on someone else's family problems. He'd swung by Rose's on the way to the appointment with his parole officer that morning to talk to Mase, whose injuries had kept him home from school. He'd tried to pry out of Mase who'd jumped him and why, but the kid wasn't talking. Not about the fight, anyway . . .

"You gonna fix things with Lily?" he'd asked, aiming the remote like a laser and flipping through the TV channels at warp speed. It was a good way to avoid looking at the older brother attempting to put his nose smack where it didn't belong: in his business.

"Don' change the subject," Gitan had said.

Mase's gaze, slitted by the swelling, settled on him, and Gitan found it a little amazing how uncomfortable it made him. "She's sweet, Gitan, an' she's got class. Where you gonna find somebody like her who'll have anything to do with you?"

"Thanks a hell of a lot," Gitan said. "Maybe I ain't lookin'. Besides, how I decide to deal with Lily is my business, not yours." He didn't admit to the kid that he'd already made up his mind not to deal with Lily at all. He had nothing to give her but trouble, and he'd given her plenty of that in the past. There was no way he was going to screw with her future.

"No need to get bent out of shape; I'm curious, that's all. You gonna see her again?"

"Mason." There was a low note of warning in Gitan's voice that his brother blithely ignored.

"I saw the look on her face when she saw you, man. I still can't believe you didn't tell her you got an early release. It'd be like not tellin' *Tante* Rose—like not tellin' me."

Gitan couldn't quite bite back his angry reply. "Did I ask you to butt into my business? What the hell are you, anyhow? Fifteen? You're a kid, and a stupid kid at that. You don' know shit about it." He took a slow, deep breath, and found the reserve he needed, then got to his feet. "You listen to Rose, and take care of those ribs. I'll stop by after work to see how you're doin'."

"Don't bother on my account," Mase answered, the sullen teenager once more.

It hadn't been an easy start to his morning, and it hadn't helped that he'd been ten minutes late getting to work thanks to Mase's meddling. Sometimes, prison seemed easy by comparison to life on the outside. . . .

Dragged out of his bunk while sleep was still in his eyes and the mist rose off the Mississippi, lying heavy and white as cotton over the fields. Breakfast, then he was marched out to work the fields, eight hours a day, five days a week, for a pay rate of four cents per hour.

The routine had been monotonous in the extreme, the labor backbreaking, but the hours he'd spent free of the concrete cell had been a welcome change. He could feel the heat of the sun on the back of his neck, smell the wet wool smell of the river and feel alive again, the exotic perfume of freshly turned earth reminding him painfully of home. A few yards away, a correctional officer assigned to supervise his work gang sat on an overturned white five-gallon bucket, his rifle cradled in the crook of his arm as tenderly as if it were an infant. Another sat a bay gelding not far away, his shotgun a grim reminder that any man fool enough to try and run wouldn't get far. . . .

Learning to appreciate the little things he'd once taken for granted came easily. It was acceptance that had been exceptionally hard for him in the beginning. Life at the Farm was restrictive, tightly regimented. He ate when they said he could, and he slept when they allowed, and the smallest privilege was earned through months, sometimes years of exemplary behavior.

He'd learned to hone his natural reticence and

suppress all emotion. Letting hopes rise too high meant an inevitable crash. Depression was equally dangerous because it suggested a vulnerability he couldn't afford to own, and survival was everything. The necessary transformation from free man to inmate had occurred so slowly, so gradually that it seemed to happen one atom at a time and in the end was so thorough there wasn't a single trace of the young man who'd stepped off the bus in the prison yard the morning of his twenty-first birthday. Life at Angola was hard, and there had been times when Gitan wished he hadn't survived the injuries he'd sustained the night he broke into Justin Martin's study.

He remembered the black rage that had rampaged through him when he'd glanced through the French doors and saw what was happening; he could still see the shock on the older man's face as he pulled him off Lily. If he thought about it—and he forced himself to think about it, to drag up every detail because he couldn't afford to forget—he could feel the repeated crunch of bone under his fist until he lost all feeling in his hands, was covered in the mingled blood from his lacerated knuckles and the blood of his victim, and still he didn't stop.

He remembered the beating vividly, he remembered Lily pulling at his arm and begging him to leave, he felt her desperation in every cell of his being . . . and it was the last thing he remembered . . . the last thing he'd felt that night, and for days afterward.

When he had awakened on a Thursday, three days after the attempt he'd made on Justin's life, his lungs were on fire and a long row of staples held his chest cavity together. Each breath felt as if it would be his last. The physician's explaining that a bullet had pierced his chest cavity, lodging in the pericardium, the membrane surrounding his heart, still had the surreal feel of a half-forgotten dream. The surgeon had been matter-of-fact without being kind. "Young man, you're damn lucky to be alive," he'd told him. "Most patients don't survive an injury like yours."

Gitan hadn't felt lucky. He'd fumbled with the oxygen tubes before pulling them off, and tried to whisper Lily's name only to find he couldn't speak. He'd lain there in the bright light of the ICU, gasping like a fish out of water while the physician motioned the guards forward and administered a sedative while they pinned his arms to the hospital bed. *As if he could have put up a struggle.* He had no strength, he had no wind, and his future had disintegrated and blown away on the night wind. *Where was Lily? How was she?*

The office door opened, then slammed with enough force to jar the corrugated metal building and to bring Gitan back from the past. He finished burning the rod before juicing down the welder. Ruben's anger didn't faze him. The older man enjoyed throwing his weight around, but he was mostly bluster. He shouted, he swore, he gave orders, he flexed his biceps, the guys in the shop scattered, and Gitan went on with his work. "I thought I told Arley to finish up the weld on this project?"

Gitan removed the hood and set it aside, then took off his sweatband and wiped his face with it. "Arley's used to a MIG welder. I told him I'd finish it for him. I had a little time to spare."

Ruben pushed out his chin, hellbent on hanging on to his foul mood. "Used to a MIG welder," he growled. "What the hell am I payin' him for? God-damned candy ass. He doesn't do enough around this place to make it worth my while to keep him on. I swear, if he wasn't my mother's cousin."

"Nepotism does have a down side."

Ruben snorted. "Jesus, Gitan. Why don't you just buy me out? You've got the skill to run this place single-handed. Christ knows we'd all be better off. You could tell Hugh to kiss your ass, and I could spend my days on a bass boat, with a cold six-pack and no goddamned relatives to give me grief." He blew out a breath, as if he'd run a mile, and Gitan realized he just needed to unload. "What's with kids these days, anyhow? Willie burns through his allowance in a few days and he's got nothin' to show for it. I've tried to talk to him, but he doesn't hear a word I say. Came in this mornin' just to tell me he quit school. Like I ought to be proud of him for it. Nine months from graduation and he quits. Just like that, and he doesn't have enough brains to know he just did somethin' really stupid."

"Dealin' with kids ain't easy," Gitan said. "If you're lookin' for advice, I'm a poor choice."

"That's right, you've got a kid brother to look out for. Hey, I heard he got roughed up. How's he doin'?"

"Cocky, pissed off at the world in general, and me in particular, but he'll live. Me, I ain't so sure."

Ruben rubbed at his chin with a knuckle. "You find out who's responsible for beatin' on 'im?"

"Mase, he ain't talkin'. Don' want me messin' in his business—not that I blame him. At his age, I wouldn't have wanted that, either."

"Pride can get folks in a pile of trouble." Ruben sighed. "But, hell, maybe in a way it's a good thing that he's not inclined to share that information. You can't afford any complications, and sometimes a man's temper can get out of hand. Like that poor devil they found over at the old church on Catfish Point. The priest, Father Dugas. Hell of a thing to do a man like that. I don't know much, but I'd have to say whoever killed him must have been out of his head."

"Maybe, maybe not." Gitan shook his head. "Michel was a good man, with a good heart. Whatever it was brought this on, it had to be personal. Damn shame, though. I don' think Michel ever hurt anybody in his entire life. He sure as hell didn't deserve what he got."

"Yeah, that's right," Ruben said, almost as an afterthought. "Father Dugas was a friend of yours."

"Guess you could say that. We spent a lot of time together when we were kids." He'd been more than a friend for the past few years, Gitan thought. He'd been his priest, he'd heard his confessions, he'd administered Holy Communion to a soul that was lost, and he'd kept him connected to Lily, and to the world. In an odd way, without Michel, Gitan wasn't so sure he'd be on the outside right now. It seemed strange, to think of the young priest who'd befriended him behind prison bars in context with the chubby, shy kid who'd hung around with Lily . . . and stranger still to know that some sick son of a bitch had hung him upside down on a church altar and slit his throat like a sacrificial lamb.

"Shit," Ruben said suddenly. "What are we doin' inside on a beautiful day like today?"

"It's Friday. We work regular hours on Friday, remember?"

"No, I mean it. Wouldn't you rather knock off early and go fishin' than to clean up Arley's mess? What say we make this a long weekend?"

He fished in his pocket and came out with a wad of bills, peeled two off, and handed them to Gitan.

"What's that for?"

"Call it a bonus. Go on. Take it. You've more than earned it. Now, get the hell out of here, why don't you?

And don't forget to pick up your check at the office on your way out."

Ruben stayed in the shop for a few minutes, but the silence was deafening to a man uncomfortable in his own skin, so he walked to the back of the shop to send Arley and the others home.

Father Julius Murdoch met Hugh in a dark-paneled office, the large windows of which overlooked the gardens where Father Bernaud continued to toil. "Nice view," Hugh said, taking a seat in front of the large glass-topped desk. The red leather chairs were obviously good quality, and far more expensive than anything the sheriff's department could afford.

"Yes, it is, thanks largely to Father Bernaud. He's an excellent gardener and has a true love of growing things. He says that being close to nature helps him to appreciate God's universe more fully."

"He also says that Michel Dugas was a radical, and that they didn't like one another."

Murdoch raised his heavy gray brows. "Father Dugas may have expressed views on occasion unpopular with Father Bernaud, but I assure you it was nothing personal."

"You're sure about that?"

"I am positive that Father Bernaud held no ill will toward Father Dugas." Father Murdoch spread hands that were well manicured and softer looking than Lily's. "If the reports I have read of Father Dugas's death are in any way true, it would have taken more brute strength than Father Bernaud possesses to achieve such an end."

"Stranger things have happened," Hugh allowed, unwilling at this point to rule anything, or anyone, out.

"Do you know of anyone else who might have disliked Father Dugas enough to want him dead?"

"I do not."

The priest met Hugh's stare without flinching, but that didn't mean the man was innocent. Hugh had interviewed cold-blooded killers who could spin a lie with a straight face. His gut reaction was that Murdoch was hiding something, though whether that something pertained to Dugas's murder was pure speculation at this point. He knew only that he wanted to rattle him, that he wanted him to know that the Church had no hold on the Angelique Sheriff's Department. He wanted to give him something to think about. "You wouldn't tell me if you did know," Hugh said. "Secrets told in the confessional stay in the confessional. Isn't it true that a key element to a priest's profession is based on the keeping of secrets?"

"The sanctity of the confessional is protected by the Church and by the state of Louisiana, but that has nothing to do with this, because I don't have the information you're looking for." He got to his feet. The interview was over. "Father Dugas's private quarters are this way."

Murdoch accompanied Hugh to the elevator that took them to the second floor, handed him a key to Michel's room, then left him.

Michel's living quarters consisted of a narrow room with a bed and a desk and a television set. The bathroom was down the hall, shared by the other residents of the second floor. His clothing still hung in the closet, a half dozen black coats and matching pairs of trousers, a tan-colored terry bath robe, and three pairs of shoes placed neatly on a shoe rack. There were other, more casual items, too. Khaki Dockers, and a couple of short-sleeved shirts, a pair of silk pajamas tucked in a dresser drawer alongside his boxer shorts, and socks—some black, a few pair striped, and one purple pair that looked new that had a Mickey Mouse allover print. Lying beneath them was a birthday card from his niece, Lorali.

Hugh went over everything in every drawer, and even tipped up the mattress to see if there was anything hidden between it and the box spring. He peered into and under everything. From the contents of the room, he might have been led to believe that Michel led a dull, austere lifestyle. Yet appearances were often deceiving, and there was something hidden somewhere in Michel's recent past that was a motive for murder. He just had to find it. "Squeaky clean," Hugh said, picking up the phone and sliding the desk calendar from underneath. "We'll see about that."

Lily went to Michel's mother's house to offer her condolences in person and to tell Mrs. Dugas what a positive influence Michel had had on her life. Somehow, she felt it was crucial that Elaine understand that her son was loved, his tragic loss mourned, yet the effort seemed puny, a tiny and insignificant ripple in a sea of shock, grief, and anger. Elaine Dugas was under heavy sedation, and there was concern that her heart might not withstand the strain of her son's funeral mass the next day.

Lily spoke quietly with Leonie, Michel's older sister, while Leonie's two-year-old twins played underfoot. "My brother loved kids," Leonie said. "And now he won't get to see them grow up, and they won't remember him."

"I wish there was something I could do." As she said it, she realized how lame it sounded. What could she

possibly do to lessen Leonie's pain, or Elaine's? Or
Mary Nevers's? All Mary had wanted was justice. But
she'd been ignored, pushed back, considered a throw-
away, an ex-hooker and recovering drug addict. Lily
couldn't help Mary, and she couldn't help Michel's
family.

"You see the headlines today?" Leonie asked, her
round face striped with moisture. "The sheriff
promised to keep us informed, right after he questioned us about whether Michel was gay, or straight."

Lily glanced at the newspaper Leonie shoved at her.
The headline blared: SECRET LIFE OF MURDERED PRIEST EX-
POSED. "I'm so sorry."

"Yeah, me too. Guess he found out about Keith.
Him and Michel were real tight when they were in
seminary together." She sighed, brushing a lock of
black hair off her forehead. "That was yesterday. It
doesn't seem like much of a coincidence this piece
of shit leaked when it did, now does it? You know what
really stinks? Hugh's gonna try to make this look
like Michel asked for it. Like he was somehow responsible for his own murder! Great way to take the
heat off himself and his cronies down at the sheriff's
department." She dabbed at the tears on her cheek,
liquid outrage at the injustice of the situation they
found themselves in. First Michel was murdered,
now he would be vilified in the media, his lifestyle
brought into question, and all Lily could say was how
sorry she was.

*I'm sorry, Mary. We'll get justice for this outrage. We'll shout
until they hear us! But there was no justice, just a second rape
by a system that was supposed to look out for victims . . . and
Mary Nevers quietly slit her wrists, and quietly died.*

"Why do folks have to be so judgmental?" Leonie
wondered. "What's it matter that my brother was

gay, anyhow? He was a good man, and a good priest, and he helped a lot of people. Why can't they focus on that?"

Lily shook her head. She didn't have any answers, and all she could do was promise she'd take it up with Hugh.

"You can talk till you're blue in the face, Lily," Leonie told her. "Just don't expect it to do any good."

Lily couldn't argue the point, and she left the Dugases' small house on Conti Avenue a short while later for the drive to the low, white stucco building with the illuminated sign that proclaimed: ANGELIQUE SHERIFF'S DEPARTMENT. Lily didn't bother speaking to Hugh's receptionist, and she didn't pause to knock. She stalked in and threw the paper she'd taken from Leonie in front of him. "Tell me you didn't leak this filth to the press!"

"Afternoon, Lily. I'm fine, thank you. I'd ask how you are, but I'm afraid that's obvious." He barely glanced at the headline before tossing it aside, then leaned over and pressed the button on his intercom. "Amy? Bring me a refill, will you?" Then, pinning Lily with that direct blue gaze of his, "Coffee?"

"I don't want coffee, Hugh," Lily ground out. "I want to know if you're responsible for this hatchet job."

"Oh, it's a hatchet job, is it? And what makes you think I'm responsible for it?"

"Leonie told me you questioned her about Michel."

Hugh shrugged. "It's an ongoin' investigation. I questioned a lot of folks, including you. But, since you asked so nicely, without jumping to conclusions and maligning my character without due cause: no, I did not leak Dugas's sexual preference to the papers. If you want to blame someone, you'll need to look else-where. I will, however, be talking to Michel's homosexual lover as soon as I can locate him. I assume you know about Mr. Green, though you neglected to share that piece of information."

Lily lifted her chin. "It was none of your business."

A sharp look. "Everything pertaining to Michel Dugas's life happens to be my business. If he trimmed his pubic hair the day before his death, then I need to know that. Everything, no matter how small or insignificant. Is that clear enough for you, Lily?"

"Disgustingly so," Lily said.

"Good, because I don't want to have this conversation again, and I sure don't need the embarrassment of having to arrest my own wife for interfering with an investigation." He sat back in his leather chair and regarded her calmly. "Now, unless you want to stay for some Chinese takeout, I have work to do."

Matter-of-fact. All business . . . but something told her that he was telling her the truth. Besides, it wouldn't have served the investigation to out Michel. "I'll leave. But first I want your word that you'll do your best to find Michel's killer."

"Lily, for Christ's sake."

Amy Bellefonte rapped softly, then hovered near the doorway, unsure if it was safe to enter with the coffee Hugh had requested. Amy . . . who'd slept with him and then bragged about it. "Damn it, Hugh," Lily said quietly. "You owe me that much."

"Oh, I'll do my best. You can bank on that, because it's my job—not because you asked me to." It was all Hugh had give her, and Lily left his office dissatisfied. He might not have betrayed Michel's loved ones by passing along private information, but he hadn't done anything to discourage it, either . . . or to ease her mind. The last thing Lily needed when she emerged from the sheriff's department was four flat tires.

Flat wasn't quite accurate. There were several cuts in the outside walls, deep, gaping cuts. They'd been slashed. "Great. Just great." She could have gone back inside and reported the incident, but she wasn't sure she could tolerate another confrontation with Hugh. She was in the process of digging in her handbag for her cellular phone when she heard tires scrape on the crushed shells of the parking lot.

"Hey, sugar. Something wrong?"

His warm, deep voice rippled over Lily's senses. Unable to help herself, she drank it in. For just an instant, Lily flashed back to happier times. Muggy summer days that seemed bright, even when overcast, as long as the four of them were together. She turned and saw him, behind the wheel of a pickup. The truck was an older model, but the black paint was shiny, and the intricate spider's web that decorated the hood was a more colorful replica of the one etched into the skin of his shoulder. "I've got a flat—four flats, actually, but it's nothing I can't handle. I've got my cell. I'll call someone." She dug in her handbag. "I *thought* I had my cell."

"Why don' I have a look?"

"It's okay, really. I'm sure you've got to get back to Ruben's."

"Ruben gave me the afternoon off." He pulled in beside her car, slipped the transmission into first, and turned off the engine. When he got out of the truck and came around the bed, she caught an involuntary breath. Gitan exuded an aura of power, and it was all the more heady for the fact that he took it for granted. The boy Lily had first idolized, and later loved, had undergone a complete metamorphosis behind penitentiary walls . . . and though she could catch traces of the old Gitan in the man he was now, they were so subtle Lily wondered if she imagined it.

He'd changed, and he was more devastatingly handsome than ever before. But there was something else, a quiet sense of purpose, that had been lacking all those years ago, a definite air of danger that she felt, and which warned her away . . . but could she listen?

He dropped easily onto his heels and examined the tires. "*Mon Dieu.* They aren't just flat, Lily. Somebody slashed 'em. Looks like you pissed somebody off bigtime. You happen to have some idea of who did this?"

"I've been in town less than forty-eight hours. The only people I've pissed off are Rose and Hugh. I have a hard time imagining your aunt slashing my tires, and Hugh's methods are a little more subtle."

"You're in a fix, *cher.* If it was just one, I'd change it for you, but four ain't as easily taken care of. I can give you a lift, though."

After their last conversation, Lily was reluctant. Last night he'd been cool and indifferent, and though a part of her couldn't blame him, she wasn't anxious to go through that again. She'd gotten on with her life, and he'd moved on, too. . . . Or so she thought, until he turned that dark liquid gaze on her, and Lily faltered. "Aunt Virginia's shop is just a few blocks away. I'll walk there and catch a ride with her."

"You could do that, I guess. You could even walk back in there and ask Mr. Button-down to give you a ride in his squad car. Don' know about you, but me, I don' trust him all that far. No tellin' where he's been." Gitan got to his feet, dusting off his hands. "Or . . . maybe you could climb on up in the cab of my truck and let me drive you home. I'm legal, I got the photo ID to prove it, and we both know where I've been.

C'mon, Lily. What've you got to lose? I'll be nice. I promise." A half beat later, "Unless, of course, this old truck ain't good enough for a class act like you . . . or maybe you're afraid of what might happen if you're alone with me?"

"Is that a dare? Because that's the way it sounds." The idea of being close to Gitan made her thoughts race and her heart beat a little faster, and the fact that he could still push her buttons didn't help. She'd never been able to resist a dare, had never gotten past the need to prove that she was just as smart, just as tough, just as fearless as anyone, and the glint in his black eyes said he knew it.

"Guess it is. I'm thinkin' you're too chicken to let me drive you home. Maybe you're afraid what folks'll think if we're seen together." His hard mouth curved slightly, and the dimples flashed in his cheeks. "Or maybe you're worried you won't be able to keep your hands to yourself."

"I'm so not chicken," Lily shot back, "and the only concern I've got is that your massive ego might be contagious." Tossing her bag on the seat and with a glare at Gitan, Lily climbed into the pickup.

"Now, that's the Lily I remember. Never shrink from a challenge."

He drove through town, but instead of turning onto Mill Creek Road, he took a left onto a little-traveled track and parked on the breast of the levee. The truck didn't have air conditioning, but there was a constant breeze off the bayou that made the hot afternoon bearable.

"Bayou's nice this time of day," he observed, but he didn't offer an explanation as to why he'd parked on the levee instead of taking her home as he'd promised.

A full range of possibilities ran through Lily's mind, from the lurid to the benign.

With Gitan, anything was possible, and the suspense was killing her. "My turn was a quarter of a mile back."

"I know. I remember where your aunt lives. I guess I'm not ready to let you go just yet."

Lily glanced at him. He was impossible, in some ways as frustrating as Hugh. At least where Hugh was concerned, there was never any doubt where she stood. Gitan was as changeable, as unpredictable as the breeze off the dark water. Unfortunately for him, Lily was in no mood to play games. "Gitan, why are we here?"

He turned slightly toward her, resting his right arm along the top of the bench seat. The maneuver put his fingertips a mere inch away from her nape, so close he could reach out with almost no effort and touch her. She shivered. She remembered his touch, the gentle way his hands slid over her skin. . . .

"I couldn't forget last night," he said, his expression gone serious.

"That makes two of us. Both you and Rose made it very clear that I was intruding. Believe me, it won't happen again."

"Rose had no right to make you feel bad," he said. "And neither did I. You rescued Mase, and I'm grateful. It took a lot of guts for you to bring him home."

Lily turned away, her gaze fixed on the bright glimmer of sunlight on the water. "I've survived worse," she said with an uneasy laugh. "I was married to Hugh, remember? Your aunt doesn't frighten me."

"I'm not surprised. Nothin' scares my Lily."

The words "my Lily" seemed to come from him so effortlessly and sounded so natural . . . as if he'd never stopped thinking of her that way. *His Lily.*

Lily glanced back at him, suddenly unsure of herself, unsure of everything. It was over between them. It had been over for years. She'd married and divorced his best friend, and he'd made a new start without her . . . So why the electricity between them? She could feel it in the warm, moist air . . . tense, terrifying. Nothing scared her? "I wouldn't be so sure," Lily muttered. The strength of her feelings for Gitan scared her spitless. The hand on the back of the seat flexed, his fingertips grazing her damp skin, and they both froze.

Or at least she did. It might have been better if she'd moved away, given him a shove—something. But she didn't move. Couldn't seem to breathe.

His fingertips lingered on the skin of her nape, his touch light, teasing. "I'd forgotten—how soft your skin felt. Like velvet. I used to think about it—try to relive it, but I never did get it right."

He hadn't been able to remember, and she couldn't seem to forget. "How *is* Mase?" she asked, as much to distract herself from the play of his hand on her skin as anything.

"He was all right when I saw him this mornin', but Rose has probably smothered him by now. I've told her a thousand times not to hover, but she can't seem to help herself."

"She loves you both."

"She does that, but it ain't so easy to take sometimes. Mase just wants to be a kid, and I get that. Guess we all want somethin'."

Lily spoke without thinking. "What do you want?"

"Me? My needs aren't complicated. A sturdy roof to keep off the rain, a good cup of coffee, the freedom just to be. There's value in that. What about Lily?"

Lily took a deep breath and released it on a sigh,

moving away from his touch. "I suppose I just want the world to make sense. I want to know who killed Michel, and I want to know why because not knowing is unacceptable."

"I'd like to know that Lily Martin is finally happy."

A brittle smile. Another moment with him and she would break. "There's no such thing as happy," she said, convinced. "At least not in this lifetime. Now, if you don't mind, I'd like to go home."

He pulled in Virginia's drive and Lily got out. No awkward goodbyes, no guilt, no recriminations—at least none that were spoken. "Thanks. For the ride, I mean."

"Anytime," he said easily. "Guess I'll see you around."

CHAPTER SIX

Lily had always had trouble sleeping. She couldn't remember a time in which she didn't dread the coming of night. As a child she would lie awake, listening to the creaks and groans of the house, fearing the sounds of his footsteps in the hall.

Only the daylight hours were relatively carefree, because with Sharon's drinking, there was always an opportunity to slip away from the house on Kyme Road undetected. Away from the oppressive atmosphere of the house, she and Michel sought out Hugh and Gitan.

Hugh wasn't really liked, but he was tolerated. Gitan was the sun around which the three of them made their daily orbit. Even as an adolescent, Gitan had been charismatic, and at least a portion of the attraction for Lily had been his absolute fearlessness. Sometimes Lily's life seemed ruled by her fears, yet with Gitan, she'd always felt safe. Then one day the unthinkable happened, and Gitan was torn from her life.

During college she'd sought therapy for the nightmares, and a year and a half later she still had no concrete answers, other than the hatred she'd had for her father.

Daddy had been the monster in Lily's mental closet. His blistering rages, his verbal abuse of her mother, the way everyone in his life jumped at his command, and far worse. Somewhere deep down there was a part of Lily that didn't want to know the root cause of her sleepless nights.

The little voice inside her insisted she let it lie. And she had.

Some insomniacs self-medicated, some sought medical intervention, but Lily ran. If she was wired, she put on her cutoff sweats and running shoes, and ran until her lungs were on fire and her veins throbbing with every pulse of her racing heart.

The payoff was exhaustion, and exhaustion brought dreamless sleep. But not last night. For what seemed like hours, she had lain awake watching the darkness of a moonless night change its somber aspect in favor of varying shades of gray. Daylight didn't burst upon the land; it came gradually, by degrees. Enlightenment came the same way, on a graduated scale so subtle that often one failed even to notice its arrival.

As Lily slipped into her Nikes, she didn't feel very enlightened. Michel's funeral was later that morning, and she was dreading it. She coped the only way she knew, setting out in the warm, sweaty darkness, fighting to fall into the rhythm and pushing through the searing pain of muscles and lungs pushed to their limits.

A mile down the levee, Gitan cradled his coffee mug in one hand and gazed into the misty darkness. The rain that had threatened for days wouldn't hold off much longer. He'd always had a sixth sense when it came to storms, perceiving when bad weather was imminent. A quirk, or a talent, whatever one wished to call it, even the thick concrete walls of Angola couldn't block out the certainty that heavy weather was on the doorstep. There had been times when it had become an irritant, having the knowledge of the storm but not the freedom to brace against the wind, or to feel the rain on his face. There was only an occasional flash of lightning through the window, a distant rumble of thunder that faintly underscored the moan of an inmate down the cellblock, caught in the throes of a dream—though good or bad was anyone's guess.

In those first dark months there had been many sounds, most a man hoped to block out; the soft grunt of carnal pleasure as one inmate serviced another's needs, a choked and sorrowful weeping, the leak of a soul in unbearable pain into the cold concrete of the cell block.

He'd missed so many things that before had been taken for granted. The steam of the shower gathering in the close confines of a bathroom, the hush that came over everything just before twilight fell. He'd missed Rose's singsong laughter as she beat his mother at gin rummy for the third time in a row on a steamy Saturday night in Annie Boudreaux's kitchen. He'd missed the soft swish of his mama's calico skirts as she danced with his papa on the back porch to music from a transistor radio, and most of all, he'd missed Lily.

A sip of black coffee, and he heard Virginia Martin's whisper, pleading and insistent against the continuous beep of the cardiac monitor. To this day he had no concept of the passage of time during that bleak period dominated by a morphine drip, when days were measured in the lessening of the intensity of the searing pain threatening to consume him, of the worry on the faces of his parents as they became convinced that he'd live. *"Bobby, you've got to hear me."*

He might have opened his eyes, but his recall was hazy concerning the details. Somehow, the desperate edge in Virginia's voice penetrated the drug-induced haze that enveloped his brain. Her face loomed close, larger than it should have been, slightly distorted, as if he were seeing her refection in a carnival mirror. *"She doesn't remember. Lily doesn't remember."*

Sometimes he wondered what life would have been like if he hadn't listened to the voices of reason battering him from all sides. Even now, he and Lily might have been living in Mexico, far from the ghosts of Angelique Past and the house on Kyme Road. Speculation got him precisely nowhere, because what was done was done, and there could be no going back. His regrets, until recently, had been few because he had known that Lily was okay. She'd moved on, first to Hugh, and then to California, and from all indications, she'd been thriving until a few months ago when she'd been assigned to the case of a sixteen-year-old debutante accused of killing her father. . . . From that moment on, everything had begun a long downhill slide.

She was still having problems of some sort; that much was evident. She was thinner than she should have been, and it was clear from the dark smudges beneath her blue eyes that she still wasn't sleeping.

From somewhere in the distance came the sound of a woman running, the methodical and determined pounding of feet connecting with the earth. The first few raindrops fell and the wind picked up, making the treetops dance and the moss sway hypnotically. Lightning split the clouds and struck a dead tree on an island mid-channel. Sparks flew and birds scattered, and the runner kept coming. She was determined; he had to give her that. As the rain came harder, she seemed no more deterred by the storm than he was. He listened a moment longer than he should have, and as he turned to walk off the levee slope, Lily materialized from the heart of the deluge.

She started when she saw him standing there, faltering for the space of a breath, sufficient to throw off her stride. When her right foot came down, she skidded on the rain-slick grass and went down like a sack full of rocks. Before she could do more than scramble to a sitting position, he was there, sitting on his heels beside her. "Hey, *cher,* electrifying entrance. You didn't break your pretty little ass in that fall, did you?"

Lily glared at him, indignant. "My ass is completely intact, no thanks to you! What in hell are you doing out here so early? No one gets up before dawn around here."

"I do . . . and looks like you do, too. What are you doing runnin' on the levee all by your lonesome before daybreak? You runnin' *from* somethin'? Or just runnin'?"

He'd turned the tables on her effortlessly, and Lily blushed. "Running helps to relieve my insomnia."

"You can't sleep, and I don' want to. Ain't we the perfect pair? What would you say to a cup of coffee? It's pretty damn fine coffee, if I do say so myself."

"I really should get going. Besides, I'm soaked."

"Mass ain't till eleven, and you ain't gonna get any drier sittin' here in the rain. C'mon in and have a cup of coffee. Ol' Gitan, he don' bite." He flashed her a

grin, and the warmth in Lily's cheeks flooded downward, into her chest. "Not hard, anyhow."

She hesitated. It was an honest invitation: she
sensed that, and she'd had little more than a sip of
juice that morning before setting out. The thought
of a good cup of coffee was damned appealing. Gitan
offered a hand to help her to her feet. Lily's gaze
shifted from his face to that hand, the thumb of
which was smeared with deep blue paint. Hard hands.
Strong hands. Hands that labored to make a living,
and she couldn't fault him for that—yet what did she
know about him? Seven years was a long time. Hugh
had warned her that he'd changed, and so had her
Aunt Virginia, and while Hugh's motives were always
suspect, she couldn't say the same for her aunt's.

"Come on, *cher*. It's just coffee." He jerked his
thumb over his shoulder. "There's a phone in the
kitchen. You can call my parole officer if you like.
She'll vouch for me."

"Don't be ridiculous," Lily said, feeling rather foolish herself as she accepted the help he offered. She'd
forgotten the warmth of his hands, the gentleness
he'd always shown toward her, as if she were somehow
precious. Was it still there? Or was she imagining it?
Then, she was on her feet, and he let go. "Coffee does
sound good. I sure hope it lives up to your bragging,
and my expectations."

"You become a connoisseur while you were away?
Maybe I should be worried?" He was quiet as they
walked down the levee slope and across a yard dotted
with live oak and sweet gum. A modest house, one
story, two bedrooms, living room, kitchen, and a
bath. "It's not Mill Creek Road, or L.A., but it suits my
needs. C'mon in. Make yourself at home."

He scoured the coffeepot with steel wool, though

it already sparkled, then rinsed and filled it with cold water. "The secret to good coffee in one of these is to start with a clean pot. Rose, she's scandalized I bought this thing. 'How you gonna make *café* without a French press, Gitan?'" he said in a fair imitation of Rose's liquid patois. "Granted, it's not Rose's fantastic brew, but it ain't too bad. That woman, she's spoiled, but I owe her a lot."

"Mason?" Lily guessed.

"Mais, yeah," he said quietly, somberly. "Mason. Don' know what to do about him. I truly don'. Sometimes I feel like I'm drownin'. There's a good kid in there somewhere, but I sure as hell don' know how to reach him."

Lily leaned against the old-fashioned white porcelain sink. "You remember what it was like to be his age. Maybe it isn't as bad as it seems."

He snorted his derision. "I remember what it was like, and that's what worries me. Jesus, I wish Daddy was here. He'd know what to do, and Mase, he needs that solid example to follow. What he's got ain't so solid, you know?"

"I'm no authority on family, that's for sure," Lily said with a sigh, "but I know that Mason idolizes you."

"Yeah, but what am I gonna teach him? That you get your ass to see your parole officer on time, with no excuses? Keep your nose to that grindstone, because you lose that job, and it's big-time trouble?" He shook his head. "Shit, I apologize. This sure as hell ain't your problem, and I didn't mean to unload on you. You've got enough on your mind already. What's Hugh got to say about the investigation into Michel's murder?"

"He asked me some questions, but you know Hugh: he doesn't give an inch."

"I know Hugh . . . and I also know Lily Martin. The

girl's all heart, and that's what has me worried." For just an instant, he softened, leaning against the sink where she stood, inches away. She could smell the scent of his soap as he leaned a little closer, feel the warmth that surrounded him. An instant's hesitation, then he reached out, cupping the curve of her cheek in one broad hand and slowly, gently, touched her mouth with his.

That first contact in eight years was poignant, bittersweet. Lily closed her eyes, afraid the ragged edge of her emotions would show as she clung to him. Her fingers found the hard line of his jaw, and the coffeepot gurgled and belched fragrant steam, jerking her painfully back to reality.

"I've thought about doin' that for so long," he murmured, then kissed her again, his mouth moving hungrily over hers. All caution, all gentleness evaporated in a cloud of sexual steam.

Lily strained to get closer. She rose onto her toes, pressing into him, her soft breasts flattening against the hard sinewy wall of his chest, her hands everywhere at once. She couldn't get enough of him. Then, the phone rang, and with a low ground-out curse, he pulled away. Her breathing less ragged now, Lily found a mug in the cabinets overhead and poured herself a cup of coffee.

"I guess so," Gitan told the caller. "But you tell him I said he needs to go back to school after—no skippin' school. It don' look good when he does that."

Lily sipped her coffee and moved past Gitan to the living room to give him some privacy. The house was a rental, and must have been furnished by the owner. It contained an assorted group of odds and ends, illmatched, but clean and in good order. A few personal touches had been added here and there, by Rose

Boudreaux, Lily guessed. A print of Christ in the garden on one wall, a small wooden crucifix on another, an embroidered pillow placed carefully on the sofa. Lily knew instinctively that Gitan didn't spend his time in this room.

Without thinking, she moved slowly down the hall. The room on the right was all but empty with a twin-sized bed and an old dresser. The last room, opposite, was larger, with a neatly made double bed and a handsome armoire made of curly maple. The armoire was obviously an antique, but lovingly cared for. In a shadowy corner where the light of the window failed to reach stood a sheet-draped easel, but there was no clutter of paints or brushes. She'd thought that he'd given up the idea of pursuing his dream, but maybe she'd been wrong about that.

Curious, Lily caught the hem of the cloth, lifting it up and over the easel. A younger version of herself stared at her over one bare shoulder, her expression slightly coy. It was so beautifully lifelike that it took her breath away, left her speechless. The painted image seemed to emit a light and a warmth all its own, to pulsate with life.

He'd come up behind Lily while her attention was focused on the portrait, and stood so close that she could feel the hot kiss of his breath on her nape. "You're trespassin', sugar. It's dangerous territory, too."

She'd seen his cool and distant side, she'd felt him push her away, and now this. . . . "Why, Gitan?" Lily asked without turning away from the portrait.

"Why is it dangerous for you to be here with me? My house? My bedroom? I think we both know that, don' we?"

"I meant the portrait. Why did you paint it?"

She turned to face him and Gitan shrugged. "Why's

a man do anything?" He took a deliberate step back, leaning against the bedpost. The bed was an antique four-poster that had seen some wear, but the mosquito netting draped over it and puddling onto the floor lent it a shabby elegance.

The T-shirt he was wearing had been cropped at the waist, and it rode a few inches higher than the waistband of his jeans. He had washboard abs and skin that was smooth and tanned. He was long and lean and dangerous, and there had never been a man who affected her as he did. With the shadow of a beard darkening his chiseled jaw, and his hair just a fraction longer than it needed to be, Gitan was sexy, exotic, untamed, and there was no place for her in his world.

Or was there? There had always been something between them, an unspoken connection that required no acknowledgment or explanation. For a moment while she stared at him, Lily was convinced that the link between them still existed, that it was still strong, still very much alive.

"That isn't much of an answer."

Gitan didn't say anything. Reaching out, he toyed with the damp hair curling at her nape, perhaps as intoxicated as she was by the shadowed intimacy of the bedroom. "You don't get it, do you, *cher*?" he asked, his voice quiet, suddenly robbed of that teasing tone he'd used previously. "I had to. It was the only way to get you out of my head . . . out of my heart."

Lily's breath caught in her throat. She had no right to ask. It wasn't fair. Yet she had to know. "Did you?"

"I think you know the answer to that." His fingers slid along the curve of her neck, toyed with her ecru top's spaghetti strap, slipping it over her shoulder and down. His dark head lowered and he kissed the gentle curve where her neck met her shoulder.

A lingering kiss. As the heat of his mouth scorched Lily's skin, she felt the last shred of caution fall away and turned into his embrace, her fingers eagerly threading through the thick dark silk of his hair.

She wanted him, just as she'd always wanted him. She wanted to feel his skin warm against hers, his body rising above her on the bed. She wanted to sleep beside him at night, and wake in his arms, and that was impossible. "Gitan, I have to go. Michel's funeral is this morning and you can't afford to be late for work."

He would have stolen one last kiss if she hadn't moved away. "Come back later this afternoon."

"I can't. I have to help out at the Dugases' after the services."

"This evenin', then?"

Lily drew a shaky breath. With a little distance between them, she felt more in control, less likely to do something crazy. Something they both might come to regret. Things were too unsettled between them, and he couldn't afford an added complication in an already complicated life. An unsteady laugh. "I'm not sure that's a good idea. I need to get my life back on track, and so do you. We can't recreate what we had, Gitan. It ended years ago, and too much has happened since then."

"If it was over, you wouldn't be here. Admit it."

Lily said nothing as she walked away. She was almost to the door when he called her name and stopped her in her tracks. "Lily? You never said—do you like the painting?"

"Yes, I like it. Did I ever look like that? Beautiful . . . innocent?" She didn't wait for his reply. Another moment and she would lose it completely. She just turned and fled.

Gitan followed as far as the screen door, where he

stood, watching her retreating figure. "God help us both, Lily. You still do. . . ."

Twenty minutes before the Dugas funeral was scheduled to begin, Hugh got a call from the dispatcher that there was an accident near Sandy Flats. It was Deputy Crebs's day off and Fred Rally was manning the station, so he took the call himself. When he arrived on scene, the fire and rescue team was already in the process of using the Jaws of Life to peel three critically injured teenagers from the metal deathtrap that moments ago had been a light-colored sports car. Covered with mud and mangled to the point that make and model were difficult to immediately determine, the demolished vehicle rested on its roof in a roadside ditch. Fifty yards to the rear, skid marks showed where the car had left the road and had become airborne.

The rescue crew managed to extract the driver, and Hugh, on his knees in the mud beside the wreckage, helped slide the backboard under him. The kid hadn't been wearing his seat belt, and his head had gone through the windshield. Covered in blood, his nose broken, and his eyes swollen shut, the boy couldn't be ID'd without the help of his driver's license. JIMMY HELVETIA. Hugh had attended high school with James, Sr., who had a raised ranch in the housing development on the next street over from Hugh's apartment. Jimmy was a good kid, polite, respectful, quick with a grin . . . and unless Hugh's gut instinct was wrong—and he hoped like hell it was—he was a bona fide DOA.

Sam Redmond worked feverishly trying to revive the kid as the other two men worked to get the front seat passenger free. From the area of the backseat came a continuous animalistic scream. "The girl in the front passenger side's already gone," Hugh said. "Let's get this fuckin' tin can open and get that kid out of the backseat while she's still breathin'! C'mon, damn it! Get a move on!"

Hugh spent the next hour lending a hand on scene, rerouting traffic so that Life Flight could land in the middle of the two-lane blacktop. The kid in the backseat was unidentified, but still breathing when she was loaded onto the helicopter for the short flight to a trauma unit in Baton Rouge. He finished at the scene of the carnage, made a few phone calls, then a personal visit to the Helvetia home to break the unwelcome news. Then he went home.

Amy Bellefonte, the same Amy who brought his morning coffee at the office and fielded calls for him, met him in the apartment's kitchen. She was wearing one of his long-sleeved white shirts and nothing else. The louvers were half-closed, enough to cast the dip of her navel and the light brown thatch between her thighs in mysterious shadow. She had a nice body, high breasts that weren't overly large, and a trim waist. Her shoulders were smooth and pale in the dimness as she shrugged out of the shirt and let it fall, and her gray eyes full of a need Hugh read and understood.

Without a word, he dropped his keys on the counter and lay the thick manila folder marked "Dugas, Michel" beside it. When he turned back, Amy pushed away from the doorway where she'd been poised and padded on bare feet to where he stood. "I heard about the call. You okay?"

He'd had a bellyful, but he didn't say so. "Sure, why wouldn't I be?" Prying dead kids out of mangled metal was a regular occurrence. "Just part of the job." An easy reply, but it sounded clipped and tense.

"I can make you forget all about it."

"I need a hot shower. I'm covered with mud."

A smile played around the corners of her mouth, and her eyes went all smoky and full of want. "Mind if I join you?"

He thought about that for a moment, while she toyed with the buttons on his shirt, slipping them through their holes, her fingertips gliding lightly through the hair on his chest. Her every move was suggestive, the images that flashed through his mind erotic. Amy was low maintenance, and he liked that.

"It'll ease some of your tension," she said, "make you feel better."

A nice thought, but after the day he'd had, he doubted it was possible. Because of the accident, he'd missed Michel's funeral, and he wondered if Lily had attended alone? Or had Gitan gone with her?

Amy read him well, knew him well, and might have been the only woman on the planet to accept him for who he was. "Come on, Hugh. We're so good together, an' you can close your eyes and call me Lily if you want to. Hell, you know I don't mind."

Hugh's lids lowered, his fingers grazing her jaw, sliding down to rest on the curve of her throat. "You're a bitch, you know that?"

She met his gaze evenly, unafraid of the hand that hovered over her jugular. "Maybe . . . but I won't leave until you ask me to." Then she took his hand and led him to the saunalike steam of the shower.

Two hours later, Hugh was alone. His relationship with Amy was simple. She wanted one thing from him, and she didn't make demands he had no intention of meeting. The sex was infrequent, discreet, and sufficiently hot to sustain him until the next time he came home to find her naked in his kitchen. She had her own life, a husband she loved but no longer desired, and needs that brought her to his door, and to his bed. When it was over, she got dressed and went back to her life, until desire met opportunity and brought them together again.

No emotional connection, and he didn't have time to waste on guilt. Especially now, with the pressure building for him to solve the Dugas case. In death, Michel had created a stir which in life he couldn't have equaled. Since Michel had always been quiet and unassuming to the point of timidity, Hugh had been unable thus far to arrive at a motive that made any sense.

Louisiana was largely Catholic, and most Catholics had an ingrained respect for the priesthood. It was considered a sacred calling. For the faithful, a priest was marriage counselor, psychologist, confessor, and negotiator with the Almighty. They christened infants, united lovers in matrimony, and blessed the sick and the dying. In some instances, a good priest was considered part of a parishioner's extended family, beloved by young and old alike. Yet in Michel's case, someone had hated him enough to end his life.

Seated on the leather sofa in the living room lit only by a table lamp, Hugh sucked the smoke of a cigarette into his lungs and squinted at the papers and photos on the coffee table in front of him.

The very first thing he'd done during the initial examination of the scene was to determine where and how the killer had entered and exited the scene. There was only one set of tire tracks recent enough to have been made the night of the murder, and the casts had matched Michel Dugas's car, which had

been found abandoned and half submerged in a
water-filled roadside ditch a half mile from the scene.
If prints had existed, the water damage to the car's interior had dissolved them. But there was nothing
else to be found, and it was apparent that the killer
had entered the crime scene one of two ways: on
foot, or by water.

As for trace evidence found at the scene, the list was
extensive. Cigarette butts, a half-smoked joint found
under the front pew, a variety of hairs, short, long,
medium length, processed and otherwise—made obvious by the lighter or darker roots . . . and something
that appeared to be an animal bone. The church,
abandoned and neglected for at least twelve years, was
a forensic nightmare. Everything had been properly
collected, processed, and catalogued, then turned
over to the Louisiana State Police lab for analysis, but
there was a better than ever chance that most of the
debris had been at the scene long before the murder
and would be of little use in the investigation.

There had always been rumors of parties at St.
Bart's, and the evidence indicated the rumors were
fact based . . . but there were rumors of other goings-
on out there as well . . . something bigger, darker,
more unnerving. There was always talk about voodoo,
the occult, and Satanism, though personally he didn't
buy into that sort of thing. Besides, unless he was mis-
reading the photos that were spread out before him,
Dugas's killer had been working alone. In the crime
scene photos dust and debris littered the floor of
the chapel . . . years of it, and the footprints he'd
found by using an oblique lighting technique were numerous, yet only three sets of prints were recent.
Two of the three were athletic shoes.

Hugh had already had a good look at Mason

Boudreaux's shoes, and the Gonzales kid's, too. Both sets were identified in the diagrams he'd made using the photographs. The remaining set of footprints were highly suspect.

Three sets of footprints and obvious drag marks, marred with blood spatter. The size, shape, and distribution of the blood spatter indicated that Dugas had been incapacitated by a blow to the back of the head and, in all probability, unconscious when the killer dragged him into the church. Some of the blood evidence had been almost obliterated by Dugas's own passage into the chapel, yet enough remained to tell the story. The uncompromised stains were circular in shape, and roughly the size of a dime. Heavy bleeding, not unlike that caused by a head wound, that came from above at a ninety-degree angle. The blood smear on Dugas's trousers confirmed that the actor had lifted the victim by grasping his ankles and walking backward to the altar where the victim was laid out like a sheep for slaughter.

The rest of it was clear. The vic had been hamstrung as he lay on the altar, so escape would have been impossible. Then as he slowly bled out, he'd been tied by the ankles and hoisted over the heavy, exposed beam overhead. The forensic boys had found sufficient DNA on the rough wood of the cross to indicate that at some point Dugas had come to, and had been at least partially aware of what followed.

Had he been conscious when the spikes were driven through his wrists and the arches of his feet? Hugh wondered. Had he stared his murderer right in the eye, begging for his life to be spared when his throat was slashed and it finally ended?

The scenario certainly fit the evidence. Somewhere

in the back of his mind, Hugh could hear the priest's screams. It was the sort of end capable of breaking the hardest man and leaving nothing but a moaning, terrified, quivering mass of muscle, blood, and bone. "One thing for sure. Whoever did this wanted him to suffer. I'd sure as hell like to know why."

The crime scene indicated careful planning. They hadn't come up with a single print that didn't belong to those kids. Shuffling the mess on the coffee table into some semblance of order, Hugh found Michel's desk calendar and laid it atop the untidy pile. Because of the accident that afternoon, he'd barely had a chance to glance at it until now. There were counseling sessions scheduled, and several late-season softball games by the St. Bart's Saints, a youth activity Michel had organized. Father Murdoch's birthday was duly noted and circled in red, but only one notation jumped out at Hugh, grabbing and holding his attention. *September 15, Gitan, Ctfh Pt.*

Gitan hadn't mentioned a meeting the night Hugh dropped Mason at the Chop Shop. In fact, he hadn't said much at all. Hugh remembered the ex-con's reaction—or rather, lack of reaction when he'd leaked the news of Dugas's murder. A lack of response in any person close to the victim who should have been surprised by that person's demise was a definite red flag, and said person automatically became suspect.

Gitan hadn't been close to Michel that Hugh was aware of, but they weren't strangers, either. Michel had made regular visits to Angola to see him, the only other person in Angelique besides Gitan's family who had. After Gitan's release six months ago, Michel had continued the visits: Rose Boudreaux's place, the Chop Shop. . . .

The question was why?

What had been behind the visits?

Concern for a lost soul?

Some perceived connection from childhood that existed only in the priest's mind?

Or did the visits have something to do with Lily? Though she'd never spoken his name during their two-year marriage, Hugh had always suspected that she hadn't gotten over the Cajun. *Oh, he'd had her body—briefly,* Hugh thought. But there was not a shred of doubt in his mind that Gitan had never quite relinquished his hold on her heart, and that certainty was like a gaping wound in him that refused to heal. A painful reminder that no matter how hard he worked, or how great his accomplishments, he would never quite measure up to Gitan.

He ground his cigarette out in an ashtray brimming with butts and stared at the notation.

September 15, Gitan, Ctfh Pt.

September 15th. The day Michel was murdered.

Ctfh Pt.

Catfish Point.

Hugh's pulse picked up its pace as he realized that he'd just gotten his first solid lead. The victim had scheduled a meeting with a convicted felon near the scene of the crime the day of the homicide. A felon with an undisputable history of violence.

Without hesitation, he picked up the phone. "Fred, it's Hugh. Listen, you're about due for your break, is that right? How about you swing by Gitan Boudreaux's place and invite him down to the station. Tell him I want to talk to him. And Fred, don't take *no* for an answer."

CHAPTER
SEVEN

Hugh took his time getting to the office. He knew Fred Rally would have picked up Boudreaux an hour ago, but he wanted to give Gitan time to stew properly before the interview. Maybe a little time in the hot seat would loosen him up a little, and it definitely gave Hugh the upper hand.

When Hugh walked in, Gitan was seated in a chair in front of the new desk Hugh had purchased the day he was sworn in as sheriff. The old relic his predecessor had been so fond of had been turned into kindling wood. Its replacement was better suited to a man of his position. It was larger than the old one, shinier, and more imposing. Boudreaux, however, seemed unimpressed. He didn't even bother to come out of his easy slouch, or uncross his booted ankles.

"Nice boots," Hugh said, taking a seat in his leather executive's chair. "What do they go for these days? A hundred? One fifty? You seem to do well, for an ex-con fresh out of prison."

The Cajun reached into the pocket of his jeans and took a stick of chewing gum out of a half-depleted pack. The black tank-style T-shirt he wore revealed more brown skin than it covered, and Hugh wondered how many hours he'd spent pumping iron in the prison yard. His drawl when he answered Hugh was slow and easy. "You have a reason for askin' Fred to drag me down here? Other than to discuss my wardrobe?"

"Oh, I've got a reason, all right, but we'll get to it in a minute. You aware that Lily's back in town? Dumb question, I suppose. You've already seen her, that right?"

Gitan shrugged, and the web tattoo moved and stretched as if blown by a gentle bayou breeze. Prison tattoos signified a lot of things. Ordinarily a web was a design white supremacists were partial to, but those webs were simpler, less detailed than the one Boudreaux had chosen, and usually worn on the elbow. This one had nothing to do with racism. It was the only thing Hugh could be sure of.

"I gave her a lift after somebody slashed her tires yesterday," Boudreaux said. "Happened right outside in your parking lot here at the station. Imagine that."

That rankled. Hugh stiffened. "It's the first I've heard of it. Why the hell didn't she report it?"

"Maybe she figured she'd had enough trouble for one day and didn't need the hassle she'd get from you."

"For old time's sake, I'll try to forget I heard that."

"Fred said this was important," Gitan said, coming out of his chair. "Looks like he was wrong about that. Since I haven't done anything to give you cause to bring me down here, I'll say *adieu*, and leave it at that."

As he started to get up, Hugh sat back, his chair creaking. "Sit down, Gitan. Stay a while."

"Get a life, Hugh, and stop tryin' to fuck with mine."

"I said, sit down."

Gitan's shoulders flexed, and the movement rippled a chain of muscle right down to his fingertips. Hugh had a good idea he would have liked to come out of that chair and turn things physical, like the old days, but he didn't. Instead, he forced himself to relax.

"Maybe you'd care to explain the nature of your relationship with Michel Dugas?"

The Cajun gave him a look that said, *Maybe you'd care to kiss my ass?* but he answered a bit more politely. "Michel was a friend; it's that simple."

"Funny, I don't recall you two bein' all that friendly before you got sent up."

"People change, Hugh. Or maybe I should correct that statement for you. Some of us do."

"Is that why you were gonna meet with him the day he was murdered?" Hugh leaned forward. "Because you were such good friends?"

If Gitan was shocked that Hugh knew about the meeting, he didn't show it. In fact, he didn't even blink, and his dark stare was steady and cold as flint. "I agreed to meet him because he asked me to, but Ruben wanted me to stay over and finish up the design on the Logan job. I clocked out at eleven thirty-five and went straight home."

"Did you talk to him that evening?"

The Cajun shrugged. "I called his place as a courtesy, but I got the answering machine, so I hung up."

"What time did you make the call?"

"Jesus Christ," he said. "I don't know—nine P.M., I guess. I don't keep a detailed log of my activities, and at the time I had other things to think about."

His impatience was evident, but that's all it seemed to be: impatience. Still, Hugh wasn't satisfied.

"It was important enough for Michel to make a note

of the meeting with you at Catfish Point. Hell of a co-incidence that he planned to meet you there—what? Three or four hours before he was murdered at that same location."

"You're right about one thing," Boudreaux said. "It's a coincidence. Michel and I both enjoyed droppin' a line in the water every now and then. It's a good way to kick back and relax, and it's peaceful on the water at night. You ought to try it sometime. Lot of folks fish out that way, and if you were as up on the goin's-on in this parish as you like to think, you'd know that."

"Coroner puts the time of death between ten P.M. and two A.M. If you clocked out at eleven-thirty, it makes it possible for you to have gone to Catfish Point and killed Michel."

"You want to find your perp, you look for motive, Jack. Me, I had no reason to want to hurt Father Dugas." He came slowly out of his chair, a bigger man than Hugh was, stronger and more muscular, more self-possessed, and Hugh felt the worm of a life-long envy turn slowly inside him. Gitan walked from the room, without permission to leave, without another word, without glancing back.

The message was clear. Hugh was no match for him, no threat, despite his position as sheriff or the power it afforded him, and that burned.

Hugh took a pack of cigarettes from the drawer and tapped one out on the back of his hand. He hung it from his lower lip, reaching for his lighter. "Fuckin' asshole." The sharp inhalation of nicotine-laced smoke took the edge off his anger, but it did nothing for the realization that he was soundly back at square one.

Without motive, he didn't have probable cause, and Gitan's being a convicted murderer was not reason enough to get a warrant for his arrest . . . even if the thought of putting him back behind bars was enough to make him salivate, and the only way he knew of to save Lily from herself.

The rain hadn't ceased for an instant through morning or afternoon, but as Lily pulled up to the curb in front of Virginia's shop, it lightened to a barely visible mist. It was six P.M. on what might possibly have been the longest, most difficult day of her life, aside from the day Gitan had been sentenced. At eleven that morning, she'd sat in the pew at the new St. Bartholomew's Catholic Church and listened to the old priest conduct the funeral mass. She'd knelt when called to, bowed her head, and gone through the motions, but she hadn't prayed, and when she'd lifted her gaze to the crucifix that graced the rear wall of the sanctuary, over the altar the dialogue of a disillusioned nonbeliever rang in her head.

Damn you! How the hell could you let this happen?
Why didn't you do something to stop it?
Michel devoted his life to you! And you let him be sacrificed! How can you call yourself a savior when you wouldn't save him?

She left the sanctuary with the other mourners an hour later. Many went home to a late dinner. Lily went to the cemetery and stood a few paces behind Leonie and her mother, and the other members of Michel's family. The small circle of mourners, each sheltered by a large black umbrella, stood stoically while the casket was placed in the Dugases' crypt for the traditional year and a day along with the bones of countless generations of Michel's family. When the crypt was sealed, the old priest spoke to each family member privately, then at last, paused before Lily.

"Don't bother," Lily had said quietly, her voice tight, full of the pain that never seemed to ease. "There's nothing you can say that will make his dying any easier to swallow."

The old man's eyes seemed to focus slowly. He stared at her for a moment; then recognition dawned. "Why, you're Lily Martin. Justin and Sharon's daughter. You were close to Father Dugas—as children, and afterward."

"He was my best friend."

"You are bitter for someone so young. But then, I suppose it is your grief that is talking." He paused, took a breath, and drew from some inner well of priestly piety. "No death goes unnoticed in the Kingdom of Heaven, and Father Dugas's passing won't be ignored. He's precious to the God he served. You should try to take comfort in that knowledge."

"Comfort? You've got to be kidding. The only comfort I could get from this situation is knowing that the creep who did this will pay for what he's done." She'd turned her back and walked away, aware that he lingered in the rain to watch her go.

There was always a reception held after a funeral, and the Dugas family had opened their small house to friends and relatives. Lily had lent a hand in the kitchen, staying long after the crowd began to thin. Then she went home to the house on Mill Creek Road, but the house was dark, and the red beans and rice Edna had prepared for dinner sat cold in the fridge. Virginia apparently hadn't been home yet, so Lily drove back to the shop to make sure nothing was wrong. The bell attached to the door jingled as she walked in, but the showroom was deserted. "Hello? Is anyone here?"

No one answered, but there was a shuffling sound

coming from the rear of the shop. Not a threatening sound, yet it was alarming given that the door was open and no one was around. Lily walked through the gallery to the storeroom in back, turning on the light as she entered. Virginia was sitting on the floor, a cardboard box beside her and a pair of antique porcelain dolls in her lap. She didn't look up immediately, and when she did, she seemed startled, like a deer caught in the glare of oncoming headlights. "Aunt Virginia?"

"Aren't they just lovely?" she said, her voice softer than it normally tended to be, wistful. "They don't make dolls like this anymore, you know. I'll have to hide them, or Justin might break them. He's always so angry. I don't understand why he's so angry."

A chill of foreboding crept along Lily's spine. "Daddy's dead, Aunt Virginia. Don't you remember?"

A moment's confusion, then the veil seemed to lift. She blinked, glanced around, and hurried to put the dolls away. "Yes, of course, I remember."

She made a move to rise, and Lily reached out to help her. "Aunt Virginia, is everything all right? No one's out front, and the door was unlocked."

"Good heavens, what time is it? I'd better hurry and get ready, or I'll miss Michel's service."

Lily drew a deep breath and, reaching out, took Virginia's hand. "It's after six. Supper's waiting."

"After six? But it can't be!" She glanced at her wristwatch and shrank back against the shelves. "Oh, dear. The time got away from me. I'm so sorry, dear. I'm so dreadfully sorry. How will you ever forgive me?"

Lily tightened the grip on her aunt's hand with her left, patting it gently with her right in an effort to calm her. "There's nothing to forgive. Nothing at all. Come. I'll take you home."

A few hours later the house on Mill Creek Road was quiet. Edna Mae had returned after Lily's call, and came prepared to spend the night. Virginia had retired to her bedroom earlier, but not to rest. Above their quiet conversation, the sound of footsteps, the creak and groan and telltale squeak of the floorboards could be heard—forward and back, forward and back—a short pause by the window, and forward and back.

Edna Mae's gaze drifted to the ceiling overhead. Lily could tell she was worried. "Did you speak to her about this?"

"I tried." Lily sighed. "She assured me she's fine, but I could tell the episode frightened her. If you could have seen the look on her face when I found her. I've never seen her like that." She stopped, unwilling to add her own concerns to Edna Mae's. Edna Mae had been in Virginia's employ for years, and their relationship went far beyond employer and employee.

"I have seen it, child. My own mama's mind got weak before she turned eighty. That was before they had a fancy name for it. It was a hard thing to live with, and I had my sisters to share the burden, and to cry with. You're all alone in this, aren't you?"

"I'm fine, really." What she didn't say was that she was shaken. Virginia had always been the one steady force in her life. Her safety net. No matter what happened, no matter how bad things became, Virginia was there to rely on, to give sound advice, support, and love, and the thought of losing her was terrifying.

"Don't you go tryin' to sweep this under the rug. You got a lot on your plate right now, losin' your job, an' all."

Lily glanced sharply up, but the older woman just smiled and patted her cheek with a work-worn hand. "Now, you know you can't fool Edna Mae for long. I know things." She chuckled softly. "Drives Miss Virginia crazy, too." She allowed herself a deep chuckle, then sobered again. "No need to worry. She won't know anything till you're ready to tell her . . . but Miss Lily, you've got to promise to take care of yourself. All this stress ain't good for nobody, and you're stretched far too thin as it is. You want me to warm up some of that red beans and rice for you? You know it took first prize last year at the Angelique cook-off, that recipe."

"Maybe later," Lily said, hugging Edna Mae. "Thank you for being here. I appreciate it, and I know she does, too."

"What are old friends for?" Edna Mae said with a sad smile. "Listen, why don't you go out for a while? Clear your head? I hear the zydeco's hot down at the Pink Cadillac Saturday nights. Might do you good to have a little fun, and there ain't nothin' you can do here."

Lily hesitated, then picked up her car keys and went out.

In high school Gitan ran track and played football. He hadn't been big enough to be a lineman, so he ran the ball because like everybody said, "Dat Boudreaux boy, he sure as hell can run." Sports had given him an outlet for his pent-up energy, and somewhere in the back of his mind he'd believed that if he worked hard enough to excel, there'd been the chance that he'd win a scholarship to a university. It had been the only way college would be an option for him. Times were tough then. With layoffs at the refinery where his daddy worked, a mortgage, and his mama's poor health, he had to find his own way financially. Hugh seemed to resent Gitan's dedication almost as much as he resented his growing interest in Lily.

"How 'bout we take off tonight and go to the drive-in? The Taylor twins put out on a regular basis. We could steam the windows up on your old man's car but good!"

"Can't," Gitan said. "Got a track meet this evenin'."

"I s'pose you're dragging Lily along?" Hugh's jealousy, never buried terribly deep, surfaced, souring his tone.

"Pickin' her up on my way there. What's it to you?"

"Ain't nothin' to me!" Hugh shot back. "What's it to you? You two doin' the nasty? Shit, never imagined she'd turn out to be so easy! Hey, man. Level with me. How was it? She go down on you yet? Always did think that mouth of hers was made to be wrapped around a man's rod."

Gitan reacted before Hugh had time to choke out one more syllable, grabbing him by the throat, pinning him against the restroom stall. "It ain't like that, Hugh, and if I so much as hear you breathe her name to anybody else, I'll make you wish you hadn't. You got that?"

"Yeah, I get it! Jesus! You in love with her, or somethin'?"

Gitan let him go and shook off the urge to throttle him. "What if I am?" he said quietly. "It ain't nothin' to you."

Gitan pushed away the memory, but he couldn't shrug off quite that easily the feeling that there was trouble on the horizon. He went to the fridge and poured himself some ice water, then made his way to the screen porch in front, sinking down onto the old chaise lounge, stretching out. From where he lay, he could see the stars peeking through the breaks in the live oak's foliage, and now and then he could feel the damp breeze kiss his hot skin. Closing his eyes, he breathed in the scent of rain on the shiny, dark leaves of the oleander, the heavy, oily smell of frying catfish drifting from a neighbor's kitchen windows, and thanked the God who had given him back his freedom for another day in paradise.

Somewhere between sleep and reality, the screen door opened and Lily walked in. He'd dreamt of her so often that he was certain that's what it was—a dream. Lying motionless, hesitant to move for fear he would wake and she would vanish, he drank her in. Moisture sparkled in her hair like tiny diamonds, coaxing curls from the short ragged wisps at her ears and her nape, turning her skin dewy. For a moment she paused, as if trying to decide if coming here was the right decision; then the moment passed and she walked to the chaise and knelt down beside it. "Lily?"

"Sssssh," she said, putting a finger to his lips.

Then he realized that it was no dream. Her touch was more tangible than any fantasy, cool and soft, as gentle as the kiss of a night breeze on warm skin. "I had to come," she said, framing his face with her hands, brushing her lips against his. The kiss was tentative, a taste of the past, a hint of a promise of the night ahead, and it wasn't enough for her. There was an ache in her deep blue eyes he recognized and understood, an unspoken need to be held and touched, to feel wanted, and loved, and safe, if only for a little while. "Please, don't send me away," she said, her voice a mere whisper, and kissed him again, this time more deeply.

The plea touched him. He had sent her away, turned his back, because she'd been hurt enough, and she'd been vulnerable. "Nobody's sendin' you anywhere you don' want to go, *cher*," he replied, his arms slipping easily around her, his hands sliding down to the gentle curve of her ass. She fitted against him so naturally, hand in glove, that it failed to register how dangerous a situation they were in. She had a jealous ex-husband in a position of power who happened to hate the air he breathed. A word to his parole officer that he was involved with the daughter of his victim, and he could land his ass in some serious hot water. Somehow, that knowledge paled further with each kiss Lily claimed, with each new move of her hands on his skin. He sensed how important it was that she lead this encounter wherever it was destined to go, so he didn't push to take control, or try to rush her to completion.

Lily didn't have Gitan's patience. She'd fought the urge to come here as long as she could, and finally she gave in to impulse. That's what it was: an insanely illogical impulse, an itch she had to scratch. She didn't just want him; she needed him. She needed to feel his hands on her skin; she needed to watch as he rose above her. She needed to feel the play of hard against soft, and warm against cool. More than anything, she needed to feel alive again, vitally important to someone, even if it lasted only for a moment or two. Morning would come soon enough with glaring clarity, and she would be forced to face her mistakes and poor judgment, but tonight in the soft shadows of his screen porch, with the fireflies drifting outside, incandescent green specks against the black velvet night, she refused to think about the consequences of her actions.

"Baby, are you sure this is what you want?" he asked softly.

She answered by lifting the hem of his tank top and peeling it from him, following the trail of the fabric with her lips. She couldn't get enough of him, couldn't get close enough to satisfy the hunger burning a hole through her vitals. "I've never been so sure about anything."

"*C'est* alright," he said, taking her mouth with his as he shifted positions, gathering her into his arms. One by one, Lily's shoes were removed and discarded. When her tan silk blouse, jade green slacks, and pale jade bra and panties became a careless pile on the floor, she reached out, opening the rivet at the waistband of his jeans, undoing his fly, so that he filled her hand, and in turn, her body . . . and Lily turned her face into the curve of his throat, content to block out the rest of the world.

Long after, Lily lay in his arms, sated, content, letting her palms glide across his shoulders and the spider's web tattoo. "This wasn't here before."

"I got it the week after my release. *Tante* Rose kept the money I'd been saving when I got sent up, so I had a little to live on." He caught her hand and kissed each finger, then kept it against his cheek as he went on. "A spider's web is like life, *cher*. Strong, yet fragile—beautiful, but something most folks take for granted. Kinda like breathin'. It's so automatic that you don' realize how important it is . . . till you have to fight to do it."

Lily frowned and, bending, kissed the heavy ridge of scar tissue that ran the length of him, from collarbone to just above his navel. Somewhere in the shadows of the dark porch, a woman's scream echoed, the report of a gunshot, a man's laughter. The scene that flashed behind her eyes was crazily distorted. Justin Martin falling, blood on her hands, and Aunt Virginia.

"You alright?"

She nodded once. "Yes. Just fine." Then she sighed as his hand slipped down and he found her again, and all thought of the past melted into the ether.

Outside, the headlights of a car moved slowly by, no threat as the light failed to reach as far as the house, and neither one noticed that as it approached the drive, the brake lights glowed red for a fraction of a second. Hugh gazed at the dark-colored compact. Lily's car, nosed in behind Boudreaux's truck, and no lights on at the house. He reached for his cigarette pack, his movements a little too quick, a little too forceful. "Well, well, well," he murmured, shoving a cigarette between his lips, pushing in the cigarette lighter. "It sure as hell didn't take him long."

CHAPTER
EIGHT

Lily was gone next morning when Gitan woke, almost as if she'd never been there at all. There was only the lingering scent of her perfume on his skin and the memory of her kiss. A tepid shower and a change of clothes and the fantasy faded and life went back to normal.

It was Saturday, but he always put in some overtime in the early morning hours. Ruben was flexible when it came to Gitan's work schedule. He never hassled him for showing up an hour late when he met with Suzanne Stone, his parole officer, and when something came up concerning Mason, he let him clock out early. In turn, Gitan stayed late several nights a week, and came in on Saturday mornings.

He was the jack-of-all-trades around the Chop Shop. Aside from his skill with the airbrush, he could use the torches and weld as well as any certified man on the premises, and in a pinch, he did some fabricating, a trade he'd practiced at Angola after graduating from field work. Quick to pick up a technique the first time out, there wasn't a machine in the shop that he hadn't used in the last six months.

He was dependable, finishing whatever project Ruben assigned to him on schedule, if not beforehand. Ruben told him often that he was the most indispensable man he had working for him, and when Suzanne came by the shop to check on how he was doing, she always got a good report.

If Mason stopped by to "hang," nothing was said. This morning, he was bored with Rose's fussing over his healing bruises, and decided to loiter for a while. The kid poked around the scrap pile at the rear of the shop, looking for anything he could salvage and finally coming in with an old fender and a pair of bent forks. Ruben had remarked to Gitan that it would take the boy an eternity to build a bike that way. Yet Gitan knew that where Mase was concerned, he would find a way to make it happen and surprise everyone in the process. The kid had some kind of potential.

"Hey, Mason," Ruben said, glancing up from his parts inventory when the boy entered the shop, letting in a blast of intense heat and bright sunlight. "What'd you find out there?"

"Fender and some forks," Mase said. "But I need to know what you're askin' for 'em."

"Seems to me I should be payin' you, instead of the other way around. I got to pay to have that junk hauled to the scrap yard, you know, so you're actually doin' me a favor by takin' it off my hands."

Mase cocked a hip, his brow furrowed. "Got to want somethin' for it, yet I'll allow it ain't worth much." He pointed out the poor condition of the forks, the shrewd negotiator on the scent of a steal of a deal. "I pay my own way, and I don' take no char-ity. Gitan can vouch for that fact."

Gitan snorted. "Guess I'll remind you of that when you start drivin' and decide to hit me up for gas money."

Ruben winked. "You need spending money, you come see me. If you're half as talented as Gitan, I'll be happy to put you to work."

Mase's expression brightened. "I can't paint like Gitan can, but I can mask, and I'm pretty good at basic body work."

"Is that right? You busy this morning? There might be something you can lend a hand on after all." Ruben turned slightly, motioning to a relic sitting in a corner with a tarp half slung over it. "You see that bike? It's not exactly a chopper, but it would make a nice little set of wheels for some kid just startin' out. You interested in tacklin' the project?"

Mase turned cagey. "I might be. Depends, though. What's in it for me?"

"Experience, for one thing. You get to come in and spend whatever time you have on it—after school, on Saturdays. Familiarize yourself with the tools, and with the rules of the shop. Do a good job and you get to keep the bike. We'll transfer the title when she's finished."

"Ah, man! You serious?"

"Dead serious, but only if your brother and your aunt say it's okay."

Mase glanced at Gitan, and a cloud of doubt passed over his angular face. But Gitan just shrugged. "It's Ruben's shop and his bike, and I got no beef with it. Besides, if you're gonna hang around, you might as well be busy, instead of buggin' the hell out of me."

"Then, it's settled," Ruben said. "You start by break-ing it down. Take it apart, piece by piece, but keep it organized. After it's all refurbished, repainted, and the chrome redone, you're gonna have to reassemble it, and you need to know what bolts go where. Tools are in the standing red tool box. You got a question, you ask Gitan. He's gonna be shop foreman while you're working here, so you got to answer to him, and do as he says. That's Chop Shop Rule Number One. You got that?"

"Shit, yeah—I mean, yes, sir! I got it." Mase headed toward the bike, carefully removing the tarp and surveying the treasure buried beneath.

"That ought to keep him busy for a while," Ruben said with a laugh. "I should have asked you first if it was okay, but he's a damn nice kid. I wanted to do somethin' nice for him."

"Well, you didn't have to, but thanks. I appreciate it, and I know he will, too."

Ruben smiled, but there was a trace of irony in the expression. "Kind of reminds me of Willie at that age, only with half the attitude. I don't know what happened to that kid, but somewhere along the way he got screwed up. I don't mind tellin' you, Gitan—he worries me."

Ruben's secretary buzzed him on the intercom. "Mr. Early? Telephone call on line three."

"Well, hell, better get back to it. Listen, how close are you to wrapping up the work on the Williams bike?"

"I'll do the last of the detail work today, the clear coat on Monday, and she'll be ready for assembly. If everything goes off without a hitch, I figure end of the week."

"Who the hell would figure somebody would want to put the Virgin Mary on a chopper?" Ruben shook his head. "Only in Acadiana."

As Ruben disappeared into his office, Gitan caught

Mase's attention. "You gonna be okay out here by yourself?"

"Better than okay," Mase replied. "Man, can you believe this?"

Gitan smiled. "Yeah, I can believe it. He's a generous man. You might want to thank him when you get the chance. I've got some stuff to do in the booth. Yell if you need anything, but don't just walk in."

"Gitan?"

He'd started to walk away, but turned back. "Yeah?"

"Thanks," Mase said. "You could've said no, but you didn't."

Gitan walked to where Mase sat and squeezed the boy's shoulder, about as much physical contact from an older brother that a fifteen-year-old kid would tolerate. "No need to thank me. Everybody deserves a chance. Now, it's up to you to show the man what a Boudreaux can do. Be back in a little while. Don't forget, we need to be cleaned up and out of here by one."

It was tempting to hang back and watch to make sure Mason toed the line and resisted goofing off, but Gitan had seen the look on the boy's face when Ruben had offered him the bike. A little responsibility, a little freedom might be just what Mason needed, and that meant trusting him. If he screwed up, there would be plenty of time to land on him. For now, he had to give him the same sort of opportunity Ruben had given him when he'd shown up at his door, an ex-con fresh out of prison. Ruben had given him a chance to prove himself, and Gitan had done his best to show the man he'd made a wise decision.

As he mixed a small amount of paint and put the finishing touches on the religious icon, he lost himself in the process of overlaying a translucent hint of gray on the top of the folds in Mary's robes to create the illusion of light, of deepening the shadows to purplish black to create depth, and lost all track of time. When he was into the process, it was as if he disappeared. The movement of the gun was steady and sure, his touch feather light, and all conscious thought ceased as pure instinct took over so that the work itself seemed to live and breathe.

A crash from the main shop stopped him cold. Gitan put down the gun and turned off the compressor, heading for the shop and the source of the racket. The stand of metal shelves where small hardware was stored lay on its side. Nuts, bolts, and clamps were scattered over the concrete floor.

As Gitan reached the shop, Willie Early lifted his foot and kicked the bike Mase had been working on onto its side, and Mason tore into the older boy, landing a solid punch to Willie's mouth. Willie shook his head and blood flew. Then Gitan pulled them apart and put himself between them. "What the hell's goin' on in here? Mason?"

"Nothin'," Mase said, reluctant to rat on his worst enemy.

"Sure didn't look like nothin'," Gitan said. "Willie, what have you got to say for yourself?"

"I don't have to tell you shit!"

"Check that attitude," Gitan warned the older boy. "I asked you a question. I want an answer."

"Yeah? Well, fuck you, convict!" He hawked and spat an inch from Gitan's boot.

Gitan could smell beer on the kid from several feet away. It was barely afternoon, and he wondered if alcohol was the only thing he had in his system. His clothing was rumpled, and his eyes bloodshot—he looked wired, from the frenetic energy that rippled from him in waves, to the cut on his knuckles that was just beginning to heal. "Looks like a nasty gash you got there—what? Two, three days old? How'd you come by it?"

Willie threw his head back, his expression belligerent. He had a heavy grudge against the world, and everyone in it, and he was too spoiled, or too stupid, to know it would only bring him trouble. "It's none of your goddamned business."

"It is if you happened to cut your knuckles on my brother's face."

Willie's slitted gaze slid from Gitan to Mason. "That what he told you?"

"He didn't tell me anything. I come in here and find you bustin' up his bike. What's it look like to you?"

"It ain't his bike. It's mine. My name's on the title, and I'll torch the goddamn thing if I feel like it."

Mase turned around and kicked the tire of the overturned motorcycle. "Let him have it. Be goddamned if I want anything that belonged to some half-baked motherfucker, anyhow."

Gitan put a finger in Mase's face. "That's enough out of you." Then he turned back to Willie, bracing his hands on his hips, his feet slightly apart. If Willie made a move, he wouldn't hesitate to put him on his face on the concrete floor. Willie was under twenty-one, and that might not go down well with Suzanne, but he'd deal with the situation first, and face the consequences later.

"You take up the ownership of the bike with your daddy," Gitan told him. "He's the one gave it to Mase. But you do it on your own time. You feel like making trouble, you better plan on doin' it far away from here. You come around here, disrupting my work, and you're gonna have to deal with me. Now, get the hell out of here."

Willie hesitated, lingering a few seconds and clearly wanting to challenge Gitan, only the superman glow from the beer and the drugs seemed to be fading. "I'll see you later," he said to Mase, then turned his back and left.

Left alone with Gitan, Mase hunched his shoulders. "Willie was one of the four, wasn't he?" Gitan asked.

Mase didn't answer directly. "I'll put the tools away and clean up the mess I made, but I'm not comin' back. Tell Mr. Early I said he can keep the bike."

Mason's life was divided into two sections: the first had the feeling of a warm and secure bubble, the good times plucked out of seven' years worth of memories . . . a time when his parents were alive, and his older brother wasn't so damned anal.

The sound of his mother's voice as she laughed at something Rose said, the smell of chicken frying, and the snap of sheets drying on the backyard clothesline. He remembered enjoying a good-natured tussle with Gitan in the grass under the live oak tree, and their father's warning to Gitan "not to get too rough with the young 'un."

The memories had been dragged out so often that they'd grown worn and faded around the edges, like a photograph too often handled. There were times when Mase thought it might have been kinder if he couldn't remember better times at all.

There was no way to miss what you'd never had in the first place. He loved his aunt and was grateful she'd been there after his parents had died, but she didn't seem to get that he needed space. She was way too clingy, and sometimes she treated him like a two-year-old. He couldn't even hang with his friends without her breaking out the cookies and milk.

When they'd gotten word that Gitan was going to be part of an early release program for inmates they considered low risk, Mase thought things would get better. But the Gitan who got off the bus from Angola wasn't the older brother Mase remembered, the one he'd wrestled with in the grass.

Prison had changed Gitan. He'd never talked a great deal, but his silences now had a brooding, intense quality that worried Mase sometimes, and he couldn't help wondering what was going on in his head.

Gonzales lit a cigarette and leaned back against the limb where he was perched. "Boudreaux, you're as moody as my sister, Alicia, when she's PMS'n. What the hell's wrong wid you?"

Mase left off doing a rapid succession of chin-ups long enough to throw his friend a dark look that was more like his older brother's than he knew. The loss of the bike had stung. In six and a half months, he'd turn sixteen. Gitan had his Harley and a customized truck he'd built from the ground up, and Rose had her Oldsmobile, but he didn't have anything of his own and now he never would have.

He knew it wasn't Gitan's fault, but having the promise of the bike for that hour was worse than not having it at all, and he had to lay the blame on someone. "Or somethin'," he said cockily, dropping to the ground and working to catch his breath. They both waited, letting the silence settle between them again. "It's Gitan, you know? He don' act right."

"What do you mean, he don' act right? He seems okay to me."

"You don' have to deal with him. He's on my case

twenty-four-seven, with no let up. 'Don' do this, Mason. Don' do dat.' It's always somethin'. Sometimes I think they took my brother away and sent somebody else home in his place. He looks like Gitan, and he sounds like Gitan . . . but it ain't him. Hell, I don't know who he is anymore. Lately, I almost wish he hadn't come back at all."

Gonzales shrugged. "Shit, man, think about it. My sister, she locked me in the closet once and I thought I'd piss my pants till Mama let me out. I thought about killin' Alicia for it, but I couldn't take bein' locked up for real. Besides, he's almost thirty. Thirty's old. Old people worry about stupid stuff, like taxes and property values. Could be you're expectin' too much."

"Could be," Mase allowed, but he still couldn't grasp what had happened to change a man so much that he barely resembled his former self. "I just wish he wouldn't act like a whupped dog that's got to beg for scraps. Especially when it ain't so."

"The Martin chick ain't seconds, dat's for sure," Gonzales said, crushing his cigarette out against the trunk of the sweet gum, then flicking it onto the growing pile at the base of the tree. "She's hot, all right. Hey, you think she goes for younger men?"

"Shit!" Mase snorted at the thought. "Even if she did, Lily's too damn classy for the likes of you!" He couldn't help thinking, though, that she would be good for Gitan—good for him, too, in a roundabout way. With Gitan focused on Lily, he'd be less likely to be breathin' down Mase's neck twenty-four hours a day.

Tucked away in Mase's mind was something he shouldn't have seen. He'd come on them by accident, a week before the trouble started. They were lying in the tall grass in a secluded spot where Gitan liked to fish, but this time there was no pole in evidence.

Gitan was stripped to the waistband of his jeans, and even that was open . . . and Lily's blouse had mysteriously come undone.

As Mase had watched, Gitan bent over her, whispering something Mase couldn't quite catch in rough-voiced Cajun French. She'd reached up, stroking his face with her hand, and the look on his face in that instant had been something Mase had never forgotten. It stuck in his mind now, the way he'd looked as Lily touched him. It was the last time he'd seen his brother truly happy. "Listen," he said, suddenly. "I gotta go."

"C'mon, Mase, I thought we were gonna chill for a while! Hey. Hey! Where the hell you goin'?"

"There's somethin' I gotta do, that's all. I'll catch up with you later!"

Lily had begun her day with a burning need to get home. The few hours she'd spent in Gitan's arms had been more perfect than she could have imagined, and she'd been reluctant to spoil it by having the cold light of day shine down on what felt like a dream. She'd given in to impulse and gone to him, and the fear of how he might react, or what he might say afterward, was cause enough for her to want to escape. She'd slipped into her bra and panties, her slacks, blouse, and shoes, then picked up her car keys. At the door, she'd glanced back and the image of Gitan, one arm flung above his dark head, his hard face softened in sleep, stayed with her throughout the morning hours.

For once, Virginia had set aside her stubbornness and agreed to stay home and rest if Lily opened the shop for the "Saturday morning crush." Anything to convince Aunt Virginia to take better care of herself. "The crush" consisted of the Smith sisters, Molly and

Regina. The sisters were well into their seventies, and chatted quietly as they fingered the antiques with white-gloved hands, closely examined several pieces, but bought nothing.

Nobody else darkened the shop door, and at three P.M., Lily dutifully locked up and drove home. The previous day's storm didn't lessen the humidity, and the heat index was unusually high for September. The temperature was 86 degrees Fahrenheit, but with 70 percent humidity, it felt more like 95, and there was a good likelihood of more thunderstorms in the forecast. When the heat index soared, those who could afford to stayed indoors. Traffic this afternoon had slowed to a trickle and the rangy fifteen-year-old who turned at Lily's approach and stuck out his thumb stood little chance of catching a ride.

At fifteen, Mason Boudreaux closely resembled his older brother. The glossy dark brown hair, the color of black walnut stain, had only a hint of a wave, and the sweatband that crossed his forehead was a touch of color borrowed from Gitan. There were differences, too, physical and otherwise: a vulnerability about his mouth that Gitan didn't possess, a slight roundness to his chin, and the battle he seemed to be waging to define who he was. As she slowed the car, she pushed the control for the power window, and it whirred as the glass disappeared inside the doorframe. "Mason? What on earth are you doing out here?"

The boy's smile was broad and bright, despite the sharpness of Lily's tone. "Walking, and hopin' for a lift."

"Get in. I'll drive you wherever it is you're going."

"The ride doesn't come with a lecture about the dangers of hitchin', does it? 'Cause I've had enough of that crap to last a while."

Lily shook her head. "Well, it *is* dangerous, but I

have a feeling you wouldn't listen anyway, so I'll save that privilege for your family."

He opened the passenger door and slouched into the bucket seat, all smiles. "Man, that air sure feels good."

"Seat belt."

"You're kiddin' me, right? I don' need to buckle up. Ain't goin' far."

"You do in this car," Lily said with a don't-mess-with-me look.

"Jesus, you sound like somebody else I know. Do this, Mason, don' do that—you'd best not go where I've been, or I'll kick your scrawny a—" He stopped, mid-sentence, his face flushing. "Sorry."

"Would this wise man have a name?"

The boy just snorted. "He's got a name, all right, only when I'm mad at him, I can't repeat it in front of a lady. Wouldn't be polite."

"It might be wise not to say it in front of Gitan, either," Lily told him, smiling as he laughed. "You haven't said where you're going."

His laughter subsided and he was all seriousness again. "Seven-Oh-One Mill Creek Road."

"You're going to see my Aunt Virginia?"

"Actually, I was on my way to talk to you. If you got the time, that is."

It hadn't been easy for Mason, and Lily knew what it was like living under the shadow of something ominous, struggling to go through the motions and pretending that everything was normal when it wasn't. Maybe that was why she felt a pang of empathy when she looked at him, a strange sort of kinship. "It sounds serious."

"Yeah, sort of. I saw you at the funeral mass yesterday. *Tante* Rose got us a seat in the last pew. I guess Father Dugas was a friend of yours."

A sad smile. "Yes, he was."

"You got connections back in California, Lily? I mean, now that the funeral mass is over, you must be makin' plans to go back there?"

"I'm afraid I haven't decided yet. There are a few things here in Angelique that I need to take care of first." She still didn't have any idea who had killed Michel and why; then there was Virginia's health to think about. Besides, there was very little to go back to.

"You got someone there? Like a husband, or a boyfriend?"

Lily caught the hopeful note in his voice and glanced his way. "Mason, what's this about?"

A shrug. "Nothin' much. I just thought I'd let you know Gitan's available, if you're interested. You two were tight back in the day."

"Yes, we were close," Lily admitted, "but that was a lifetime ago." The conversation made her uncomfortable. It was true that she'd been to the house on Mayfly Street last night—*run,* she had *run* to the house Gitan rented on Mayfly Street . . . but Mase couldn't know it. There was no way a kid his age could understand what Lily herself couldn't comprehend. She met and held his gaze, needing him to understand. "We can't go back, Mase."

"What are you sayin'? That you don' still care about him?"

"Of course, I care!" Lily blew out a frustrated breath and ran a hand through her hair. "I can't believe I'm having this conversation with a fifteen-year-old kid."

"Okay, so maybe I'm a kid, but I ain't stupid. Gitan still loves you, Lily."

Lily shook her head, refusing to listen. "I don't

expect you to understand, but sometimes caring about someone just isn't enough. Our lives are different now—we're different. It wouldn't work—not even if I wanted it to."

"And you don'—want it to."

Lily couldn't answer. She wasn't sure what she felt, and she was too tired to think logically.

"C'mon, Lily. He needs you."

Lily laughed, but it sounded weak and uncertain. Pathetic. "Gitan doesn't need anyone, aside from his family," she said, her voice low, intent. "And he doesn't need the problems that getting involved with someone like me might bring. He has to be careful, and I'm not willing to be the cause of his losing his freedom. I won't ever let that happen again." It was the millionth time that day that her mind had replayed that particular argument, and the first time she'd said it aloud.

"He's allowed to have somebody care about him," Mase argued. "He's allowed to be happy. Ain't no law that says he has to be miserable and alone the rest of his life."

"No. There isn't," Lily agreed. "But that happiness can't include me. End of story." There was no missing the finality in her voice. She stopped at a stop sign a few hundred feet from her door. Mase opened the door and got out.

"Thanks for the lift," he said, but his tone said, *Thanks for nothin'.*

"Mason, wait!" Lily called after him. "At least let me take you home!"

"Don' worry 'bout me. I'll know the way!"

Lily let him go. She didn't have much of a choice. She watched as he cut across a yard and disappeared into the trees; then she drove home. Virginia came onto the porch when Lily pulled into the drive. There was color in her cheeks, and her blue eyes were bright. She looked like her old self, and for a moment Lily convinced herself that nothing was wrong. "Wasn't that the Boudreaux boy? Bobby's little brother? Don't know that I recall seein' him so far from town before. What's he doing out here all by himself?"

Trying to do the impossible, Lily thought. "He was hitchhiking. I gave him a lift. I wanted to take him home, but he got out and ran."

"You say something to make him mad?"

"Probably."

"Well, don't let it bother you. Kids that age are so emotional. If he's angry, it won't last long." Virginia frowned. "I sure hope he gets home all right, though. There are dreadful things goin' on around here. Makes it so a body doesn't feel safe in her own home."

Lily hoped Mason would get home safely, too. The Boudreaux family had seen enough tragedy. The last thing they needed was more difficulties.

Much later that night, a single light burned in a house across town. The bathroom was on the second floor, and though he knew it was unlikely that anyone could see inside, he didn't try to squash the impulse to cover the window with a large bath towel.

Better safe than sorry, and he knew what sorry felt like. He wished now that he had waited. That he'd drowned his anger with a bottle of scotch, or smashed the big-screen TV in the first-floor den. He wished with the clarity of hindsight that he hadn't sought him out so soon after he'd found out what had happened to the boy. But he hadn't waited. He'd discovered by chance that afternoon where he would be, before his world came crashing down around him. A chance comment from a third party that became useful later, and he'd stalked the man as if he'd been nothing more than an animal. Undeserving of mercy. What mercy had he shown when the rape occurred? How many young lives had he destroyed with his perversity? Pedophiles could not be redeemed. It wasn't an illness. It was pure evil, the corruption of innocence an unforgivable sin.

He wasn't a killer, not really—he was an avenger. If he'd gone to the authorities, it would have ruined lives already tainted, and the Church would have tried to do what it had always done in the past. Father Dugas would have been given a reprimand and sent to another diocese where he could ruin other children. There would have been no justice, no end to it.

So, he took matters into his own hands, and now those hands were stained with a blood he could not seem to wash away. He scrubbed them now with bleach and detergent, the nail brush he used turning the skin raw. He told himself that it was his imagination, but somewhere in the back of his mind, a rusty stream swirled clockwise down the drain.

If someone should notice. If someone should see, his life would be over.

CHAPTER NINE

There had been a burglary overnight, and a shooting. At two-thirty A.M. the call had come in that a young black male had allegedly tried to rob a convenience store on Rapier Street by using a smash-and-grab method.

Unfortunately for the young looter, the owner, Isaac Aubrey–living in the apartment above the store— had an aging Pomeranian with a bladder problem, and the man never left his apartment after hours without carrying what he referred to as "insurance," a chrome-plated .38.

"Tippy" asked to go out, and while she was watering the lawn, the store alarm tripped, Aubrey rushed from the shadows, and the kid ran, his arms full of whatever he could carry. He made it a total of thirteen paces before Aubrey drilled him between the shoulder blades.

Hugh cited the shooter for carrying an unlicensed firearm, but he hadn't arrested him. Hugh's opinion on the matter didn't enter into the equation. However unpalatable his actions, Aubrey had been defending his property against an unlawful invasion. In the great state of Louisiana, a man had every right to use deadly force when protecting his property or his person against a credible threat. Whether an unarmed thirteen-year-old kid stealing an armful of merchandise and running in the opposite direction from the shooter could be deemed a credible threat was certainly debatable.

Jamil Montrose was clinging to life in the ICU, and his doctors were saying that, should he survive, he was unlikely to walk again. Hugh didn't let it bother him. He was a career cop, and a certain amount of ugliness came with the territory. He drank his cooling coffee and made a few calls. Michel's homosexual lover still hadn't surfaced. Friends and acquaintances had no clue as to his whereabouts—or at the very least, they weren't talking. That morning, Hugh had issued an APB on him. Thus far, he was wanted for questioning, though Hugh was frankly more than a little curious as to why he'd disappeared, rather than answer a few questions about his relationship with the deceased.

Crebs knocked, then partially opened the door. "We heard back from the footwear expert in Baton Rouge."

"Well, don't just hang around the doorway," Hugh said without glancing up. "Get your ass in here—and try not to disappoint me."

Crebs slid into a seat. "The latent prints at the Dugas crime scene were made by a size eleven high-topped Wolverine work boot. I called the manufacturer, and three stores in the parish sell this particular boot."

"You get me any names?" Hugh asked.

"I'm gettin' to that. Amos's Outfitters downtown

sold a pair to a local resident last week, days before the murder. One Rose Boudreaux." He paused; then another thought occurred. "Which reminds me. A Boudreaux boy was tagged for shoplifting a bottle of wine at Santee's Market. I sent Fred to pick him up."

Hugh sat back with a grin. "First the work boots, now this?" He glanced at his desk calendar. "For a minute, there, I thought it was my birthday."

"What do you want me to do about the boots?"

"Well, I've seen Mason's shoes. He wears a size nine, tops; and I kind of doubt Rose would have something like that in her closet, so I'm going to assume they belong to Gitan. In fact, he was wearing a similar work boot when he was in here the other day. If Mason's on his way here, and the kid gets a phone call, care to wager which Boudreaux shows up for the kid?"

"My money's on the old lady," Crebs said. "If Gitan Boudreaux suspects he's being considered for a role as main actor in Dugas's passion play, he'll skip."

"A fool and his money." Hugh fished a cigarette out of his pack and lit up. "Nope. Mr. Got-It-All-Together ain't goin' nowhere. He's too busy putting his life back together to run."

Crebs shrugged, a big man with a chrome-dome do, and a face that was wholly unremarkable. If that didn't provide enough strikes against the deputy, he was from Wisconsin. "You come up with a motive yet?"

"Now, did I say Gitan was a suspect?" Hugh asked, the soul of innocence. "You just make sure our young shoplifter gets the nicest room in the house, will you?"

"You serious? You gonna put a fifteen-year-old kid in a holding cell?"

"This is the third time in a week he's been in some kind of trouble. A look at life on the inside might do him some good. Besides, I don't want any interference when his brother arrives."

"You're throwin' lit matches at a powder keg," Crebs told him.

Hugh smiled. "Every man needs a hobby."

Crebs shrugged. "Just be careful not to push the man too far without just cause."

Hugh didn't care for his reply. "I appreciate the advice, Deputy, but who runs this place?" He picked up the photograph of the boot prints. The forensic team had lifted the latent prints using adhesive paper, which they'd smoothed over to collect the light layer of dirt. Then, using a mixture of crystal violet and distilled water, the technicians had stained the print, making it clearly identifiable. Clear acetate preserved the shoe print for evidence, and everything was photographed. Crebs was waiting to be dismissed, and sat at ease. It was one thing Hugh liked about the man. He was unflappable, and didn't get bent out of shape over minor difficulties. In fact, there were times when Crebs seemed immune to stress. "Take a look at this," Hugh said, handing him the photograph. "See anything unusual?"

"The right foot shows an uneven tread. I might think its cause was a misstep, except that the pattern was repeated." Crebs frowned at the series of photographs that followed, each carefully numbered and documented as to its position. "Could have been due to him struggling to drag the vic. Dugas wasn't exactly a lightweight, if you know what I mean."

"Or maybe it's something peculiar to our murderer," Hugh suggested. "Like an injury."

"Dugas didn't have defensive wounds. He knew the guy who did this. Coroner surmised that he was struck from behind, and that was that."

"I'm not sayin' the injury had to have occurred the

night of the murder. Could've even been years old, but there's something about that right foot."

A shrug. "Could be you're right." The deputy stood. "That all you need?"

"That'll do for now."

Crebs went out, closing the door. Hugh's cigarette had burned down to ash in the ashtray while he stared at the photograph. He reached for another and heard a commotion outside in the reception area. Amy was arguing with someone, a one-sided argument that seemed to be getting closer. "Do you have an appointment? If you don't have an appointment, then you need to come and sit down—"

"No time for that."

"Sir, Sheriff Lothair is busy!" Amy's voice grew louder, almost frantic. "You can't just walk into his office!"

The door opened, and Gitan Boudreaux walked in. Amy, red-faced and obviously flustered, peered around one of his broad shoulders at Hugh.

"It's all right, Amy. I've been expecting Mr. Boudreaux."

"You want to tell me where he is?" Gitan demanded.

"Have a seat, Gitan. Make yourself at home. Stay a while." A flick of his lighter, and a second later Hugh shot a stream of smoke into the air between them. He knew Gitan's lungs had been compromised by the bullet from Justin Martin's pistol, and he really didn't care. "You stayed here for a month or so, prior to your sentencing; is that right?"

Gitan braced one brawny hand on a hip and leaned slightly forward, not quite in Hugh's face, but hardly polite. "No disrespect for your position, *Sheriff*—you want to mess with me, that's fine. But don' play games with my family."

"No games, Gitan. Mason is safe and sound in a

holding cell. Looks like he's headed down a dangerous path. Figured it might not hurt to shake him up a little before I handed him back. I'd think you'd thank me for that."

"I'll thank you once he's out of that cell."

Crebs appeared in the open doorway. "Amy said you might need help—"

"Help? Why, Gitan and I are old friends," Hugh said, his blue gaze meeting that of his adversary. Gitan was pissed, and Hugh took a certain amount of satisfaction from being able to rattle him out of his usual calm. He glanced up at Crebs. "Bring Mason Boudreaux out of the holding cell, will you? Tell him his brother's here to retrieve him. That ought to cheer him up."

Crebs turned and went out, and Hugh tapped the photo he'd been examining. "You see this photograph? That's a footprint lifted from the old church at Catfish Point—the Dugas crime scene. Those prints were made by a size eleven Wolverine work boot. No distinctive wear patterns on the soles, which means the boots were new."

Gitan didn't take the bait. "What's it got to do with Mase?"

"With Mason? Nothin'. But maybe it's got something to do with you. I happened to notice you were wearing work boots the other day, and they looked new. Size eleven."

"You're reachin', Hugh. Reach too far, and you'll fall flat on your face."

Hugh fingered his chin, his blue eyes narrowing slightly. "What's that you Cajuns say? *Peut-être que oui, peut-être que non?*"

"Ain't no 'maybe yes, maybe no' about it," Gitan told him, "and this is startin' to feel like phase two of the conversation we had yesterday. What's the matter? You can't find a legitimate suspect, so you decided to make one up?"

"Oh, I've got a suspect all right. In fact, I'm lookin' right at him."

Outside the office, Lily had just raised her hand to knock. Virginia had received a fine that morning for a violation of the parking ordinance by parking outside her own shop. Lily, certain that Hugh was behind it, had come in person to settle the dispute, or to kill him. She nearly took a step back when she heard Hugh's words; then Gitan turned, their gazes met, and Lily froze in place. "A suspect? For what?"

The tension didn't leave him, but his voice was easy and drawling. "No sweat, sugar. It's more of Hugh's petty bullshit, that's all. Don' let it concern you." He turned for one last glance at Hugh. "I'm gonna get Mase and go. You send your flunkies to my house, they better damn well have a warrant."

Gitan brushed past Lily, who stood staring at Hugh in total disbelief. It didn't take long for the shock to wear off and her instincts to kick in. "What the hell is going on here?"

"You asked me to do my best for Michel, and that's exactly what I'm doin'. You should be happy about that."

"I should be happy that you're implicating an innocent man? He had nothing to do with Michel's murder, and you know it!"

"I *don't* know it, and neither do you! He killed one man—what's to stop him from killing another? Jesus, Lily! I don't know how you can look at him without seeing your daddy lying dead on the floor!" Ignoring her, he hit the intercom button. "Amy, would you get Judge Malcolm on the phone?"

Lily's mind whirled with a confusing array of images. *The gun in Justin Martin's hand, the murderous expression on his face. He was beaten and bruised, and bleeding, and ready to kill. There was a flash, an explosion, and somewhere a woman screamed a desperate denial. Gitan seemed to fall in slow motion. Blood. Blood on her shirt, on her face, on her hands. So much blood! Two bodies, not one. Two men and so much blood . . . and Virginia's voice. My God, Lily. Lily, can you hear me? Oh, Jesus. Oh, Jesus. . . .*

Her head swam and her vision seemed distorted. She could feel her heartbeat vibrate through her body. Panic crowded her chest cavity, squeezing her lungs, rising up the back of her throat. It was so hard to breathe! In a moment she would run screaming into the street. "This is insane!"

"It's called the process of elimination. If there's no blood spatter on his boots, and they don't fit the pattern, then we keep looking. If he's innocent, like you say, then he's got nothing to worry about—and neither do you, apparently. You can go right on doing whatever it is you two do."

"So that's what this is about? You're getting back at Gitan for some imagined slight?"

"Oh, it's anything but imagined." He sat back, waiting for Judge Malcolm to take the call.

"Do you have any idea what a dangerous game it is you're playing?" Lily demanded. "It's not a competition, Hugh, where you can cheat to win. It's his life."

He dug in a pile of papers on his desk and came up with a fax which he thrust into her hands. The sender was the warden at Louisiana State Penitentiary. The content: a list of dates and times when Father Michel Dugas had visited with prisoner number 4623. "Gitan Boudreaux met with the victim once a month every month, beginning in the period when Michel went to seminary and ending when the inmate was paroled."

"That doesn't prove anything!" Lily insisted.

"And they kept up that association after his release, after his return to Angelique," Hugh insisted, the expression in his blue eyes unforgiving. "In fact, there's a notation in my possession written in the victim's own hand that indicates they had a meeting scheduled for the night of the murder at Catfish Point. Did you get the significance of that, Lily? Gitan claims he missed that meeting, but I have no proof of that."

Lily shook her head. He was pathetically transparent. He'd set his sights on bringing Gitan down, and he wouldn't stop until he succeeded. His dogged determination to ruin someone he'd once considered his closest friend disgusted her. More than that, she found it frightening. Gitan had a dark history, and given that, there was a chance that Hugh could succeed. "It's all circumstantial. It won't stand up in court, and you know it."

"Not yet. But it's a foundation based on fact. Facts that could very well add up to a motive for murder." He sat back, regarding her with a guarded but level expression. "Do you know anything about this, Lily?"

"I know that you're dead wrong."

"You were Michel's closest friend. His confidante. What do you know about his relationship with Gitan? What in hell was going on between them?"

"I don't know," Lily admitted, "and if I did, I sure as hell wouldn't tell you."

Amy Bellefonte's voice came over the intercom, smooth and seamless as silk. "Sheriff? Judge Malcolm on line two."

"Shut the door on your way out." Hugh's expression

was closed. He'd stopped listening. "Roy? It's Hugh. Listen, I need a favor."

Lily went out but she didn't close the door; she slammed it so hard the glass rattled in its frame, then broke free and shattered on the hardwood floor. Her stomach churned, and for a dread-filled moment she thought she was going to lose it. Then she flung through the double doors and the heat hit her in the face like a blast from a furnace. She made it as far as the parking lot before she realized she'd forgotten her reason for being there in the first place. Aunt Virginia's parking violation . . . but at that moment, nothing and no one could make her go back inside.

Father Bernaud didn't answer the evening call to prayer. He heard the faint tolling of the bell, but he didn't heed it. Father Murdoch would understand, and there would be no repercussions beyond his brethren in Christ expressing how deeply they felt his absence. Much was afforded his age, and his long service to the people of the parish. He was highly respected, and no one among his colleagues in the small religious community living at the rectory realized that the time he spent on his knees in the dirt was his private penance. A man could keep secrets from other men, but he could not keep secrets from God.

God knew all. Every thought. Every deed and misdeed. Every sin, merely contemplated by the meek, or by the bold committed. God's light shone into the darkest corner of the soul, and he could only pray feverishly that he would not be judged too harshly.

His gardening helped. It was good to labor and be busy, and he felt that perhaps bringing beauty to this holy place would somehow compensate for the ugly stain upon his soul, in a sense upon his hands as well. Hands that were raw from his constant weeding. He paused for a moment to catch his breath, saw Father Murdoch watching him from the window of his office, and nearly flinched. Murdoch was an astute man. Did he know? Did he know what he was thinking? He shivered at the thought, despite the perspiration soaking his white short-sleeved shirt and coursing in thin runnels over his face.

Not until Murdoch turned away did the tension drain from his body into the soil. The strain of the past two weeks had been almost more than he could bear. His appetite had bled away as surely as Father Dugas's life's blood had, pooling on the cypress plank floor of the old church. He did not sleep well, and in the rare moments when he did drift off, he suffered the torment of dreadfully vivid nightmares—images of Father Dugas being hoisted aloft and nailed to the large rough wooden cross at the old sanctuary . . . His eyes looked dead, clouded with white and gazing blankly, and the flies had blown his naked body so that there was barely an inch that did not writhe or wriggle. Shockingly, his mouth still worked, pleading, pleading for mercy.

And then his face slowly changed, and his hair lost its color, and it was no longer Father Dugas, but he who begged for mercy . . . But the young woman standing before the altar gazing scornfully up at his bloated body had no mercy in her heart to give. Her hatred seemed to shoot from her blue eyes and pin him to the cross. The finger she pointed at him was accusatory, her cry echoing through the abandoned chapel, so that there was no escape, none. *I hope you rot in hell.*

Crouched in the dirt, with the sickening smell of

earth and dampness rising all around him, Father Bernaud nearly wept in frustration. He had done the funeral mass and the graveside service as the bishop had requested, but no one could ever know how greatly it had cost him to see Justin Martin's daughter.

Lily Martin had consigned him to hell only in his nightmares, but her determination to see justice done for her friend was almost as frightening, and he had to decide what, if anything, he could do about it.

He wiped the dirt from his hands with his handkerchief, carefully avoiding the rope burn between his finger and thumb. Then he set to his work again. There were so many weeds this year.

"I heard last week that William Gunn's in trouble again." Edna Mae passed the candied carrots to Virginia and chided her when she declined. "Don't you turn up your nose. Just have some. They're good for what ails you."

"I'm not so sure they've made a vegetable that'll cure what ails me," Virginia grumbled, but she took the serving dish and ladled some of the vegetables onto her plate. "Well, give over, now that you've gotten what you want. What did old William do now?" William Gunn was a legendary figure in the parish. He was ninety-six years young, and completely incorrigible, with numerous run-ins with the law.

"Robbed a bank. Can you imagine?"

"At his age?" Virginia said. "How'd he get caught?"

"He forgot where he parked the getaway car."

Virginia laughed. "You're making that up!"

"God as my witness. It was in today's paper."

Lily looked on as the two women chatted over a leisurely supper and thought how normal everything seemed. All three of them were equally determined to ignore Virginia's appointment to see her physician the next day. After the episode with the dolls the day of Michel's funeral, Virginia had finally given in to Lily's urging and agreed to make an appointment, though she was still insistent that nothing was wrong. Lily fervently hoped her aunt was right. She wasn't sure how she would cope if anything happened to Virginia Martin.

Her silence drew both women's notice. "Miss Lily, you haven't touched that roast beef. Somethin' wrong?"

"Now that Edna Mae mentions it, you do look a little pale. Are you feelin' all right, dear?"

"I'm sorry. I'm afraid I don't have much of an appetite. Difficult day."

"Oh, dear. You saw Mr. Personality today." Virginia didn't try to hide her concern. "Did he give you a hard time over the parking violation? I do wish you'd let me handle it. There's nothin' I'd love more than to take his head off. He's high on my shit list these days."

"Hugh was just being Hugh, that's all. Gitan was in his office when I arrived."

"Rose Boudreaux's nephew. Probably pickin' up his little brother," Edna Mae said. "He got tagged for shopliftin' at the market this afternoon. Matter of fact, I was there when it happened."

What little remained of Lily's appetite dissolved. She put down her utensils and stopped all pretense of trying to eat. "Would you both excuse me? There's something I need to see to."

"Certainly, dear." Virginia presented a cheek to be kissed. "Don't forget to take your key. Edna Mae and I are going to bingo at the fire hall this evening."

Lily grabbed her car keys and went out. It was almost dusk when she arrived at the house Gitan rented on Mayfly Street. She found him in the living room, picking up the pieces of a broken picture frame. Furniture lay overturned and the odds and ends of his orderly existence were scattered through the house like so much trash. He glanced up when Lily walked in, but he didn't speak. "Hugh," Lily said.

He carefully replaced the photo of his parents, now devoid of a frame, on the end table. "Crebs and Fred Rally. Fred kept apologizing, but Crebs outranks him and they were both under orders from their superior."

"This is my fault," she said. "I'm sorry, Gitan. I'm so sorry. For everything."

Gitan shrugged. He was shirtless and barefoot, fresh from the shower. Small droplets of water dotted his shoulders from his still-wet hair, glistening almost as brightly as the gold crucifix he wore around his neck. "You got nothing to be sorry for, *cher*. Hugh had a problem with me long before you came along. He found an opening, that's all, and he took advantage of it." He shrugged his bare shoulders and the web on his shoulder moved and flexed. "Could have been worse. I'm here, instead of locked up, and they didn't break anything that can't be replaced. I can put things back and sweep up, and since he got what he wanted, maybe he'll leave off for a while." Bracing one hand on his hip, he gave her a sidelong glance. "That why you're here? You come to evaluate the damage?"

"Not exactly. It's about Mason. I just heard."

"Mase," he said softly, rubbing the left side of his jaw. "Now there's a deep subject that's got me at a loss. *Dieu*, Lily, I swear that kid's gonna drive me insane. I don' know how to get through to him, or what makes him do the crazy shit he does."

Lily took a deep breath and tried to slow the thunder of her pulse. She wasn't sure why the thought of telling him about her conversation with his brother made her so nervous, but it did. Or maybe it wasn't about the conversation at all. Maybe it was about last night, and seeing him so soon after. Anything could happen. Anything at all.

It wouldn't be smart to fall into bed with Gitan again, but if the conversation took a seductive turn, she wasn't at all sure she would be able to resist. There was so much unfinished business between them, too many things that they'd never gotten the chance to say. She'd been so certain that it was too late, that what they'd shared had ended a long time ago. Now, she wasn't so sure. "Normally, I wouldn't have an answer. This time, I just might be able to clue you in. I ran into Mason earlier. In fact, he was hitchhiking, and I offered him a ride. He said he was on his way to Aunt Virginia's house."

"Mill Creek Road? What for?"

"He wanted to talk, about you and me." She shook her head and laughed. "Somewhere along the way he seemed to get the idea that your happiness involves me. I tried to explain he was way off base, but I'm afraid it wasn't what he was hoping to hear."

"So he went downtown and stole himself a bottle of wine." He turned a chair back onto its legs and sank onto it. "I s'pose it's because of everything he's been through, but he needs to stop tryin' to control everything. Some things you gotta relax and just let be." A soft, derisive snort. "Listen, you want some coffee? I was gonna make a pot once I cleaned up the mess. I'd offer you a beer, but it's contraband where I'm concerned. No alcohol, no firearms, no contact with other known felons, and I can't leave town without permission. Kinda like being a perpetual twelve-year-old, only without all the ragin' hormones."

He smiled and Lily felt the effects of it right down to her toes. She was still standing just inside the doorway, as if she were ready to turn and run. Pushing out of the chair, he walked to where she stood. "Gitan—about last night—"

There was something about a man who was fresh from the shower that she found unbelievably erotic. Half dressed with the rivet at his waist undone, the smell of soap and water, the taste of cool, clean skin . . .

"What about last night, *cher*? Oh, you mean that thing we had on the porch? Bein' a man of heightened sensibilities, I wasn't gonna mention it . . . but since you brought it up, maybe we should talk about it—"

"I don't think we should—see one another again—alone, like that, I mean."

"I'm with you on that, *cher*, a thousand percent," he said, sliding his hands around her waist, pulling her closer so that he could steal a taste of her lips. "No tellin' what might happen, 'cause I don' think you're out of my system yet. Last night was just too good."

Locking his hands behind her, he lifted her off her feet, kissing her in earnest. Lily's objections dissolved in that instant; she sighed her surrender, her arms around his neck.

"What do you say we take this discussion into the bedroom?" Gitan asked, kissing her again. Bending slightly, he slipped an arm under her knees and started for the bedroom. He hadn't taken more than a step or two when something outside the living room window caught his attention. It was just a flash, and he couldn't shake the feeling that somebody was there, watching. He set Lily on her feet, took a step toward the window, and the whole pane of glass exploded into the living room.

CHAPTER TEN

No matter how long or hard Lily argued, she couldn't convince Gitan to report the vandalism. He didn't want the sheriff's department or her ex-husband involved in something he considered his business. He didn't indicate that he suspected Hugh of somehow being responsible for the broken window, but Lily wasn't stupid, and her own suspicions led her in that direction.

Hugh had always been jealous of Gitan, and it hadn't stopped after their marriage. By that time, Lily had come to accept that Gitan was far beyond anyone's reach, and had done the best she could to get on with her life. For Hugh, there seemed to be no getting past it. Even behind prison walls, with little hope of an early release, Gitan had loomed large as a threat.

Lily had never understood Hugh's possessiveness, but there was no doubt that it still existed. He'd proven that fact again and again. But was his jealousy strong enough to make him stoop to petty vandalism?

Or did the brick have a deeper meaning? Had it been a warning of some sort? She didn't want to think so, but he'd sent his men to trash Gitan's place on the flimsy pretext of retrieving potential evidence. Lily was incensed. Abuse of power was one thing; destroying private property and endangering the lives of others was quite another.

"Do you have any idea who might have done this?" She was cleaning the cut on his chest just below the collarbone with an alcohol solution.

He shrugged and a trickle of scarlet broke from the gash and ran down over his chest.

"Keep still. I just got the bleeding to stop."

"Sit still, while you got your hands on me. How am I supposed to do that?"

Lily tried to ignore the comments, though it wasn't easy. He'd always had charisma, that hypnotic unidentifiable something that drew people to him and kept them there. She didn't just see Gitan walk into a room; she felt it. Her every sense would ratchet up several notches, she would notice small details, like the way his hair curled the slightest bit when damp, smell the scent of his soap, thrill at the smoothness of his voice, be completely aware of him instantaneously. "I still think you should see a doctor. It's a deep cut. It needs stitches."

"They'd ask questions I don' feel like answerin'. Got to keep a low profile, *cher.* I'm an ex-con who can't afford trouble."

"Well, whether you can afford it or not, it looks like you've got it. You're the victim here. Just because you were in prison doesn't mean you don't have rights."

"That's a fine concept you got there, but you and I both know it don' always work that way. Shit rolls downhill, baby, and this ain't a big enough deal for me to want to risk it. Besides, it's nothin' you need to worry about."

What he meant was, he'd handle it in his own time, in his own way, without outside interference. Somehow, the thought made Lily almost as uneasy as did the knowledge that someone hated him enough to put a brick through his living room window. "You still haven't answered my question."

"Maybe one of my neighbors objects to having a nondrinker, nonsmoker, nonparty animal who minds his own business livin' in the neighborhood. I don' know. Maybe one of the local kids decided to test my restraint and his courage . . . or maybe Mase is still pissed at me for comin' down so hard on him. I had him scrubbin' the restroom at the Chop Shop with a toothbrush for stealing that bottle, stupid-ass kid."

His making light of the situation didn't make Lily feel any better, and she could only wonder if he was telling the truth, or attempting to protect her from what was happening. There was a lot she didn't know about him, like the close relationship he'd had with Michel. Michel had never mentioned making visits to the prison. One each month, and their association had continued after Gitan was paroled. Yet, he hadn't attended Michel's funeral mass, and he hadn't mentioned meeting Michel the day of the murder. He'd kept it all a secret . . . and she couldn't help wondering if there was anything else he was keeping from her.

He took her hand in his. "You got more on your mind than a little broken glass. What's wrong?"

"Hugh mentioned that Michel made regular visits to the prison, yet Michel never told me. In all the years he went there, he never mentioned it once." She drew the edges of the cut together, securing them with thin strips of surgical tape. "Why is that?"

"Michel kept it quiet because I asked him to." Reaching out, he traced a path from her temple to the corner of her mouth. "I didn't want you wastin' your life waitin' for me."

"That doesn't explain your connection to him. You were never close."

"We may not have been tight, but I didn't dislike him, either. It's not complicated. The man went out of his way to be kind, to offer a hand when I needed it most, and I felt I owed him because of it. It's as simple as that." He watched her for a moment, his dark eyes concealing all but what he wished her to know. "That answer didn't satisfy you, 'cause that wasn't all Hugh had to say. He told you I was supposed to meet Michel at Catfish Point the night of the murder. Ain't that right?"

Lily's mouth went dry. "Did you?"

His expression changed subtly as he withdrew the finger teasing her cheek. His voice as he gave her what she wanted was clipped and cold. "Michel wanted me to meet him there, but Ruben asked me to work. He had an appointment he couldn't break, so I told him I'd stay late. I was at the shop all evening. When I left there, I came straight here. I was alone, so there's no one to corroborate my statement or provide me with an alibi. Hell, I didn't exactly know I was gonna need one or I would've arranged somethin'." He pushed a hand through his hair, a gesture that betrayed his impatience with the direction the conversation, and the evening, had taken. "Level with me, Lily. What's this really about? You askin' me this stuff because of what Hugh said . . . or because of what Lily Martin's been thinkin'?"

"I don't know," Lily replied. She finished taping the

wound together, cut the tape, and stepped back, suddenly unsure what to do with her hands.

"You feel that way, then maybe it's time for you to go."

She turned to leave, and Gitan made no move to stop her. He just watched her from the doorway until her taillights disappeared, then walked out to the shed behind the house to find something to board up the window until he could replace the broken window glass. The brick lay where he'd placed it, on the coffee table. It was common red brick, the kind that was easily had from a hundred crumbling abandoned buildings in the parish, and it could have come from anywhere. As for who'd thrown it, he could think of at least three people he knew of who weren't happy with him at the moment. Mason, Hugh, and Willie Early.

Mason, he could pretty much rule out. He was family, and man enough at fifteen to confront him openly when he had a beef with him. Hugh was a possibility, yet as sheriff, with a murder investigation in full swing, he already had his hands full. Besides, Hugh was never quite that unimaginative when it came to getting his pound of flesh, and while he wasn't above twisting the law till it screamed uncle, he wouldn't resort to breaking it and risk ruining his career. He enjoyed running things a little too much for that. Which left him with Willie Early, or the possibility that someone in the neighborhood objected to having a convicted murderer living in the neighborhood and had decided to let him know he wasn't welcome here.

As he cleaned up the broken glass, Gitan thought about Justin Martin and all the misery the man had caused during his lifetime. Lily was on edge, and he wondered if the problems Michel had mentioned during their last conversation were real, as he'd claimed.

"I'm worried about Lily," the young priest had said. "When she sleeps at all, she's having nightmares."

They were at the Chop Shop, it was mid-afternoon, and Ruben was out of town on business. Gitan had come in to put in his hours sweeping up and organizing the tools and spare parts. "Everybody has nightmares, Michel. And Lily, she's had 'em all her life."

"This is different," Michel had insisted. "She's dreaming about her father, about that night. Her recall is starting to surface."

Gitan had clenched his jaw, and it was a moment before he could gain control enough to reply. "Ain't nothin' I can do about that."

"I've got to tell her. If she remembers on her own, there's no telling what will happen. Gitan, you've got to release me from my promise. I wouldn't ask if it wasn't for Lily—"

Gitan had looked up from what he was doing, his expression cold. "Like hell! You're bound, Michel. You repeat what I told you during confession and you might as well renounce your vows!" He shook off his anger before facing him again. "Lily don' know what happened that night, and if I can help it, she never will. Trust me, it's better this way."

Michel wasn't satisfied, and he didn't fold in the face of an anger that could have rolled over him as if he were nothing. Gitan didn't like it, but he respected it, *then, and now.*

He blew out a breath, dumping the glass in the trash and returning the dustpan and broom to the hallway closet. Then he went into the guest room, where he had put the easel and new canvas, and tried to put his demons to bed for the night.

CHAPTER ELEVEN

"Lily! Lily Justine! Where the hell have you gotten to?"

It was half past eleven on a warm summer night and Lily should have been in bed asleep hours ago. Instead, she watched and waited, hoping desperately to see Michel's face appear outside her bedroom window. If Michel came for her, she would summon the courage to climb down the tree, and they would run hand in hand to the cane field across the road. Daddy wouldn't think to look there because he had a fear of snakes, and sometimes the six-foot-long black snake Gitan called "Gran'daddy" hunted mice in the cane. Lily knew Gran'daddy wouldn't hurt anybody, but Justin didn't know, and that gave her some place to hide when he remembered she existed and came upstairs to look for her.

Most of the time, he ignored her. Too busy bragging to her mother about the deals he'd made that day, or what went on at the country club, and who had said what. When he was home, Lily became a different person, slipping quietly from room to room, afraid to make a noise and draw his disapproving stare, or worse. Sometimes Lily wished that he would just disappear, and then she could have a new daddy, someone quiet and strong, like Mr. Boudreaux with big hard hands but a gentle touch, or soft-spoken and affectionate like Michel's father. . . .

Then she would catch herself and feel that small twinge of guilt that got smaller every time his footsteps sounded outside her room, reminding herself that he was her daddy and she was supposed to love him . . . and she did, but she hated him, too, hated the heat in his hands, the cruel pinch of his fingers. Hated the way he made her feel when he touched her, uncomfortable in her own skin, a bitter and frightened person in a little girl's body.

When she was with Michel, and Gitan, and even Hugh, she could shake off that Lily Martin and become someone else. Gitan, who had at first frightened her, made her feel safe. There seemed to be nothing on earth that he feared, and he looked out for her and Michel while pretending not to. But she wasn't with her friends now. She was alone, and she feared the footsteps coming up the stairs more than the bite of a cottonmouth or the sting of a black widow spider.

"Lily?" His voice was pleading now. Lily gave the open window and the dark beyond it one last glance, then ran to the closet, squeezing behind a stack of boxes and making herself as small as possible. The door to her bedroom opened. Mama was out for the evening and wouldn't return until very late. Through a crack between the boxes and the wall, Lily could see the narrow shaft of light beneath the closet door. As long as the strip was rectangular, she was safe. She wanted to close her eyes as she had when she was very small, and pretend she didn't know, didn't see, but she forced herself to look, her heart beating so hard she thought he would surely hear it.

"Lily? Lily, damn it, it's your daddy! I know you're here!" An angry sound, almost a sob. "Lily, please."

Then the narrow rectangle of light became two, the closet door silently opened, and eleven-year-old Lily wanted to die. . . .

Covered in cold sweat, heart thundering in her chest, Lily sat up, fighting for air. Fear was so thick in her throat that for a moment she feared she'd strangle on it. *It was a dream. Just a dream. He was dead, and she was no longer a child, no longer vulnerable. No one would ever hurt her like that again! Gitan had seen to that.*

Or had he? She had no memory of what happened to end her father's life, no clear memory at all beyond Justin's attack and the beating that followed when Gitan broke through the French doors. The autopsy had revealed that her father's cause of death had been a massive internal hemorrhage caused by a single stab wound that severed the aorta just above the diaphragm. It had been two weeks before the doctor would allow Sheriff Vance Pershing to question Gitan, and even then he could barely whisper monosyllabic answers.

Virginia Martin had provided the only clues to what had occurred that night, and her statement— along with Gitan's fingerprints on the murder weapon—seemed to corroborate Gitan's admission of guilt.

Lily hated having to rely on secondhand accounts of the events that night. She'd been there in the room, a witness to everything. She should have remembered. Yet she didn't.

It was like having a black hole where her memory

should have been, a missing piece that kept the other puzzle pieces from fitting properly into place. Threading her fingers into the short, damp hair at her temples, she drew up her knees and rocked slightly, forcing herself to concentrate. Forcing herself to dredge up images of that fateful night that anyone else in her position might have tried their best to forget.

There were some aspects of that night she did recall. Like the feeling of fear and impatience as she waited for her parents to leave the house. They were going to meet friends at the country club, and she could hear Justin shouting at Sharon to hurry. He was tired of waiting, and she should have been ready to go an hour ago. Lily heard her mother's reply in her mind as though it had happened yesterday; then the door closed and the car pulled down the driveway.

She felt her excitement rise as she pulled the suitcase from under the bed. It was packed and ready, and all she needed to do was meet Gitan. They were going away, as far away as they could get on the money he'd saved. If they were careful, he'd said, they might even make it to Mexico. She had no doubt that her parents would attempt to track her down and drag her back home to Louisiana, and since Gitan was twenty and she was only seventeen, he was risking jail time. If they could be together, it would be worth it.

All they had to do was get out of Louisiana, Lily remembered thinking. As soon as they were safely out of the state and beyond her father's reach, she would dye her hair dark, and buy some colored contact lenses. Three months was all they needed. Three months, and she would turn eighteen.

She saw herself hurry down the stairs. She was halfway to the meeting place when she realized she'd forgotten her locket . . . the locket Gitan had given her for Christmas. Unwilling to leave it behind, she turned her car around and drove back to the house.

Lily's eyes were closed as she forced herself to mentally walk back up the sidewalk and into the house. Up the stairs, to her bedroom. The locket was lying where she'd left it, on the dresser. She quickly fastened it and left the room again. She went down the stairs, unaware that the door to her father's study was open.

"Goin' somewhere, Lily?" His silhouette loomed large and dark against the soft light coming from the doorway and the brass lamp on his desk. He was several paces away, but she could smell the whiskey on his breath.

Lily knew a second of panic. He'd destroyed her innocence, turned a childhood that should have been bright and carefree into something dark and ugly. If she let him, he would destroy her one chance at escape, at happiness. "I have a math test tomorrow," she'd said, fighting to keep her voice steady. "Michel's going to help me study, and I'm already late."

"What you doin' hangin' 'round with that little faggot?"

"Daddy, don't. Please."

"Now, there's a word I don't hear from you near enough." Lily saw him lurch forward, and though it was only a memory, her pulse accelerated. "Bet you say it often enough to that Boudreaux boy, don't you? You like it when he lays his hands on you? You got a taste for the bayou, Lily?"

"No! No, no, no, no, no, no, no, Daddy, please, no . . ."

Lily had vivid recall of the attempted rape. She remembered his hands on her, and heard the sound of cloth being torn, and seams coming undone. She remembered sinking her nails into the flesh of his face as she tried to fight him off, but it only seemed to fuel the violence in him and he hit her hard across the mouth. She cried out in fury and frustration—then the sound of shattering glass.

The security alarm tripped and started wailing. Justin glanced up, cursing, but couldn't get away fast enough. Gitan pulled him off her and hit him, and he kept hitting him, and hitting him, and hitting him. Lily saw the blood, on her father, on Gitan, on her hands as she begged him to leave. "You have to go. Please. You have to get away now. If you wait, he'll find you, and there will be trouble. Please, oh God, you have to listen!"

"Not without you. I'm not leavin' you here with that crazy son of a bitch!"

She pulled at his arm: she remembered that vividly. "Go to Mexico like we planned. As soon as I turn eighteen, I'll come to you. I promise. But you have to go."

There was barely a noise as Justin regained consciousness and came up off the carpet with the .38 he kept in the drawer of his desk. He didn't say anything. He just leveled the gun at Gitan and pulled the trigger.

Lily knew there was more, but all she seemed to get were fragmented images. Pieces of that same puzzle that didn't make any sense. Gitan flat on his back on the floor, his white T-shirt awash in scarlet. A keening scream that must have been her own, and Virginia's voice. "Oh, God. Oh, God, no. Please, no!"

Lily didn't realize she had cried out loud until Virginia's light, insistent rapping sounded in the hall. "Lily? Lily? Are you all right?"

Lily shook off the remnants of the memory, slid off

the bed, and opened the door. Dressed in her pink chenille robe, even with the hallway light at her back and her face in shadow, Virginia's deep concern was still evident. "Darlin', I thought I heard you cry out. Are you all right?"

"Sorry," Lily said. "I didn't mean to wake you." She pushed the hair off her forehead with a hand that shook. "I've been trying to remember—the night Daddy died—Gitan, and you. I just can't seem to get it straight in my mind." Lily hugged her arms tightly to her body, still unnerved by the disturbing memories, perhaps more so by what she felt was missing.

"Sugar, you don't want to dredge it all up again. Bring everything back. Wouldn't it be better to just let it go? To move on?"

"That's just it," Lily said with a shaky laugh. "I don't think I have a choice. I can't move on with a piece of my life still missing."

She took Lily's hands and led her to the bed. "Honey, I'm not sure this is healthy."

"I get that," Lily said. "But neither are the nightmares. One way or another, I have to resolve this."

"All right, then. If you think it will help." Virginia sighed, ill at ease with giving her what she wanted "You know that I got there after it was over. Your father was already gone, and Bobby—I wouldn't have bet a nickel on his chances of surviving. I picked up the phone on the desk and dialed the emergency number for an ambulance, but the alarm had gone off and the sheriff's deputy arrived first. Bobby's life was in God's hands, so I took care of you. Honey, you were so out of it. I was terrified—I wasn't sure you'd ever be the same again."

"There was blood on my hands, my blouse, my

jeans. It seemed to be everywhere. A sea of red, and I couldn't tell whose it was."

Virginia frowned. "Then, you do remember?"

"I remember Daddy shooting Gitan. He fell to the floor, unconscious. With a bullet lodged in the membrane surrounding his heart, how could he have gotten back up to kill a man? Where would he have found the strength? I'm sure he must have been in shock by then, and if he was, then it was physically impossible for Gitan to have killed Daddy."

Virginia was quiet, waiting. "Baby, of course you don't want to believe that Bobby killed Justin. He might have been a heartless bastard, but he was still your father. And you loved Bobby—but there were three people in the study the night Justin died. If Bobby didn't do it, then who did?" As it dawned on her, she put fingertips to her temple as if a sudden ache had suddenly appeared there. "Lily, no. Dear God, you can't think—"

"Humor me, please. Walk me through it. What did you see when you got there? Maybe somewhere in it all I'll find the trigger, a word, an image—something that will unlock it for me, and it'll all come flooding back."

Virginia gave in with a weary sigh. "I just hope it doesn't make things worse. You do realize, though, that you're askin' a woman to recall events from eight years ago who can't recall what she had for dinner last night." It was her final ploy to avoid broaching a subject she would rather have forgotten. When she realized Lily wouldn't give an inch, she gave her what she wanted. "When I arrived, everything was pretty well over. Justin was lying a few feet from where Bobby fell— there was blood everywhere, from both of them. I checked your father for a pulse and found none, then went to Bobby. He was barely alive, and his skin had a sickly blue tinge to it. You were crouched beside him, rocking back and forth with this blank look on your face. Covered in blood. It was smeared on your hands and your face, it soaked your clothes. At first I thought you'd been hurt, too; then I looked into your eyes and realized that most of your hurt was on the inside. Two ambulances came that night. You went to the hospital, too, but I drove you. Sharon met us there. Someone had called her at the country club—the deputy, I think."

"The weapon," Lily said, "Gitan's buck knife. Where was it when you arrived?"

Virginia shrugged. "Why, lying where Gitan dropped it, I guess. He must have pulled it free after he stabbed your father; I don't know. Maybe he intended to stab him a second time, and just ran out of strength. Not like Justin wouldn't have deserved it— may he burn in hell."

"None of it makes sense."

"There's no making sense of any of it," Virginia replied, her voice growing softer, gentler. "The only thing I know for sure is that Bobby did what he did that night out of love for you. I've heard it said that when the situation requires it, an ordinary person can find the strength to do the impossible. And Bobby Boudreaux was never ordinary." She squeezed Lily's hand, her smile sad. "He still isn't, which concerns me, I admit. But that's a different worry altogether."

"What about the evidence? Is it possible something was overlooked?"

Virginia thought about that. "Well, I suppose that anything is possible. Vance Pershing was out of town that night, and the deputy was new. I recall that he didn't stay more than a few months after that. I do remember reading that he had secured the weapon, but before they had a chance to go over the scene again, Sharon had a hired man tear up the carpet and burn it. So anything that they didn't find on the scene that night was lost to them. Still, there's no disputing a confession. And the murder weapon corroborated Bobby's statement to the police." She paused to search Lily's face. "Does that help at all?"

It helped, Lily thought. As Virginia had said, there had been three people in the room that night: the victim, and a man so badly wounded that he was near death—incapable, Lily felt certain, of doing the murder he'd confessed to, and for which he'd been punished. Which left only her.

"Yes," Lily said. "Thank you. I know you hate to talk about it."

"Anything for you, sugar." Virginia put her arms around Lily and held her close for a few brief seconds before releasing her again, and Lily saw that her eyes were moist. "Try to get some sleep, baby. I'll see you later." She patted Lily's cheek, then got up and walked from the room, closing the door quietly behind her.

Lily changed her pajamas and lay staring at the dark rectangle of the window. Gitan hadn't been the only person in the room with motive to kill her father. She had hated him for the things he'd done to her, but had she hated him enough to plunge a knife into his body and watch while he bled to death?

Lily didn't know. What she was sure of was that her love for Gitan had been so strong that the thought of losing him had nearly destroyed her. If Justin had closed in for a second, killing shot, she would have given her life to protect him—or perhaps, taken one.

It was the only thing that made sense . . . that she'd killed her father while Gitan had lain unconscious, and that he had taken the blame in order to protect her. Instead of bringing relief, it made Lily sick to think of the lives she had ruined. If it was true, then she'd cost an innocent man his freedom, and there was no way she could ever hope to repay him for his sacrifice.

Michel Dugas had weighed more than two hundred pounds, and had been five feet ten inches tall in his stockinged feet. Not exactly a lightweight by any means, and Hugh was having a hard time imagining how one man could drag what was, hypothetically, dead weight far enough into the air to position the body as it had been positioned when it was found.

It had taken some doing, but he'd rigged a large sandbag to Dugas's weight and hauled it to Catfish Point, along with the same type of one-quarter-inch polypropylene rope used by the perpetrator. He'd damn near emptied the station of personnel, and he could tell by the look on their faces that everyone but Crebs thought he'd lost it, especially since some smart-ass had penciled eyes, nose, and mouth on the sandbag with a black permanent marker. The two vehicles—Hugh's unmarked dark blue Pontiac, and Crebs's red and white pickup—pulled in at roughly the same time. Hugh stepped out of the car, wearing a black T-shirt and jeans as opposed to his usual shirt and tie. "Okay, folks. Lets get this show on the road."

Crebs lowered the tailgate, and the three of them hauled out the sandbag and cargo dolly. It took only a moment to drag the dummy into the old building and position it under the beam above the cross. The rank smell lingered in the chapel, despite the cross-ventilation from the broken windows, and Hugh knew that the best thing would be to demolish the building. The crime scene ribbon wouldn't keep the curious away for long, and the last thing he needed was for this place to become a sort of weird tourist attraction for curiosity-seekers and the mentally unhinged.

Grabbing the coiled rope, Hugh threw it up and over the beam, then turned to Crebs. "That look about right to you?"

"On the mark. You want me to go first?"

"Let's start with the lightweight first. She's lookin' a little green." He inclined his head in Amy's direction. She had her face as close to the broken window as she could get without endangering herself, and she was gulping air. When Crebs whistled sharply, she glanced back. Hugh crooked a finger. "Give it all you got, sugar."

He handed her a pair of leather gloves to protect her hands—the same sort of glove the killer had worn to aid him in his macabre task, and to prevent leaving any prints at the scene. She slipped them on, grasped the rope, and pulled with all her might, but the dummy didn't budge. "Go on outside," Hugh told her. "I'll give a yell if I need you."

She turned and all but ran for the exit, and in less time than it took Fred Rally to step up to the rope, he heard the sounds of her losing her Danish and coffee. Crebs shook his gleaming head. "And I was going to ask her if she wanted to join us for a brew after we were through here. There's one idea shot in the ass. So much for equality in the workplace."

Hugh ignored his second in command. "You're what, Fred? Five-eight?"

"Five-eight and three-quarters, and a hundred sixty-two pounds."

Hugh noted it all on his notepad. Rally was average

height, with an average build, with the exception of a small paunch above his belt. He grabbed the rope and pulled till the tendons stood out in his forearms and neck, and his veins popped.

"Come on, Fred, haul on that sum-bitch!" Crebs said. "Jesus Christ, you're gonna kill that dummy, and you want to finish it before he comes to."

The bottom of the sandbag was face level when he lost his grip and the rope slipped through his hands. He let go and jumped back with a pseudocurse, being a non-profanity-using churchgoer, and the dummy narrowly missed Crebs's foot.

Crebs flexed his big hands. "Stand back and let me show you boys how it's done. Height six-two, weight one ninety-seven, body fat zero." As Fred guffawed, Crebs donned leather gloves and began to lever the sack upward, not stopping until the top was level with the horizontal beam of the cross, but when he tried to tie it off, the knot slipped, and so did the sandbag.

Hugh pocketed his notepad and pen. "That's all I need for today. Crebs, drop Amy at the office. I'll meet you back there later."

Neither man argued. Rally followed Crebs out, chatting about what a pity it was that the old church had fallen into such a disgraceful state of repairs. Hugh waited until he heard Crebs's Hemi crank to life before grasping the sandbag and dragging it back to the door. He looked around as if he'd just stepped inside. It was dark, but he knew the place, and knew what he needed was here. He didn't need light to determine that there was nothing and no one to witness what he was about to do. Then grabbing the bag once more, he dragged it to the beam and, working quickly, threw the rope over. It took two tries, but he got it and threw it a third time, looping it around to prevent slippage. There was no way to simulate the mutilation of Dugas's ankles, so he attached the metal hook through the nylon mesh harness that held the bag and inched the dummy into the air. He didn't think about what he was doing. He thought about his motive, and he thought about the need to work quickly and efficiently so he didn't get caught.

The hundred-foot rope had been sufficient to reach the wrought iron railing that ran the length of the altar, with only a ten-foot separation in the center to allow passage for the altar boys and the priest. Keeping the rope taut, he looped it through and tied it in a double half-hitch knot strong enough to hold a butchered steer, or the body of the murdered priest. Finally he finished and stood back, sweat pouring over his face, running into his eyes to blur his vision. He was winded, and he could feel the strain in the uncontrolled quiver of his muscles, but he'd proven that it could be done. Wiping the sweat from his eyes with a bare forearm, Hugh took out his notepad and wrote: *Hugh Lothair, ht. 5'1", wt. 175.*

Just as he'd thought. Size didn't matter half as much as the level of determination.

Rose Boudreaux stepped through the back door of the house on Tupelo Avenue and sat down on the wooden steps to have a smoke. She didn't allow herself but one or two cigarettes a day, because tobacco was bad for the lungs, and she never smoked inside for fear it would somehow harm Gitan, or influence Mason. It didn't matter that Gitan appeared the picture of a healthy and virile young male; Rose still worried that something dreadful would change that, something like his having a sudden relapse, or that

Martin girl getting her hooks into him again. *Ca pourrai arriver.* It could happen.

Lily Martin was trouble, make no mistake about it, and Rose found herself wishing that Gitan would find himself a nice girl from the neighborhood, like Harriet Chapin, who lived down the street. She'd seen how Harriet looked at him, and she suspected that despite the girl's strict Catholic upbringing, she might be able to quickly get beyond Gitan's troubled past. It was something to think about. As for Mason . . . She was truly at a loss, and her heart was heavy because of it.

She put a cigarette between her lips, flicked her disposable lighter, and someone tapped on the inside of the storm door's window glass. Rose nearly jumped out of her skin, or at least that's how it felt. Then the door opened, and Gitan stepped outside. "You sneakin' a smoke? Doc Trelawney tell you that was okay?"

Rose waved a hand in dismissal. "That doctor. He ain't much older than you. How do I know he's even got a legal degree?"

"He's old enough to know cigarettes'll bring you no good. Besides, the degree's framed and hangin' on his office wall. I've seen it." He sat down on the steps beside her. "Where's that damn kid?"

"You shouldn't call him that. You should never damn anybody, Gitan. Never know who's listenin'. Could be, it'll bring bad luck." Rose put the cigarette carefully back in the pack, and slipped both pack and lighter into the pocket of her housedress. "Mason, he's next door, at the Gonzaleses'. I made him go with me down to the market to apologize."

"I'll bet he liked that."

"He handled himself pretty well. Like a man. Your daddy would have been proud."

Gitan wouldn't cut him any slack. "Daddy would have whupped his ass with his belt for stealing in the first place. You're too easy on him, Rose. He can't just do whatever he damn well pleases and expect to get away with it."

"And you're gonna sit there and tell me you never stole nothin' when you were his age? I seem to remember you stealing apples from the roadside fruit stand. You never got a whuppin' for it."

"I never got caught." Gitan gave her a level look, and Rose could see the concern in his dark eyes—concern for Mason. "And look where it got me. I don't want him havin' any more trouble with the law, that's all."

"You're too hard on him, Gitan. And that ain't all. You're too hard on yourself, too. You didn't get into that mess all by yourself."

"Rose." One word, but it was a warning.

Rose ignored it. "What'ch you doin' givin' that girl the time o' day for now, when all she did was bring you grief?"

Gitan massaged his forehead with one hand. "Let's don' go there, all right? Been a tough day already, and the last thing I need is you bustin' my chops about something that's none of your business anyhow."

Rose's expression clouded. "Then, you *are* seein' her?"

"I didn't say that. I said I didn't want to talk about it."

Mason emerged from the house next door and stood for a moment, as if trying to decide whether to approach, or to run. As Gitan stood, the teen hunched his shoulders in his threadbare Black Sabbath T-shirt, thrust his hands into the pockets of his jeans, and crossed the grassy expanse separating them. "What do you want? Didn't I clean the shitter to suit you? We all know what a perfectionist you are. Sure wouldn't want to disappoint you."

"Mason!"

The boy skated a glance in Rose's direction, but remained stubbornly unapologetic. *"Dieu!"* she said. "I give up! On both of you! Stubborn right down to the bone, that's what you are!"

She disappeared into the dim recesses of the house, and in a moment, Gitan heard the angry rattle of pots and pans. "You're in for it now. You know she's gonna cook somethin' you hate. That's the number one rule, Jack. Don' piss off the cook."

Mason hitched up his jeans and sat. "S'pose I'll have to apologize. Seems like that's all I get done these days."

"Yeah? Well, maybe if you didn't work so hard at screwin' up, you wouldn't have that problem. All the same, while you're at it, you might just add Lily to that list."

The cloud lifted, and Mase's whole aspect brightened. "You saw Lily?"

"Get that look off your face, kid. There wasn't anything to it."

Mase squinted through the late afternoon sunlight filtering through the boughs of the sweet gum. "Yeah, right. Tell me another one, why don' you? She came to see you, or you went to see her. Either way, that's somethin'."

"She came to the house when she heard about you bein' in hot water. She thought I needed to know about your conversation, and she was right." Gitan shook his head. It was easy to see that one thought, and only one, had stuck between the kid's ears. He'd made the link between them, and he was determined to make more of it than existed. He wasn't sure he could explain it clearly enough to get through to Mason, because he didn't totally understand it himself. "Damn it, kid, it ain't like that. Lily and I are friends, that's all. She's got a lot goin' on, and the last thing she needs right now is you puttin' your nose in her business." He clamped a hand down on his brother's shoulder in an attempt to gain his full attention. "That means you stay away from her aunt's place on Mill Creek Road."

"I hear you," Mason said, but Gitan couldn't be sure he would listen.

"Rose took care of the mess you made, so things are square with the market. Only trouble is, they don't want you on the premises."

"What? How am I supposed to get a sports water after school?"

"I don' know. You figure it out. You done the crime. Guess you'll do the time."

Mason pulled a face. "Thanks for nothin'."

Gitan got to his feet. "No problem. That's what family's for—to let you know when you're bein' stupid. Besides, you wouldn't respect me if I let you off easy."

"Shit," Mase said. "Who you kiddin'? I don' respect you now." He huffed an exhalation as he watched his brother cross the yard and head down the dirt track alley that separated Tupelo Avenue from Mayfly Street. His being banned from the market was something he hadn't even considered, and a definite downer, but not everything to come out of his problems the previous day had been negative. Lily had gone to Gitan's place on Mayfly Street. That fact loomed larger than anything his brother had said, far larger than his denials.

It wasn't lost on Mason that Gitan hadn't said he

wouldn't be seeing Lily again. Mase knew for a fact that he wasn't seeing anyone else, and Lily hadn't been in town long enough to hook up with anybody. There was also his brother's rare good mood. He hadn't come down on him hard at all today, an unusual occurrence for Gitan. "Say what you want," Mase said to himself. "I gotta feelin' it ain't over yet."

CHAPTER
TWELVE

Gitan put the finishing touches on the Virgin Mary fenders and gas tank, then turned out the lights and sealed off the bay so that nothing could mar the mirror gloss of the clear coat. Arley had had a run-in with Ruben earlier concerning the bike's assembly.

The delivery of the transmission had been delayed by two days, and when the part arrived, it wasn't the one they'd ordered. Arley had received most of the fall-out for not staying on top of the situation, but the truth of the matter was that the boss's temper was shorter than ever these days. Ruben had threatened to fire Arley—despite his family connections—if no real progress was made by the end of the day. It was reason enough for Arley to be working late.

It was eight P.M. when Gitan entered the shop. Arley was mounting the transmission—or trying to—and sweating bullets as the shop's clock ticked a rhythmic censure on his lack of progress. "How's it goin'?"

Arley shook his head. "Shit, man, don't even ask.

I've bolted this bitch down three times and stripped the threads twice. It just doesn't want to seat right. If Ruben hadn't already threatened to can my ass, I'd fuckin' quit, but it's a matter of principle, you know? Hell, I been fired from better places than this."

"You try modifyin' the mount?" Gitan asked. "Strange as it sounds, sometimes a good smack with a mallet does wonders."

"You serious?"

Gitan shrugged. "Hit the mount, not the tranny. If it don' work, we build another one."

"Nothin' like takin' out my frustration on this monster." Arley lifted off the chrome-plated transmission and whacked the mount hard with the mallet. When he tried it again, the part slipped right into place. "Jesus Christ, will you look at that?"

Arley bolted it into place, then straightened slowly to his full height. "I don't know about you, but man, I'm beat. What do you say we call it a night and get to work on this first thing in the morning? My old lady's gonna think I got hit by a bus, I'm so fucked up from bendin' over this thing." Arley limped to the vending machine and brought back two cans of Coke. The small silver flask he produced came from his hip pocket. Popping the top on one can, he took a swallow, added some liquid from the flask, and offered the flask to Gitan. "Jim Beam—it's good for what ails you."

Gitan took the Coke, but declined the whiskey. "No thanks. I'm good."

"You're good, all right," Arley said, lifting his can in a mock salute. "But I sure as hell wish you'd slow down a little. You're makin' the rest of us look bad in front of the boss."

"Just doin' my job, that's all."

Arley tipped his soda can for a long swallow. "The talk around here is that you had a visitor last night."

Gitan glanced at the older man. "What do you know about it?"

A shrug. His white T-shirt hung on his thin frame like an oversized gunnysack. "Not a lot, but you might want to talk to Willie. I hear he wasn't too happy about yesterday. A few of the boys were down at the Pink Cadillac havin' a brew, and they overheard him runnin' his mouth in the parkin' lot."

"What's Willie doin' down at the Cadillac?" Gitan asked. "He's not old enough to get served."

Arley threw a glance at the doorway, then lowered his voice just in case. Ruben had come in two hours ago, disappeared into his office, and hadn't come out since. "He might have trouble gettin' served, but he's got other reasons for being there." He tapped the side of his nose with a finger. "If what I hear's true, then the kid's got a serious habit. Could be why he's in here every other day to shake the money tree."

Gitan set aside the soda can, unopened. He just didn't have much of a thirst at the moment. Cocaine and Willie. It made sense. "Anything else I need to know?"

"Just keep your eyes and ears open. I've got a feelin' this ain't over yet. That kid's got a hell of a mean on him. Makes me wonder how the hell somebody with so much goin' for him ends up being such a waste." He jabbed a thumb at his own chest. "Hell, Gitan, if you and me had the kind of opportunity this kid's throwin' away with both hands dropped into our laps, we'd be well on our way to ownin' this place by now." Rocking up onto the balls of his feet, he went for the long shot, aiming the empty soda can at the garbage can ten feet away, sinking a perfect ringer. "Damn, I'm good. I'm also outta here. Keep it clean, bro."

Gitan said nothing, just put away the tools and carefully covered the bike with a tarp. He was about to turn out the lights when the main door opened, and Lily walked in. "Hey, *cher.* You come down to buy a bike? If so, you need to come back tomorrow. Shop's closed."

She looked rattled, the shadows under her blue eyes more noticeable. Tension rolled off her in waves, and he had the strange impression that it was the tension that kept her from total collapse. She walked to within a few feet of where he stood; her arms crossed over her handbag, she hugged it against her body.

"You okay?"

"No. I'm not okay. Aunt Virginia's been hospitalized. Doctor Trelawney wanted to run some tests." She made a gesture with one hand, unable to say more.

He laid the last wrench in the drawer, then closed it. "I'm sorry to hear that. She gonna be okay?"

"I guess so. He wants to rule out an arterial blockage. Something about an obstruction possibly causing low oxygen levels to the brain—then they'll go from there. I'm not sure there are any positives in a situation like this—either, or—it all sucks."

"I don' imagine she's too happy about this."

"She's already threatening to sign herself out and go home."

"But that's not all that's botherin' you. There's somethin' else." He could see it in her face, the way she looked at him, as if she wished she could peel back his skin and look inside him. "What's wrong, Lily?"

Lily laughed, a humorless and self-deprecating sound. "Nothing. Everything. Things are . . . starting to surface . . . images . . . memories, I think . . . and what I'm seeing doesn't jibe with what I know about the night my father died."

"What sort of memories?"

The change in Gitan was subtle, but Lily saw and recognized it. The sudden wariness, the guarded way he chose every word as he tried to keep from upsetting her fragile emotional balance. "Blood, Gitan. Blood on my hands, my face, my clothing! The smell of it thick in my nostrils."

He shifted his weight, bracing a hand on his hip. "Why you doin' this?"

"Because I have to! Because I have to know the truth, or it'll drive me insane!" She caught her breath and calmed enough to drive her point home. "There were two bodies on the floor of my father's study that night. I know that now. *Two*, Gitan, not one. I remember Justin firing the gun and I saw you fall."

"Lily, for Christ's sake!"

"There was so much blood, and you didn't move. I thought you were—I thought you were dead. You were still and white and—"

He walked quickly to where she stood and she knew he would try to stop her from saying it. "C'mon, *cher.* Let it go. You can't change it. It's over and done with, and you got to let it go."

Lily shook her head, unable to stop now. She'd come too far. "You didn't kill him. You couldn't have. *You* were physically incapable of stabbing him . . . but I wasn't."

He grabbed her shoulders and shook her hard enough to silence her. "Stop it! *Dieu*, Lily! What's wrong with you? Is that why you came back here? To relive this shit? Jesus Christ. It ain't worth it. You hear me? It ain't worth it! Go back to L.A. Get on with your life."

What life? She had no life. She had no future. The only thing she had was a glimmer of truth, a clue to a mystery that had haunted her for eight long years. Everything that had happened since, every decision she had made had been based on the outcome of that night. Getting at the truth wasn't just important. It was everything. "Get on with my life," she said with a watery laugh. "That's almost funny. I killed my own father and sent an innocent man to prison for it. How do I live with myself—"

"I killed your old man because he needed killin'! He asked for it!" It was almost a shout. She saw him check himself, regaining control as effortlessly as someone turning off a light switch, and she envied him the ability to turn off his emotions. "You think too damn much."

She managed to pull herself together, but it was an illusion. She was walking a fine line, and they both knew it. On one side lay a dark and terrifying abyss; on the other, sanity—if she stumbled, it was anyone's guess which way she'd fall. "That argument might have worked when I was seventeen. Good luck getting it off the ground today. I'm just not that gullible."

"So that's it?" he said, releasing her, stepping back. "First you buy into Hugh's theory about me bein' involved in Michel's murder, and now you think I took the rap for somethin' I didn't do?"

"I don't just think it," Lily said quietly.

He shook his head, weary of the argument. "Fine. If it makes you happy, you believe it. But I know the truth."

"That's it?" Lily asked, unsure what she'd expected. "What else you want from me, *cher*? You want me to confess to the Lindbergh kidnappin'? There's an unsolved crime you were wonderin' about? *Mais,* yeah, sure—ol' Gitan, he done it. There, you satisfied?"

Lily watched him for a moment, her heart in her throat. Then she turned and ran from the shop, ignoring the voice—*his* voice, calling out behind her. "Damn it, Lily, wait!"

Lily was beyond hearing. She'd parked near Virginia's shop three bocks away. She'd promised Virginia she would make sure the place was locked down tight and the CLOSED sign turned out in the display window. Then, thinking the walk would clear her head, she'd set out to find Gitan. At some point during their confrontation, night had fallen, and the overcast sky and thready fog drifting in off the bayou nearly swallowed the halo from the dusk-to-dawn street lamps. Only a faint grayish blue shone in shallow puddles on the sidewalks, failing to penetrate the deeper shadows and lending an eeriness to the evening that had been missing earlier.

Somewhere in the mist, a young man's laughter rang out, too distant to provide any comfort. She heard voices, but they were lost somewhere in the fog. The mist rising off the bayou seemed to alter everything. Streets that were familiar and friendly in daylight felt foreign and sinister on a night like this. Lily's footsteps echoed off the pavement . . . but as she paused for a second at the corner to look for oncoming traffic, she noticed that the sound didn't stop. A chill chased down her spine as she glanced back. A man dressed in dark clothing with a hat pulled low on his brow ducked into a doorway and disappeared.

Lily let go a breath. "Get a grip, Lily." Her confrontation with Gitan had upset her, and she was letting her imagination run away with her. As she neared the street corner and glanced at the oncoming traffic, she caught a dark blur in her peripheral vision, heard the rush of movement. Something struck her hard between the shoulder blades; Lily pitched forward, tried to catch herself, but couldn't. She landed hard in the street, directly in the path of an oncoming car, and then came the screech of tires on pavement, the glare of the headlights, the blare of a horn. . . .

"Lily!" Gitan sprinted down the street, in front of the car, scooping her up as the driver laid on the horn a second time.

Lily sat in the same chair in the same kitchen Gitan had occupied when she'd cleaned the cut he'd sustained when the window was broken, feeling more than a little foolish. "You don't have to do this. It isn't necessary. It's just a few scrapes and bruises. I think I'll live."

A clean white towel padded the table's surface. Gitan held one of her hands in his and poured a thin stream of hydrogen peroxide over the abrasions. "No sense in takin' a chance. We can't have you gettin' some sort of infection."

"I could have taken care of this at home," Lily said. She felt foolish for doubting him. He'd never been anything but good, a positive force in her life.

"What are friends for, anyhow?" he said, blotting the moisture from her palm with the edge of the towel.

Lily laughed at the irony of it. "Is that what we are? Friends?"

He glanced up, without a hint of a smile, the expression in his dark eyes candid. "Sure, why not? Always been. You, me, Michel—even Hugh. Hell of a lot of history between us. A few years away don' erase that."

"A lot of tension." Lily swallowed the lump of painful emotion that had lodged in her throat, but it was persistent and refused to go away completely. It made her voice sound tight, constrained. "I'm not going to apologize for tonight, because I'm not sorry." She lifted the hand that was already bandaged and gently touched his face with her fingertips. "You can deny it all you want, but I just don't believe you. It's just the sort of thing you'd do for someone you cared about—take the blame, take the rap, do the time. It kills me to think of you in Angola, to know I put you there."

He silenced her with a finger to her lips. "Let's don' drag that up again. Not tonight." His touch was gentle. "We're okay right now. That's all that matters."

He was sitting beside her, his chair pulled close to hers. It was an easy thing, to reach out and touch him again, only this time her touch lingered. His skin was like heavy silk, smooth, tawny, and flawless, warm under her hand. He reacted to her nearness, to the slow glide of her fingertips over his skin, a slight, involuntary tension that gripped him, and then he relaxed, threading his fingers into the short curling hair at her nape. "You got no clue what you do to me," he said softly.

"No?" Lily replied, so close she felt his slow intake of breath at finding out she was more than willing to play the game. "Well, why don't you show me? Right here . . . right now?"

He grasped her fingertips, kissing each knuckle. "Why not? I got the time, *cher,* if you do."

Lily just smiled, the last remnants of the evening's upset melting away. She got up slowly, her short black skirt riding high on her thighs as she straddled his knees. "I can make the time, but I need to know that I'll be well compensated for it."

"What do *you* think?" he said, slipping a hand under the silky black fabric.

Lily thought she'd be a fool to walk away. He made her feel whole and alive, vital and wanted. More than that, where Gitan touched, Lily burned.

"You need these, sugar?" he asked, reaching up under the skirt to hook his fingers in the elastic of her black thong panties. With his help, they glided down and Lily kicked them free. "Oh, yeah," he drawled. "That's so much better." With hands on her hips, he urged her back to lean against the table; then his head dipped and the heat of his kiss seared her flesh, forcing an involuntary shiver from her.

Much later, in the shadows of the antique bed, Lily lay listening to the heavy thud of her lover's heart, reliving the moments just past in her mind . . . Gitan peeling her clothing from her body, piece by piece, a slow and sensuous striptease that ended with their clothing lying in a careless pile at the foot of his bed. The look on his face as he lifted her, guiding her legs around his hips. Then, their bodies joined, he lowered her onto the mattress and proceeded to eradicate the last shred of Lily's inhibitions. . . .

"You want to tell me what happened tonight?"

Lily sighed. "Before or after our argument?"

"Don' even try to dodge the question. You know exactly what I mean."

She shrugged, sitting up. "I don't really know. I just wanted to get back to my car and go home, but everything changes on a night like this. Sound echoes. I could hear someone laughing far away, and then footsteps. At first I thought they were mine; then I caught sight of someone behind me. I didn't really think he was a threat. I guess I was wrong about that. He hit me from behind, and I fell."

"You see what this guy looked like?"

Lily shook her head, then hugged the sheet closer to her. Talking about it brought it all back. In her mind's eye she felt the hard shove, saw the head-lights, heard the blare of the car's horn. . . . "He wore a hat that threw a shadow over his features, and some sort of overcoat, or raincoat."

"That's kind of overdressed for a night this warm, don' you think?"

"I didn't think about it at the time," Lily admitted, "but now that you mention it, it does seem suspicious."

"What about his build?" Gitan asked, intent on prying every bit of information from her.

Lily frowned, picturing the sinister figure coming out of the light fog. "Medium height, not heavy. The coat he was wearing hung on him."

"Medium height. Like Hugh, maybe?"

Lily laughed. "Like Hugh, but not Hugh. He's a real prick sometimes, and he's impossible to deal with, but he wouldn't hurt me—not like that. Besides, he doesn't own a raincoat."

"That you know of."

"Gitan. I'm serious," Lily said. "If it had been Hugh, I would have smelled tobacco, and there was none—not a whiff."

Gitan had an arm around her shoulders and his hand played over the soft skin of her neck. "Hey, I'm just tryin' to figure out who would want to kill you. You've only been in town a week."

"It was random—it had to be. Just one of those things that happens for no reason."

"I'm not so sure I buy it, Lily." His voice was a deep rumble in his chest. Masculine. Incredibly sexy.

Lily bent to kiss the satiny scar that cleaved his chest. "I saw a man push a little girl in front of a bus in L.A. When the police asked him why he did it, he said he was sending her to God." She paused a few seconds to listen to the thud of his heart. Somehow, the sound was comforting. "There's one more thing."

"What's that?"

"I had the weird impression that he was lost."

"What do you mean, lost?"

"Like a homeless person."

Gitan wasn't satisfied. "I still think I should have a little talk with the sheriff. He owes me one. He never did give me back my work boots."

Lily rose up just enough to meet his gaze. "I'm the one who was pushed, so it's my place to deal with Hugh. There's no reason for you to get involved in this, and I don't want him to know I was here. He could make things uncomfortable for both of us."

"I can handle Hugh," he said calmly.

"Yeah, I know," Lily whispered. "That's what worries me." Hugh had a badge and just enough power to be dangerous. Gitan had a record and a murder conviction, and it wouldn't matter to Hugh that Lily was convinced he'd been innocent of the crime. He could harass him, provoke him into confrontation. He could even manipulate the system to send him back to prison. Hugh was an SOB with an agenda, and if he was bent on payback, he had just enough clout to ruin both their lives.

The hand caressing her shoulders moved lower, sliding along her spine, tracing the cleft in her ass till his hand was just where he wanted it to be. "Hey, woman," he said in a sexy rumble. "This is my bed, and Hugh ain't welcome here. Put him out of your head and come on up here and give me a kiss."

Lily kissed him, wrapping her arms around his neck, fitting her body to his and sighing as he groaned deep in his throat. Then she raised her body to impale it on him once again, and for a while all thoughts of Hugh, or the incident that might have ended her life that evening, were forgotten.

The rectory at St. Bartholomew's was surrounded by street lamps and the lawn lamps lining the main sidewalk. He chose a path less well lit and approached through an unlocked side door. Once inside, he swept off the low crowned hat and black slicker, and nearly collapsed. *Dear God. Oh, Heavenly Father, forgive me!*

Sweating and nauseous, he sat down on the stairs, clutching the clothing he'd used as a disguise and rocking his body back and forth as he had when he was a child. "Oh, Father, forgive me."

He hadn't realized he'd spoken aloud until the foot sounded on the stair, and above him a disembodied head appeared above the banister. "Father Bernaud, are you ill?"

"What?"

Father Aristide was new to the priesthood and still wore the glow of a man with a calling.

Had he ever looked like that? Full of truth and innocence. Goodness. It made him sick to realize how far he'd wandered from the flock, and he wondered if God would ever welcome him back? Or if his sins were unforgivable?

The young man descended as far as the landing, cautious in case his condition were contagious. "Are you ill? Shall we seek medical attention? I can summon Father Murdoch. I saw him not five minutes ago coming from the chapel."

"No. No, I am fine, really. I'm shaken, is all. I wit-

nessed a mugging tonight. I was walking, and someone pushed a young woman into the street." He
nearly choked on the lie, and was forced to swallow
it down. When he continued, his voice was oddly
strained. "It is sickening to see what humanity has
been reduced to, but I'll be fine very soon."

"And how is she?"

"She?" For a moment he was confused.

"The victim of the mugging? Was she hurt?"

"No. No, I don't believe so. But it had the potential to be serious—very serious, indeed."

"It was fortunate that you were there to help."

"Yes, fortunate." *So fortunate. The Martin girl had been
fortunate to have spoken as she did at the crypt, and fortunate
that he had followed her from the motorcycle shop. He hadn't
meant to harm her. Only to frighten. But his own fear had
taken over, and the situation had gotten so out of hand.*

Heavenly Father, forgive me!

*God was stubbornly silent, and thus he turned to Mary,
the Merciful.*

"Come," Father Aristide said gently. "I'll help you
to your room."

"Thank you," Father Bernaud managed to whisper,
but it did not shut out the voices in his head. "You are
too kind."

In his room, he closed the door, fell to his knees, and
vomited. He'd been driven by desperation to try and
frighten her. He'd seen her determination to uncover the truth, and he'd known in his heart that she
presented a larger threat to his safety than the sheriff's department did. It was no secret that most homicides were solved within the first forty-eight hours. And
as the days ticked by, the possibility grew stronger
that Father Dugas's killer would go free. It was a
dreadful thing, to wish for justice to be thwarted, but

he did wish it. If the killer was taken, and talked, then motive would be established, and the trail could lead back to him.

Kneeling on the floor, he retched until his stomach was empty, and still the spasms racked his frame, his thoughts reeling backward to that night, the night after Father Dugas was murdered. . . .

It was very late, but he was awake, and kneeling for hours in the dimly lit chapel. He was getting old, and he was keenly aware that before too many years passed he would be forced to answer to God for his transgressions. Prayer did not lighten his soul. Nothing could, but he hoped that God would hear and have mercy.

Head bowed over his folded hands, his rosary dangling through his fingers, he heard someone slide into the pew behind him. "Don't turn around. If you look at my face, I might feel the need to hurt you."

"What is it that you want?"

"To talk. To unburden. I came here because it's the only place I could go. You are bound by the Church, and by the law to keep the secrets told to you."

"This is true. Confession is sacrosanct."

A sigh. The man was agitated, and Father Bernaud had the strange impression he was close to breaking down. "Bless me, Father, for I have sinned."

"Would you rather enter the confessional, my son? For privacy's sake."

"There is no time. I killed a man last evening. I took a life in the most horrible way possible."

"Go on. I am listening."

"He was one of your own, but he deserved killing. He deserved being treated like the animal he was. When I think about what he did to my boy—"

"I see."

"You don't see. There's no way you could under-stand. He stole my boy's innocence. He ruined him! He deserved what he got. He deserved it!"

In that instant, he recognized the voice, and a chill swept over him that raised the hairs on his arms. "I shall pray for you, my son, and for your immortal soul." The man slid from the pew and hurried off. The doors of the chapel closed behind him, and Father Bernaud collapsed trembling onto the pew. He'd recognized that voice, and he knew that whoever's life he had ended, he'd killed the wrong man.

CHAPTER THIRTEEN

The analysis of the work boots belonging to Gitan Boudreaux was inconclusive. There was only one accidental characteristic, due to the newness of the boots and the light wear: a tiny cut in the tread on the outside of the right foot not visible on the prints taken from the church because of the way the murderer had placed his foot. Hugh didn't like it, but it was a stretch for even him to believe that the killer had walked with a hitch in his step just to avoid leaving a tiny clue from a nick on the boot's sole that he probably hadn't even known existed. Of course, there were two ways to look at the lab results. While they couldn't prove that Gitan had played a role in Michel's murder, they also didn't totally eliminate him as a suspect.

But as far as Hugh was concerned, Gitan still didn't have a motive, and that was the thing that bothered him most.

He knew that Gitan Boudreaux and the victim had had regular contact for a number of years, and Ruben

Early, Gitan's employer, had also substantiated that Michel had stopped by the shop regularly to see the ex-con. Gitan had shrugged if off, saying that Michel was his friend and his priest, and that was as far as it had gone.

Hugh didn't buy it, but he couldn't ask Michel, and Gitan wasn't going to confide in him. All he had left to go on at this point was speculation. What the hell did the two men have in common, besides a childhood connection that had never been close to begin with?

Lily.

Hugh turned the notion over in his mind. Lily had always been the linchpin that had held the four of them together. If not for Lily, he and Boudreaux might have fallen out soon after their association had begun. He had never quite understood why they had hung out together in the first place, except that Boudreaux had collected people as easily as he'd collected baseball cards . . . and as strange as it seemed, Hugh had always wanted what the other man had. It had been that way with everything.

He'd envied Gitan's physical prowess because as a kid, he'd been on the scrawny side. He'd envied his ability to charm, and later, he'd envied him Lily. If not for her being involved with Boudreaux, he and Lily might never have gotten together, and it was a near certainty that they would never have married. Marrying Lily had been important to him because it had been taking the competition one step further. He could admit that now that the divorce was finalized. And he still wanted her—for all the wrong reasons— just like Gitan.

Maybe that's it. That's the connection. Boudreaux's association with Dugas had something to do with Lily.

But what?

Michel hadn't exactly helped to keep the two in contact with one another. Hugh knew Lily's history nearly as well as Lily herself did, and she had lost contact with Gitan shortly after he had arrived at Louisiana State Penitentiary. As far as Hugh could tell, they'd had no other contact until after Michel's death and Lily's return to Angelique.

Crebs knocked, then stuck his head into the room. "Sheriff?"

"You're smilin', so it must be good."

"Oh, it's good, all right. I did a little trawling last night at Zula's Crystal Palace, and it paid off, big-time."

Hugh sat back, his chair squeaking. "Zula's? The gay bar? Crebs, you *do* know that there are certain types of personal information that should *not* be shared in the workplace? I believe this falls under the category of 'don't ask, don't tell.' If you've got extra large pink lace in your closet at home, do me a favor and keep it to yourself."

"It was strictly work related," Crebs assured him.

"Spill it," Hugh said. "I can see you're anxious."

"I spoke with the bartender, a fellow Wisconsin native who happens to be straight as an arrow, and told him I was looking for Green, the vic's boy-toy. He knew him, and from the sounds of it, he's a regular. I slipped him a twenty and my card, and he just called. Looks like we have an address."

Hugh sat up. "Well, what the hell are you waitin' for? Go pick him up, and take a copy of the warrant with you."

Forty minutes later, Crebs returned with Keith Green. Tall, but slight, he had the look of a walking cadaver, and the light in his eyes was almost too bright. Hugh motioned for him to take a seat—

quickly, before he fell down. He sort of folded into the chair, a bag of bones with so little muscle it was a wonder he could hold himself upright, but that didn't stop him from challenging Hugh's authority. "I know my rights," he said. "I don't have to say anything without my attorney present."

"You can have counsel present if you want, but that will delay things. I'm afraid the phone lines are down."

The phone in the outer office made a sick-sounding bleat, and Green pursed his lips in disapproval. Hugh shrugged. "I never said we couldn't take calls; we just can't make 'em. Maybe you've got a cell phone on you?"

Green seemed to fold a little further in on himself, as if he were shrinking into his chair. "They discontinued my service. I was hospitalized two months ago, and I can't work. No insurance, and the cocktail is so expensive. I just can't afford it."

The man was dying of AIDS, and they both knew it. He should have been in bed somewhere, being seen to by family, or in hospice care instead of hanging around in nightspots and wandering the streets. Physically, it would have been impossible for Green to hoist Hugh's ninety-pound grandmother a sixteenth of an inch off the ground, let alone haul a heavyweight like Michel Dugas into the air. "My sympathies on your situation. You can call a lawyer if you want, but it really will slow things down, and all I want is to have a brief conversation. Give me thirty minutes of your time, and Deputy Crebs will drop you off at your apartment. You've got my word on it."

"Talk. About Michel." His eyes glistened, and he swiped at them angrily with the back of a blue-veined hand. "I didn't kill him, if that's what you mean. I could never have hurt him. I loved him too much for that."

Hugh scribbled notes on a pad. "You had a relationship with the victim?"

"It wasn't sexual, if that's what you mean."

Hugh looked up. "Then what kind of relationship was it?"

Green tilted his chin up and sighted along his razor-thin nose. "The best kind. We loved one another, and if not for the Church, we would have been together. Before Michel, I didn't believe that kind of love was possible. Quite the irony that no matter how much Michel loved me, he loved being a priest even more. Do you know what a calling is, Sheriff?"

"Oh, I know what a calling is, Mr. Green, but that doesn't exactly answer my question."

"Michel had a true calling. He was a child of God, and worldly things came second with him, after his service to his Lord. His feelings for me fell into the latter category. Seeing him, being near him, but knowing we could never have a life together was too painful, so I left the Church—"

"Did you and Michel stay in touch?"

His bony frame lifted and fell in a shrug. "He called infrequently at first. Then I tested positive for H.I.V. I suppose he felt sorry for me, because he made it a point to come around, just to see that I was taking care of myself."

"Dugas was a prince," Hugh murmured. "We all know that."

Green didn't seem to take offense. "He wasn't the type of guy to desert a friend in need."

If Green was to be believed, then Dugas was deserving of sainthood, and the interview didn't yield much. Dugas had called Green a few days before the murder, and though he said Michel had sounded troubled, he didn't know why. Hugh did glean a few facts he hadn't known—that Dugas had been coaching a youth softball team a few months before his death, and counseling troubled teens. By comparing that information with Dugas's desk calendar he came up with a few names, but only one screamed loud enough to catch and hold his attention: Mason Edward Boudreaux.

Crebs had given Green a ride back to the cheap hotel where he was staying, and Hugh, feeling the need for a change of scene, grabbed his jacket and keys. He was seated at a corner table at the Pink Cadillac, with a shrimp po'boy, fries, and a cold glass of sweet tea when Gitan walked in.

Hugh watched with mild interest as Gitan caught Amalie by the arm and whispered something in her ear. He pointed to Hugh's table, then walked over and sat down. "Hey, coon-ass. You supposed to be in an establishment that sells liquor? Isn't that a violation of your parole?"

A lazy shrug, and that damned spider's web caught Hugh's eye. He could have chosen anything to put on his body, but he'd opted for a black widow spider crouched on a glistening web. Now what the hell was that supposed to mean?

"Drinkin' alcohol's a violation of my parole. I'm havin' what you're havin' and couldn't ask for a better witness to my exemplary behavior. The sheriff? The only way it could get better than this is if the warden showed up."

Amalie brought a platter of boiled crawfish and a glass of tea, and with a wink in Gitan's direction, left the table. Hugh got serious. The company had ruined his appetite. "What do you want, Gitan?"

"It's simple, really. Some conversation while I have lunch. Man's got to eat." He doused the crawfish in hot sauce and pulled one apart, pinching the tail and biting into the fleshy pink meat with strong white teeth. "Somebody tried to hurt Lily last night. She stopped by the shop, and when she left, she was followed. Whoever it was pushed her into traffic."

"Why the hell am I hearin' this from you, and not from her?"

A dark, level glance. He didn't look at Hugh like he was looking at the sheriff of Angelique, someone who could end his freedom. He looked at him the way he'd looked at him all of his life, like he was privy to Hugh's thoughts and disdained him for it. "Because she'd rather do just about anything than talk to you. Go on, Hugh, tell me you're surprised by that. You know, you can only beat a dog so long before it turns on you, or a woman."

"I never laid a hand on Lily in anger."

Another shrug to show him he could have given a flying fuck for his denial. "Maybe not literally, but there are a lot o' ways to beat somebody down. It ain't always necessary to use your fists."

"Goddamned son of a bitch," Hugh ground out, half coming out of his chair. His fingers itched for the feel of his pistol's grip.

"Go on, pull that piece. But you're gonna have to lie your way out of it. Somehow I don' think two old friends havin' a friendly conversation over a hot meal adds up to justifiable homicide, especially when you're the only one who's packin', and I don' pose a threat. All I want to know is where you were last night. It's an easy question. You got an answer? I'll take my crawfish over there and leave you alone to finish your sweet tea."

"Fuck you. I don't owe you shit."

"Your mama know you use that kinda language? Or maybe that's where you learned it." A flash of white teeth in a dark-skinned face. "I know you've been keepin' tabs on Lily. I know you saw her car in my driveway the other night, and the very next day, I got a brick through my living room window. Imagine that."

"And you think I did it," Hugh said with a laugh.

"As in threw it yourself? Gettin' your hands dirty ain't your MO. But I gotta admit, your name did come to mind in connection with all of this. A broken window's vandalism, but pushin' somebody into traffic might just constitute attempted murder. What kind of term does that carry these days?" He thought about that for a minute. "A cop on the inside. Wonder how long you'd last?"

"If you intend to make an accusation against me, you'd better have a dozen eyewitnesses to back it up." Hugh leaned forward across the table, lowering his voice so that only the man he was addressing could hear. "I run this town, and I've got a reputation that's Teflon clad. You get what I'm sayin', coon-ass? It wouldn't matter if you had concrete proof: you couldn't make it stick. You're a convicted murderer, an ex-con, and there's not a man in the whole damned state of Lou'siana that would take your word over mine."

Gitan's dark eyes glittered dangerously. "Maybe not, but that big-time sheriff, he bleeds, just like me. You hurt Lily, and I swear to Christ, they gonna be wonderin' which piece of Hugh to pin that badge on."

Hugh sat back with a nasty smile. "I'm gonna pretend I didn't hear that. Call it a favor for old time's sake. Call it whatever you want—you threaten me again, the mess you were in over Lily's old man's gonna look like a cakewalk by comparison." He got up, threw down his napkin and a ten-dollar bill, and left the table without once glancing back, and without telling Gitan where he'd been the night before.

The door opened, and Mason walked in, hesitating, then heading for the table where Gitan sat reflecting on his conversation with Hugh. Without a word, he slid into the chair Hugh had vacated a moment before. "Am I crazy, or were you havin' lunch with that asshole?"

Gitan threw a stern look at his younger brother, but he wasn't in the mood to play surrogate father. "That's Sheriff Asshole to you. And no, we weren't having lunch together. I brought my food to his table because I wanted some information from him."

"Damn, those look good." Mase helped himself to a crawfish, pulling off the tail for a mouthful of tender meat, sucking the head.

Gitan sighed. "Mason, we got to do somethin' about that mouth of yours. If Rose hears you, she'll pitch a fit."

Another crawfish, doused with hot sauce. "Man's got to have at least one vice to keep the chicks interested, and I ain't old enough to drink."

"When's illegality ever stopped you?"

"Very funny. You said you needed information," Mase said, reaching for the platter again. "How come you didn't come to me? Don' I know just about everything there is to know that goes on around here? Sheriff, he ain't got nothin' over on me, and dat's a fact!"

"Hey, maybe you'd like some crawfish, huh, Mason? 'Cause it looks like I'm not all that hungry." Gitan shoved the plate across the table and watched the boy dig in. "What's put you in a mood to socialize? I'm usually lucky to get a growl out of you."

"You remember what tomorrow is?"

"Yeah. It's Tuesday."

"Stop bullshittin' me, man. You know as well as I do that tomorrow's *Tante* Rose's birthday. I was thinkin' we ought to do somethin' nice for her, kind of as a thank-you for everything she's done for us."

"You want to buy her somethin'." Gitan reached into his back pocket and pulled out his wallet.

"I was thinkin' of a birthday party. Nothin' too fancy, just a cake, some ice cream, and a few guests."

"Sounds nice, but who's gonna do the legwork on this thing? I got to work."

"If you want to finance it, I'll be happy to handle the details."

"'Lay down the cash, Gitan.' Do I look like a banker to you?"

"Hey, man. Now ain't the time to get cheap on me," Mase said around a mouthful of crawfish.

Gitan shook his head. The kid was shrewd; he had to give him that, and he had all the makings of a very successful con man. He would have been lying if he'd said it didn't keep him awake nights. "How much is it gonna cost me?"

"Hey, just you remember, she's your aunt, too."

"How much?"

"Hundred bucks'll do it," Mason said so matter-of-factly that Gitan merely suspected he was being fleeced. "That way, I can pick up a few supplies, and get her that rosary in the jeweler's window. You know, the fancy black one, with the gold-plated chain. She sighs every time she passes their window. 'Course, if you can't afford it—"

Gitan opened his wallet, counted out five twenties, and laid them on the table between them. He watched Mason reach for them, and put one finger on the pile to prevent him from taking them. "You've got to account for every penny. No beer, no cigarettes, and no weed. You got that?"

Mason looked indignant. "Cut me a break, man! This ain't for me. It's for Rose. You know what your trouble is? You've lost your faith in humanity. Think I'll skate on outta here before I get too corrupted."

Gitan rose halfway out of his chair, and Mason ran to the door, laughing. "No worries, Bro! I'll handle everything."

"*Mais,* yeah, *brother,*" Gitan said softly. "That's what worries me." Yet he couldn't quite suppress a smile. He'd come here to try and shake Hugh up enough to find out if he'd had anything to do with Lily's near miss the night before, and though the conversation hadn't gone quite the way he'd planned, Mason's arrival had been a nice surprise. Something had put the kid in a good mood, and damned if they hadn't had a moment in which they'd actually connected, a rare enough occurrence these days.

"Now there's something you don't see every day: a smile on Gitan's handsome face." Amalie piled the plates and flatware onto a tray and swung it up to balance it on one hand. "You need anything else, sugar?" She licked her painted lips and the implication was clear.

"Not unless you can spice up my afternoon with some scuttlebutt." He paid for the meal and slipped her a twenty.

"Gossip?" Her dark eyes lit up. "Who we dissin', darlin'?"

"I don' know. Why don' you tell me? Looks like somebody 'round Angelique don' like me. You work evenin' shift too, sometimes? You hear anything that's been said?"

"I might have," she said with a coy smile. "A certain

dawg with a lot o' cash isn't exactly a fan, if you know what I mean. Hangs out in the parking lot."

"Willie Early."

"See that," she said with a smile. "You didn't need my help after all. Listen, if you decide you want to liven things up some night, stop by. I get off at two-thirty on Friday and Saturday nights. Got a thing for bad boys, that's for sure."

"I'll keep that in mind." With a wink, Gitan left Amalie and the Pink Cadillac behind.

"Did you know that I'm NPO, until tomorrow after those tests have been run? NPO . . . nothing by mouth—I won't even be allowed to have coffee! How on earth does one survive without their morning coffee?"

As Virginia continued to grumble, Lily smoothed the blankets on the hospital bed. Her private room was nice enough, but decorated in hospital drab. Beige walls. Not beige beige, but a shade sufficiently light to keep the patients from being remotely interested, let alone from getting excited. The blankets were white, the walls plain, and the window devoid of any window treatments. The décor was, in a word, clinical.

"It's only for a few hours," Lily assured her. "And I'll ask the nurse to be sure you have coffee as soon as they say it's okay."

"Goodness knows when that might be," Virginia grumbled. "Those papers they made me sign gave them leave to poke and prod and torture me at their leisure." She set down her overnight bag and groaned. "Why am I doin' this again? Oh, that's right, because I'm a little forgetful. You know it isn't like I've forgotten my name, or where I live." She sank down in the chair by the bed and sighed. "I'm sorry, sugar. I know I'm bein' a big baby about this, and I should just shut up and play dead for the nice young doctor and his bored young female assistants." She pulled a face. "Have you noticed how young they all are? Don't doctors have to go to college any more? Some of them look like they're fresh out of high school."

"Yes, they have to go to college, and medical school, and an internship, and residency," Lily said with a smile. "They may look young, but they've got training and experience." Lily took Virginia's hand in hers, patting it reassuringly. "You have every right to be upset about this, even to be a little nervous, but it's important that you stay and see it through, because I don't want to lose you."

"Oh, darlin'. I'm not goin' anywhere—at least not until I've had my coffee." She chuckled lightly. "You know Edna Mae's stoppin' by later with some sliced ham and red-eye gravy. Gonna sneak it past the nurses' station. She's bein' so nice to me it's almost scary." Another laugh, this one easier. "It almost makes all this fuss worth it." She shook her finger at Lily. "But don't you tell her I said that."

"Your secret's safe with me," Lily said. "Look at the time. I've got to go. I promised Michel's sister I'd stop by St. Bart's rectory and pick up his belongings."

"Call me later?"

Lily kissed Virginia's cheek. "I promise." She felt only a little guilty for not telling her aunt what had happened the night before. Nothing raised the blood pressure like finding out a loved one had been involved in a close encounter with an SUV. It was a single, freakish incident, and it was over. There was no point in upsetting anyone by relating recent history when it had no basis in the past, and no bearing on the future.

Yet as she left the hospital parking lot, she could almost hear Gitan contradicting her. *You don' know that's true.*

"It was a transient, hopped up on drugs," Lily argued. "I'm sure of it."

But the truth was, she wasn't sure.

By midafternoon, Hugh was cooling his heels in Father Murdoch's office. Anything but a patient man, he nosed around the office, opening drawers that weren't locked, picking items off the bookshelves, looking at them, and putting them back. He had just taken a book off the shelf when the door opened and Father Murdoch stepped into the room, hesitated for a half beat, then offered his guest a bland smile. "Sheriff Lothair. I'm surprised to see you again so soon. How can I help you?"

Hugh flourished the book he was holding. *"Demons of the Dark Ages.* That's some interesting reading material you have here."

Murdoch seated himself and got comfortable. "I'm a collector, and of course my library is accessible to all who live and work here, so it serves a dual purpose. Are you personally interested in religious texts?"

"Not particularly. I'm always curious, though, to see what a man likes to read. You can tell a lot about someone's personality by the books on their bookshelves. *Lucifer Throughout History. The Inquisition. The Suffering of Mankind.* That's some dark and depressing stuff. Do you read before bed? How do you keep from having nightmares?"

"I read whenever a moment presents itself. Knowledge is power, Sheriff."

"So is money, Father."

A shrug. "That's true in your world, I suppose. As for sleeping, my conscience is clear."

"Funny you should use that reference," Hugh said, putting the book back in place and moving to sit down, so that he could more closely watch Father Murdoch's face. You could tell a lot by a man's expression, if that man had nothing to hide and was open and honest. If his face gave away nothing, it was usually because he was keeping secrets. "I've known a lot of kids, and most have nightmares. Untroubled sleep at an early age is usually pretty rare, since kids know they're vulnerable. Monsters under the bed, the stranger down the street, the boogeyman . . . common stuff. Serial killers, though—they sleep like babies. So, you could say that untroubled sleep has more to do with lack of conscience than a clean slate."

"You have a unique point of view, Sheriff." Murdoch folded his hands on the desk blotter. His impatience was showing. "This conversation has been entertaining, but I'm afraid I have a full calendar this afternoon. Perhaps you'd like to get to the point of why you're here? I assume it's about your investigation?"

"It's come to my attention that I may not have gotten all the details of Michel Dugas's duties—as a priest, I mean. He was counseling kids?"

"Actually, he was a favorite among the parish young people. Father Dugas was a good listener, and he cared. He was very good at relating to them on their level."

"So, you're saying he was like a big kid?"

"Well, that's an odd way of putting it, but yes. I can't say enough good about Father Dugas, Sheriff."

"Just curious, but were you aware that he was a homosexual?"

"No, I wasn't aware. Are you suggesting that Father Dugas's sexual orientation had something to do with his death?"

"Murder," Hugh corrected. "Michel was murdered. Let's don't gloss over that fact. As to whether his preference for men over women as objects of his desire was motive for murder, I haven't arrived at anything concrete yet. But I can't rule it out, either. I would be very interested in knowing if there have been any complaints concerning molestation lodged in this diocese against St. Bart's."

"There have been very few dioceses that have not been affected, but anything occurring here happened long before I came to serve at St. Bartholomew's, before Father Dugas gave any thought to becoming a priest."

"And you would, of course, be forthcoming if it had."

"If there were incidents, you would have been the first person I notified. Church policies have changed, and are far more open now than in the past. We have recognized our failings and we have corrected them."

At gunpoint, Hugh thought. Or, more literally, under the glaring scrutiny of the journalistic spotlight. He stood. "Well, if you don't mind—or even if you do—I'd like to verify your statement. You'll provide me with a list of the children Dugas counseled, and the kids on his softball team. You can fax it to my office no later than this afternoon." He handed Father Murdoch his card and walked out.

The spacious corridor was shady and cool, serene with the gentle tolling of the bells, and hardly the place he expected to run into Lily. She breezed through the Gothic double doors, lighting up the space with her golden good looks, and filling Hugh with sharp regret. He'd always wanted her in some fashion: as an awkward kid he'd wanted her to look at him the way she looked at Gitan, with a glowing hero worship shining in her blue eyes because he knew it would have made him feel bigger than he was, strong and invincible.

As a teen, he'd wanted to own her, to know she was his and only his; he'd wanted to be her first and her only . . . and even though he had won the chance to court her after Gitan was sent away, had claimed her as wife and partner for two years, he still felt that gnawing ache deep in his chest, a hunger that was so acute it was as if he'd never had her at all. Never stood a real chance with Lily as long as Gitan Boudreaux drew breath somewhere in the world. That sense of loss bewildered him even as it haunted him, and he had no idea what had gone wrong.

As she caught sight of him standing silent and still in the shadowed hall, there was a hitch in her sure stride, a narrowing of her gaze, and she looked ready to run. Then he saw her steel herself for whatever would happen next and gain steam again. "Hugh. I didn't expect to see you here."

"You mean you were hoping you wouldn't run into me," he said, unable to help himself, though he softened his tone to lessen the impact. She didn't reply, just shifted the strap of her bag on her shoulder, and he knew she was bent on escape. In that instant he would have done anything to keep her there a second longer. "I saw Gitan a little while ago. Actually, we had lunch together." A pause. "Funny, how the mere mention of his name makes your eyes light up."

"Damn it, Hugh, will you just stop!" She would

have stepped around him, but he closed his hand over her forearm, holding her there.

"Why didn't you tell me that somebody slashed your tires outside the station? And why the hell didn't you report that somebody tried to kill you last night?"

"Don't make it sound like some sinister plot when it wasn't. He pushed me, I fell, and he ran off."

"Yeah?" Hugh said. "Well, Gitan made it sound more serious than that. In fact, he seemed to think I had something to do with it."

"Did you?" she asked, then seemed to regret it. She shook her head. "I'm sorry I said that, but I have to admit, the thought did cross my mind. There are times when you're so bitter—I'd be lying if I said it didn't concern me."

"You'd be bitter, too, if you'd lost what I lost." He tried to draw a full, unencumbered breath, but the tightness in his chest wouldn't let him. "He makes you feel alive, doesn't he, Lily? That's what it is that's so different."

No sharp denial, no plea for him to cease his badgering. She just lifted her chin to look him right in the eyes and without sympathy gave him the truth. "Yes."

This time, when she shook off his hand and walked away, he let her go, but he couldn't quite resist the urge to watch her retreating figure until she disappeared into the stairwell. Then and only then did he turn to go.

CHAPTER FOURTEEN

Lily was busy trying to downplay the incident on the street the night before, determined to brush it off as some random act of weirdness by an anonymous psycho, but Gitan wasn't so sure. Angelique was a different world, compared to L.A. In a small town where everyone knew their neighbors, as well as their neighbors' business, strangers didn't go unnoticed. The closest thing Angelique had to a homeless population was Addy Morrison, an old eccentric who roamed the streets with a shuffling walk, muttering to himself. But even Addy had a home, and lived with his spinster sister. Ada Morrison was a deaconess at the First Presbyterian Church and didn't allow alcoholic beverages in her home, so Addy spent most of his time as far away from Ada and her needlepoint and lace-edged doilies as his slow-moving gait would take him.

Gitan had known Addy all of his life, and he was certain that Addy hadn't pushed Lily into the street. But someone had, and he wanted to know why.

Lily didn't have enemies, unless he took Hugh into consideration . . . or the mix-up between Mason and Willie Early and his friends that had occurred shortly after Lily had arrived in Angelique. Hugh was a logical choice, due to the level of hostility that existed between him and Lily. It was no secret that Lothair could be ruthless, but would he stoop to trying to hurt Lily?

Gitan didn't know, but Lily didn't think so, and she knew Hugh better than anyone.

As for Willie, Gitan realized he'd made an enemy when he'd thrown him out of the shop, but his suspicions didn't stop there. There was a damn good chance Willie had been the one who had thrown the brick through his window, and if Hugh hadn't been behind Lily's near miss the night before, it was likely that Willie had been. Lily had described her assailant, and the description didn't fit, but that didn't mean shit. Willie Early had access to a ready supply of cash and he could have hired someone else to do the deed.

Mase hadn't talked about the beating he'd taken, or named the boys responsible, but Gitan was certain Willie had been involved, and if that was the case, then he was the one Lily had cut off at the knees in front of his friends with a well-aimed jab to the larynx. If that wasn't enough to tip the scales, a nose full of coke could do strange things to a man. If Willie had thrown the brick, then chances were that he'd seen them together and had decided that they were too large a threat.

But they weren't exactly together. She'd come to him a couple of times, and the sex had been hotter than hot. It made him ache just thinking about it . . . but sex and commitment were two different things. Lily might want his arms around her deep in the night, she might crave the thrill of something forbidden and risky, but that was as far as things went. She wasn't ready for anything permanent, and neither was he. Maybe, Gitan thought, they never would be.

Life was too damned complicated for him to even think about it.

Mercy Blue's voice echoed in his head, a mere whisper compared to what it had been the first day he'd heard it. He'd been flat on his back in the infirmary, still too ill to be housed on the cell block. Mercy was a lifer convicted of raping a white woman, a crime he swore he hadn't committed. Gitan was in no position to judge anyone, not that it mattered a damn one way or the other to him. The old man provided a welcome distraction from counting the ceiling tiles, or chasing his worries about Lily and his family around in circles.

"Boudreaux," he'd said, "you too new to realize it yet, but you need to be educated, and you need it fast. Things different in here, cause ever'body's too sick to care 'bout what the man next to him's doin'. Out dere in de gen'ral population, it's a different world. Dat's where de big dogs are, and they try their best to tear a new man to pieces and divvy up de meat. You listen to me, and you might just do okay. Pay attention, and you'll live long enough to learn the ropes."

"I guess you're gonna give me all the advice I need. That right, old man?"

"I might, if you act right. Piss me off, and you on your own. Rule Number One . . . Don't think about tomorrow. You concentrate all you got on gettin' through today. Today is what matters most. In here, it's the only thing dat matters."

The voice faded. Mercy had taught Gitan everything

he'd needed to know to survive Angola, and they'd become friends. Then, once he was certain Gitan knew what he needed to know to survive, he'd quietly succumbed to the lung cancer that had kept him a permanent fixture in the prison infirmary for months. They'd buried him in the prison cemetery on the grounds at Angola. Gitan had been well enough by that time to walk to the prison cemetery and watch as his fellow inmates lowered the plain pine box into the ground.

Aside from how to survive on the inside, Mercy had taught Gitan that life was short, and freedom precious. It didn't really matter that he couldn't remember a time when he hadn't loved her. He wouldn't use emotional strings to hold her . . . because he loved her enough to let her go. *Freedom was precious. Freedom was everything . . . but not just for him . . . for Lily, too. . . .*

Evening came and Gitan showered the sweat and grime from the workday away and put on his jeans and a T-shirt Mase had given him for Christmas. Hugh's deputy had brought back his boots an hour ago, grunting when he asked what the results of the lab tests were. No satisfaction from that quarter, but no arrest warrant, either, so he had to assume that Hugh hadn't been able to manipulate the evidence to make a match. He finished dressing, combed his damp hair away from his face, and rode the Harley to Tupelo Avenue.

Mason was loitering near the front porch when he arrived, conspicuous in a white dress shirt and dark trousers. He viewed Gitan's casual dress with skepticism. "What? You ain't got nothin' better than that?"

Gitan frowned down at his jeans and T-shirt.

"What's wrong with this? I ain't goin' to mass, and this ain't no funeral. Besides, when did you become the fashion police?"

"I just figured you'd want to look your best, is all."

"Tonight, this is my best. Where's Rose?"

"She took Miss Jean from next door to look at some fabric for curtains. It had to be done today, too. Imagine that."

"Where'd you learn to be so manipulative, Slick?" Gitan wondered, cutting him off before he could answer. "Never mind. I don' want to know. But you sure as hell know how to work it, I'll give you that. Just make damn sure you use those powers of yours for good and not evil or I'll land on you so hard you'll think you got flattened by a semi."

Mason glared at him. "You might want to watch your mouth this evenin'. *Tante* Rose, she deserves the best for her birthday." He craned his neck for a better look at the package tucked under his brother's arm. "What'd you get her, anyhow?"

"Guess you'll find out when she does." Gitan moved past Mason into the house. A vase with fresh-cut flowers had been placed on the coffee table, but unless he was mistaken, the flowers looked suspiciously like the ones in Rose's flower garden. Gitan looked around. "Tell me you didn't use my hundred dollars to hire a clown and rent a pony."

Mason shook his head. "Go on, make fun. You ain't seen nothin' yet."

Mase cut through the house and out the back door. Curious, Gitan followed. A pair of long tables had been set up on the lawn under a striped canvas tent, then spread with a pair of snowy tablecloths. John Long from down the avenue was busy hanging Chinese lanterns from the boughs of the sweet gum tree, which had been strung with brightly colored streamers, but stopped long enough to shout a hello to Gitan.

Gitan turned a skeptical eye on Mason. "How'd you manage all this?"

Mase positioned a radio on the porch and tuned it to Rose's favorite station. "You ain't the only Boudreaux with connections."

"Is that supposed to set my mind at ease? 'Cause it sure as hell don'."

A car door opened and closed in front.

"Hey, she's back." He opened the back door and disappeared in the direction of the kitchen. A few seconds later, Miss Jean appeared, Rose's voice floating out behind her, "I don' know why on earth we need to be lookin' at the flower garden this time of the evenin'. You know it's almost time for *Wheel of Fortune*, and I like to play along."

Miss Jean made a face. "Oh, Rose, it'll only take a minute or two, and you know your beds are the nicest in the neighborhood."

"Well, they do look good this year, that's for sure!" Rose stepped outside and, glancing up, saw Gitan and a small army of friends and neighbors standing under the sweet gum. "What on earth? Gitan—what is this?"

Gitan shrugged. "Guess you better ask Mason. It was his idea."

As Rose turned to find her youngest nephew, the door opened and Mase stepped out, carrying a cake large enough to serve everyone, complete with candles. "Happy Birthday, *Tante* Rose."

"Oh!" The exclamation was all she could manage. She waited until Mase set the cake in the center of the table to throw her arms around him. She hugged him, kissed his cheek, then scolded, "A bakery-bought cake? You know it won't hold a candle to my *grand-mère's* recipe! *Comme si!*"

"The idea was to get you out of the kitchen," Mase said. "It's your birthday. Besides, Gitan's loaded. Well, maybe not so much as he was yesterday!" Mason laughed.

"Gitan works hard for his money, and don' you forget it! But thank you, anyway. Both of you. I'm so blessed." She put her arms around Gitan, sniffing. "Well, let's cut that cake and see if it's worth eating."

The food was gone and the party in full swing when Lily appeared, a vision in blue jeans and a white linen shirt. Her hair curled slightly at her nape and in front of her ears, and there were small diamond studs in her lobes. She was gorgeous, and she was taking a hell of a risk coming here. She and Rose weren't exactly on friendly terms.

As soon as Mason saw Lily and changed positions, maneuvering closer to his aunt, Gitan understood, and he was hard-pressed to decide whether to kick the kid's ass first, or congratulate him for his genius in the art of manipulation, and save the ass-kicking for later.

Lily's glance clashed with Gitan's, then slid away as she placed a beautifully wrapped package with the other gifts. When she stopped in front of Rose, Gitan saw his aunt stiffen, and the gathering went still except for the sad old song playing on the radio. Mason leaned in close, "She's a guest, *Tante* Rose. I asked her to come."

"Happy Birthday, Miss Boudreaux," Lily said.

Rose couldn't have looked more affronted if Lily had slapped her. "It was—till now."

Gitan saw the hurricane coming, and moved to shield Lily from his aunt's wrath. "You just don' get it, do you?" Rose screeched. "I pay the taxes on this property. This is my house, and I don' want you here!"

"If you're gonna yell at someone," Mason said, "then yell at me, not Lily! Comin' here wasn't her idea; it was mine. She came because I asked her to! What's wrong with you that you can't see?"

"I see more than you know!" Rose said, stricken by her favorite's criticism. Tears sparkled in her dark eyes, but her expression remained bitter. "I see what's happenin', and I don' like it one damn bit! It wasn't enough that you tore this family apart once?" she demanded of Lily. "You got to do it again? What kind of woman are you that one of my nephews ain't enough? You got to have them both? What kind of woman are you?"

"Damn it, Rose!" Gitan snapped. "That's enough!"

Rose stiffened. "Gitan? You would talk to me that way? My own brother's son? You'd turn against your own kin for Lily Martin when I stood beside you through everything?"

"Don' listen to her," Gitan said, grasping her arm, leading her away. "She doesn't know what she's sayin'."

"Tell him lies!" Rose screamed. "Poison him against me!"

Behind them Mason exploded. "Shut up! You hear? Just shut up! Lily didn't do anything! She didn't do anything! It's you! You're the one ruinin' everything!"

"Mason Edward!" Rose tried to catch Mase by the arm, but he pulled roughly away, his features twisted with anger and disgust.

"Stay away from me!" He took a small jeweler's box from his pocket and flung it on the ground at her feet. "Here's your present—you got what you wanted! I hope you're happy, 'cause you're the only one."

The box flew open, the rosary spilling out to glitter on the grass as Mase broke and ran.

They reached the drive and Lily pulled away from Gitan. "I shouldn't have come, but Mase made it sound as if she wanted me here."

"There's no need to apologize. You didn't do anything. It was Rose. There was no call for her to speak to you that way. No damn call for that at all." He reached for her, but she eluded his grasp. "C'mon, *cher.* I'll see you home," he offered. "After last night, I don' want you roamin' around alone."

Lily pulled from his grasp. "Go after Mason. I couldn't bear it if he got into trouble again because of me."

"Lily—"

She walked away, quickly. "Just go. I'm not a little girl, and I don't need you to protect me. I don't need anyone." She opened the driver's door of her car and slid behind the wheel. In the time it took Gitan to run a hand through his hair, a sure sign of his agitation, she was gone.

Rose stood on the inside of the screen door, watching. "You're not going after her?"

Gitan had had enough. He spread his hands wide. "What if I am? You're family, Rose, and I love you, but I'm not fifteen, and you don' get to tell me what I can or can't do. Mase is right! You owe Lily an apology. What the hell'd she ever do to you?"

"She tore this family apart! Nothin' but grief's gonna come of this, Gitan! You mark my words! Nothin' but grief!"

Gitan swung his leg over the Harley's seat. It had a kick-starter that didn't always cooperate, but this time it took right off. He checked Mase's usual haunts, but the kid was nowhere to be found, and his friends claimed they hadn't seen him. After an hour's search, he found himself at the last place he should have been: Lily's door.

She must have heard the bike's throaty purr, because before he could ring the bell, the door opened. "Did you find him?"

He shook his dark head. "My guess is he don' want to be found."

Her blue eyes were large and luminous in the dim oval of her face, and even the shadows couldn't hide her concern. "What are you going to do?"

An uneasy shrug. "Not much I can do. He'll come home when he's good and ready."

"But you're worried about him."

"Yeah, I'm worried," he said, his voice softening slightly. "But not just about Mase." Reaching out, he traced the curve of her cheek to the hollow beneath with the pad of his thumb. "You worry me plenty. I lie awake at night, wonderin', is Lily sleepin'? Or is she lyin' awake, thinkin' 'bout things better left alone?"

Lily shifted uneasily against the door frame. She wasn't comfortable with his knowing her so well. She didn't want him reading her thoughts, looking into the dark recesses of her soul.

Slipping a finger under her chin, he tilted her face to the right, then the left. "Funny. You don't look fine. In fact, you look like a woman with far too much on her mind. Well, baby, you're in luck. Doctor Gitan, he got the best medicine for what ails you." He made a dramatic flourish with one hand, indicating the shiny black and glinting chrome beast parked menacingly in the driveway. He'd bought it years before—before things had begun to unravel, but Lily had been wary of it then, and was wary of it now.

"Oh, no."

"No! What'd you mean, 'no'?"

"No," she said. "I am not getting on that thing. Not for you—not for anyone."

"It's freedom, Lily. The wind in your hair, the hum of the road. It's like flight without the airplane." He sighed. "C'mon, sugar. Don' you wanna be free?"

Lily shook her head. "What about road rash?"

"I'll protect you," he said easily. "When was the last time you cut loose and just went with the flow?" He raised a brow in silent question. "See there. It's been so long you can't even remember. You went to California and you forgot how to have fun."

Lily heard a door open down the street and knew Mrs. Iberson had walked out onto her porch. "Miss Martin? Is everything all right? Is that man bothering you?" Mrs. Iberson was in her seventies, a retired schoolteacher who lived with a pair of Doberman pinschers. The dogs were with her now, leashed and sitting like statues at her feet.

"Yes, Mrs. Iberson, everything is fine, and no, he isn't bothering me." *Fine. Everything is fine. But it wasn't fine, and it was getting harder and harder to pretend.*

"Live a little," Gitan said softly, persuasively. "We can ride by the sheriff's station and wave to your ex-husband. It'll keep him up all night."

Lily laughed. "You're so sadistic."

"Yeah, and you love it."

All of Lily's instincts screamed for her to say no, but there was something inside her that whispered she would spend the rest of the night—maybe even the rest of her life regretting it.

"I'll let you drive." He took her hand, lifting it to his mouth, dropping a kiss on her knuckles.

"Me drive? You must have a death wish."

His dark eyes narrowed slightly, masking the glint

in the ebony depths. "No death wish, I just got it bad
for Lily Martin." He leaned in and nibbled her earlobe.
The heat of his mouth seared her flesh, made her
think of a shadowy bedroom and Gitan rising above
her. Lily shivered. "Take a risk, sugar. Live large—
unless, of course, you're scared to get on that bike with
a bad-ass like me."

Lily closed her eyes as past and present blurred together. He could be so damned persuasive . . . always
there, urging her on to take risks, encouraging her
to ignore her fear, to live life. Always . . .

The two of them raced ahead, Gitan and Hugh,
pushing each other as they competed to be the first
to reach the Indian bridge that crossed a narrow inlet
of Bayou des Cannes. It was less than a dozen feet from
bank to bank, bridged by a fallen tree, but danger lay
in the muddy shallows beneath. It was a favorite spot
for gators, lolling in the heat of a midday sun. Twelve-
year-old Lily was terrified of alligators. She couldn't
count the times she'd crouched down beside Michel,
listening to Gitan spin tales of the huge gator that lived
in the swamp, a true man-eater that could swallow a
whole dog in a single bite, or bite a man in half with
a snap of his jaws. The stories stuck with Lily, told in
Gitan's softest, most frightening voice and punctuated
by his trademark, "You know I might steal a little once
in a while, but Gitan, he never, ever lies!"

Hugh hooked a foot in front of Gitan's ankle and
yanked, knocking him on his face. "First man on the
log!" he crowed. Gitan reached the other side and
smacked him hard.

Lily looked at Michel, who watched with wide eyes.
"Maybe we should just go home," he said, quietly, so
the others wouldn't hear and know he was too frightened to continue. "Mama wouldn't be too pleased if

I got gulped down by a gator, and I surely do hate the thought of her bein' upset with me."

Lily's insides twisted and writhed at the thought of going home before she was forced to. It was something she wouldn't admit to anyone, but she feared her father far more than the gators, and the gators were a near-crippling preoccupation with her. When life at home became nearly unbearable for her, she would dream of alligators, only they were half man, too, with pinching fingers and Daddy's sometimes pleading, sometimes angry voice. "It's so early," Lily argued. "And maybe it isn't as scary as it looks. Like a trip to the dentist, when you think he'll use the drill and it's just to get your teeth cleaned instead? Tell you what . . . I'll go first, and you can hold my hand. If we fall, at least we'll be together."

From the far shore, Gitan coaxed the two younger members of their ragtag little band, while Hugh nursed the nosebleed he'd earned. "C'mon, Lily! Step on up and don' look down! Michel, you can make it, man!"

"They're both too chickenshit to walk the Indian bridge!" Hugh said, his brow clouded and expression sullen. He wiped his streaming nose on the hem of his T-shirt. "Don't know why the fuck you bother with those two, anyway!" He had obviously found his second wind because he got to his feet and tucked his hands into his armpits. "Bock, bock, bock!" he cried, flapping his arms like wings. "Bock, bock, bock! Hey, Chicken Lily, bet you think the sky's falling!"

"You kiss my ass, Hugh Lothair!" Lily told him. "I'm not afraid, and neither is Michel!"

Hugh's face reddened, and his blue eyes flashed his anger. "That's some big talk for a girl. Let's see you walk the bridge!"

Lily stepped onto the log, and on the bank a few

yards distant, a sluggish gator began to move toward the water.

"C'mon, *cher!*" Gitan shouted. "Show him what you got!"

Lily pushed down her fear and took a step as the gator slid into the water.

Somehow, through sheer tenacity, she made it across and Michel, rather than leave her, found the courage to follow. . . .

The memory faded. Lily blinked. It had always been that way, with Gitan leading the way, inviting her to try new things, to dare far more than she otherwise would have, to risk it all. What was life without risk? She'd risked it all when she walked away from Hugh and cut ties with this place, gambling everything on a new start. A new place, a new job, a new life . . .

And look how it had turned out.

Somewhere along the way, her perfect plan had begun to unravel. She'd been assigned a high-profile case, and she'd blown it. The DA had called it a "make or break" opportunity, a wealthy young socialite accused of killing her father, allegations of sexual abuse, a mind so traumatized that one day it just snapped. The irony of what followed had been almost laughable. She'd thought she could handle it. She'd thought she was tough enough to get past old ghosts to see that justice was done. She'd been fully prepared to walk into that courtroom and portray the accused as a spoiled rich girl who had taken a life and deserved to be punished . . . then, she had looked into the girl's eyes and saw herself reflected there, and it all fell apart.

Haunted by half memories of the night her own life had come undone, Lily continued to tread dangerously uncertain ground. One misstep, and she could easily be lost.

Even worse, she could take Gitan with her.

History repeating itself.

"Do you remember the Indian Bridge that crossed the inlet? It took everything I had not to turn and run. I was terrified of falling, afraid of the alligators— kind of like now—only this time I'm not just afraid for myself. I'm afraid for you."

"You know there's no need for that."

"That's not what I see. I came back to Angelique because I'd lost a friend who was everything to me." She smiled sadly. "Miracles happen, and I found another. I don't want to lose him, too. You've already sacrificed too much for me."

He leaned back onto his heels. "This about Hugh?"

Lily put every ounce of conviction in her tone that she could muster. At the peak of her career she'd been able to sway a jury and make them see the light, because the outcome of the trial had been her absolute focus. Now, her focus had to be untangling the mess her life had become.

Like it or not, Hugh was a primary factor in all of this. He would take down Gitan just for spite if things continued to escalate between them. Yet, maybe with some distance between them, there was a chance he would come to his senses and drop his vendetta. Rose's scathing criticisms had brought it all home to her earlier that evening, and for the first time since her arrival, she saw things clearly. Gitan had too much to lose. "It's not about Hugh. It's about me, it's about Michel, and it's about doing what I feel is right. I can't afford to go on being selfish, and neither can you."

He still leaned in close, his hand braced on the door

frame. As he bent to kiss her, Lily stepped back, closing the storm door.

Message received.

He stepped back, and the look on his dark face cut Lily to the quick.

She didn't watch him leave, afraid her resolve would melt and she would beg him to come back. Instead, she went inside, closing the door, leaning against it, her dry but burning eyes closed as she listened to the Harley rev to life. A few seconds later, he was nothing more than a mechanical purr in the distance, and Lily could only pray she'd done the right thing.

Mason wasn't sure why he'd chosen to come back here. It was weird enough in the daylight; after dark he half expected to see the Crypt Keeper hanging around, or to interrupt a bunch of Satan-worshippers, complete with black robes and cowls that hid their faces, human sacrifice, and all the rest. Just the thought creeped him out, and he was starting to regret his spur-of-the-moment choice of a place to hide out.

He should have dragged Gonzales with him. That would have made better sense, but it was too late for that, and he couldn't go back without being found.

Gitan would be out looking for him, checking his favorite haunts and interrogating his friends. For once, Mason couldn't blame Gitan. He was just doing what he felt he had to do, only Mase wasn't ready to face Rose. No way could he look at her without speaking his mind, and calling her a bitch would just land him in more hot water . . . even if it was true.

He'd put a lot of time and effort into the evening,

and for once his motives had been completely unselfish.

All he'd wanted was to bring his family together. Why couldn't anyone see that?"

Mama and Daddy were gone, but Gitan was back home, and if Rose would just forget about being pissed at Lily, things could be good again. Maybe even better than good. Lily was the one for Gitan. She could make him happy, like his old self, and it would almost be like he'd never been away at all.

So he'd done a little scheming to make it happen. So what? Everybody needed a good shove now and then. Besides, it was the end result that mattered, not how they all got there. It might have worked, too . . . if Rose hadn't opened her mouth and ruined everything. . . .

So caught up in his thoughts that he didn't stop to think about what he was doing, he pushed through the doors of the abandoned church and took several steps into the sanctuary before he realized the building wasn't empty, and he wasn't alone.

A voice that cut through the stillness, desperate and filled with emotion, pleading for forgiveness. To run would have been the smart thing, but Mase recognized the voice.

"Bless me, Father, for I have sinned. . . ." He was down on his knees in the filth, his face buried in his hands, and from where Mase stood, he could see his shoulders shaking. Seconds ticked by. Mase wanted to run, but he couldn't seem to peel himself away from the man's tearful confession. What he was hearing didn't make sense. He didn't make a sound, didn't dare draw a breath as he listened, but it didn't matter. The kneeling figure seemed to notice he was no longer alone and turned eyes on him that burned with torment.

"You were the one," Mase said with amazement. "You killed Father Dugas?"

"Son, you shouldn't have come here," he said, getting to his feet. "Why did you have to come here?" He didn't give the boy time to answer, lunging at him, wrapping big hands around his throat . . . and he could tell by the disbelief in Mason Boudreaux's eyes as he squeezed the breath from his lungs that he didn't even know he was dying.

CHAPTER FIFTEEN

"Is that a taxi out front? It is. It's a taxi." Edna Mae pushed the curtains aside to peer out the window. She had a permanent squint, but she was too vain to wear eyeglasses. "Well, dear me, that pot on the stove is about to boil over! Miss Lily, why don't you see who that is while I check the rice?"

The phone in Virginia's hospital room rang, and rang, and rang. Portable phone in hand, Lily walked to the window in time to see the driver open the rear passenger door. Virginia stepped out, and Lily hung up the phone. The door opened as she reached the foyer and the cabby set her overnight bag inside, accepting the bill Virginia tucked into his palm with a smile and polite "thank you, ma'am."

Virginia breezed into the house as if nothing out of the ordinary had just happened, as if she took a taxi home from the hospital every day. She bussed Lily's cheek as she passed down the hallway to the kitchen.

Stunned, Lily followed. "Aunt Virginia? What are you doing here?"

"Well, that's a silly question, sugar. This is my home. Where else would I be?"

"In the hospital, undergoing a battery of tests?"

"Oh, that. It's nothing that can't wait until a less busy time. Did you realize that the Annual Crawfish Festival is next week? It's a big draw for tourists, and I have a ton of work to do to prepare for it. Work that won't get done with me lyin' on my back in some hospital room."

Lily frowned. There was more to it, she was certain. Virginia's tone was a little too bright, a little too carefree. "Does Dr. Trelawney know you checked yourself out?"

"He does," Virginia replied, busying herself filling the bag she always carried with her to the antiques shop with fruit and bottled water. "I left him with a bug in his ear, and he richly deserved it. Do you know that he insisted I see a specialist? A neuro-something-or-other who specializes in psychological testing. Psychological testing, mind you! He's got a lot of nerve, and I told him so; then I gathered my things and came home."

"You paid that doctor for his opinion and you're not gonna hear it?" Edna Mae snorted. "Why am I not surprised?"

Virginia rounded on her housekeeper. "Spoken like someone who wasn't being subjected to a long list of indignities! I have my pride, you know."

Lily stepped between the two women in an attempt to defuse the tension. "Aunt Virginia, what did the doctor have to say?"

"Oh, just some mumbo jumbo about my arteries bein' clear." She shook her head, reaching into a cupboard for a coffee cup. "Clear arteries are supposed to be a good thing—and he doubts *my* sanity? Incompetent quack." She shook a finger at Edna Mae, who clucked her tongue in disapproval. "Not a word out of you. I pay you to be my ally, not my enemy, and I am *not* going back there."

Lily pressed her fingertips to the center of her forehead. She'd lain awake for hours, unable to forget Rose Boudreaux's accusations, worrying about Mason. Then, when she'd finally drifted off, she'd dreamt about Gitan's being sent back to prison, a dreadful dream from which she'd awakened in a cold sweat, heart pounding. The effects of the nightmare had proved impossible to shed. "No one's going to force you to do something you don't want to do," Lily assured her. "But I'd still like to hear Dr. Trelawney out before closing that door completely."

Virginia set her chin stubbornly, and she refused to give an inch. "I've listened to him all I'm goin' to." She went to the freezer and took down the Rocky Road. "Edna Mae, why on earth did you take this down?" she asked, lifting the coffee cup. "You know I can't drink coffee this late in the morning. I've already had one cup, and too much caffeine gives me the jitters." She placed the cup back in the cupboard, triumphantly closing the door. "Ice cream, anyone?"

Edna Mae planted a fist on one hip. "At ten-thirty in the morning?"

"I can tell time," Virginia assured her. "But who made the rule that I can't have ice cream for breakfast if I want? I'm done with worryin' over what's appropriate, and what's not! To hell with rules and convention. I'm gonna live life while I can. Maybe I'll even have two scoops and we'll call it an all-out rebellion. Lily? You'll have some, won't you?"

Lily shook her head. The very thought made her nauseous. "No, thanks, but you go ahead."

"After last night, she's probably had her fill of cake and ice cream for a while," Edna Mae said cryptically.

Virginia looked at Edna Mae, then at Lily. "Something happened? Worse, something happened that you're keeping from me?"

"You gonna tell her? Or should I? It's all over town, you know. I found out when I went by the market this morning to pick up some collard greens. Better she hears it from you than from some old gossip with time on her hands."

"Too late for that," Lily muttered. There was damn little that went on in Angelique that didn't reach Edna Mae's sharp ears eventually.

Virginia frowned, looking a good deal older than she had a moment ago. "Lily Justine, what is goin' on around here?"

"Mason invited me to his aunt's birthday party," Lily admitted. "It was a special request—or so he claimed—that she had made. Only he wasn't exactly telling the truth, and the whole thing blew up in his face—and mine."

"Blew up how?" Virginia asked.

"Rose Boudreaux seen our gal and went off like a Roman candle, that's how."

"Bobby's aunt? That big-mouthed, controlling old harpy?"

Edna Mae looked smug. "That's her, all right. Never did like that woman."

Lily's head felt as if it would split wide open if she didn't get away for a little while. She needed to escape Virginia's indignation, and the dilemma of what to do about her refusal to have the tests she obviously needed. She'd been on the verge of calling

Gitan all morning to be certain that he'd found
Mase, and that he'd managed to smooth things over
with his aunt, but she'd been reluctant after turning
him away as she had last night. She was rapidly becoming the queen of mixed signals and feeling
slightly schizophrenic. Sleep with him, then keep him
at arm's length, let him make love to her till she was
weak in the knees and then push him away. She
didn't want to do that. He didn't deserve to be
treated carelessly, and he didn't need the added
complication of involvement with someone as
screwed up as she happened to be.

As she'd always been.

What would he have done with his life if he'd
stayed away from her?

What would he have become? Would he have his
degree? Would he have his own studio? The recognition he deserved?

But he hadn't stayed away, and their association,
their love affair, had not only nearly destroyed him,
it had cost him seven years of his life. "I'm going out
for a while," Lily said, as much to stop the circuitous
path her thoughts had taken as to simply get away.

"Out where, sugar?"

"I don't know."

"Well, when will you be back?"

"I don't know." She grabbed her keys and all but ran
from the house, but even with the radio blasting and
miles of highway behind her she couldn't quite squash
the idea that there must be some way to make sense
of the mess her life had become.

She drove to the sign welcoming visitors to Jeffer-
son Davis Parish, pulling off onto the shoulder where
she sat for a long time before she turned the car
around . . . and she still had no answers.

* * *

Early leaned in, concentrating on the phone call he was making. "Gene? It's Ruben. Listen, when you gonna have an answer for me? Four days? Why four days? What'd you mean the application has to be put before the board? We've always done business on a handshake before." He sucked his breath in through his teeth and tried to get a grip on his rising anger. "Look, you know I'm a good risk, so what's the problem?" Closing his eyes against the pile of unpaid bills in his "in" basket, he pinched the bridge of his nose. "Standard procedure. Yeah, I get it. You'll let me know? Thanks." He hung up the phone, muttering, "Thanks—yeah, thanks. Thanks for nothing."

A light tap of a knuckle on his door frame. Early glanced up, startled. "Gitan. You need somethin'?"

Gitan Boudreaux was the most capable, hardest-working man in the whole damned shop. He went about his business without Ruben riding his ass, and he was as respectful as he was focused.

This afternoon, however, he looked distracted. "I hate to do this, but I've got to ask for the afternoon off. I need to talk to Hugh at the sheriff's department."

"Is Lothair still givin' you grief? Cause if he is, I can talk to him, ask him to back off. The man's a persistent pain in the ass."

"No. It's nothin' like that. Actually, it's personal business. Mason didn't come home last night."

"Mason? No kidding? I'd expect that of Willie, but Mase is a good kid." He sat back in his chair and the leather creaked. "You don't think he's in some kind of trouble?"

Gitan raised a hand and absently rubbed the back of his neck. "To be honest with you, I don' know what to think. He had an argument with Rose and ran off, and we ain't seen him since. Rose, she's beside herself with worry, and I've got to do what I can to fix it."

Ruben nodded. "Sure thing. Take the afternoon, and let me know what happens. I know what a worry kids can be."

"Thanks, Ruben. I appreciate it, and I'll make up the hours as soon as I locate the kid." Gitan went immediately to the sheriff's department. It was almost one o'clock, but the sheriff was just breaking for lunch. Ignoring Amy, Hugh's receptionist, Gitan walked right in, not even bothering to knock. He figured Hugh owed him that much for having his skinhead deputy trash his place when he "searched" for potential evidence that was right out in the open.

Hugh's muffuletta was halfway to his mouth when Gitan slid into a chair. "Now, why do I get the feeling that this is going to totally obliterate my appetite?"

"I need to talk to you about Mason," Gitan said. "He didn't come home last night, and Rose is convinced he's in some kind of trouble."

Hugh bit into the olive salad sandwich, chewing and swallowing before answering, reluctant to let anything spoil that first succulent bite. "Shirley Moseby makes *the* best muffuletta this side of N'awlins. As for Mason, I wouldn't be surprised if Rose is right, considerin' trouble is pretty much his MO. What is it about you Boudreauxs, anyhow? Always in some kind of hot water, always givin' somebody grief. Hell, even Rose isn't immune to it. I heard about her landin' on Lily, and I sure as hell didn't like it."

"Well, for once we agree on somethin'," Gitan shot back. "What the hell are you gonna do about findin' Mason?"

"Not much I *can* do, other than file a missing

persons report. Since he's a juvenile, we can waive the standard twenty-four-hour waiting period."

"A piece of paper ain't likely to locate him, now is it? That takes manpower, and you aren't gonna expend it in a search for him, because he's just a Boudreaux, ain't that right, *mon ami?*"

"File the report, Boudreaux. Deputy Crebs'll help you, but do me a favor and get out of my face. By the time I finish this sandwich, and before the ink dries on the report, Mason'll be back at Rose's with a joystick in his hand. You know it, and I know it." He flipped on the intercom. "Amy, ask Deputy Crebs to get his ass in here."

"Sheriff?"

"Mr. Boudreaux wants to file a missing persons on his brother, who happens to be a juvenile. Take care of it, will you? And warn everybody in the outer office that I intend to drill the next idiot to walk through this door before I finish this sandwich."

Gitan sat with Crebs, answering questions and watching the man type the report into a typewriter. A typewriter. There was just one computer in the building, and it was in Hugh's office. Crebs used the hunt-and-peck method of typing, two fingers only, and proved so interminably slow that it took every ounce of self-restraint Gitan had to keep from taking hold of him and shaking the snail's pace right out of him.

"Name of missing person?"

"Mason Edward Boudreaux."

"Age, height, weight, and physical description."

"Fifteen years of age. Five feet eight inches tall, weight one hundred forty-five pounds. Dark hair, dark eyes, a slight scar on his chin from wrecking his bicycle when he was twelve. He had five stitches."

"Where did you last see the person in question?"

"The Boudreaux residence on Tupelo Avenue."

And all the while, Gitan's mind was elsewhere, leaping ahead, questioning. Where the hell was Mase? Was he pulling this stunt to get attention? To shake Rose up? Because it sure as hell was working. Or was he hurt somewhere? Had he run off? Beyond the parish? Headed for Baton Rouge, or worse, New Orleans? He could lose himself in the city, and they wouldn't find him unless he wanted to be found. But would he do that to his family? Disappear without a trace?

It sure as hell didn't seem like something Mase would do. He was just fifteen, but he'd always been fairly responsible, except when his temper got in the way. The two of them may have had their problems, but Mase loved Rose. She'd been the closest thing to a mother to the boy since his own mama died. Gitan just couldn't imagine Mason wanting her to fret over him for more than an hour or two . . . until his temper cooled, and he calmed down.

Crebs finished writing the report. His ruddy face was shiny with sweat, despite the air conditioning and the slow-moving fans overhead. But then, he was a northerner, a Yankee, unused to the heat and humidity of southern Louisiana. The accent was a dead giveaway. "I'll file this, and if he turns up, we'll call you."

Gitan left the station unsatisfied, but it was Hugh and Crebs he was dealing with, so his expectations hadn't been all that high going into it. All he was doing was trying to cover all the bases. This way, if Mase ran and got picked up outside the parish, they'd already know he was missing. If not—hell, he didn't want to think about everything that *could* happen, so he kept on looking.

* * *

Back at the sheriff's department Hugh stared glumly at the muffuletta lying only moderately touched on the Styrofoam plate. He picked it up with both hands—the things were too damned big to do otherwise—brought it to his mouth, then put it back on the plate. "Crebs!" he yelled, not bothering with the intercom. "Get the hell in here!" Size twelves scuffed against the linoleum, and Hugh wondered why his deputy never lifted his feet.

"Sheriff?"

Sheriff. Not boss, or Hugh, or hello asshole. Always respectful, even though he knew the man didn't like him—and even that irritated him. "I want your take on this situation. What are the chances the Boudreaux kid is anything *but* a runaway?"

Crebs shifted the toothpick from side to side in his mouth by rolling it with his tongue. "Slim to none. He's probably holed up at a friend's place, or he's hitched a ride to a relative's. He'll be back before sundown, or they'll get a call; I guarantee it."

"You just echoed my thoughts exactly," Hugh said, sounding disgusted. "So, why do I have this sinking feeling where my appetite was before Gitan walked in here?"

Crebs jammed a meaty thumb over his left shoulder. "I got some Tums in my desk—"

"Yeah?" He feigned hopefulness just for the sheer hell of it. "Well, take your Tums and get bent. I've got shit to take care of." Crebs went back to his desk and Hugh got down to business, and eventually all thought of Mason Boudreaux and his whereabouts faded before the more pressing problem of finding Michel Dugas's killer. He jotted down the facts one more time, hoping when he saw it in his own handwriting, it would jar something loose.

He glanced once again at the fax from St. Bart's that Murdoch's assistant had sent. There was a long list of names culled from church records of the youth softball team, listed in chronological order for the past three years—the length of time Dugas had been serving and coaching at St. Bart's. The names were easily recognizable, familiar names around Angelique. Hugh knew most of their parents, aunts, uncles, and cousins, and he wondered if one of them had a motive for murder. Crebs had a duplicate list and would be back out conducting interviews this afternoon, along with Sergeant Fred Rally.

The second list was brief. A half-dozen kids, all boys, ranging in age from twelve to seventeen. Johnny Eckland, Tim Rosal, Jimmy Martinez, Remy Fontaine, Mason Boudreaux, and William T. Early. None of the names really surprised him, except for Willie Early, Ruben's kid.

Willie had a 1969 Pontiac GTO Judge that looked showroom-new, and mighty deep pockets for a kid who didn't have a job. Hugh had caught him drag racing near Sandy Flats the previous summer, but he'd let him go with a warning and a call to his daddy. The boy had been drinking at the time. Ruben had promised it wouldn't happen again.

And it hadn't. Or, at least Willie hadn't been caught.

Nobody liked Willie much, including Hugh. The kid had a truckload of attitude, but so did Mason Boudreaux and a whole shitload of teenage kids he could have named. Attitude was nothing new to teenage boys, but something about these kids in particular had caused their parents or guardians to seek counseling, and he intended to find out what that was.

He flicked the intercom button, then picked up his suit coat. "Amy, I'm goin' out. If an emergency crops up, have dispatch call my cellular."

"Will do, Sheriff. Is there anything else?"

"Not at the moment."

Hugh started at the top of the list and worked his way down. By two that afternoon, he was satisfied that the first three kids didn't constitute leads. Johnny Eckland was being raised by an elderly grandmother who had found a pack of condoms tucked away in the corner of his sock drawer, and panicked. Tim Rosal had religious leanings, and was genuinely interested in the seminary. Michel had been "kind enough," Rosal said, to speak with him honestly about what it was like being a priest. The kid was still sitting on the fence, but Hugh left his house and crossed his name off the list. The Martinez kid was heavily into drugs, presently in rehab, and his father was just plain angry. He put a question mark beside Martinez's name, jotted down a few observations, and moved on.

It was nearly four-thirty when Hugh knocked on the door to Ruben's office and answered the call to "come in." Ruben had a hand pushed into his short scrub of graying hair and was punching buttons on a desk calculator while the machine pushed a rolled printout onto the desk. Early held up one finger and continued to crunch numbers for a full sweep of the second hand on the office clock. Finally he finished the tally and sat back, but he looked anything but at ease. "Sorry to keep you waiting, Hugh. What can I do for you?"

"Rough day, Ruben?" Hugh asked.

"Rough day in a string of rough days," Early said. "You'd think I'd be used to it by now. It just doesn't get any easier. It was a real tough summer in a business sense, and now that things are finally starting to turn around, I get a summons to appear in court. The ex-wife has decided that she needs an adjustment in her alimony. Honestly, she took one of my nuts in the settlement. Now, it looks like she wants a matched set." He shook his head. "Oh, hell, I don't need to tell you about this. You're divorced, right?"

"Lily didn't want alimony," Hugh replied. *She'd wanted her freedom. She'd wanted an end to the constant fighting. She'd hated the adversarial tone their relationship had taken. The pathetic part of that is that I don't know how to do anything else.*

"No alimony. That's fucking amazing."

"Maybe," Hugh said with a shrug. He hadn't come here to talk about Lily, their marriage, their divorce, or his never-ending disappointment in the way things had worked out. "You got a few minutes? I need to ask you some questions."

"Sure thing. Mind if I ask what it's about?" Ruben folded his hands on the top of the desk, hands that were visibly irritated. The palms appeared cracked, and in a few places, his knuckles had broken open and bled a little. It was obvious he'd cleaned them up, but there was no concealing the damage.

It was one of those small details that Hugh picked up on and found impossible to ignore, even though it didn't mean anything. "Willie's name came up in the course of the Dugas murder investigation."

Ruben's weariness seemed to weigh a little more heavily upon him. The furrows at the corners of his eyes seemed deeper somehow, and his shoulders were hunched. "You're kidding, right? I mean, Willie's an irresponsible little shit sometimes, but he couldn't kill anybody."

"Relax, Ruben," Hugh said. "I didn't say he was a suspect. Somethin' wrong with your hands?"

For one split second, Early looked startled, like somebody caught doing something they shouldn't do; then almost as fast as it had appeared, his surprise was gone, replaced by an almost too casual attitude. "Oh, this? It's from the acetone. I tore the engine on the Indian apart and soaked it in the solvent to clean it, but I got some on my hands. It's hard on the skin, but hell on old grease and grime. That baby's as shiny as a new penny. It's no big deal. I can always grow new skin, right?"

A short bark of a laugh, maybe a little nervous-sounding. *Nervous because of the shape of his hands? Or because of his mention of Willie?*

"You said Willie's name came up in your investigation." His voice sounded tired, Hugh thought. Not just tired—exhausted. "Level with me, Hugh. What's this about?"

"It's come to my attention that Willie was bein' counseled by the deceased. You've been havin' problems with him for a while?"

"Only every day or so." It was said jokingly, but there was no trace of humor in that rock-hard face. Hugh knew a little of Ruben's background. An ex-marine who'd been in Saigon when it fell to the North Vietnamese, he'd been married twice, and had started his family late in life. He must have been in his forties when Willie was born. He'd kept in shape, though, and he was strong as an ox. It was a little amazing that he couldn't seem to handle one seventeen-year-old. "I seem to recall something about that," Ruben said. "But that was months ago. The ex-wife thought it might help him gain perspective."

"You didn't agree?"

Early shrugged. "I suppose you could say I'm from the old school. I don't believe a man should whine, whether it's to a psychiatrist or his priest. Everybody's got problems. Kids today—they just don't seem to be able to handle anything. Maybe if they had to stand alone once in a while, they'd learn to take responsibility. Can't say I cared much for her choice of counselors, either. No disrespect, but he seemed a little light in the loafers, if you know what I mean?"

"How long did Willie get counseling from Dugas?"

"Six months, maybe? I don't know, exactly."

"During that time, did you ever notice anything odd pertaining to his meetings with Dugas?"

Another shrug. "It didn't help straighten him out, if that's what you mean. Damn kid." Early's heavy brows came together. "Hey, wait a minute. You're not suggesting—you think that fucking pansy put the moves on these kids?"

"I'm not suggesting anything, Ruben. I'm saying it's a possibility, that's all." And that was all Hugh was likely to say. "So, you were aware of Dugas's sexual orientation before Willie started counseling?"

"Weren't you?" It wasn't an answer, and the man seemed to realize it a half beat later. "Yeah, I knew. It was kinda hard not to notice. Not exactly overloaded with testosterone, if you know what I mean? A little too soft looking, a little too sensitive. Maybe I've got a sixth sense about these things, but yeah, I knew, and I didn't care much for the wife sending my son to spend time with him. Kids are impressionable."

"You never did answer my question, Ruben. Did you have reason to believe that Michel Dugas made sexual advances toward Willie?" Hugh knew that he was pushing the envelope, but sometimes it was the only way to get results.

"No. Willie would have told me if he had," Ruben insisted.

Hugh pushed back in his chair and fixed the bigger man with a level look. "Correct me if I'm wrong, but a minute ago you indicated that your relationship with Willie was strained. Now, you're tellin' me that he would have felt comfortable confiding something of a highly personal nature in you? Which is it?"

Ruben's scowl never wavered. "I'm his daddy. He would've told me if somethin' like that was goin' on. You can take my word for it and drop this, or you can talk to my lawyer. It's your choice, Hugh. Either way, we're through here."

"Just askin', Ruben, and yeah, I'll take your word for it. I've got no reason not to." Hugh closed the notepad on which he'd been jotting notes and stood.

Ruben released a breath and his anger evaporated. "So, when are you gonna let us build you a bike?" he asked, the affable businessman once again.

"On my salary?" Hugh just laughed. "That's funny, Ruben. Real funny."

Ruben walked out with him, stopping at the garage door. "Good luck with the investigation. I sure hope you find what you're lookin' for." He watched Hugh Lothair as he got into his car and drove away, checking to see if the sheriff glanced in his rearview mirror. Not even once. Then, he frowned down at his hands.

The house on Kyme Road was closed for the summer, but Lily still had a key. Parking her car in the circular drive, she got out and stood for a few minutes, staring up at the dark windows, as if she might glimpse a small and unhappy face gazing down at her, or hear Michel's tap on the window glass, the rattle of the tree branches against the house as they made their escape. But all was quiet and still, the only sound the buzz of a lawn trimmer running somewhere in the distance.

Time was supposed to heal wounds and change perceptions, but Lily's wounds were fresh, and the house that seemed so large, so scary when she was little was still a place of dread. Her pulse accelerated as she inserted the key in the lock, and a lump of dread the size of her fist had lodged in the pit of her stomach. It took every ounce of courage she possessed not to get back in her car and drive away. "You've been running away all your life," she said softly, "and where has it gotten you?" The door latch fell under her hand and the heavy mahogany door swung slowly inward. . . . *"Welcome home, Lily," the heavy shadows beyond the open door seemed to whisper. "It's been far too long. . . ."*

Lily took a deep breath and stepped over the threshold and into her past, closing the door.

The window shades were drawn to keep the sunlight from fading the draperies and furniture while Sharon was away, turning the interior shady and dim. The air conditioning was set high at eighty degrees in order to conserve electricity and because comfort wasn't a consideration in an unoccupied house. The unit helped take some of the moisture out of the air and kept the woodwork from gathering mildew, but it wasn't much help with the stale smell that had invaded the place.

For a moment, Lily stood inside the foyer, wondering what had possessed her to come here in the first place. What did she hope to find? Had she made a mistake? Did she really expect to uncover some revelation that would erase the past and make her whole again? When had she become so naive? So unrealistic?

As she walked from room to shadowed room, she

gained no new insight into what had happened the night Gitan was shot, and her father murdered. There was only the silence, unbroken except for the sound of her footfalls, and the soft continuous swish of the air pouring from the registers.

From the foyer, to the living room, the formal dining room, and kitchen. Lily ran a finger across the marble countertop. It came away covered in dust, and her mother's words, from the letter she'd received the week before Michel's murder, seemed to echo through the empty rooms.

> *Sugar, I just can't tell you how refreshing it is to not have to wage a constant battle with mold, mildew, and lichen. Normally, I come back to Angelique for the holidays, but this year I may just stay put. After all, I've little family left since Justin's unfortunate death—with you off in California—did you realize the current governor of California was an actor? How tacky! And the earthquakes! Why, how ever do you sleep at night?*

Lily had smiled at her mother's innocent question. Why, how ever do you sleep at night?

I don't sleep, mostly, but it has nothing to do with California's earthquakes, and everything to do with the ghosts of Angelique.

Sharon was clueless, and always had been. She hadn't known about the monster she'd married because she went out of her way to avoid unpleasantness. Anything that might upset her was carefully shunned, including the bruises on her little girl's arms and her terror of bedtime. If a worry arose, it was quickly put to sleep with a double martini, minus the olive.

Others, however, *had* noticed.

"Hey, cher, what happened? You're all black and blue!" Gitan's voice.

Lily closed her eyes, surprised at the sharp stab of emotion welling up inside her.

"I fell," Lily heard herself say, a voice small, but brave, and only she understood what the lie she'd been ordered to tell cost her. . . .

She wandered like a wraith, back down the hall, stopping at the study door, unsure she wanted to go in. She checked the thought. It wasn't about want. It was about need. She needed to know what had happened here the night Justin died. She needed to know everything that had happened, because right now she was unable to tell the truth from well-meaning lies.

The truth shall set you free. Or, destroy you, Lily thought. Either way, she had to know. Bracing as if for an assault, she turned the knob and walked in.

The room was little changed, except for the silvery blue carpet. The original carpet had been white.

White carpet, red blood . . . The image lodged in her mind, shimmering like a heat devil in the distance, threatening and surreal. . . .

He was dead.

Gitan was dead, and she was floating a few feet above him, looking down at his still, pale face, looking down at the pathetic figure curled into a fetal position near Gitan who must have been herself, then into Virginia's worried face. "My God, Lily. Sugar, can you hear me?"

She couldn't reply. The shock had been too much. She seemed incapable of rational thought, incapable of anything. Gitan was dead. He was dead. That dreadful knowledge was all that mattered and there was nothing beyond it but a gaping black void. Lily stared into the darkness inside her and knew it was warm and safe. Without a struggle, without a shred of resistance, she turned and embraced it, but as conscious awareness faded, she had the vague impression of something unsettling happening on the outside. Raised voices, angry but indistinct, followed by the scream of a siren in the distance.

Voices . . .

Now, Lily grabbed onto that. She remembered voices.

Too far away, too indistinct for her to determine who they belonged to or what was being said. One had to have been Justin's; the only thing she could be sure of about the second voice was that it hadn't been Gitan's.

CHAPTER
SIXTEEN

Rose called the sheriff's department every hour on the hour, demanding to speak to Hugh personally, but Hugh wasn't in. The nice young sergeant was polite and very sympathetic, and he did his best to reassure her that everything would work out without making promises he couldn't keep. The police were experts at being noncommittal. "We'll do the best we can to find your nephew, Miz Boudreaux. I think the sheriff may be out looking right now."

The sheriff, whether he was looking for Mason or not, didn't inspire confidence in Rose. She remembered him as a boy, and he'd been a mean little shit. Besides that, he didn't speak French, which in her eyes meant he wasn't to be trusted completely. She had no idea why Gitan had ever given him the time of day, except that Gitan had been a good boy, generous to his friends, loyal and tolerant, a lot like Mason.

Mason, at times, was too tolerant, too forgiving. The Martin girl was a fine example. He had somehow

gotten it into his head Lily Martin would be good for
Gitan, that they belonged together, and he'd been
working toward that end with all the subtlety of a
steamroller. "Over my dead body," Rose said, angry
all over again just thinking about it. This whole mess
was that Martin girl's fault. If she'd stayed away from
the party, then none of this would have happened, she
wouldn't have said what she said, and Mase would be
at home where he belonged.

"Holy Mother, hear my prayers," she said, standing
vigil on the screened porch. "Keep Mason safe, and
bring him home. He's a good boy, and I can't bear
the thought that something might ha—" She clapped
a hand over her mouth, unwilling to speak the words
for fear they would come true. "Just hear my prayers,
that's all, and send him home. Just send him home."

Rose's prayers went unanswered.

Mason didn't come home that night, and neither
did Gitan. He'd been in and out of his truck so often
that day that he swore he had blisters on his ass.
He'd combed the neighborhood, knocking on doors
and asking the same questions again and again. He'd
gone to the Pink Cadillac to talk to Amalie, but she
hadn't seen the kid, either. She promised to keep an
eye out and let him know if Mase turned up. When
he'd exhausted every possibility, he'd taken his boat
out onto the bayou, checking his brother's favorite
fishing haunts, but he found nothing.

When he dragged home near dawn the next day,
Rose met him on his screened porch. She was standing at the door looking out, and he could see that
she'd been crying. Her eyelids were swollen and her
handkerchief was wadded in her hand.

"Is there news?" Gitan somehow managed to

squeeze the question past the lump of dread in his throat.

She shook her head. *"Non,* but I was hopin'—"

She'd been hoping he would pull off a miracle, walk in the door with the kid, and everything would be just like always. He'd managed to do it half a hundred times since he came home from Angola, dragging his kid brother back to the straight and narrow, ragging on him about his grades, skipping school, and mouthing off. But this time it was different, and he seemed to be fresh out of miracles.

Fatigue rode him almost as hard as his worry did, and the nagging insistence deep in his gut that something was terribly wrong. He did his best to spare Rose his concerns, knowing she had enough of her own without his adding to it. He accepted the steaming mug she handed him, inhaling appreciatively before taking a sip. *"Merci.* Nobody makes coffee like you."

Her hand fluttered to her face, then down again, as if operating independently from the rest of her and unsure exactly what to do. "I brought my French press from the house. I didn't know what else to do. I've scrubbed the kitchen floor three times, and the house just feels so empty—" She broke off, and a tear rolled down her cheek. "Mother of God, Gitan. What we gonna do? This is my fault. I never should've landed on him so hard. Not after him makin' such a fuss over an old woman's birthday."

Gitan set the coffee aside and put his arms around her. "We're gonna find him, that's what we're gonna do. We'll find him, and I don' want you beatin' yourself up over this. You did the best you could for him— for the both of us. Nobody can fault you for carin'."

She nodded, breaking away, strong again. "You drink that coffee. I got sandwiches in the kitchen, spicy chicken on fresh-baked French bread. None of that soggy white stuff they sell at the market. Did you talk to Mason's friends?"

"I went down the list you gave me, starting with the Gonzales kid. He says he ain't seen him. Same with the rest. Nobody's seen him. It's like he dropped off the planet."

Rose wrung the wrinkled scrap of white linen into a tight knot. "Did you call that Martin girl?"

"I spoke with Virginia. Lily wasn't home, and she didn't know where she was. She said she hadn't seen Mase, but she'd give Lily the message as soon as she gets in. She's got my number. Someone will call if he shows up over there." Mason's showing up at Lily's place was a distinct possibility, and they both knew it. He'd gone to a lot of trouble to get Lily to the birthday party, and it had blown up in all of their faces. It was likely that he'd try to apologize, or maybe even try again. The kid didn't give up easily; he had to give him that.

"You don' think he's run off for real?" Rose asked, putting voice to a question that had lingered in the back of Gitan's mind all day.

"Might be the best thing for us if he did, since the cops are keepin' an eye out for him. Kid his age can't exactly blend in and get lost." *Unless he made it to New Orleans, where anything could happen.* Kids hit the streets and got lost. It happened all the time . . . It just couldn't happen to his little brother. "Somebody'll notice him and ask questions."

She latched on to his reassurances and took whatever comfort she could from them. *"Mon dieu,* you're right, Gitan, and I should be home if they call. You gonna get some sleep, eh? You're wore out."

"I'm good for now. Think I'll grab a shower before

I head back out, though. A little hot water and this high octane of yours and I should be good for a few more hours." He lifted the mug in a salute, then took a sip. "Go on home. I'll call if I hear anything."

Rose stood on her toes to kiss his cheek, then wiped the lipstick smudge away with her fingertips and hurried home, leaving Gitan to face his fears alone.

Hugh wiped the steam from his bathroom mirror with the heel of his hand, then reached for his razor. It was five minutes of six in the morning and he hadn't slept. The lack of rest showed in the deepening of the creases at the outer corners of his eyes— eyes which were as bloodshot as a drunk's at the end of a two-day bender. He hadn't been drinking, though he'd reached a point when he'd grabbed a Heineken from the fridge. He'd opened it, put the bottle on a paper napkin in lieu of a coaster, and it sat there, sweating the napkin wet, and warming by slow degrees to a state of unpalatability.

Absorbed by the facts of the most difficult case of his career, while the hours ticked by and the night fled before a rising red sun, he went over and over the material spread out before him until he couldn't look at the photographs or diagrams or scrawled notations without seeing two of everything. He'd dragged his sorry ass to the shower and stood with hot water sluicing over his face until the water heater gave up the last ounce and the stream grew tepid. And still, he couldn't shake the feeling he was missing something, some minute detail that would break this case wide open.

He didn't have a fucking clue as to what that was.

The more he reviewed the crime scene photos, the

more frustrated he became. The report from the forensic pathologist had come back the afternoon before, and had basically said they had enough trace evidence to bring into question a little less than half of the town's resident population. If there was anything of value in the samples, they hadn't identified it yet. The only blood at the scene had belonged to the victim. The rope had been clean, and the person who'd used it had worn gloves, probably leather ones.

No help there, and it was back to square one.

Most homicides had one of two common denominators somewhere in the equation: sex or money. As far as he could tell, money didn't factor into Michel's death. Priests weren't big on bank accounts, and Michel had been no exception. A few hundred dollars in a savings account and a modest insurance policy with his mother as beneficiary were the extent of Michel's assets. The amount had been so small that it would barely have covered the costs of his funeral . . . and though at times murder could occur for little more than pocket change, Hugh was as certain as he could possibly be that that wasn't the case with the Dugas homicide.

Victims were shot or stabbed, or sometimes beaten over money.

They weren't crucified.

The person who had killed Michel had gone to great lengths to dehumanize him. The manner of death hadn't been merely unusual; it had been extreme, and he couldn't seem to get past the idea that there was a direct link between the manner of death and the victim's occupation. Not just a religious man—a priest, a man who had taken a vow to serve God, while serving the community.

Hugh had never been particularly interested in

religion, but he'd done his homework and knew that, while the practice of crucifixion dated back to 500 B.C., it had become a common method of execution during the Roman Empire. While Jesus had been the highest-profile victim to be killed in that particular fashion, it was Peter, an apostle, whose death had caught Hugh's attention.

Peter, the most popular of the twelve apostles, had been crucified, also. Yet, unlike Christ, Peter had been suspended from the cross upside down because he had felt unworthy of dying in the same manner as his savior.

Michel Dugas, a deeply devoted servant of Christ, had also been crucified upside down.

Like St. Peter.

Was there a connection . . . or was it just a bizarre coincidence?

Dugas had been strung up like a deer, the nylon rope strung through deep cuts between his ankle and Achilles tendon. There was significance in that. Not only would it have been excruciatingly painful for the victim, and a lot of trouble for the doer, it had been important that the victim be treated as an animal to slaughter.

Why?

Because it had been important to emphasize that Dugas was un-Christlike, more animal than man. Unworthy of a noble death?

Yet what about the motive? It had been driving him nuts for days. He'd turned it over in his mind endlessly, looking at every possible angle, obsessed about it, and gnashed his teeth at not being able to figure it out, yet in deconstructing the scene and events piece by piece he still couldn't seem to get past the two initial factors in most homicides. Money and sex. And if it wasn't money . . . then it was probably sex.

It was the only thing that made sense, and the hardest thing to confirm. As a priest, Michel had taken a vow of celibacy. Hugh snorted, tapping a cigarette out of his half-depleted pack and lighting it. He may have taken the vow, but that didn't mean he had kept it.

He inhaled and blew smoke out through his nostrils, all of his attention on the notes he'd been jotting down. "SEX" was written in large block letters, then underlined three times. Michel's ex-boyfriend, Keith Green, had claimed that his relationship with Dugas had been platonic because of Michel's devotion to his calling . . . but the possibility existed that Green didn't know everything. In fact, maybe he hadn't known Dugas as well as he'd thought.

Hugh had spent a good portion of the previous day interviewing the parents of the kids with whom Dugas had had prolonged contact. He'd listened to the parents talk about the murdered priest in glowing terms, and he'd been unable to detect even a hint of animosity or bitterness toward the priest. The regret that Dugas had met with such tragedy seemed genuine at first look. Not that he was about to leave it at that. He would interview each of them again, but not until he'd spoken to Rose Boudreaux and her eldest nephew.

In Hugh's opinion, the Boudreauxs were ass-deep in this . . . or at least Gitan was. Not only did he have a connection to the victim, he was determined enough to carry out the difficult task of hoisting an unconscious victim of Dugas's size off the floor and into the air without the aid of an accomplice. There was also no doubt that Mason Boudreaux was one troubled teen. The question was: were Mase's problems serious enough to provide Gitan with a motive for murder?

At six thirty-five that morning Hugh stopped at the café on Catalpa Street and bought a coffee. Bonnie Pinto took his money without a word. He'd arrested her brother six months ago for simple assault on the eve of her wedding, and he'd been unable to make bail or attend the ceremony. Bonnie carried a grudge longer than anyone in the parish, and hadn't spoken to him since.

For the sake of perversity, he went out of his way to drop by on her shift and indulge in a one-sided conversation, to which she stubbornly refused to reply. "Hey, Bonnie. Nice mornin', isn't it? How's Henry? I haven't seen him in a coon's age. You tell him I said hey." He lifted the Styrofoam cup to his face and took an appreciative sniff. "Coffee sure smells good this mornin'. Have a real nice day, now, you hear?"

Bonnie had a face as sharp as a hatchet and looked even more sour when Hugh went whistling from the café than she had when he'd walked in. He'd never liked her, so it didn't affect his mood one way or the other, and even before he opened his car door, his thoughts had returned to the investigation, the evidence, the interviews, the unanswered questions.

Something was missing, some crucial piece of the Dugas puzzle that kept it from falling into place. Unfortunately, the more time that passed, the less likely it was that the case would ever be solved.

It was the one facet of police work that Hugh had never reconciled himself to. He hated loose ends, especially when they had the potential to soil an otherwise blemish-free record.

Lily had accused him of being obsessive often enough, and maybe on some level he was, because this morning he couldn't let it go. Almost before he realized what he was doing, he'd taken the rutted track that led to Catfish Point and the old church. He'd been to the crime scene several times since the discovery of the body, but never quite so early in the morning.

Could be he'd turn up something new if he went over the scene of the murder one more time. Everything looked different this time of day. The angle of the light shifted and perspective changed, details became more glaringly apparent, and sometimes a man's luck could turn around unexpectedly.

Sometimes . . . but not today.

It was apparent almost as soon as Hugh stepped from the air-conditioned car and into the warm, moist morning that something wasn't right. The first thing he noticed were the few unbroken glass windowpanes, an opaque black in the sun-dappled morning light. Then, as he moved through the waist-high weeds, he realized the opaque mass was undulating.

Flies. Thousands of them, as attracted to the sickening smell of decomposing flesh as Hugh was repelled by it. Taking his neatly folded handkerchief from his pocket, he made his way to the front entrance. A few feet away, a bicycle lay discarded in the weeds. The decal on the back fender read: *The Chop Shop.* Below the decal, carefully lettered in black paint, were the initials *M.B.* Pushing the vestibule door open with the aid of the clean cloth to avoid leaving or marring any fingerprints, he walked in, careful to note where he stepped. The noise of the swarm was louder now, the scene like something out of a B-grade horror flick.

The body had been laid out as nicely as anything

Hugh had ever seen at Homer Folley's funeral parlor. His arms were crossed over his chest, and a jacket placed carefully under his head like a pillow. Hugh stood a moment longer, looking down at the body of the boy; then he went outside to use his cellular phone to dial the station and Crebs's extension.

His deputy answered on the first ring. "Angelique Sheriff's Department, Deputy Crebs speaking."

"Crebs, it's Hugh. We've got another body at the church at Catfish Point. I want the white coats all over this as soon as you can pull it together, but for now we need to keep a lid on this. Make the calls, then get your ass over here. Not a word to any outsiders—I don't want this to leak. I'll secure the scene until you get here."

At twelve-thirty P.M. the body bag was loaded into the coroner's van and driven away. Crebs stood talking quietly with the photographer, and though neither knew the victim personally, the mood at the scene was somber. Hugh emerged from the inside of the building where he'd been for the past two hours, overseeing the removal of the remains, observing every step of the collection of evidence from the sidelines. There was no room for mistakes on this one, and it was crucial that nothing was overlooked, no short-cuts taken.

Everything by the book.

Hugh was the last man to leave the church, and he personally loaded the abandoned bike into the trunk of his car. Upon leaving the scene, Hugh went home, showered, and changed, and put the clothing he'd been wearing in a garbage bag and set it out with the trash. Even if the items were sent to the cleaner's and they somehow managed to get rid of the stench, they would carry the memory of the morning he found a

fifteen-year-old kid in a place where he shouldn't have
been. A kid who wouldn't be going home ever again.

After several cigarettes and a quart of black coffee,
Hugh got in his car and drove to Mayfly Street. Gitan's
truck was in the driveway, the hood warm and the keys
still in the ignition. He'd been out looking for his
brother, and he would have resumed the search had
Hugh not dropped by to save him the trouble.

The coffee turned acid in his stomach . . . or maybe
it was the objectionable task of being the bearer of bad
news. It really didn't matter how he felt about the
Boudreauxs . . . how much he hated Gitan, there was
no getting around the unfairness of Mase's murder.

He lifted his hand to knock and at the same time,
someone moved in the deep shadows of the house.
Two days' growth darkened Gitan's jaw and made him
appear harder than ever. His dark hair was tousled and
his dark eyes looked as tired as Hugh felt, tired and
wary. "You mind if I step in?" Hugh asked. "It's hot
out here, and this might take a while."

Gitan hardened his jaw. Hugh Lothair at his door,
looking like he hadn't slept. Somewhere deep
inside, the hope he'd been determined not to lose
sight of shriveled and died. There was news about
Mase, or Hugh wouldn't have come personally, and
it wasn't good.

Gitan didn't reply, just turned his back and walked
to the kitchen. The screen door opened and closed.
Hugh followed. "Why do I get the feelin' I'm not
gonna want to hear what you got to say?" Gitan said
quietly.

There was no easy way to do this, but Hugh wasn't
an easy man. He didn't shrug it off on one of his
grunts; Gitan gave him that much. It took guts, and
while he could respect that, he didn't have to like it.

"It's about your brother," Hugh said. "I know you've been lookin' for him."

Gitan's gaze was level, without a flicker of emotion. He knew because he was empty, like someone had turned on a tap and drained him of every last drop of sensation. He walked and he talked, and he responded on cue, but he was dead inside . . . as dead as his little brother. "And you're here to tell me I can stop lookin'."

"Mason's dead, Gitan."

"How?"

"I went by the church at Catfish Point this morning. I found a bicycle abandoned outside in the weeds. The kid was inside the building. He'd been gone a while. No official word yet, but if I was to hazard a guess, I'd say a day or two."

"That wasn't what I asked, Hugh."

"Nothing has been determined yet—"

"Fuck the official shit and level with me," Gitan ground out. "How did he die?"

Hugh took a breath, but he didn't look away. His gaze was steady and unflinching, his expression hard as flint, as hard as his blue eyes. "Off the record. It's a homicide."

It was a little surprising, Gitan thought, how he just kept on breathing. His lungs pulled air in and pushed it back out. His heart continued to beat and his pulse was even. It was his brain that was having the most difficulty.

Mason gone.

Dead.

He could stop looking for him, worrying about him. Rose could stop fretting. The kid could come home. Dead. What did he do with this? Where could he put it? How in hell would they ever be able to get beyond this moment?

Hugh was speaking, and Gitan had to force himself to listen. "I can only speculate at this point, but it's my opinion that Mason was in the wrong place at the worst possible time. Someone was in the church— someone he wasn't supposed to see there."

"Who the hell would kill a fifteen-year-old kid?"

"Someone he knew. Someone he recognized. Someone with too much to lose to let anyone see him in a place where he shouldn't be . . . the scene of another homicide."

Or someone who had it in for him, someone who had found an opportunity to hurt the kid, and hurt him bad. Gitan wouldn't say it aloud. He didn't trust Hugh to do his job, to take it seriously enough to do what he'd sworn he'd do when he took the office . . . to uphold, to protect, to serve more than a wealthy and influential few.

What had he done to find Michel's killer? He'd gone through the motions and made it look like he was doing his job; then he'd used it to his advantage to harass an innocent man because of some time-worn vendetta that had never made sense anyhow.

Now, Mason was gone. Mason . . . a Boudreaux, and Gitan couldn't count on the Sheriff's Department to find his killer. He couldn't expect Hugh to do anything but express his condolences for the sake of appearances, shove the case file in a drawer, and get on with business as usual.

The truth was: he couldn't trust Hugh. Period.

But Rose would need answers, and he would see that she got them, one way, or another.

"What do you plan to do about this?" Hugh seemed to read his thoughts, though he'd become an expert at hiding his emotions, any hint of vulnerability, behind an unreadable mask. For the past eight years, keeping people out had been a matter of survival. It was now, too.

"Do? Seems to me that's the question I should be askin' you." Smooth, easy, emotionless. "You're what passes for the law around this place. Somebody crucified Michel, and now you tell me my little brother, he's dead too. Murdered by the same unknown assailant— that's the technical term for it, right? Unknown assailant? What happens next? What is Hugh Lothair gonna do while I try to explain to Rose why the kid she loves so much is gone? You gonna actually look for whoever did this, or you gonna come knockin' at my door, tryin' to pin this on me, too?"

The question raised the other man's hackles. Gitan could see it, sense it. His voice turned brittle, sarcastic. "You tellin' me you killed Mason? Did you, Gitan? Did you kill your brother?"

Gitan took a bottled water from the fridge, but he didn't offer his guest any. "I'm tellin' you that if you've got information, then spill it. Otherwise, get out. I've got things to take care of that don't involve you."

For once, there was no attitude and no argument. Hugh left the way he'd come in, and in a few seconds his dark-colored compact backed out of the drive. Gitan picked up the phone, and put it down again. Some things just had to be seen to in person, and Rose deserved so much more than that, so much more than he could give.

Lily had come in before dawn, and didn't emerge from the shaded cocoon of the Red Room until Virginia had gone and the house was quiet. She didn't know if she slept, though she may have dozed, and fatigue was a yoke on her shoulders she couldn't seem to shrug off.

Edna Mae was on the back porch, shelling peas for the evening meal. A plastic sack full of ear corn sat near the old woman's feet. She glanced up when Lily sat down on the porch swing and reached for the corn. "Now, Miss Lily. You'll ruin your pretty hands."

"I haven't shucked corn since I was little. My friends used to steal a few ears from the farm down the road, and I would eat some, raw and milky, but I never took any myself. I was always too worried about gettin' caught, and what would happen if I did."

"There was reason for that, I suppose. Your daddy was a hard man."

Lily laughed. "You should have been a diplomat, Edna Mae. My daddy was a lowlife."

"Black folks learn from the cradle how to be diplomatic 'round a powerful white man. It's called self-preservation."

"You know, I'm not sorry he's dead," Lily said. "I just wish his death hadn't destroyed so many lives. Like ripples in a pond . . . the rough water just keeps coming. It's like there's no end to it."

Edna Mae sighed. She was quiet for a while, thoughtful, and when she finally continued, her voice was softer with a note of confidentiality that she generally saved for a few select family members and women of color. Edna Mae didn't have a problem with white folks, Lily knew, but she didn't always trust them, either. Not even the ones she knew well, and cared about more than she should have. "Sometimes there's just no makin' sense out of life. Things happen—sometimes bad things. If we could foresee them, we might be able to stop them, but nobody can do that, and all we can do is try to live with whatever comes. Take Miss Virginia, for instance. Doctor Trelawney's been tryin' to reach her all day. If she'd given him the number at the store, she could have kept me from knowin' and blabbin' about those tests. But she didn't, and it's just one of those things."

"Doctor Trelawney gave you the results?" Lily said with a frown.

"No, darlin'," the housekeeper said. "He just said it was an urgent matter, and to have Virginia or her representative call his office." The peas she shelled plunked softly into the growing pile in the bottom of the bowl. "Representative . . . isn't that like the power of attorney Miss Virginia had you draw up a few years back when she thought she'd have to have gall bladder surgery? She's such a chickenshit when it comes to hospitals."

Lily raised her brows. "Why, Edna Mae, what *are* you suggesting?"

"Me? I'm not suggesting anything. I'm just sayin' that sometimes you got to take the bull by the horns. Miss Virginia's runnin' away from something awfully hard. I'd like to know what that something is." She clucked her tongue. "Honey, if she sick, then she needs to get treatment. They do miraculous things today. But a body's got to give 'em half a chance to help out."

"She'll be angry with both of us," Lily warned. But she knew Edna Mae was right. If something was wrong, then they needed to know. Running away never solved anything, because sooner or later, the problem surfaced and insisted upon being dealt with. She was living proof of that.

The thought of her employer's anger didn't faze Edna Mae. She shrugged. "Mmm. I expect that if she get mad, she'll get glad again, sooner or later. I ain't scared of her . . . are you?"

An hour later, Lily pulled in against the curb in front of Virginia's shop and got out of her car. The OPEN sign was turned toward the window, but the lights were off and the door was locked. Virginia's car was parked in its usual spot, so Lily used the key Virginia had given her when she was eleven and walked in. The bell attached to the door jangled pleasantly, stirring a flurry of dust motes and sending them dancing in the shaft of sunlight pouring through the door's single glass pane. Faint sounds came from the back room, sounds of slow movement, and Lily's stomach clenched as she remembered the episode with the antique dolls. There was a part of her that wanted to run rather than face what lay beyond the curtained doorway—the same part that ran and ran, and couldn't ever seem to run hard enough, long enough, fast enough to escape her problems.

She could turn around now and walk back through the front door, locking it on her way out. She could get in her car and drive home and pretend she didn't know, and maybe she'd wake tomorrow and everything would be normal. . . .

Exactly what she'd been doing all of her life. It hadn't worked then, and it wouldn't work now.

Her steps were measured and even and unhurried, but they didn't lag as she pushed aside the curtain and entered the back room. Virginia, seated at the worktable in the center of the storage room, glanced up. Her gaze was unclouded, and for an instant Lily hoped Trelawney had been wrong. "Sugar, what on earth are you doin' here in the middle of the day?"

"I'm visiting my favorite aunt, and it's almost evening."

"I'm your only aunt," she reminded her. "But I suppose that's an oversight that's permissible. Being a favorite anything can't be bad, now, can it?"

Lily smiled. "If I'd had a dozen, you'd still be my favorite." She walked to the worktable and glanced at the photograph album in front of Virginia.

"A lot of memories on these pages," Virginia said, her expression softening. She was a handsome woman, instead of being merely pretty. Silver blond hair and deep blue eyes. Any makeup she wore was subtly applied, enhancing a beauty that was as timeless as it was natural. In her sixties, and hardly a wrinkle. "A lot of history. Just look at Justin. He had such a sweet look about him—those blond curls and fat baby cheeks. Who would have thought he'd turn into such a bastard?"

Lily stepped closer, close enough to gaze down at the black-and-white photograph Virginia indicated. "I spoke with Dr. Trelawney today," she said quietly.

The hand turning the page faltered the smallest bit before finishing its task. "I hope you gave him a piece of your mind on my behalf. He ought to be ashamed for all the nonsense he tried to put me through—"

"Aunt Virginia, I know about the preliminary diagnosis."

"He had no business tellin' you when it's pure nonsense! Alzheimer's disease—what on earth kind of name is that, anyway?" Her forced smile wavered and a groan escaped her. "I promised myself I wasn't going to indulge in theatrics, and by God, neither will you."

Lily walked around the table where Virginia was sitting on a stool, and put her arms around her. "No theatrics. I promise. But we are going to deal with this. We have to."

* * *

Angelique was a quiet town, largely untouched by the kind of senseless violence that plagued the inner city, so the news of the boy's death spread like wildfire. Community mattered here, as did family, and there were few households left unaffected by the murder of one of their own, especially someone so young. Parents who were normally lax about their kids' being abroad after dark imposed curfews, and even the grumbling which resulted from the stricter controls was subdued as it sank in that there was a nameless, faceless killer walking the streets . . . a man brazen enough to kill a priest *and* a high school sophomore.

The sheriff's department did its best to squash the rumors of a connection between the two homicides, but once it leaked that Mason Boudreaux had been discovered in the old church at Catfish Point, everyone with half a brain was able to connect the dots, and the picture it made was a terrifying one.

No one was safe, and something had to be done about it. The Committee for the Beautification of Angelique elected a pair of spokeswomen to express concerns to Sheriff Lothair personally, but after twenty minutes, they were ushered to the door. The PTA had gotten together with a few of the more militant soccer moms and were picketing the building with signs that said, "Take Back Our Streets," but on Mayfly Street and Tupelo Avenue, Mason's family was largely unaware of the unrest their personal tragedy had triggered.

Gitan spent a large part of the afternoon seeing to the necessary arrangements. He'd put on dark trousers, a white shirt and tie, and escorted Rose to

Homer Folley's funeral home to discuss the memorial service; then he'd driven Rose home again and sat with her for an hour while she restlessly fussed with anything she could find to occupy her hands, no matter how mundane. When the house was spotless, she put on her dark blue dress and drove to mass at the new St. Bartholomew's. Gitan went home, knowing she would stay to light a candle for Mason, and to keep a silent vigil for his soul.

Rose found some measure of comfort from her God, but for Gitan there was no comfort, and no distraction. He sat in the dark kitchen, the only light in the room the orange glow of the power indicator light on the coffeemaker, trying to figure out what had gone wrong.

Mase had been pushing the boundaries for months and with them, pushing Gitan's buttons. There hadn't been any overlooking the fact that the kid had been angry. They'd been at odds almost since Gitan had stepped off the bus that first day, and he'd made no effort to change it. He'd been so determined to keep Mase from making the same sort of mistakes he had made, and in the end all he had done was alienate him.

And now he was gone, and not only was there nothing he could do to change that; there was nothing he wouldn't give to see him breeze through the door and make a beeline to the fridge for a cold can of his favorite soda. Gitan kept it on hand just for Mase, but Mase wouldn't be raiding his fridge anymore.

He wouldn't cut class, or use profane language, and he wouldn't play matchmaker between him and Lily. He wouldn't get a learner's permit, or a driver's license, or attend his senior prom. He wouldn't graduate from high school, have a steady girlfriend, or get married. He wouldn't ever live up to his potential, because he'd been taken away before he'd been given half a chance.

Murdered.

He'd been murdered.

In Gitan's mind, there was no getting around it. In the case of a car crash or sudden illness, you could blame it on fate, or call it a tragic accident. Rose would have said with a sigh that "the Lord had called him home." But Mason's death hadn't been accidental. He'd been strangled. Hugh had called earlier to pass along that piece of information, confirmed by the coroner.

Cause of death: homicide.

Manner of death: strangulation.

Someone had wrapped their hands around the kid's throat and squeezed the life from him. The same sick someone who'd hung Michel Dugas upside down from a cross.

A strong man with big hands.

He'd gone back to the funeral home after Rose had driven to mass and he'd talked Homer Folley into letting him view the body. Folley was reluctant, but in the end he looked into Gitan's face and relented. He'd warned him about the condition of the remains to prepare him, then led the way to the small building in the back of the lot. He'd opened the cold drawer, unzipped the body bag, and stood back while Gitan stared into the face that had always been a near mirror image of his own.

Mase lay on a cold slab . . . his skin discolored, face swollen. The body would be washed prior to embalming, but it would still be a closed coffin. Decomposition was swift in the subtropics, and the damage was irreversible.

That didn't stop Gitan from reaching out to stroke

the boy's dark hair, but it was lifeless and straw-like. He pulled his hand back, balling his fist, lowering it to his side, and saw the bruises on Mason's throat.

Massive bruising from big hands.

The murderer was a man who not only happened to be exceptionally strong, he was conscienceless. From the way the bruises were placed on the throat, he had to have been facing Mason, looking into his eyes when he killed him.

How the hell did anyone justify killing a kid?

How could this pissant take an innocent life and then go on living? Going through the motions, making it all appear normal and ordinary?

It was easy. You closed your mind to it, and got on with the process. You distanced yourself from the victim by blaming them for their own deaths . . . and you justified the act a thousand different ways during those quiet moments when the guilt crept in.

Gitan had seen it often enough at Angola, where the majority of the inmates who had taken lives claimed to be innocent, misunderstood, unjustly accused, and unjustly punished. *It wasn't my fault. It just happened. They shouldn't have been there. If they hadn't been there, if they hadn't resisted, if they'd given me what I wanted, it never would have happened.*

Knowing the drill, having had close contact year in and year out with the dregs of society, understanding how the taking of an innocent's life could be rationalized didn't make things easier. If anything, it made it worse, because Mase's life was worth a thousand of the man who'd taken it, and because he'd had so much to live for. He'd had family, he'd been loved, and for his potential and his worth to be trivialized for the sake of convenience was unacceptable.

He'd heard it all before, and he knew what

to expect, if Hugh managed to land the prick responsible.

With Hugh involved, it was a mighty big "if," accompanied by a shitload of risk. *"Did you kill your brother?"* The question seemed to echo in his weary mind, magnifying with each repetition, blocking out everything . . . *Did you, Gitan? Did you kill your brother? Did you kill your brother? Did you, did you, did you kill your brother?*

"Stop it. For Christ's sake—just—stop."

He was sitting at the kitchen table when Lily walked in. The kitchen was dark, but the absence of light seemed somehow appropriate. Such intense grief couldn't bear the light without compounding the pain. She'd never known him to break down, not at his sentencing, not at the prison, and she knew the damp tracks on his bearded cheeks had little to do with him, and everything to do with a young life that had ended far too prematurely. God help them all, she felt the deep, inconsolable ache of his loss, his bewilderment at what to do, his anger.

Without a word, she knelt beside him, touching his bare arm, gently, letting him know he wasn't alone in his misery.

Slowly, like a man coming out of a deep sleep, the throes of some all-consuming dream, he lifted his dark head and opened his eyes. Reaching out, Lily smoothed the dampness from his face with her fingers, then put her arms around him and pressed her cheek to his. "I'm sorry about Mase. My God, I am so sorry."

It seemed the right thing to do, the appropriate thing, to press her lips to his cheek, his temple, his brow, and as she did so her own problems receded for a little while, fading into the background. This was all about Gitan. He had to know that he mattered, that he didn't need to carry this burden alone. It wasn't about commitments or promises. It was about everything he'd done, and everything he had been to her over the years. He sighed a little when she pressed a kiss to his forehead, pulling back to consider her. "Where's this goin', *cher*? 'Cause I'm not in the mood to play games."

Lily sat back on her heels. His face was a dark, expressionless mask just slightly above her. Only his eyes registered the pain with which he was struggling to cope. "I'm here because I care—about Mason . . . about you."

He rubbed his left temple with his fingertips, as if he could somehow erase the tension gathering there, ease the heavy throb of his pulse that showed beneath his skin. "Mase, he's beyond anyone's help now. Nobody can fix things, or make it better. Me, I don' want anyone's pity. Not even yours."

"This has nothing to do with pity," Lily insisted. "I know how strong you are, but I know your heart, too, and when you say you're just fine, I can see the lie. I've certainly told it often enough myself to recognize it. I want to help, if I can. I'm worried about you." She shrugged, embarrassed. "Sometimes your intensity scares me. I guess it always has."

He didn't argue the point. There was no light in the room, no reason to hide old hurts, or new ones. There was room between them for nothing but truth. "You wanna help, but what are you willing to do, *cher*? You gonna stay the night to make sure I don' do somethin' stupid?" Leaning forward, he kissed her deeply and Lily could feel his reluctance to let go. "Think about it before you answer, Lily. 'Cause you walk into that bedroom, you don' leave till the sun's high. No runnin' from the scene of the crime. Not this time."

Kneeling between his knees, Lily reached up, threading her fingers into the soft hair at his nape, pulling his head down to meet her kiss. There was nothing to think about. Nothing to consider. She couldn't bear to leave him, and Gitan knew it.

One kiss, and then another, and his body took over, shoving all thought far into the background. His physical hunger was far greater than anything he'd ever experienced, the desire to lose himself in Lily almost overwhelming. "All those years I was in lockup, I'd wake up shakin' and covered in sweat because I'd been dreamin' of you." He slid his thumbs over her cheeks, then framed her face with his palms. "When the news came that you'd married Hugh, I tried to accept it, get past it. It didn't work because it couldn't work . . . There was never anyone but you in my life, and I knew there never could be."

"Gitan . . ."

"*Non, cher* . . . don'. Don' say anything. I already know, and it doesn't matter." He pulled her closer and kissed her, then kissed her again. She was his until the sun rose, and it was enough.

Gitan took her hands, helping her up, and together they found their way to the bedroom. Without turning on a light, she kicked off her heels and, while he watched, peeled away the silk dress she wore. Gitan's blue jeans followed, and there was nothing but hunger between them.

Lily sighed when Gitan turned her to face the full-length mirror standing in the corner opposite the portrait. She watched from the cover of lowered lids as his arms came around her, dark hands exploring pale golden skin, seeking, finding, worshipping. Mes-

merized by their reflection, she watched her arms
cross over his, her hands gliding with his over her
curves. The woman in the mirror arched against the
hard, tanned, and tattooed male body molded to
hers, her head tipped back and her eyes slitted. She
could feel her temperature rising, tiny beads of perspiration forming on her upper lip, her pulse accel-
erating steadily until the thunder of her heart
reverberated through her.

They were opposites on the outside, hard against
soft, dark and light . . . but on the inside they fit so
closely together that they were almost indistinguish-
able from one another. One heart, one mind, one
soul—one purpose.

Gitan bent to nuzzle the curve of her throat. She
was warm to him now, pliant, and he could have
done anything he wanted to do, yet his only thought
was to please her. One perfect night. Sexual communion in the midst of great sorrow, the satisfying of
mutual need, a silent, unspoken pledge that they belonged to one another, at least for tonight. With
great care, he lifted her, then joined her on the bed,
one by one eliminating her every inhibition, until the
shuddering end came. Exhausted, Lily slept the sleep
of a weary child for the first time in a long time, safe
in her lover's arms.

CHAPTER SEVENTEEN

Hugh had always been a hands-on kind of guy. He liked to get into the trenches and get fully involved in an investigation even when he didn't have a personal stake in the outcome, but with this case, it was definitely personal. He couldn't really say why Mason Boudreaux's death had gotten to him, but it had. It wasn't like he and Gitan were friends. Far from it. But he'd known Mason all of his life.

The boy had been seven years old when Gitan began serving his sentence, and much younger when Hugh and Gitan had been hanging out together, always rivals, nearly inseparable. Hugh could remember the kid's dark hair and big brown eyes. Unlike Gitan, who had always seemed so serious, Mason had had an engaging smile which he flashed often to his advantage. Even as a kid, he'd known how to take a situation and turn it to his advantage. It was a talent he'd carried into adolescence, a talent which had worked well for him until he'd met head-on with a situation he'd been unable to manipulate or control.

Now he was dead, and once again Hugh found himself attending the preliminary examination and autopsy of someone he'd known personally. It rankled.

"I don't believe I've ever had such an unusual request," Homer Folley said. The older man seemed to gain a good six inches in height when he put on those green scrubs he wore to conduct his gruesome duties as coroner. "I thought that fingerprints disappeared from skin almost as soon as they were made."

"From living skin," Hugh replied. "Postmortem is a whole new ball game. Perspiration or movement can destroy a fingerprint, but the body begins to cool as soon as the heart stops beating, and corpses don't perspire . . . but then you'd know all of that."

"You think the killer touched the body after death?" Homer's tone was conversational, even as he placed the plastic tent over the boy's naked body. "He was fully clothed when he came in."

"Just a hunch, that's all." It had to do with the crime scene and the care with which the body had been positioned. The jacket used to pillow the boy's head, the folded hands: it all indicated remorse. He knew what he was looking for, and with any luck at all, he'd find it.

Homer stood back from the stainless steel autopsy table. "Why don't you do the honors, Sheriff? I'll observe."

Hugh had everything he needed in a twelve-inch square cardboard box. The lamp was something he'd grabbed from his apartment, a small reading lamp minus the shade. He lifted it from the box and plugged it into the AC outlet, positioning it inside the tent and slipping the bottom half of a soda can which he'd cut with the tin shears over the bulb. With the apparatus in place, he added a small puddle of Super Glue to the dish the bottom of the can made, and turned on the lamp.

"Well, I'll be darned. You learn something new every day," Homer said, more to himself than to Hugh. "What now, Sheriff?"

"Now, we wait."

Hugh didn't realize how tense he was until his beeper went off and he actually started. "That's the office, and I need to take it. Do me a favor, Homer. Don't touch anything until I come back."

Within ten minutes, Hugh and his improvised device had pulled off a minor miracle. The plastic tent was dismantled and the AC current to the lamp cut. Hugh checked the boy's hands and wrists first, then moved to his throat, finding a few white smears, but nothing he could use. As he moved to the kid's face, the break for which he'd been praying dropped into his lap. There, on the boy's right eyelid, was a clearly defined thumbprint.

The do-er had crossed the kid's arms over his chest, put a pillow under his head, and closed his eyes.

Using his own digital camera, he zoomed in close and shot the memory stick full, downloading the photos into a notebook computer to assure he'd gotten the clarity he needed. Normally, he would have used tape to lift the print, but because decomposition was fairly advanced, there was too much skin slippage to allow it.

He had what he wanted, yet Hugh stayed for the autopsy. Cause of death was asphyxiation by manual strangulation. The pressure applied to Mason's throat had been so intense that it had fractured the U-shaped hyoid bone at the base of the throat. The overkill brought on by rage so in evidence in the Dugas killing was noticeably absent in Mason's case. All damage had been limited to the boy's throat. There was no evidence of sexual assault, or any other physical violence. He had been silenced, not slaughtered.

Hugh was all too aware that the coroner's findings would be of little comfort to Mason's family. Rose was grieving and Gitan was angry. But was he angry enough to do something insanely stupid?

"Why the hell do you care?" Hugh wondered aloud.

He was in his car and halfway back to the station when he realized it wasn't road kill he was smelling; it was him. He was a small town sheriff who was getting used to the smell of dead bodies, and the last thing he needed was another killing.

The last time Gitan had evened the score, Lily's old man had ended up wearing a toe tag. Not that he cared if Boudreaux ended up serving a life sentence, but he sure didn't need another homicide on his hands. He'd run his campaign on a platform of restoring law and order, and a rash of vicious unsolved murders would be an indelible stain on his record.

Talking to the man was not an option, so he settled for putting himself in Gitan's shoes and trying to guess what he might do. The first thing was about trust, or rather a complete lack of it. Gitan had never given Hugh credit for having enough intelligence to come in out of a soaking downpour, and he wasn't going to trust him to find Mason's killer, or Michel's. He was also not the sort of man to let something this personal slide.

Someone would pay for killing his brother. Gitan would see to it, and in the process he would make Hugh look like a damned inept fool for not being able to keep a lid on a deteriorating situation.

Hugh didn't like it, but all he could do was step up the investigation and hope he got the break he so desperately needed before the whole thing exploded in his face. He sent a copy of the photo files of the fingerprints found on Mason's body directly to AFIS, Automated Fingerprint Identification System, but they came back empty. He even compared them to Gitan's prints, on file from his arrest, and taken again right before he got out, but he didn't get a match, and he could almost hear Lily's *"I told you so!"* The print on Mason had a distinctive break on the right thumb's center swirl in the form of a slight scar.

Hugh didn't give himself time to feel disappointed; he just kept pushing the leads he had, hoping that something would give. He felt sure he had the motive, but thus far, he'd been unable to shake any new information loose that would lead to the conclusions he'd drawn about Dugas's murder being sexually motivated. He'd gone over his half of the list twice, and compared notes with Crebs, and not a single whiff of impropriety had arisen to spark another lead. Of course, that didn't mean it wasn't there. Depending upon the cultural background and personal views of the person, sexual abuse was sometimes viewed as being shameful—especially when the victim was a healthy young male.

"What would you do if you were raped?" he'd asked Crebs point-blank earlier that morning. It was something he'd been thinking about most of the night, and had been unable to get out of his mind since.

"Me? You're kidding, right?"

"Humor me, will you?" Hugh had said. "Forget that you're invincible for the time being, and pretend there's somebody bigger and stronger than you out there. What would you do?"

"I wouldn't confide it to you, that's for sure."

"Exactly," Hugh said. "You wouldn't talk about it, because you would be afraid of what other people might think. That it was your fault. That you asked for it—or worse, you enjoyed it."

Crebs's expression disintegrated into a scowl. "I only went into that gay bar once, and it was strictly business. Now, if you'll excuse me, I need to adjust my thong."

The memory of the conversation faded, but his conviction that he was on the right track remained unshaken. "If you can't get in through the front door, go in through a window." He might not be able to crack the facade presented by the kids' families . . . but he could damn sure go back to Murdoch and shake that tree a little more forcefully. He still hadn't gotten past the initial impression that Murdoch knew more than he was telling. Maybe if he kept at him, he'd get results.

The sanctuary at the new St. Bartholomew's was softly lit and smelled of candle wax and incense. It was Father Bernaud's favorite place on earth, aside from the garden, the only place he found solace. The only place he felt safe. He came to the sanctuary each morning, before he had breakfast and went to the gardens. He came to speak to his savior and to plead for mercy and for salvation. Prayer was supposed to lighten man's load; confession by its very design eased the wearisome burden on one's soul.

Every morning, Father Bernaud knelt before the altar, his gaze fixed mournfully on the life-sized statue of Christ on the cross with head bowed and crown of thorns, and feverishly prayed. Near silent outpourings of a tormented soul which bore too great a burden, a man who had sinned against his savior, against his parishioners, against humanity and was tormented because of it . . . but it all fell upon deaf ears.

He knelt until his knees were raw and his joints too stiff for him to rise, and still he saw no relief from the terrible burden he carried. The weight of the guilt bowed his back and furrowed his brow until he appeared years older than his actual age, but he couldn't unburden except to his Lord, and he couldn't be sure until death took him whether or not his God had turned His back upon him.

If his secret were known, he would be despised, banned from the parish, perhaps imprisoned . . . and at times like this, alone in the dim, flickering candlelight, with only the soft weeping of a few faithful kneeling to pray, he wondered if it would not be easier to bear than this?

His daily search for atonement was more difficult physically than any prison work detail could possibly be. He was truly, utterly lost.

This morning, the weeping inside the church raked his raw nerves and left his spirit bleeding. The middle-aged woman tipped a face to the crucifix that was tearstained and swollen, and her litany of sorrow was just loud enough for Father Bernaud to hear. "Not my Mason. Blessed Mother, please. Not my Mason—not this way. How'm I gonna live with this? How'm I gonna live with what I done?"

Father Bernaud recognized the name of the one for whom the woman wept. Mason Boudreaux, a young man—no more than a boy, really. Another life senselessly taken.

Another innocent who'd fallen victim to a killer . . . and where did it stop?

Where did it stop?

It stops with you. A voice so quiet, so solemn and earnest, whispered in his ear, and he was so convinced of what he had heard that he turned to look and to determine its origin, but the pew behind him was empty. There was no one on either side of him, no one near enough to have spoken in such a way and have him hear it, and it shook him to the soles of his shoes.

I'm an old man. A weak man. I don't possess the strength to do what is right.

No answer came, not a whisper, not a shout, not a breath of argument. The shadowed church remained silent and still except for the Boudreaux woman's weeping.

Father Bernaud blessed himself hurriedly, clawed his way upright with the help of the forward pew, and stumbled from his seat, nearly tripping over the kneeler. His upset was so great that he couldn't bring himself to break his fast. Instead, he retreated to the gardens, working feverishly in the damp soil.

Hours later, Father Murdoch found him in the garden. The calla lilies were glorious, flanked by begonias in yellow, peach, and pink, their leaves glossy and lush. "We missed you at breakfast. There's speculation as to why you avoid the others."

He stabbed at the loose soil repeatedly, his movements angry and exaggerated. "I avoid them because I can't bear to look them in the eye. Honest men with open hearts, and my heart is neither open, nor honest."

Murdoch ignored the admission. "You have done a marvelous job with the beds, Father Bernaud. I have never seen such prolific blooms."

"I can't take credit. The soil is rich in nutrients. If

we planted a cat's tail, we could grow a new cat. It's a pity that poor woman in the chapel cannot grow a new nephew. Shattered lives are not so easily replaced as dead blooms. Pinch off the exhausted heads and the plant soon sprouts another. The Boudreaux boy is gone forever, and his aunt grieves so. It cuts my heart to see it."

"Yes, I heard the news. It's tragic."

"This morning, I was praying in the chapel, asking forgiveness for the harm I have done, and I asked where it would stop. You'll think me mad, but someone, something, answered me."

A wry glance, almost scornful. "Are you feeling quite well? Perhaps you've had too much exposure to the sun?"

"I don't feel well. I haven't felt at ease with my myself since Father Dugas—" He glanced quickly around to see if he had been overheard, then lowered his voice. "Since Father Dugas came to me with his suspicions shortly before his death."

Murdoch pursed his full lips in disapproval. "I thought we agreed not to speak of it again. There is so much at stake."

"There are lives at stake," Father Bernaud whispered frantically, "and I can't keep it to myself any longer. The burden is too great." His watery blue gaze wandered to the curb where a slick-looking young man was just closing the door of a dark-colored car. He carried a jacket over one arm, and wore a shoulder holster for the firearm under his left arm.

Murdoch, standing beside the older man who knelt in the dirt, reached down to stroke the old man's cheek. "Think carefully," Murdoch cautioned. "What's done is done. Do not compound the situation with a second betrayal." The hand left Bernaud's face as

Murdoch turned to greet his unwelcome guest. "Sheriff Lothair, back so soon?"

Hugh focused for one second on the old man kneeling in the dirt. The old geezer seemed agitated, but he'd always been pretty nervy and there was no telling what had passed between him and Murdoch in the moments preceding his arrival. Father Bernaud was touchy about his flower beds, and probably resented the interruption. Dedicated gardeners took matters pertaining to dirt, mulch, and fertilizer very seriously. Personally, Hugh preferred dandelions. No fuss, no muss, save the juice for more important matters . . . like murder. Still, when in Rome. . . He bent slightly, pointing to a spot between two verdant blooms. "Looks like you missed something."

The old man glanced up, and Hugh saw that he was trembling. Had he been trembling the last time he spoke to him? And did the noticeable palsy have its roots in old age, or something else? "I beg your pardon?"

"Chickweed, right there. Make sure you get all of it, or it'll ruin the whole bed. Its insidious and it'll take over everything."

Father Bernaud looked as if he would answer; then Murdoch stepped smoothly in. "Do you garden, Sheriff?"

Hugh snorted. "Not a chance, but my grandmother does. She's eighty-three and in better shape than any of us. I swear it's got something to do with all that horse manure."

"More likely, it's the activity," Murdoch said. "Have you come with a purpose in mind, or are you just admiring Father Bernaud's handiwork?"

"I don't do anything without a purpose, Father Murdoch. Not having a goal is a complete waste of time. Take the Dugas investigation. You know, it's kinda funny, but I spoke with the kids Dugas counseled, as well as the kids from the softball team, and I'm getting a very different picture from the one you painted for me of your brothers in Christ. You told me there has been no history of sexual misconduct that you're aware of, but I'm not so sure you're telling me the entire truth." It was a lie with a kernel of truth. Not one of the families he had interviewed had indicated a hint of scandal, yet he was fairly certain that Murdoch was stonewalling. It was a gut-deep feeling and the only thing that made sense.

"I believe we've covered this area before, and I am not sure how else I can help you," Murdoch said.

Hugh kept his focus on his target. There was something there; he could smell it. The method he employed with difficult subjects was direct and relentless; like a pit bull terrier, he latched on and wouldn't let go. "You can help me by leveling with me."

"To the best of my abilities, I have already done that, Sheriff. I'm not sure what it is you want from me. I can't give what I don't have."

Hugh produced the large envelope he'd carried with his suit jacket. "Tell me, Father. Have you ever seen a crucifixion? I don't mean those bloodless depictions in sixteenth-century paintings; I'm talkin' the real deal here." He took the photos of Dugas's bloated naked form from the envelope and thrust them into Murdoch's hands. "Go on, take a good look. I insist."

Murdoch's gaze was drawn involuntarily downward, his eyes widening as he caught a glimpse of the graphic scene and tried to shove them back at Hugh. "Dear God."

"Man did this, Father Murdoch, not God. A man who's still out there, still willing to kill to cover up this crime. A man you're protecting with your silence, which makes you just as guilty as he is." He snatched the photos back and thrust them in front of Murdoch's face so that the only way to avoid them was to close his eyes. "How angry do you have to be to do that to a man? How furious do you have to be to want to make a man suffer like Michel Dugas suffered?" He put the crime scene shots back in the envelope and settled back into his heels, his stance sure and solid. "Most homicides come down to one of two common denominators: sex, and money. Michel was a priest, so we know this wasn't about money. That leaves one thing—*one.*"

Hugh was watching Murdoch's face, but he could see Father Bernaud in his peripheral vision and saw him falter and abruptly sit down in the lush green grass. Instinct kicked in. Hugh left off his target for the time being. "Father Bernaud? Are you all right?"

The old man was breathing heavily. Sweat poured down his face. "No. No—I don't believe I—" His face turned dusky and he fell onto his side in the flower bed.

Hugh put two fingers on his carotid artery. "Jesus Christ, he's got no pulse." He dug out his cellular phone and handed it to Murdoch. "Nine-one-one, right now! Tell them it's a possible cardiac arrest— the subject isn't breathing on his own." He flipped the old man onto his back, folded his jacket and put it under his head, cleared his airway, and began to administer CPR.

Rose had her religion, and Gitan had a deep, dark emptiness. It was a little startling that he could feel nothing, aside from a cold numbness in his chest. Air filled his lungs and was expelled with mechanical precision. He remained aware of his surroundings, especially the increased humidity that made the late September heat so oppressive, but it didn't seem to matter without Mason there to bitch that the air conditioner was on the fritz again. Ruben had closed down the shop for a day or two due to personal problems, but he'd stopped by the house to express his condolences and sent a large fruit basket to Rose's house on Tupelo Avenue that no one was likely to eat. Ruben seemed to think he was doing him a favor by giving him time off, but the truth was, he might have been better off not having so much time to think.

When he was deep into a project, he could forget himself and just create the effects he wanted. Without the work, there was no losing himself, and no escape from the incredibly bewildering awareness that his baby brother was gone. The only solace he'd found, the only reprieve he'd had was the momentary forgetfulness he'd found in Lily's arms.

He watched her get dressed from the cool comfort of the bed. Watched her adjust her stockings and slip into her shoes, and thought about what he would do once she left him. The coroner hadn't released the boy's body, so there was plenty of time to find the answers he needed, and he knew where to start. Willie had a history of making trouble that went back several years. He was a kid destined for a bad end who resented his old man, and who'd never let an opportunity to make Mason's life miserable pass him by.

That's what this was about . . . opportunity.

He'd run into Mase and something had happened. Maybe he hadn't originally intended to take a life, but the end result was the same. He didn't know how this tied into Michel's murder, or even *if* it did, but he intended to find out.

Lily ran her fingers through her short hair, her gaze finding his in the mirror. "Are you going to lie there in bed? Or get up and have coffee with me?"

"That depends," Gitan said.

"On what?"

"On what's in it for me? Looks to me like you're leavin'. I was thinkin' that maybe if I waited right here, you'd come back around."

Her reflection smiled at his. "It's tempting," she admitted. "You're the only man I know who looks that good wearing nothing but a smile and a tattoo."

He got out of bed and walked naked to where she stood, slipping his arms around her, pulling her in tightly to him, so there could be no doubt as to how much he wanted her, needed her . . . especially now. "If I look that good, then why you leavin'?"

She sighed, leaning back and letting his warmth envelop her. "Aunt Virginia isn't doing well. The doctor is afraid it's early dementia. She has a consultation with a specialist today, and I can't let her face this alone." She turned in his embrace, kissing him like she meant it. "I'm worried about you."

"Don' worry, *cher.* I'll manage. I always do." He buried his face in the hollow beneath her ear and inhaled. He needed to remember this moment, remember the way she felt, and smelled, and tasted because after today the memories would have to sustain him. "You're the best thing that ever happened to me, you know that?"

She laughed, the sound laced through with irony. "I don't know how you can say that after everything I've cost you—"

"My Lily's a bright light in a sea of darkness. Never

forget that. All you got to do from this day on is shine." He set her from him, gave her a smile. "You go. Virginia's waitin'."

"You'll be here?" she asked. "I'll call."

"I'll be here." He kissed her, a tender reassurance that all was fine when it was anything but fine. "See you later."

Lily left without coffee, and Gitan did too. His first stop was Rose's place on Tupelo Avenue. She wasn't home, but she rarely locked her door, so he walked right in. The house was quiet—too quiet. Normally, the TV set would be blaring MTV and Rose would be in the kitchen, shouting for Mason to turn the volume down, but not enforcing it if he didn't listen.

The set's 19-inch screen was black. The remote lay forgotten on the coffee table, and a plaid flannel shirt was draped over one end of the couch as if its owner had placed it there a moment ago on his way through the living room. Gitan picked it up, his fingers closing over the worn and faded fabric before he replaced it. The living room and kitchen were directly adjacent to one another. A trio of bedrooms and a full bath opened off a central hallway. Mason's room was all the way to the rear, the largest bedroom because nothing was too good for John and Annie Boudreaux's baby boy. Always the best she could provide for Mason.

The bedroom was neatly kept, the bed made and shoes all in a row along one wall. Mason's clothes were in the dresser and in the closet; the felt fedora their daddy had owned and wore only for the most special occasions hung on the bedpost. A place for everything, and everything in its place. . . . Gitan went through the drawers, the closet, and the metal footlocker at the end of the bed. He found baseball cards and a current copy of *Playboy* magazine, but nothing that told him why someone would want to kill his little brother.

Hugh had approached the investigation with a cop's point of view. Motive. Always motive. Logic. Like there was a reason for everything that happened. But that view was one-dimensional, and a little unrealistic. Gitan's life experience was more diverse, more realistic. There were times when no motive existed. Some men acted on impulse, killing for no more reason than the momentary thought that the opportunity to take a life existed and there was no reason not to act on it.

And sometimes they weren't men, but boys. Kids like Willie Early who respected nothing and no one.

Hugh thought that the two murders were connected. It was possible, but Gitan didn't buy into that theory. It was a little too neat a package, too easy. Not when so much bad blood had passed between Willie and Mason, or as long as Hugh was sheriff. He couldn't truthfully say how far he would trust any law enforcement type, but he didn't trust Hugh at all.

The Earlys were wealthy, and money was power, prestige—sometimes even a license to kill and to get away with it—especially when the sheriff had a tendency to look the other way when certain people were involved. Money bought a lot of things, like fancy lawyers and friends in high places. Willie didn't need a lawyer yet, and probably wouldn't if Hugh kept doing what Hugh did best. Ignoring the obvious.

Willie had been out of control for months. He drank, despite being underage, and if the rumors were true, he was heavily into illegal substances, and he had his old man's big hands. *Booze, contraband, and a self-destructive streak—but did he do it? Did he wrap his hands around your neck and squeeze?*

There were no immediate answers, only the unnatural quiet of a house that days ago had been full of life. This whole situation was far from over. In fact, his role in it was just beginning. Unearthing the truth would likely come with a heavy price tag, but it was a price Gitan was prepared to pay. "Somebody's got to speak on Mason's behalf, and ain't no way I'm gonna let this slide."

Willie Early came to the rectory after dark, and left Murdoch's office by a little-used side door at five minutes of eleven. The parking lot was empty except for his car, and out of habit, he parked it in the shadows where the overhead street lamps failed to reach. Julius Murdoch had taught him the importance of taking care of the petty details. Details were crucial. They could keep the darkest secret safe, or bring about a man's downfall. Or, in his own case, net a large amount of cash.

Stopping in the shadows by the car, he tore the seal on the envelope Murdoch had given him a few minutes earlier and counted the bills. Five crisp one-hundred-dollar bills. Never enough to satisfy him for long, just enough to keep him coming back for more. Murdoch was uneasy with their arrangement. The tables had turned on him and he knew it. One word in the right ear, and his life was over. The reputation he'd spent years building would be destroyed. Willie had danced around the threat a thousand different ways in the past weeks, since the killing. At first, when he'd realized what he'd done, he'd been a little frightened, but he'd always been fast on the uptake. A quick study. And what he'd realized in the first few days after the murder was just how powerful a seductress power happened to be. As seductive as sex.

Murdoch didn't put his hands on him now unless Willie wanted him to, and then he did exactly as he was told to do. Willie called the shots, and Murdoch didn't even try to argue.

The bright lights of the ICU were always a little startling, and Hugh found the fact that they were always on more than a little ironic. Critical-care patients were supposed to rest and recuperate, but how the hell was a man supposed to rest with an artificial light source glaring in his face twenty-four-seven? Maybe it was the quality of the drugs, he thought, following a short, round woman in a pale blue uniform through the unit and into the room adjacent to the nurse's station. She stopped at the door to glare at him. "Five minutes, and don't you upset him."

"It's a courtesy call, honey," Hugh insisted, but she wasn't buying it and he really didn't care. The old priest lay very still, his eyes slitted but open, oxygen being fed through small green tubes directly into his nostrils. "Father Bernaud, how are you feeling? You're looking better." It wasn't a lie. He was still pale, but he wasn't blue.

The man struggled to focus his watery blue eyes, a moment of confusion, and recognition dawned. He sighed, as though relieved. It wasn't a reaction Hugh got often, and it puzzled him. "Sheriff Lo—thair. You were there, in the gardens. With Father Murdoch, and those dreadful photographs. I thought it was— a dream."

"I apologize for that. I didn't mean to upset you."

A ghost of a smile. "No. It was Father Murdoch you—meant to upset."

"You're quick, I'll give you that. I can't get past the feelin' that he knows something he isn't telling. Something to do with Michel Dugas's murder." Hugh scrubbed at the stubble on his cheek and jaw with his knuckles. He needed a hot shower and a shave, and an hour's sleep, but there was no time for that. After he left the hospital, he would head back to the office. He could use the electric razor he kept in his desk drawer, but the shower and rest would have to wait. "Hell, I don't know. Maybe I'm wrong about Murdoch. In any case, it's nothing you need to worry about. You just rest and listen to the doctors, and you'll be back with your lilies before you know it."

"There is no—rest for the damned." Bernaud turned his head on the pillow, his eyes opening a fraction wider, and Hugh thought he saw fear in the watery blue irises. "Do you believe in God, Sheriff?"

"I'm afraid I don't see a great many miracles in my line of work, Father, and without circumstantial evidence, I'm a definite hard sell."

"I believe," Bernaud said softly, "and I'm—frightened."

The nurse in the pale blue uniform came in then, administering a sedative so the old man would sleep and hustling Hugh out of the room, but as he moved from the bedside, the priest plucked at his sleeve, as if anxious to keep him there a few seconds longer.

He went, reluctantly. The conversation had been downright weird. *There is no rest for the damned.* What the hell had he meant by that? Was it the drugs they were giving him to treat his illness? Or was there something more to it than that? And what had frightened the old geezer?

He left the hospital and went back to the station where he settled in with Crebs and some hot black coffee. Alan was in plain clothes and had returned to the office after an evening at a local hotspot. Hugh gestured with the mug halfway to his lips. "Want some coffee?"

"I had a couple of beers, so I'm good. I was gonna go on home when I saw the lights through the window shade. You ever think about anything other than this case?"

Hugh snorted. Ordinarily, he might have put the deputy in his place with a well-honed verbal jab, but tonight he had too much on his mind, and as much as Alan Crebs wasn't his favorite person on the planet, his concern seemed genuine. "Shit. You're kiddin', right? What the fuck else is there?"

"Food? Sleep? A social life, maybe?"

"Social life?" Hugh shook his head. "For a minute there, you sounded like my mother." He sipped his coffee and waited for the caffeine surge. "Crebs, I'm warnin' you, we are *not* having this conversation." Another sip. "Let's talk about my day, why don't we, and how much headway I didn't make? That print we lifted from Mason Boudreaux ran through AFIS and came back as not being in the database. Unidentified individual. I call that a lucky break, don't you?" He sat back in his chair, the leather creaking. "Another fucking dead end in a shitload of goddamned dead ends. What the hell are the chances of us finally lifting a print from a vic's eyelid that can't be identified?"

Crebs shrugged. "Fifty-fifty?"

"Not in my universe," Hugh insisted. "Not in my goddamned universe. This ain't gonna happen. This case is *not* goin' cold. I won't let it."

Crebs glanced at his wristwatch. "Clock's ticking. We've only got so much time on these things."

"The statute of limitations never runs out on a homicide," he said hotly, jabbing a finger at his deputy. "There's time enough, if I say so. I'm gonna find this asshole, and I'm gonna nail his nuts to that wall." He wadded a report and threw it past Crebs. It bounced off the wall and landed in the wastebasket.

"Great shot, boss."

Hugh leaned forward, the banker's lamp on his desk casting bright light on his white shirt, and throwing his face into shadow. "You get anywhere with the kids? Because I didn't. Not a morsel, not a whiff of anything out of the ordinary. I know it's there, Alan; I just can't prove it. Everybody spoke of the first vic like he'd walked on water . . . and nobody made mention that him bein' a fruit bothered them at all. We're deep in the Bible Belt, for Christ's sake. How can that be?" He thumped the empty coffee cup down on the desk blotter, his frustration showing. "I know it's there, but I couldn't shake it loose, so I figured I'd try another angle, and that blew up in my goddamned face."

"The old guy from the rectory," Crebs said, neatly sidestepping the fact that his superior had called him by his first name. "How is he?"

"Hangin' in, but scared shitless. Go figure. A priest that's afraid of meeting his Maker. And here I was thinkin' that was the main objective with guys like him."

Crebs shrugged. "Maybe he has a legitimate reason to be scared."

"Come again?"

"Priests are just men who dress funny, you know. They make promises, but they break promises, too. Just like the rest of us. Who knows? Maybe he knows more than he's telling about Dugas. They lived in the same place, right?"

"You think the old man figures into Dugas's murder? Give me a break, Crebs. They're warming his drawer in the crypt. I doubt he could hoist somebody the size of Michel off the floor, let alone overhead."

Crebs shrugged. "I'm not suggesting he was the main actor, just a minor player. Sooner or later, most murderers talk. They tell someone—a cell mate, a girl-friend, or maybe their priest."

"And as a priest he's bound by the Church and the State to keep the secret." Hugh whistled. "Talk about bein' between a rock and a hard place." He thought about that, and it made sense. The old man hadn't killed Dugas, but the possibility existed that he knew who had. "Let's say this is more than theoretical—if the murderer decided to lighten his load by con-fessing, he shifts the burden to Bernaud's shoulders. Bernaud is forced to hear it, maybe even in detail, but he can't tell, so technically he becomes an unwilling accessory after the fact. That would be a load to carry, wouldn't it? Maybe enough of a load to cause a heart attack?"

Hugh grabbed his jacket, slipping into it, noting that Crebs still wore a puzzled look. "You goin' home, Sheriff?"

"Like hell," Hugh replied. "I'm going back to the hospital to talk to that old man. With any luck, we can end this thing tonight."

Lily couldn't quite shake the feeling that some-thing wasn't right. Cold and insidious, it permeated her consciousness and kept her uneasy throughout the day. Even Virginia seemed to notice that something was wrong. They were on their way home from the specialist's in the late afternoon and she kept up a running chatter. Lily didn't hear a word. Finally tiring of the one-sided exchange, she lowered her sunglasses, glancing at Lily over the rims. "Sugar, what on earth is goin' on with you? I've been talkin' your leg off, and you haven't done more than mumble a syllable or two."

"I'm sorry, Aunt Virginia. I guess I'm too distracted to be good company today."

"This is about what happened to young Mason Boudreaux, isn't it?"

"It's hard not to think about it," Lily admitted. "First Michel, and now this—" She broke off as they pulled into the drive. "Mase was just a kid, and this shouldn't have happened. He should be hanging out with his friends, or playing video games."

"Michel was a man of God, and that shouldn't have happened, either," Virginia said. "I don't know. Maybe I'm just getting old, but this world seems so much harsher and more unforgiving than it used to be." She opened the car door and stepped out. "You haven't mentioned Bobby. Is he the reason you didn't come home last night?"

"I know you don't approve."

"I like Bobby well enough, sugar. I always did. I'm just worried about you, that's all. Where's this goin'? Is it serious between you two?"

Lily didn't know how to answer. She'd been in love with Gitan since she was eleven, and that love hadn't lessened, despite her marriage to Hugh, despite everything. Yet, she was no innocent. She knew that love wasn't always enough to sustain two people as different as she and Gitan happened to be, and there was so much that was unresolved between them. Physically, they were good together, but it had been good with

Hugh for a while, too, and the crash and burn of the marriage was lesson enough that a relationship based solely on attraction couldn't last.

There was so much emotional history between her and Gitan. So much baggage.

Maybe too much.

Her life was a mess, and she hadn't even begun to pick up the pieces. How could she give him what he needed, the kind of relationship he deserved when she hadn't been able to exorcise her own demons?

How could she live with the knowledge that she'd been the one who had almost destroyed him?

She couldn't live with it. And neither could he, no matter what he said. Every time she looked at him she would be reminded of that night, the night her life fell apart for the first time. Doubts would creep in, and it would only be a matter of time before he began to resent the sacrifice he'd made for her.

No bond was strong enough to survive such a devastating secret.

"Let's don' go there."

"I have to. I don't have a choice. But you do. You don't need to relive that night, ever again. You earned a good life." The ache in Lily's chest was a dull misery, and she knew from experience that there was no relief. Her heart ached for her own sense of loss, and for what she had to do. But most of all it ached for Gitan, who had already known so much hardship, so much hurt. So much loss.

Loss of his reputation.

Loss of his freedom.

And now he'd lost Mason, the brother he'd loved so deeply, and who he'd tried so hard to save. Mason's death was earth-shattering, yet he'd been so calm this morning. *Too calm*. It had been harder to watch than his sorrow the night before, and the thing in which most of Lily's uneasiness had its roots. He should have grieved more openly. He should have gotten angry. Demanded justice. He should have gone to the authorities and insisted on answers.

Only in this instance, Gitan didn't trust the man in charge of the investigation.

They were rivals, enemies, and as such, he wouldn't turn to him for answers.

He wouldn't trust anyone to do what he could do himself. Mason was his brother, and he hadn't been able to save him. The least he could do was get to the truth and punish the man who'd taken his life.

Lily, standing at the window in the Red Room, staring out over the cane field, felt a sudden chill that had little to do with the air conditioning. Gitan's hold on his freedom was tenuous. Any violation of the terms of his parole could mean a one-way ticket to Angola where he would be forced to serve out his original sentence. And if someone got hurt or killed in the process of uncovering that truth, it would be far, far worse.

Lily knew the stats. Angola was one of the toughest prisons in the nation. Five thousand, one hundred and eight inmates, and 90 percent of the population would die behind bars. Eighty-seven men were housed on death row, awaiting execution. Gitan had been exceptionally lucky to have been granted parole. The odds of it happening a second time were nonexistent.

"My Lily's a bright light in a sea of darkness. Never forget that. All you got to do from this day on is shine."

"My God," Lily breathed, "he'd been saying goodbye."

CHAPTER EIGHTEEN

Gitan parked at the back of the lot, where the street lights couldn't reach. From his position, he could watch the entrance to the Pink Cadillac and observe the traffic coming and going without being so obvious that he drew more attention than he wanted. Word on the street was that Willie Early was usually looking to score some coke on Friday nights, and the Cadillac was the place to be.

Gitan had no doubt that Ruben knew his son was a user, or at the very least, the man suspected. But did he know the extent of Willie's addiction? Or that his son was capable of worse things? Like murder? It was a little hard to imagine that the big man would have stood still for that, but Willie was his flesh and blood and there was no disputing the strength of that kind of connection. Unknowingly or not, Ruben had fed his son's habit with regular infusions of cash, and he'd covered up for him. But would he go so far as to shield a murderer?

It was possible, Gitan thought. Love made men do crazy things . . . like protecting a son from the consequences of his actions . . . or taking a murder rap for a crime he didn't commit. . . . Letting Lily pay for killing her old man had never even occurred to him, any more than it would occur to Ruben to let his son pay for murdering Mase. It was all about love, all about loyalty.

Mase is gone, Gitan. Dead. You can't help him. You can't bring him back. All you can do is go on from here.

But he couldn't go on. Couldn't get past it.

Someone had killed Mase, and that someone was going to pay for it. His money was riding heavily on Willie Early as the murderer.

Gitan watched the parking lot and waited. At five minutes to ten, a GTO Judge motored into the lot, cherry red with six layers of clear coat for maximum gloss. Willie got out and a small knot of patrons gathered in a huddle at the corner of the building broke apart, two of them approaching Willie. They slapped hands, and Gitan caught the exchange of goods. Money followed, and Willie pulled some weed from his pocket and lit up. "Hey, man, later. There's somebody inside I gotta see."

Willie emerged from the bar and went straight to his car, opening the small plastic bag he'd scored from his supplier a few minutes ago. He wanted a hit so bad he could almost taste it. Just thinking about it helped ratchet up his pulse several notches, and he got clumsy as he tapped some of the toot onto a mirror he kept in his console and fluffed it with a razor blade. Intent on the high which awaited him, he never even realized he was no longer alone until he was grabbed from behind. Dark, unforgiving eyes met his in the rearview mirror . . . Gitan Boudreaux, Willie's worst nightmare.

Boudreaux's arm circled his neck, his rock-hard biceps constricting his throat. Each breath was reduced to a pained wheeze. The man's left hand was pressed to Willie's skull, the pressure he applied forcing his head at an odd angle. "Toss that blade out the window," Gitan said. "Try to use it and I'll snap your neck like a dried-out wishbone."

Willie tossed the blade out the open window. "What the hell do you want? You want the toot? I'll give it to you. There's always more where that came from. Just let me be."

"What makes you think I'd bargain with a crack whore? That what you are, Willie? You'd do anything for a rush; ain't that right?"

Willie tried to swallow, but Boudreaux's choke hold was so tight he nearly strangled on his own saliva. His thoughts raced, fueled by his cravings. Boudreaux had killed before. In his mind he saw himself lying facedown in a ditch. His bladder let go, and he pissed all over his white leather bucket seat. "Jesus, man. What do you want from me?"

The black eyes in the rearview mirror flickered with amusement, and Willie knew he was playing with him, savoring his fear, drawing it out. "I want you to start this mother up and drive."

"Drive where?"

The choke hold tightened; the pressure on Willie's neck doubled. "You want to keep breathin'," Gitan warned, "you'll turn that key and drive."

Willie didn't ask any more questions, just started the car and left the parking lot. He was quiet until they reached the rutted road that led to Catfish Point.

"Make a left here."

"But it's a dead end," Willie said. "There's nothing back there but—"

"But the old church. That's right. Guess the drugs haven't completely fried your brain."

Gitan was quiet for a few seconds, and in the interim, a sob escaped Willie's throat. "What are you gonna do to me?"

"Nothin'—yet. Park the car, and toss the keys—don' just drop 'em. That's right. Now, we get out and go inside." Willie's hands trembled so violently that he couldn't manage the door handle on the first try. Boudreaux laughed at that. "What you scared of, boy? You been here before."

"You're crazy, man!"

"Maybe," Gitan said with an easy shrug. "One thing I know for sure? My little brother's lyin' on a cold slab in the parish morgue. He's dead, *mon ami,* and I'm lookin' at the piece of shit who made that happen."

Willie shook his head. "No. No, I didn't hurt him. I didn't, I swear!"

"Oh, and I'm supposed to believe that?" He grabbed Willie by the scruff and hauled him out of the car, then kicked him in the ass for good measure. Willie sprawled on his face in the dirt and came up with a mouthful of grit and loam. Tears streamed down his face. His vision swam. The dark door to the old chapel gaped open a few feet from where he lay, and he had the weird, unreasonable fear that hell lay beyond the black rectangle. More frightened than he had ever been, he broke down, weeping, but his tormentor was pitiless. He crouched beside him, grabbing a fistful of shirt, forcing him to his feet, shoving him toward the chapel. "You were on Mase every chance you got. You made his life hell—"

"Maybe—maybe I did rag on him some, but I

didn't kill him. I didn't kill him," Willie said, sobbing uncontrollably. "I didn't kill him, Gitan. I swear to Christ, I didn't kill him . . . but I know who did."

Lily searched everywhere, but couldn't find Gitan. No one was home at Rose's place; Gitan's windows were dark and the truck with the distinctive paint job gone from its usual spot. Virginia said he hadn't been by the house, but if he showed, she would do her best to keep him there. "Be careful, darlin'. I don't like the thought of you goin' out alone. Why don't you come on home? Bobby can look after himself."

Lily wished she could believe that, but she had a feeling of dread that she couldn't seem to shake, and it had everything to do with Gitan. She knew him better than anyone, and it wasn't hard to imagine him looking for Mase's killer alone. Yet it wasn't the search that frightened her; it was what he would do if he found him. Gitan's loyalty was unshakeable. He wouldn't stop to think about what he was sacrificing— he would take his revenge and face the consequences after. . . .

Unless she could stop him.

She had to find him. Had to stop him. Before it was too late.

Lily drove past the sheriff's station in the vain hope he might be there demanding answers, but there were two cars in the lot and no sign of his pickup. Finally, she went to the Chop Shop. Ruben Early's van was parked out front. Lily breathed a sigh of relief. If anyone could help her find Gitan, it was Ruben.

The door was open, the knob turning easily under her hand. Ruben was crouched by an antique motorcycle, but he glanced up as she walked in. "Miss Martin, is it? Gitan's friend?"

"Lily."

"Lily. Pretty name. You lookin' for Gitan?" He stood, wiping his hands on a rag, a big man, powerfully built.

"I was hoping he'd be here," Lily admitted. "It's really important that I find him."

"Wish I could help out, but he hasn't been by since they notified the family about Mase. Understandable, considerin'. It's a damned shame about the boy." He shook his head. "He hung around here sometimes, you know, after school and on Saturdays. He was a nice kid, and Gitan must be takin' this hard. I know he was concerned about Mase, 'cause we talked about it. I guess on that score we had a lot in common."

"That's right. Willie Early's your son. He gave Mase a lot of trouble." He'd given her trouble, too, until she'd put him on his knees with a well-aimed blow to the windpipe. And Gitan had suspected Willie of putting the brick through his living room window. . . . A chill ghostly finger ran up Lily's spine. "Ruben . . . have you seen Willie this evening?"

"This afternoon. He came by the shop. Said he was out of cash, as usual. Why?"

"No reason," Lily replied. She didn't know him well enough to confide in him, and her suspicions were just that . . . suspicions. "I was just wondering—"

Something about him changed, shifted, and though the difference was subtle, Lily suddenly felt the urge to turn and run. She resisted. He was Gitan's boss, his friend, and Gitan trusted him.

"Wondering, Lily? You mentioned Willie giving Mase a rough time; then you ask if I've seen him. I hope you're not making a connection between my boy and Mason being strangled? Because if you are, you're way off base. I'm the first to admit Willie's wild . . . but he isn't capable of killing anyone."

The warmth left Lily in a rush, leaving her cold and shaken. "Strangled?" she repeated.

Ruben's eyes narrowed. "Yeah. That's what happened, right?"

Lily laughed, but it sounded sick. "How could you possibly know that? Hugh didn't release the details of Mase's death to the press."

He shrugged his broad shoulders. "I don't know. I guess Gitan must have told me."

A sick sort of awareness swept over her. Gitan hadn't told anyone . . . not even her. "I really need to be going," Lily said. "I have to find Gitan."

The phone rang in the office. "Excuse me, one second." Ruben walked to the workbench and picked up the portable handset. "Chop Shop . . . Where the hell are you?"

Lily could hear the caller's voice, a male voice, its tone frantic, but she didn't stay to find out the details. She turned and ran, but as she opened her car door, a large hand clamped over her wrist. Lily struggled, trying to shake him off, but he held her as effortlessly as he would have held a child. "No need to rush off, Lily."

"Get your hands off me!" She tried for the same punch that had done Willie in, but he caught her free wrist and held her against him. "Let go! Damn you, let go!"

"There's no need to be frightened, Lily. I just wanted to tell you . . . I found Gitan." A heartbeat later he pinned her arms to her sides with one arm and pressed a rag to her nose and mouth. Lily recognized the sickeningly sweet smell . . . ether . . . and then nothing.

* * *

Lily's wrists were tightly bound when she came to. She was slumped on the passenger seat of Early's van, and as the fog cleared, she reached for the door handle only to find that he'd removed it. "I didn't want to hurt him," he said. "He was a nice kid."

There was misery in his voice, but Lily wasn't fooled. He was capable of anything. "Then why did you?"

"I had no choice. He shouldn't have been there."

"Shouldn't have been where? At St. Bart's?" She looked at him, and he must have recognized the loathing in her glance because his defenses rose.

"He was standing there, and he overheard, and he knew. I could see it in his eyes. He knew, and he would have gone to Gitan, or to Hugh. He would have told someone, and I couldn't risk it. I was already in too deep. I had no choice!"

Lily's heart sank. "My God. It was you all along—you killed Michel. You crucified him."

"He deserved what he got. He deserved to burn in hell for what he did to my boy! This was all his doing! All of it!" Spittle flew from his mouth and he swiped it away with the back of one hand. "I couldn't let him get away with raping my son."

Lily shook her head, her eyes burning. "Willie may have been molested, but not by Michel Dugas. If that's your motive, then you killed an innocent man."

"Willie told me. He said it was Dugas."

"Willie . . . who's such a saint? How do you know he was telling the truth?"

The air conditioner made the air in the van almost chilly, yet Ruben had begun to sweat. Lily could see the flicker of doubt, faint, but real, that her suggestion had sparked. "Willie wouldn't lie—not about something like that."

"You'd better hope not," Lily said. "That was your son on the phone wasn't it? And you said you'd found Gitan. He's got Willie, and this time it's your son's life that's hanging by a thread."

"Gitan won't hurt him if I have something to give him in exchange for Willie. Something—*someone* he'd lay down his life for." He pulled the van off the blacktop road and drove along the rutted path that led to Catfish Point. It hadn't changed much, and Lily recognized it. Then the old church came into view, and the van headlights bounced off Willie Early's car. Ruben turned off the engine and turned to Lily, showing her the pistol in his hand. "If you want your boyfriend alive, you'll do what I tell you to do."

Hugh got the call on his cellular a few minutes from the hospital. Father John Bernaud was in an agitated state and asking for him. The same nurse who'd shown him to the priest's room earlier that afternoon walked him through the unit a second time, lingering by the door to make sure he didn't force the old man to get up and do aerobics. Hugh ignored her, concentrating on the priest.

He was blue around the lips, and though he seemed to sleep, his breath was labored and his hands were infected by a restless twitch. "Father Bernaud, it's Sheriff Lothair. Sir, can you hear me?"

The old man's eyes slitted open and he almost smiled.

Hugh took a step closer to the bed, resting one hand on the railing. "The hospital called and said that you wanted to speak to me."

Father Bernaud nodded. "I must tell. It's the only way. It weighs too heavily upon me, and I can carry—the burden—no longer."

"Does this have to do with Father Dugas's murder?"

Benaud nodded. "Father Dugas discovered that a member of our order had become involved with a young man—in a most inappropriate—manner."

"A homosexual relationship?"

"This person called it a 'seduction,' but it was much more. The boy was just fourteen when it started. An innocent. The priest was not. He had been transferred from another diocese when scandal threatened, but had undergone counseling, and because of his family connections was given a prominent position at St. Bartholomew's. This happened before the scandal broke in the media, when the silence of families affected by such transgressions could be coerced, or bought." He paused, wheezing as he fought for breath. "Father Dugas confided in me that he suspected something wasn't right, though he did not name names. We had disagreed before, so I took his suspicions to my superior."

"Father Murdoch."

"Yes. At the time, I did not know that he was responsible. I did not learn the extent of his duplicity until I heard the news of Father Dugas's death."

"Why didn't you come forward?"

"He was a priest, and I was a coward. I could not help Father Dugas, and I feared how my role in such a disclosure would affect my retirement. Most of all, I feared disgrace."

"You couldn't help Michel Dugas, but you could have saved Mason Boudreaux."

Another nod. "I know, and I regret it."

"There's more, isn't there?" Hugh said, maintaining the distance and objectivity he needed to see the interview through to its conclusion.

"Shortly after the murder, I was at prayer in the chapel when someone entered to sit behind me. He told me not to turn around, but I recognized his voice. He was there to confess a ghastly transgression, the murder of the man he felt had stolen his son's innocence. Mr. Early didn't realize that he had killed an innocent man."

"Early?" Hugh said. "Ruben Early?"

Another nod. "His son, Willie, is the young man Father Murdoch molested."

Hugh left the ICU ward on the run, but as he reached the lobby, the call for a Code Blue in ICU echoed through the corridors. He got to the car and radioed the station to arrange for Fred Rally to pick up Murdoch. The lights were on at the Chop Shop when he arrived, the main door unlocked, and Lily's car was parked out front. He'd just about steeled himself to see Lily and Gitan together when he realized there was no one around.

An assortment of wrenches were scattered around the Indian motorcycle. Ruben liked to keep a clean workplace, and Hugh had never seen anything left out of place. He was the only one who touched the old bike, and he wasn't the type to leave a job before putting his tools away. Unless someone or something had interrupted him, or he'd been called away on an emergency.

But there was no emergency, or Hugh would have been the first to know about it. Except for the call from the hospital, it had been unusually quiet. *No emergency*, Hugh thought, *and Lily's car's out front.*

A coffee cup sat on the floor by the front tire, the hot liquid sending a thread of wispy steam into the air. Hugh lifted the Styrofoam cup and turned it slightly. The grease-stained prints were visible . . . The right thumb had a cut through the center swirl. The hair on the back of his neck stood on end as he dug in his coat pocket for his cellular phone. He punched in a number and listened to it ring, praying he was wrong this one time. Praying that Lily hadn't run into Ruben Early. It was a long shot that Ruben would hurt Lily, unless she'd stumbled onto the truth, unless somehow she'd figured it out.

On the third ring, Virginia picked up. "Martin residence."

"Virginia, it's Hugh. Is Lily there?"

"Hugh Lothair, you've got some balls, callin' here."

He could have come up with several comebacks, but he didn't have time to debate who had the bigger set of *cojones*, he or Lily's aunt. "A straightforward yes or no will do. Is she there?"

"No, she isn't, and the only satisfaction I've derived from this call is the 100 percent certainty that she's not with y—"

Hugh hung up on her. "Goodbye, Virginia," he said, depositing the phone in his pocket. The call hadn't brought him any satisfaction. He didn't like Virginia, and he certainly didn't like talking to her. Every time he called the house on Mill Creek Road, he was forced to run the gauntlet before he was permitted to talk to his own ex-wife.

Ex-wife. He snorted. He'd gotten it right that time. Maybe there was something Freudian in that. Lily would be thrilled . . . *if* she survived to see it.

"I did what I had to do," Ruben told Lily. "And that's all this is, too. Nobody'll get hurt as long as you do what you're told. You're gonna talk to Gitan. He'll listen to you. You're gonna convince him to give up my boy."

"And if I don't? Then what? You'll kill me, too?"

"If I have to." He secured the 9mm pistol in the waistband of his jeans, reminding her that he was armed and willing to use it. "I can make it look like Gitan did it. A lover's quarrel? Or maybe you found out that he killed the priest. Hugh tried to pin it on him, didn't he? Who do you suppose he'll believe? Me or Gitan?"

"That might have worked before you made the mistake of killing an innocent boy," Lily said. "However much Hugh hates Gitan, he'll never believe that he killed Mason, and he would never hurt me. Hugh knows Gitan almost as well as I do. He won't buy it, no matter what you say."

He pushed Lily in front of him, forcing her to walk toward the church. A few yards from the dark doorway, he jerked her to a halt, holding her by a fistful of fabric at her nape. "Gitan! It's Ruben! Open the door and send Willie out."

A moment passed. Lily held her breath. Slowly, the door creaked open and the unmistakable odor of gasoline wafted on the night breeze. Sick with fear, Lily could only watch the scene play out, certain she was about to lose everything she cared about a second time, and she didn't know how she would survive it. If Gitan harmed Willie, he would return to prison. If he let the Early boy go, Ruben would silence them both. "Gitan, he has a gun."

"No worries, *cher.* He's got it, but he won' use it. Discharge it, and this old building'll go up like a torch, and Willie with it."

"Daddy!" a voice howled from the bowels of the

building. "He soaked this place with gasoline. Do as he says!"

Something moved in the darkness and slowly took shape. A long, tall, shadow-figure leaning in the doorway, a disposable lighter in his hand. A cigarette dangled from his lips. "You know, Ruben, I ain't had a smoke in almost eight years. Doctors, they said it would cripple my already-diminished lung capacity. Hell, who listens to doctors, anyhow? I don' guess just one could hurt, do you?"

Lily felt the big man behind her flinch. "Do you really want me to kill her? This is no bluff, Gitan."

"I guess we all know what you're capable of. My brother's dead. Somebody needs to pay for that. It'll either be you—or him. You won' hurt Lily, 'cause you know what she means to me. You hurt her, and Willie, he's toast. Make a wrong move and he'll go up like that." He snapped his fingers. "Painful way to die, too. Do you s'pose it hurts as much as bein' crucified?"

Ruben pressed the gun's muzzle to Lily's ear.

"Be careful with that," Gitan warned. "You won't even have a body to bury, unlike Rose. Rose and me, we got a body for the family crypt, thanks to you. Come to think of it, I'm in no mood to negotiate with you." He bent his head, cupping his hands around the lighter.

"Wait!" Ruben said. "Jesus, don't! Don't light it."

"Let her go, and maybe I'll think about it," Gitan said quietly. He was calm and rational and he would carry out his threats. Lily knew it, and so did the man who still held onto her.

"You know the difference between me and you, Ruben? You're a desperate man, desperate to save that worthless waste of oxygen, desperate to save your own ass. Me? I ain't got nothin' to lose."

A spotlight from the patrol car hit Ruben Early dead-on, blinding him. Car doors slammed and men were moving behind the bright beam. Lily could barely make out Hugh's deputy manning the light. His other hand gripped his service revolver, braced on the door of the squad car. Another figure skirted the perimeter, making use of Early's blind spot. "Drop your weapon! Drop it, now!"

Hugh raised one hand, a signal for his officers to hold fire. "Ruben, it's Hugh. I'd listen if I were you. You're in a damn dangerous position. That's my ex-wife you've got there. You hurt her, and Gitan won't have to kill you. I'll save him the goddamned trouble." He was a mere shadow in Lily's peripheral vision, but his voice was level and confident. "It's all over. I spoke to Father Bernaud. I know everything. Father Murdoch is already in custody."

"Murdoch—"

"Willie lied to you," Hugh said. "Michel Dugas had nothing to do with what happened to him. You killed the wrong man. Now, give me the gun."

Ruben shoved Lily away from him, but instead of dropping his weapon, he put the muzzle in his mouth and pulled the trigger. The blast kicked his body back into waist-high weeds. As his body jerked once, then settled into death, some night creature, disturbed by the blast, scuttled deeper into the underbrush, then splashed into the dark waters of the bayou.

"Gitan, it's Hugh. You can come on out now. It's over." With a look of distaste Hugh stepped over the man's body and took Lily by the arm. "You okay, sugar?"

"Yeah." Lily nodded. "Yeah. Thanks to you, I'm okay."

"Well, that's a damn good thing. You're the only ex-wife I've got."

Lily laughed, a watery gurgle of sound. "Did you say ex-wife?"

"Don't make a big deal out of it, but yeah, I guess I did. Maybe I finally got the message, or maybe you're that important to me. Men do a lot of crazy things for the people they love," Hugh said. "Myself not excluded. Like this . . . go on. He's waiting."

For the space of a heartbeat, Lily faltered. Inclining his head at the shadow-man lingering by the church door, Hugh softened his voice. "He needs you a hell of a lot more than I do right now. I don't know, maybe he always did. Now, you tell me. Who's the better man?"

Lily stepped close for one second, and standing on tiptoes, put her arms around him. "I don't think I'll answer that. But thank you." She pressed a kiss of gratitude on Hugh's cheek, then turned and ran to the church. Gitan met her halfway, wrapping her in his embrace, lifting her off her feet.

Neither noticed when Hugh, flashlight in hand, brushed past them. "I hope the hell you realize how lucky you are, coon-ass. If it wasn't for the fact that I'm such a prince, your ass would be on its way back to Angola by now. Terroristic threats. Destruction of public property. What the hell is wrong with you?" He moved the flashlight's beam around the church, then fixed it on Willie, who swung by his ankles from the beam above the altar. "Hey, Crebs! Get your ass in here! You got to see this!"

"Get me down," Willie pleaded. "Somebody, please, get me down from here."

* * *

Three days later, Mason Edward Boudreaux was laid to rest in the family crypt. There wasn't a dry eye at the service, including Lily's. Rose Boudreaux's grief was sobering, and Lily knew that the woman would have collapsed if not for Gitan. It had given Lily a great deal to think about. In fact, for three days she had done nothing but think, and this afternoon she was finally ready to act. She called Hugh and set up an appointment, then called an attorney who would work on getting Gitan's conviction overturned.

It wouldn't be easy, but it needed to be done. *She* needed to do it, Lily amended mentally. *She* needed to tell the truth. For Gitan's sake, and Rose's. For Mason's memory . . . but most of all, for herself.

Gitan deserved his freedom in the truest sense of the word, and Lily loved him enough to give it to him. Virginia had argued against it, but Lily's mind was made up, and nothing could stop her.

The most difficult part for Lily was the final visit to the house on Kyme Road. She hadn't mentioned to anyone that she planned to go back there one last time, yet strangely, when she arrived, Virginia's car was in the drive.

The air inside the house was still stale and stuffy, hard to breathe, and it only seemed to heighten Lily's feeling of anxiety. "Aunt Virginia?" A low muttering came from the direction of Justin's study. There was something about the sound that raised the fine hairs on Lily's arms and at her nape, despite the warmth of the house. She walked to the study door, pushing it open. Virginia sat on the carpeted floor, close to where Justin had fallen the night he died. Her head rested on her upraised knees, her arms locked so tightly around them that the tendons stood out in her wrists. Her eyes seemed unfocused, her gaze so far away that it was terrifying.

Lily got down on Virginia's level, speaking softly, as one would to a frightened child. "Aunt Virginia? It's me, Lily. What are you doing here? Sugar, are you feelin' all right?"

The older woman looked up, startled but still far removed from reality, and her eyes filled with tears. "He's gone, you know. Justin's gone, and it's my fault. It's my fault, it's all my fault."

"No. Darling, no, it isn't your fault," Lily reassured her. "I know what happened."

Virginia shook her head. "No. You can't know. No one knows. No one saw. Bobby was dead, and Lily had gone away somewhere. There was no one to see."

"Bobby was dead, and Lily had gone away somewhere. . . ." The images assaulted Lily, fast and relentless, and for once she didn't fight it, but let them surface. With the truth out in the open, there would be nothing to haunt her, nothing to fear. She felt her father's hands tearing at her blouse. But she was fighting back, trying to get away, angry that he could spoil this night for her.

"You can't leave with that swamp rat!" Justin had shouted. "I won't let you!"

"You can't stop me! If you try, I'll tell! I swear I will! I'll ruin you!"

"Lily." Cajoling, almost a whimper. The sound of his voice made her nauseous. "Lily, baby, you can't leave me. I won't let you."

He fell on her, tearing at her clothes as he pushed her down on his desk, and Lily clawed at him, screaming until there was no air left in her lungs.

Then there had been such a sense of confusion. . . .

The sound of shattering glass, Justin's gasp of surprise as he was pulled away. Gitan, more angry than she had ever seen him, pounded Justin to a bleeding pulp. No match for a younger, stronger man, Justin fell, and Lily grabbed Gitan by the jacket, panicky at what he had done. Her father was vindictive, and he could fight back in ways Gitan had never imagined. "You have to go! Leave now, please! I'll meet you as soon as I can, but get out of Louisiana. He has connections. He won't let this go!"

"I'm not leavin' you here with that fuckin' lowlife bastard. I won't!"

The words echoed crazily in Lily's brain. She turned in slow motion, begging him, seeing too late Justin rising off the carpet, his face swollen and cut, the gun in his hand. Lily screamed . . . and screamed again as her father pulled the trigger and Gitan was knocked back by the blast. There was a dark hole to the left of his breastbone, and the white fabric of his T-shirt was rapidly turning scarlet. Blood trickled from one corner of his mouth. His eyes were slitted, but only the whites showed . . . and as Lily knelt beside him, holding him, she felt her world tilt crazily and spin out of control.

Blood. So much blood. Blood on Gitan, on the carpet, blood on her face, hands, and blouse. So much blood, and she knew he was dead. Gitan was dead. He was dead!

"You caused this, Lily," Justin was saying. "You brought it on by getting involved with him in the first place. He isn't good enough for you. You should have listened! Why the hell couldn't you just be a good little girl?"

"Be a good little girl. Come sit on Daddy's lap, and we'll play a little game. It'll be our secret. . . ."

Lily closed her eyes against the hot flow of liquid

emotion, but it leaked from the inner and outer corners of her lids, down over her cheeks, twenty-five years' worth of unshed tears.

"No. No, no, no, no-no-no-no-no-no!"

"What in hell is going on here?" Virginia's voice. Furious. "What did you do to her? Monster! What did you do?"

"Mind you own goddamned business for once!" Justin shouted. "Lily's my child, not yours!"

"Yes, she is. Your child, Justin! And you've hurt her for the last time."

"What are you doing?"

"Calling the police . . . and I'm going to make sure that they put you away!"

Through a reddish haze, Lily saw Justin shove Virginia hard, and she fell near the spot where Gitan lay. In the distance a siren wailed. A knife was in Virginia's hand, the same knife Gitan always carried, and which he'd dropped on the carpet when he fell. Virginia got to her feet, plunging the blade into Justin's chest . . . stepping back as he fell. . . .

The clouds cleared from Virginia's vision. She glanced around, saw Lily's tearstained face, and groaned. "I did it, sugar, not you. I killed him, and I'm not sorry. He deserved it. He deserved to burn in hell for what he did to you."

"The knife," Lily said. "Gitan's fingerprints were on the handle. I don't understand."

"I thought Bobby was a goner. No one could survive a bullet to the heart, and I was sure he was already dead. So, I wiped the handle clean and put it in his hand. Someone had to be here to take care of you. Nobody questioned it. But then he recovered." She lifted her gaze to Lily's. "I know it was wrong, and I don't expect you to forgive me—or Bobby. He lost seven years of his life because I wasn't strong enough to tell the truth."

Lily sat with Virginia for a long time, and when they left the house, they left together.

The office was dark except for the banker's lamp on the desk. Fred Rally was working the night shift. Seated at his desk in the day room, he played a game of solitare. Rally was a good man, and he wouldn't disturb his boss unnecessarily. Behind a closed office door, Hugh opened the bottom drawer of his desk and took out a bottle of single-malt whiskey and a clean shot glass. He kept the whiskey for nights like this, when his shift was over, but he couldn't seem to force himself to go home.

Mason Boudreaux's body had been laid to rest earlier that afternoon. Hugh had felt an obligation to attend, though he'd stayed on the fringes of the crowd. Lily had been seated with the family. Rose might not be crazy about the idea, but she and Gitan were definitely together. For once, it hadn't bothered Hugh to see her with him, and he couldn't even say why.

He poured and sipped a whiskey, enjoying the slow warmth that followed. It was the thirtieth of September, and he was glad the month was over. The end of October would mean the end of hurricane season. The humidity wouldn't lessen, but the temperature would begin to drop bit by bit, making life just a little more bearable. Crime would drop off a little, too. Tempers tended to soar along with the mercury in the thermometer, and though Angelique had its share of Halloween pranks, nothing could be worse than the month just past.

Two murders, one suicide, five robberies, a dozen domestic situations, and twice that number of DUIs. Mrs. Frazer from Oak Street had decided to play erotic games with her husband Ron on a Saturday afternoon, handcuffed him to the balcony railing, buck naked, and forgot where she left the keys. Hugh had sent the unflappable Crebs to free the bone-thin sixty-seven-year-old from his bondage, but not before half the town had strolled by for a look-see.

It had provided enough jokes in the station house to break the tension that had gripped them all for weeks, as well as the reassurance that things would eventually slide back toward normalcy. For Hugh, normal hadn't arrived yet, and he was still steeped in the many paper details and phone conversations of the recent homicides' aftermath. A lot of times, death by violence was almost cut-and-dried. The victim was discovered, the body and the scene processed, and you followed the clues to a suspect.

The Dugas case hadn't been that easy, and more than one person was in deep shit because of it. Willie Early and Father Murdoch were both facing a number of serious charges, and unless someone in the DA's office fucked it up royally, they'd be seeing sunlight through cell bars for years to come. The biggest irony lay in the fact that money had played a small but significant part in the motive behind Michel's death after all. The extent of Willie Early's greed, compounded by a seriously expensive addiction, had kept him milking Murdoch's cash cow, as well as fleecing his father. One night, during a particularly vicious argument, Willie had turned the screws on Ruben, admitting that he'd been taken advantage of by a priest. But when pressed, he had fingered Dugas, not Murdoch, not wanting the money train he was riding to come to a grinding halt. Yet, instead of triggering a truckload of guilt, it had brought on a murderous rage that had ended in a grisly homicide.

Oddly, it was Father John Bernaud who lingered in Hugh's thoughts. The ICU team had been unable to revive him that night, and Hugh thought that on some level, having unburdened, he was ready to face whatever awaited him after death. Maybe he'd found peace at last. Hugh doubted it, but wiser men than he seemed to think it was possible. From a purely personal standpoint, he preferred dealing in the everyday details of keeping a lid on the bayou town, and was content to leave theology to others.

There was a light tap on the office door.

"Come on in; it's open."

The door opened and Amy walked in, closing and locking it behind her. "Now, how did I know I'd find you here?"

"Probably because you stopped by my place before comin' over here, and found out no one was home."

"You know me too well," she said with a smile. She was wearing a sheath dress, simple, but sexy, made of a sinuous fabric that molded to her legs as she walked to his desk and sat on the corner of it next to him. "I thought you could use a little company by now. It's been a tough week."

Hugh sat back in his chair, taking her hand in his, bringing it to his lips. "Yeah, but a good one. I haven't felt this good about myself in a long time. Longer than memory serves, actually . . . and while you'll think I'm crazy, I'm not so sure I want to spoil it by doing something totally selfish." It was the one thing she hadn't expected from him, but instead of feeling like a damn fool, he felt as if he'd been standing in a swift storm breeze . . . strangely cleansed. It was a rare moment, and he found himself wanting to hang on to that. "Why don't you go on home to Charlie. I expect he'll be waitin' for you."

Her disappointment showed. "Hugh? Are you feelin' all right?"

"Never better. Now, go on. I've got some last-minute stuff to take care of."

Amy left, and Hugh settled back and poured another whiskey. Raising the shot glass, he smiled to himself. "To the future."

"You need to tell me everything. I want to know, so that we can start fresh."

"Tell you what, sugar? That you're everything to me?" Gitan was flat on his back, his dark head resting on the pillows, one arm flung above his head. The other arm encircled Lily's waist, the fingers of that hand tracing lazy circles on her bare skin. She'd filed the papers that afternoon to get his conviction overturned. Gitan had been reluctant, saying it was done and there was no going back, but Virginia insisted. The older woman had an attorney—the best money could buy, and even Hugh had allowed that there was a better than excellent chance she would get off. He had even volunteered to act as a character witness, though Virginia had refused his offer on principle. Killing Justin had been self-defense, after a fashion, and it wouldn't serve anyone to put a woman with Alzheimer's in prison.

"Hugh thought there was a connection between you and Michel that was mysterious enough to make you a suspect."

He snorted his derision. "Hugh Lothair just wanted me out of the way, that's all. There was no mystery to it. Michel was my friend, but he was also my priest. He came to the prison to hear my confession, and to bring me news about you. I'd told him that to the best of my knowledge, I couldn't have killed Justin. He had to keep my secret for me . . . Then you started to remember, were having nightmares, and he tried to persuade me that it would be best to tell you the truth. That's why he wanted to see me the night he was killed, to try and change my mind—only Ruben asked me to work and kept the appointment instead. I wish it hadn't come down the way it did. Michel was a good man, and a great friend. He loved you—I guess we all have in one way or another. Even Hugh."

He sighed, pulling her in for a lingering, sexy kiss that brought back memories of their making love just moments ago. "What's gonna happen to Willie?"

"He's been charged with conspiracy to commit murder, extortion, and a host of lesser charges," Lily said. "With Ruben gone, there's no one to pull the strings to get him out from under. He's looking at a number of years."

"And what are we lookin' at?" he wondered.

"I don't know, but I'm willing to give it a shot if you are. We'll take it one day at a time and see where we end up?"

"Right here's where we end up," he said, laughing as he rolled her onto her back and covered her mouth with his.